DEBBIE MACOMBER

An Engagement in Seattle

mira

mira

ISBN-13: 978-0-7783-3111-7

Recycling programs
for this product may
not exist in your area.

An Engagement in Seattle

Copyright © 2011 by Harlequin Books S.A.

The publisher acknowledges the copyright holder of the
individual works as follows:

Groom Wanted
Copyright © 1993 by Debbie Macomber

Bride Wanted
Copyright © 1993 by Debbie Macomber

For questions and comments about the quality of this book, please contact us at
CustomerService@Harlequin.com.

www.MIRABooks.com

Printed in U.S.A.

GROOM WANTED

To Wanda Roberts,
in appreciation for her many skills.

One

Julia Conrad wasn't a patient woman at the best of times. She paced her office, repeatedly circling her high-gloss black-lacquer-and-brass desk. She felt so helpless. She should've gone to Citizenship and Immigration Services with Jerry rather than wait for their decision.

Rubbing her palms together, she retracted the thought. She was a wreck and the Immigration people would have instantly picked up on that and it could hurt their case. She couldn't help being anxious. The future of the company rested on the outcome of today's hearing. Ultimately she was the one responsible for the welfare of Conrad Industries, the business her grandfather had started thirty years earlier.

In an effort to calm herself she stared out the window. The weather seemed to echo her mood. There was a ceiling of black clouds, thunder roared and a flash of lightning briefly brightened the room. The lights flickered.

Julia's reflection was mirrored in the window and she frowned, mesmerized by the unexpected sight of herself. Her dark hair was swept back from her face and secured with a gold clasp. She wore a dark suit with a pale gray blouse, which—in her view, anyway—conveyed tasteful refinement. She *looked* cool, calm and collected, but inside she was a mass of tension and nerves. At thirty she had a pleasant face when she smiled, but she hadn't been doing much of that lately. Not in the past three years. Her cheekbones were high, her jaw strong, but it was her eyes that told the story. Her eyes revealed vulnerability and pain.

The image of herself distressed Julia and she hurriedly glanced away. Sighing, she circled her desk once more, silently praying for patience. She was determined to get the company back on its feet, to overcome the odds they faced. Jerry, her brother, had worked with her, sacrificing his personal life the way she had hers. They'd met with a handful of small successes. And now *this*.

Both Julia and Jerry were determined to revive Conrad Industries. Julia owed her father that much. Jerry had shown such faith in her by volunteering his services. If their situations were reversed, she wasn't sure she would've been so forgiving. But her brother had stuck by her through all the turmoil.

Slowly she lowered her gaze, disturbed by that revelation. However, she didn't have the time or the inclination to worry about it. If she ever needed a cool head and a cooler heart, it was now. Two years' worth of innovative research was about to be lost because they'd allowed the fate of the company to hinge on the experiments and ideas of one man. Aleksandr Berinski was a brilliant Russian biochemist. Jerry had met him some years earlier while traveling in Europe and convinced

Julia he was the answer to their problems. Her brother was right; Alek's ideas would revolutionize the paint industry. Bringing him to the United States had been a bold move on their part, but she hadn't been sorry. Not once.

Hiring Aleksandr Berinski from Russia and moving him to Seattle—it was the biggest risk Conrad Industries had ever taken. Now the fate of the company rested in the hands of a hard-nosed official.

Julia wondered again if she should've attended the hearing at the district office of Citizenship and Immigration. She'd done everything within her power to make sure Aleksandr's visa would be extended. She'd written a letter explaining his importance to the company and included documentation to prove that Aleksandr Berinski was a man of distinct merit and exceptional ability.

Jerry, who was a very good corporate attorney, had spent weeks building their case. Professional certifications, affidavits, a copy of Aleksandr's diploma and letters of reference filled Jerry's briefcase.

Her brother had told her there could be problems. It was often difficult to renew an H-2 visa, the type Aleksandr had been granted when he'd entered the United States. The H-2 is one of temporary employment. He'd warned her that if it looked as though employment might become permanent, then Immigration and the Labor Department would be reluctant to extend the visa.

On top of all that, the case had been assigned to a particularly difficult bureaucrat. Jerry had warned her that the agent hearing their case might decide Alek had applied for the temporary visa knowing the job was really permanent and refuse to grant an extension on principle.

She checked her watch again and exhaled with impatience. Only a few minutes had passed. Annoyed with herself for the uncharacteristic display of anxiety, she sat down on her white leather chair. Everything was neatly arranged on the polished black desk. A small marble pen stand was next to the phone. The address and appointment books were perfectly aligned with everything else. Behind the desk stood her computer table, the company website pulled up, its logo prominent. Julia liked to keep her office and her world under control.

When her phone rang, the sound caught her off guard. She grabbed the receiver. "Jerry?"

"Sis," Jerry's voice greeted her. "I'm on my cell. I thought you'd want to know the decision as soon as possible."

"Yes, please."

"I'm afraid it didn't go as well as we'd hoped. They've decided not to renew Alek's visa."

His words felt like a kick in the stomach. She closed her eyes and waited until the shock had passed. It wasn't as if she hadn't known the likelihood of this verdict. The fact that Aleksandr had no proof of a permanent residence in Russia didn't help. In the eyes of Immigration Services that was a red light indicating he didn't intend to return. Furthermore, she and Jerry were dealing with a large, complex bureaucracy. In a fit of worry, Julia had tried to contact the agency herself, reason with them. She'd spent nearly an hour on the phone and hadn't spoken to a single person. She was forced to listen to one recording after another. Press a number on the phone, listen, press another one, then another. She quickly became lost in a hopeless tangle of instructions and messages.

"When will he have to leave?"

"By the end of the week, when his current visa expires."

"That soon?"

"I'm afraid so."

"Jerry, what are we going to do?"

"I'll talk to you about it as soon as we get back to the office," her brother said in reassuring tones. "Don't worry, I've got a contingency plan."

Nice of him to mention it now, Julia mused. He might've said something this morning and saved her all this grief.

Ten minutes later, her intercom buzzed; her assistant announced that Jerry was in her outer office. Julia asked Virginia to send him in and waited, standing by the window.

Jerry entered and Aleksandr Berinski followed. Although Aleksandr had been working for Conrad Industries for nearly two years, she'd only talked to him a handful of times. Even those conversations had been brief. But she'd read his weekly reports and been excited by the progress he was making. If he was allowed to continue, Julia didn't doubt that his innovations would put Conrad Industries back on a firm financial footing.

Julia and Jerry, but primarily Julia, had taken on the impossible task of resurrecting the family business, literally from the ashes. Three years before, the plant and adjacent warehouse had been severely damaged by fire; fortunately, it hadn't spread to the lab and the offices. Because of the rebuilding they'd had to do, she'd decided the line of paints Aleksandr was developing would be called Phoenix.

To be so close to success and lose it all now was more than she could bear. For three long, frustrating years, she'd hung on to the business by wheeling and dealing, making trades and promises.

Being aggressive and hardworking had come naturally to her. Jerry possessed the same determination and had been a constant help. If she was cold and sometimes ruthless, she credited it to Roger Stanhope. She'd needed to be, but Julia didn't have any more tricks up her sleeve once Aleksandr returned to Russia.

She feared that losing the business would be a fatal blow to her grandmother. No one knew better than Julia how fragile Ruth's health had become these past few months.

"You said you have a contingency plan." She spoke crisply, the sound of her steps muffled by the thick wheat-colored carpet as she stalked back to her desk. She leaned forward and averted her gaze from Aleksandr's.

The man disturbed her in ways she didn't understand. He was tall and lanky with impeccable manners. His face wasn't handsome the way Roger's had been, but rawboned and lean. His eyes were dark, the brows arched slightly, and in him she read strength and character. Unwillingly she found her own eyes drawn to his, and the shadow of a smile crept across Aleksandr's face. She focused her attention on Jerry.

"There is one way," her brother said, with obvious reluctance.

"This isn't the time to play guessing games. Tell me what you're thinking," she snapped, hardly believing he could be holding something back. Jerry knew as well as she did what kind of predicament the company was in.

Her brother set down his briefcase and motioned toward the leather chair. "Perhaps you should take a seat."

"Me?" She noted that his voice was strained, which surprised her almost as much as his request.

"You, too, Alek," Jerry advised as he moved to the opposite end of her office.

Julia turned toward him and tried to read his features in the gloom of late afternoon. The storm had darkened the sky, stationing shadows around the room until it resembled a dungeon, Julia thought.

"Whatever you have to say, please say it, Jerry. You've never worried about phrasing before."

Jerry's eyes traveled from Julia to Aleksandr, and she saw that his cheeks were flushed. He sighed. "There's only one legal way I know to keep Aleksandr in the country." Slowly he leveled his gaze on Julia. "You could marry him."

"I was hoping you'd stop by and see me." Julia's grandmother, Ruth Conrad, spoke softly, stretching out one hand. She was sitting up in bed, her thin white hair arranged in a chignon of sorts. Ruth was pale, her skin a silky shade of alabaster, her eyes sunken now with age, revealing only a hint of the depth and beauty that had been hers in years past. She was frail and growing more so daily.

The cool facade Julia wore in her role with Conrad Industries quickly melted whenever she saw her grandmother. She sank gratefully into the chair next to the brass four-poster bed and slipped off her shoes, tucking her feet beneath her.

Visiting Ruth at the family home was an escape for her. She left her worries and troubles outside. Her world was often filled with chaos, but with Ruth she found calm; the day's tension was replaced by peace and solace.

The storm outside seemed far removed from this bedroom haven.

"The thunder woke me," Ruth said in a low voice, smiling weakly. "I lay back and I could hear huge kettledrums in the sky. Oh, how they rumbled. Then I had Charles open the drapes so I could look outside. The clouds billowed past like giant puffs of smoke. It was a marvelous show."

Julia took her grandmother's hand and released a slow, uneven breath. She glanced around the room, studying the treasures Ruth had chosen to keep nearby. A row of silver-framed pictures rested on the nightstand, next to several prescription bottles. There was one of her son—Julia's father—another of the family together, plus Ruth's own wedding portrait and a candid photo of her beloved husband, Louis. A chintz-covered Victorian chair sat in front of the fireplace, a wool afghan draped over the back for when Ruth felt well enough to venture from the bed. The round table beside the chair was covered with a dark velvet cloth. Julia's picture, one taken shortly after she'd graduated from college, was propped up beside the lamp. Julia looked away, unable to bear the naïveté and innocence she saw in that younger version of herself.

"I'm so pleased you stopped by," Ruth said again.

Julia came almost every day, knowing the time left with her grandmother was shrinking. Neither spoke of her death, although it was imminent. Julia was determined to do whatever she could to make these last days as comfortable and happy for her as possible. That was what kept Julia going day after day. She spent hours talking to her grandmother, telling her about Alek's ideas, the innovations he was currently working on, her own hopes for the company. They discussed the future and how the entire industry was about to change because of Alek's vision. Her grandmother had been as impressed with Alek as Julia was. Ruth had wanted to meet him, and Julia had asked Jerry to bring Alek over. From what she heard later, the two had been quite charmed by each other.

"I've been meaning to talk to you," Ruth whispered.

She sounded so weak. "Rest," Julia said urgently. "We'll talk later."

Ruth responded with a fragile smile. "I don't have much longer, Julia. A few weeks at the most…"

"Nonsense." The truth was too painful to face, yet much too persistent to ignore. "You're just tired, that's all. It'll pass."

Ruth's eyes drifted shut, but determination opened them a moment later. "We need to talk about Roger," her grandmother said insistently.

A muscle in Julia's neck tensed, and a cold shiver went down her backbone. "Not…now. Some other time. Later."

"Might not…have later. Best to do it now."

"Grandma, please…"

"He betrayed you, child, and you've held on to that grief all these years. Your pain is killing you just as surely as this heart of mine is draining away my life."

"I don't even think of him anymore." Julia tried to reassure her, although it was a lie. She struggled to push every thought of Roger from her mind, but that wouldn't happen until she'd completely rebuilt what he'd destroyed.

"Regret and anger are poisoning you like…like venom… I've watched it happen and been too weak… to help you the way I wanted."

"Grandma, please, Roger is out of my life. I haven't seen him in over a year. What's the point of talking about him now?"

"He's gone…but you haven't forgotten him. He failed you."

Julia clenched her teeth. That was one way of putting it. Roger *had* failed her. He'd also betrayed, tricked and abandoned her. When she thought of how much she'd loved him, how much she'd trusted him, it made her physically ill. Never again would she allow a man into her heart. Never again would she give a man the power to manipulate her.

"The time's come to forgive him."

Julia closed her eyes and shook her head. Her grandmother was asking the impossible. A woman didn't forgive the things Roger had done. Roger, the company's onetime director of research and development—and Julia's fiancé—had taught her the most valuable lesson of her life. She wasn't going to turn her back on the humiliation he'd caused her. Forgive him? Out of the question. She'd rather bury herself in work, insulate herself from love, than forgive Roger.

"I want you to love again," Ruth said, but her voice was so frail Julia had to strain to hear. "I don't think I can die in peace, knowing you're so miserable."

"Grandma, how can you say that? Jerry and I are working hard to rebuild the company. We're on the brink of doing truly amazing things. I've told you about them and about everything Aleksandr's done. How can you say I'm miserable? These are the most challenging, exciting days of my life."

"None of that means much…not when you're still imprisoned in pain. I've waited all these years for you to break free and fall in love again. It hasn't happened. I…look at you—" she hesitated and tears moistened her faded eyes "—and my heart aches. I want you to marry, to discover the happiness I found. It's the only thing that's kept me alive. I've waited for your season of suffering to pass…"

"I'll never be able to trust another man."

"You must for your own sake."

"I can't, not after what Roger did. Surely you understand. Surely you—"

With what must have required supreme effort, Ruth raised her hand, cutting Julia off. "I've longed for the day you'd proudly introduce me to the man you love. I was hoping it would be Aleksandr… He's such a dear man, and so brilliant. I'd also like Jerry to find a woman to love…" She paused. "I can't wait any longer. My time is short, so…very short." Her eyes drifted closed once more and her head slumped forward.

Julia sat quietly while the seeds of fear took root within her. Love again? Impossible. Something she refused to even consider.

Marriage. To Alek.

Twice in the same day someone had suggested she marry him. First Jerry, as a ridiculous solution to their problem with the Immigration people, and now her grandmother, as the answer to her pain.

Julia stood, her arms wrapped around her. Glancing over at Ruth, she realized her grandmother was asleep. The grandmother who'd loved and supported her all her life, who'd stood by her when the whole world exploded. When Ruth had lost her son and Julia her father, when the man who was supposed to love her betrayed them all.

Julia remembered a time, long past, when she'd been a child and a fierce thunderstorm had raged in the dead of night. Terrified, she'd raced down the hallway to Ruth's room and slipped into bed with her. Even then she'd known that was the safest place in all the world for her to be.

That security had always been with her. Soon she would lose her anchor, the person who'd guided and loved her. Ruth had never asked anything of her before. Julia didn't know how she could refuse now.

Julia's request came as no surprise. Aleksandr had been waiting for it since the scene in her office the day before. If he lived to be a wise, old man he doubted he'd ever understand this country he'd come to love. Nor was he likely to understand Julia Conrad. She was a woman encased in frost, a woman with a wounded soul. He'd recognized this from the moment they'd met. She was uncomfortable with him; he knew that from the way she avoided eye contact. He hadn't had much contact with her, and he suspected she preferred to communicate through her brother.

Julia's assistant let him into the office and announced his arrival. Julia was sitting at her desk writing. When he entered the room, she glanced up and smiled.

"Please, sit down," she said politely, motioning toward the chair on the other side of her desk. "I hope I'm not interrupting your work."

For a few seconds Aleksandr didn't trust himself to speak. Her pain was closer to the surface than ever before, almost visible beneath the facade she'd erected.

"I'm never too busy for you, Ms. Conrad," he said, bowing his head slightly.

Her features seemed perfect to him, her beauty so flawless it was chilling. He noted that her creamy skin was flushed but her eyes dark and clear as they studied him with equal interest.

"I thought it might be a good idea if we talked," she suggested haltingly.

He nodded. "About my work?"

She hesitated. Not answering, she stood and moved away from him, carefully placing herself in the shadows where it was more difficult to read her expression.

"Tell me how your experiments are progressing," she said, her hands clasped behind her back. He sensed her reserve—and her tension.

Aleksandr was well aware from the notes he'd received from her that Julia had read and understood his weekly reports. Nevertheless he humored her. The additives he'd been working on for Conrad paints had impressive capabilities. His first innovation had been a simple one. Once an exterior surface was painted, if the owner wished a different color at some later date, all he or she needed to do was wash the surface with another solution, one that would be available only through Conrad Industries. It was an approach that would work on homes, cars and lawn furniture.

His second innovation had been just as successful so far. He'd developed a blend of chemicals that, when applied to a surface, would completely remove the old paint. No more scraping or heating it. A spray of the solution would dissolve it away with a minimum of effort, without harmful effects or harsh chemicals to damage the environment.

Aleksandr gave Julia a detailed description of his most recent experiments. He regretted that he wouldn't be with Conrad Industries to see his work come to fruition, but there was nothing more he could do. He was sorry to be leaving America, especially since there was still such poverty and upheaval in his homeland.

He paused, awaiting her response.

"You're very close, then."

"Within a few months," he guessed.

Her brows arched with what he assumed was surprise and delight. Both emotions quickly left her expression as she looked away. Her eyes avoided his, and Aleksandr wondered privately how many hearts she'd broken. She held herself distant, the unattainable prize of many a man, the untouchable dream of loveliness.

"Aleksandr." She spoke with a casual familiarity, although as far as he could recall, it was the first time she'd addressed him by his first name. "We have a problem… as you know."

She moved toward him, her eyes wide, and when she spoke again it was in a whisper. "We're too close to lose everything now. I can't let it happen. My brother… came up with a solution."

Aleksandr's mind churned with confusion. She couldn't possibly be considering Jerry's suggestion that they get married, could she? Only a day earlier she'd scoffed at her brother for even mentioning something so preposterous. Alek hadn't been given a chance to comment.

"I've been thinking about Jerry's idea," she continued demurely, glancing over her shoulder at him as she returned to her desk. "It seems marriage is our only solution."

Aleksandr wasn't fooled by her demeanor; there wasn't a shy, retiring bone in that delectable body of hers. Julia Conrad was too proud and stubborn to play the role well. But there was no limit to her determination.

"Of course you'd be well compensated for your... contribution to Conrad Industries. Even more than we're currently paying you. We'd be happy to double your salary. Naturally it wouldn't be a real marriage, and when you've finished with your work, we'd obtain a quiet divorce. If you're agreeable, I'll have Jerry draw up a prenuptial agreement for us to sign."

Aleksandr was convinced that if there'd been any other way to solve the problem, Julia would have opted for it. She was offering him a pretend marriage, followed by a discreet divorce.

He frowned, disliking the fact that she was trying to bribe him with money. His wages were already far beyond what he could ever hope to make in Russia. Much of what he earned now he sent to his family, while he lived as frugally as possible.

"I understand there are several members of your family still in Russia," she said cautiously. "We might be able to help them immigrate to the States if we did decide to go ahead with this marriage."

At his silence, Julia added, "*If* that's something you'd care to consider—bringing your immediate family into the country. Is it?" she prompted.

Aleksandr's voice was strained when he spoke. "My sister is unmarried and lives with my mother, who is a widow." Unable to remain seated, he stood and walked to the window, his back to her. He felt a strong desire to take Julia in his arms, but he was painfully aware that there was no warmth in her, nor would she welcome his touch.

For two years Aleksandr had studied Julia Conrad. Outwardly she was often arrogant and sometimes sarcastic. But she wasn't entirely capable of hiding her softer side. Every now and then he caught puzzling, contradictory glimpses of her. She cared deeply for her employees and was often generous to a fault. Then there'd been the day, shortly after Alek had come to America, when he'd seen Julia with her grandmother.

Julia's facade had melted away that afternoon. If Alek hadn't seen it with his own eyes, he wouldn't have believed such a transformation was possible. Julia had glowed with joy and pride as she gave her grandmother a tour of the rebuilt facilities. Alek had watched from a distance—and had held on to that image of her ever since.

Marriage. He sighed inwardly. His religion didn't accept divorce and he refused to sacrifice his life and his happiness for a business proposition.

"I wish you'd say something," she said.

He returned to the chair and kept his features as expressionless as he could. "There's much we would need to consider before we enter into this agreement."

"Of course," she returned.

"Your money does not interest me."

She seemed surprised by his words. "Even for your family?"

"Even for my family." What he earned now was adequate. Julia wasn't the only one who was proud. Alek couldn't be bought. She, a woman who needed no one, needed him, and he appreciated what it had taken for her to approach him with this offer. Alek wasn't being completely unselfish, nor was he without greed. He had a price in mind.

"Then what is it you want?"

He shrugged, not knowing how to tell her.

Restlessly she came to her feet and walked away from him. He admired her smooth, fluid grace. She was a woman who moved with confidence, sure of herself and her surroundings. Usually. But at the moment she seemed sure of nothing and obviously that disturbed her.

"I don't know what to say," Aleksandr answered truthfully.

"Do you find the idea of marriage to me so distasteful?" she asked.

"No," he told her quietly. "You're lovely."

"Then what is it?"

"I don't want money."

"If it isn't money, then what? A percentage of my stock? A vice presidency? Tell me."

"You Americans regard marriage differently than we do in my country. There, when a man and woman marry, it is for many reasons, not all of them love. Nevertheless, when we marry it is for life."

"But you aren't in Russia now, you're in America."

"Americans treat marriage like dirty laundry. When it becomes inconvenient, you toss it aside. My head tells me I live in your country now, but my heart believes in tradition. If we marry, Julia, and it would be my wish that we do, there will be no divorce."

Her breath escaped in a rush and her dark eyes flared briefly.

Aleksandr ignored the fury he read in her and continued. "We both stand to gain from this arrangement. I will remain in the country and complete my experiments. You will have what you wish, as well. But there is a cost to this, one we should calculate now. The marriage will be a real one, or there will be no marriage."

Her gaze cut through him with ill-concealed contempt. "So you want more than the golden egg, you want the whole goose."

"The goose?" Aleksandr hadn't heard this story. He smiled. "In my family, goose is traditionally served at the wedding meal. I do not know about the golden egg, but you may keep that. I want only you."

Her voice was husky when she spoke. "That's what I thought."

The phone on her desk rang just then and Julia reached for it. "I said I didn't want to be disturbed," she said impatiently. Her face tightened as she listened. "Yes, yes, of course, you did the right thing. Put me through immediately." Several seconds passed. "Dr. Silverman, this is Julia Conrad. I understand you've had my grandmother taken to Virginia Mason Hospital."

Alek watched as the eyes that had been distressed and angry a moment earlier softened with emotion. She blinked, and Alek thought he might have noticed the sheen of tears.

"Naturally. I'll let my brother know right away and we'll meet you there as soon as we can. Thank you for contacting me so soon." She replaced the receiver, stood and started out of the room, apparently forgetting Aleksandr was there.

"Your grandmother is ill?" he asked.

She whirled around, apparently surprised at the sound of his voice, and nodded. "I...have to leave. I don't believe there's any need for us to discuss this further. I can't agree to your conditions. I refuse to be trapped in the type of marriage you're suggesting. I'd hoped we'd be able to work out some kind of compromise, but that doesn't seem possible."

"I'm disappointed. We would've had fine children."

She stared at him as if he'd spoken in his native tongue and she didn't understand a word he'd said. "Children?" she repeated. A sadness seemed to steal over her; she shook her head, perhaps to dispel the image.

"I will think good things for your grandmother," Alek told her.

She nodded. "Thank you." With what looked like hard-won poise, she turned and left the office.

Alek watched her go, and the proud way in which she carried herself tugged at his heart. He wished her grandmother well, but more importantly, he wished Julia a happy life.

Knowing his time in the States was limited to mere days, Aleksandr worked well past five, when his colleagues had all gone home. He felt it was his moral obligation to do everything within his power to see that the next series of experiments was performed to the standards he'd set for the earlier ones. He wouldn't be with Conrad Industries to oversee the ongoing research, and that bothered him, but he had no choice.

The laboratory was silent, and the footsteps echoing down the wide corridor outside his office were louder than they would otherwise have been.

He raised his eyes expectantly when Julia Conrad opened the door without knocking and walked inside. She was pale, her eyes darker than he'd ever seen them before.

"Julia," he said, standing abruptly. "Is something wrong?"

She looked sightlessly around, as though she didn't know where she was or how she got there.

"Your grandmother?"

Julia nodded and gnawed on her bottom lip. "She... she had another heart attack."

"I'm sorry."

Her eyes flew upward as if to gauge the sincerity of his words. For a lengthy moment she said nothing. Then she inhaled a shaky breath and bit her lip so hard, Aleksandr was afraid she'd draw blood.

"I... I've reconsidered, Mr. Berinski. I'll marry you under the conditions you've set."

Two

"I don't want an elaborate wedding." Julia folded her arms, moving to the far side of her office. Her brother was being impossible. "How could there even be time to arrange one?"

"Julia, you're not listening to me."

"I'm listening," she said sharply. "I just don't happen to like what I'm hearing."

"A reception at the Four Seasons isn't so much to ask."

"But a wedding with guests and this whole thing about wearing a fancy wedding dress is ridiculous! Jerry, please, this is getting out of hand. I understand marriage is the best solution, but I didn't realize I'd be forced to endure the mockery of a formal wedding."

Jerry gestured helplessly. "We've got to make this as credible as we can. Apparently you don't understand how important this is—and not just the wedding, either. That's only the first hurdle. You have to make everything appear as though you're madly in love. Nothing less will convince the Immigration people. If you fail... I don't even want to think about that."

"You've already gone through this." More times than she cared to count.

"Alek has to live with you, too."

This was the part that disturbed Julia most. Her condo was her private haven, the one place where she could be completely herself. She was about to lose that, too. "But why?" She knew the answer, had argued until Jerry was seething with exasperation. Julia didn't blame him, but this marriage was becoming far more complicated than she'd ever thought it would.

"Why?" Jerry shouted, throwing his hands in the air. "I've made everything as plain as I can. Alek isn't the problem, it's you. What I don't understand, Julia, is why you're being so difficult when we're the ones who stand to benefit from this arrangement."

"You're making Alek sound like a saint for marrying me." She frowned. "And I don't see *you* running for the altar." Jerry had recently ended yet another brief liaison.

He didn't answer right away, which irritated her even more. "Let's put it this way," he finally said. "Conrad Industries is gaining far more from this marriage than Alek ever will. And," he added, "my marital status is irrelevant."

Julia rolled her eyes at that. "I offered to pay him, and very generously, too," she said.

"You insulted him. The man has his pride, Julia. He isn't doing this for the money."

"Then why is he going through with it?"

Jerry shrugged. "Darned if I know."

His words reiterated that Alek wasn't getting any bargain by marrying her. "He wants to help his family," Julia reminded her brother. She remembered Alek mentioning a sister and his widowed mother. As the oldest son, Alek would feel responsible for taking care of his family. Julia had promised to do whatever she could to bring both his mother and his sister to the United States. This marriage provided plenty of incentives for Alek, she told herself, so she didn't need to worry about taking advantage of him.

"There's more to the man than meets the eye," Jerry muttered. "I'm convinced he's not interested in monetary gain. When he read over the prenup, he insisted on no stake in the company. We're about to make a fortune because of him, and he wants no part of it."

This discussion wasn't doing anything to ease Julia's conscience. "I agreed to the marriage," she said, not wanting to stray any further from the subject than they already had. "But no one said anything about a wedding. I thought we'd make an appointment with a justice of the peace and be done with it." She walked over to her desk, opened the old-fashioned appointment book and flipped through the pages. "Friday at four is open."

"Julia," Jerry returned with a sigh. "As I've explained— we've got to make this as real as we can for obvious reasons."

"I've said Alek can move in with me." To Julia, that was a major concession. She wasn't pleased by it, nor did she feel good about tricking Alek. He'd insisted from the first that their marriage be real. He'd made it known that he intended to sleep with her; he also wanted children. Julia couldn't allow any of that. Alek didn't understand and neither did Jerry. Julia was incapable of love, the kind of trusting love a husband and wife shared. That possibility was dead, destroyed by Roger's treachery. Never again would she put her faith in a man. Alek expected her to be his wife in every way, but soon he'd learn the truth. Soon he'd know for himself how badly he was being cheated. Such deception didn't sit well with Julia, but there was no avoiding it.

While Julia admired Alek, she found herself nervous around him. He left her feeling naked, somehow. Exposed. He seemed to be able to look into her very soul. That didn't make sense, but she couldn't shake the suspicion that in some uncanny way he knew all there was to know about her.

"Immigration is going to ask about the wedding," Jerry went on. "We need proof that what prompted the marriage to Alek was nothing less than earth-shattering love. A hurried-up affair in some judge's chambers won't work. They're going to want evidence of your commitment and devotion to each other."

"A hurried-up affair at the Four Seasons will convince them of all that?" she asked sarcastically.

Jerry sighed again. "It looks better. Now, I suggest you go out and get yourself a fancy wedding dress while I make arrangements with Virginia. We'll deal with the caterers and the photographers and see to having the invitations hand-delivered."

"Jerry, this is crazy!" Julia protested. The idea of dressing up in an elaborate wedding gown, as if she were a loving bride on display, appalled her. Nor was she keen on posing for a series of photographs, like a new wife passionately in love with her husband. It was too much. "I can't go through with this," she said evenly.

"You've already agreed."

"To the marriage, yes, but not this…this circus. It's becoming a Hollywood production, a show for media attention."

"A show is what we need if we're going to fool the Immigration investigators," Jerry argued. "And trust me, Julia, this marriage will be investigated."

Julia walked over to the window and studied the street several floors below. In a moment of weakness, when her fears had been rampant and she was so deathly afraid of losing Ruth, Julia had gone to Alek and agreed to his terms. Even now she didn't understand what had prompted her. She was sick of analyzing it, furious with herself for being so weak. This morning, once her head had cleared, she'd realized it had all been a mistake. But by then Alek had contacted Jerry, who'd put everything in motion. Now, it seemed, there was no turning back.

Her intercom hummed before Virginia's efficient voice reached out to her. "Mr. Berinski is here to see you."

Julia looked at her brother in sheer panic. She wasn't prepared to deal with Alek just yet. They hadn't spoken since she'd consented to the marriage.

"Julia," Jerry prompted when she didn't respond.

"Send him in," Julia instructed her assistant, steeling herself for the confrontation.

No sooner had the words left her mouth than the door leading to her office opened. Alek walked in and his dark eyes shone brightly as he gazed over at her. A slow, seductive smile appeared on his lips.

"Good afternoon." Alek spoke to her brother first, then returned his attention to her. "Julia."

"Alek," she said briskly, surprised by how defensive she sounded.

He didn't seem perturbed by her lack of welcome. Last night she'd agreed to become his wife, accepting the stipulations he'd set. She'd been overwrought with anxiety, frightened and lost. Yet no matter how hard she argued with herself, Julia wouldn't change her mind... unless Alek wanted out. She was a woman of honor, a woman of her word. She knew he was the same way.

"I was just clearing the wedding arrangements with Julia," Jerry explained.

Alek's eyes refused to leave her. She felt her face heat and wished with everything in her that she *could* escape.

"I'd like some time alone with my fiancée," Alek said.

Julia sent Jerry a pleading glance, not wanting him to leave her. Jerry ignored the unspoken request, mumbled something under his breath and walked out of the room.

"You want to talk?" she asked abruptly. She rubbed her palms and walked away from him. Her shoulders felt stiff and her legs heavy.

"You're nervous."

Nervous. Terrified. Afraid. None of those words adequately described what Julia was experiencing. The situation had an eerie, unreal quality that she couldn't shake. Only a few years earlier she'd looked forward to being a happy bride. She'd dreamed of the day Roger would slip a wedding band on her finger and gaze down at her with love.

She felt a flash of unexpected pain, then forced herself to shake the image from her head.

"All brides are nervous," she said quietly in response to his question.

"How is your grandmother?"

"I'll be seeing her this afternoon... Better, I believe." According to the nurse Julia had spoken with that morning, Ruth had slept restfully through the night. But that had been *after* Jerry had spoken to her and said Julia would be marrying Aleksandr Berinski. Her grandmother had only met Alek once, and that had been recently. He'd obviously made quite an impression, because his name had cropped up with alarming frequency ever since.

"Do you wish to cancel the wedding?" Alek probed.

Here was her chance, handed to her on the proverbial silver platter. All she needed to do was tell him that she hadn't been herself, that she hadn't been fully aware of what she was doing. She opened her mouth to explain it all away and found she couldn't. The words refused to come. While she was fumbling for a reply, he stepped behind her and rested his hands on her shoulders. He leaned forward, gently kissing the side of her neck.

Julia froze. It was the first time a man had touched her since Roger. She couldn't move, couldn't breathe. Alek didn't seem to notice. Sliding his arms around her, he brought her against him. His breath stirred shivers along her spine and a curious warmth crept into her blood.

Alek turned her around to face him. She wasn't given the opportunity to object as he pressed his mouth to hers. His lips moved slowly over hers. She wedged her hands between them, braced her palms against his hard chest and pushed herself free. Her lungs felt as though they were about to burst, and she drew in a deep breath.

Alek didn't seem offended or surprised by her actions. His eyes danced with mischief as they sought hers. Julia raised the back of her hand to her mouth and held it there. She burned with anger. He'd done this intentionally so she'd know he expected to touch her and kiss her often after the ceremony. She was to be his wife in every sense of the word and he wouldn't tolerate a loveless, sexless marriage. He wanted her and he was making sure she knew it.

What was she going to do?

Julia stood outside the bridal shop with all the thrill and anticipation of a long-overdue visit to the dentist.

She opened the door and walked inside, grateful the saleswoman wasn't busy.

"Hello."

"Hello," Julia said stiffly, fanning out the billowing chiffon skirt of a pale yellow bridesmaid's dress that hung from a rack.

"May I help you?" came the friendly voice.

Julia revealed her lack of enthusiasm with a noncommittal shrug. "I need a wedding dress for this Friday afternoon."

The shopkeeper was petite, hardly more than five feet tall with soft brown hair. The woman was a dreamer; Julia could see it in her eyes. She, too, had once worn that same look of innocence...

"The wedding is *this* Friday?"

"I know that doesn't give me much time," Julia said, feeling foolish. "It's one of those spur-of-the-moment things."

"Don't worry," the saleswoman assured her, hurrying toward a long rack of plastic-covered wedding dresses. "Spur-of-the-moment weddings are often the most romantic."

Julia had nothing to add. She could tell that this woman was more than a dreamer; she was also hopelessly sentimental. She had her head in the clouds when it came to love, and no doubt her attitude had been influenced by her job. She dealt with women who were deeply in love, women for whom the entire world was there for the taking.

Three years earlier, Julia had been one of them. Young, enthusiastic and so much in love she didn't recognize what should've been obvious.

"I'd like a very plain dress," she said forcefully, breaking off her thoughts.

"Plain," the woman repeated slowly.

"The plainer the better," Julia reiterated, strolling about the store.

"I'm afraid I have a limited selection of plain dresses."

That was what Julia feared. "Something simple, then."

"Simple and elegant?" she asked, grinning approvingly. "Would you like to look through this rack? Choose the designs that appeal to you, I'll get them in your size, and then you can try them on."

As far as Julia was concerned, this business with the wedding dress was a waste of time. She wanted it to be over and done with so she could head for the hospital and visit Ruth.

The saleswoman led her to the appropriate display of gowns. Julia shuffled through them quickly, making two selections. Neither dress really appealed to her.

"I'll try on these two," Julia said.

The woman made no comment as she went into the back room and returned a few minutes later with the two dresses in the correct size. She took them into the dressing room and placed them on the hook.

Julia obediently followed her inside. She undressed and slipped into the first dress. It was just as the saleswoman had promised. Simple and elegant. A straight skirt made of silk, a beaded yoke and cuffs. It looked fine, Julia supposed.

"No," the shop owner said with certainty. "This one doesn't suit you."

"It looks…"

"No," the woman repeated. "Don't even bother to try on the next dress. It wouldn't suit you, either."

"Please, I don't have a lot of time."

"The dress is one of the most important aspects of your wedding. Every bride deserves to feel beautiful on her special day."

Julia didn't know why she felt like crying, but she did. Buckets of tears welled up inside her. She was grateful the woman didn't seem to notice. Brides deserved a whole lot more than feeling beautiful; they deserved to marry a man they loved. A man who loved them, too.

"Wait here," she instructed. She left the changing area and came back a moment later carrying a lovely ornate dress. The silk gown with pearls and sequins was anything but simple. Rarely had Julia seen a dress as intricate as this.

"Try it on," she said when Julia hesitated.

"I… I don't think I should."

"Nonsense. This dress was designed for someone with your body type. It's perfect. It arrived this afternoon, almost as though I'd sent away for it with you in mind."

"I don't know," Julia murmured. The woman held up the gown for her inspection. It was lovely, ten times more elaborate than the one she'd tried on earlier. Ten times more beautiful, too. It was the kind of dress a woman in love would choose, knowing her groom would treasure its beauty. Would treasure *her* beauty.

A groom who'd cherish her devotion all his life. It was the style of dress she would've worn for Roger before she learned of his betrayal. Before she'd learned what a fool she'd been.

She wanted to argue, but one look convinced her that the woman would hear none of it. Not exactly sure why she'd allowed this stranger to dictate her actions, Julia put on the dress. The silk and taffeta rustled as it slid effortlessly over her hips. She kept her eyes lowered as she turned around and the shopkeeper fastened the small pearl closures down her back.

Julia felt strangely reluctant to look into a mirror, almost fearing her own reflection. When she did raise her eyes to the glass, she was startled at the beautiful young woman who gazed back at her. It took her a wild second to realize it was herself.

Gone were the lines that told of the bitterness and disappointment she'd carried with her since her father's death. The cool, disinterested look in her eyes had warmed. The calculating side of her personality faded, replaced by the woman she'd been before she'd fallen in love with Roger Stanhope. Open, trusting, naive—too young for her years.

Unable to look at herself any longer, Julia dragged her eyes away from the graceful reflection of the woman she'd once been. The woman Roger's deception had destroyed.

"It's perfect," the saleswoman was saying with a sigh of appreciation. "Just perfect. It's as if the dress was meant for you."

Julia opened her mouth to contradict the woman, but before she could voice her objection she looked at the mirror one last time. A few days earlier she'd caught a stormy glimpse of herself reflected in her office window. She'd disliked what she'd seen, the woman she'd become, cold, uncaring and driven.

She'd quickly abandoned her self-analysis and had concentrated on what was happening with Alek and Jerry at the Immigration office instead. The events of that afternoon had resulted in this farce of a wedding.

Alek had been adamant that there be no divorce. Julia had agreed to those terms, but not in the spirit he'd intended. If it weren't for these particular circumstances, Julia doubted she would ever have married. This would be her only wedding, her one chance to wear such a beautiful gown.

"I'll take it," she said, calling herself a fool even as she spoke.

"Somehow I knew you would." The saleswoman grinned broadly.

It took an additional twenty minutes, while the dress was wrapped up and the bill paid, before Julia was able to leave the shop. Nervously she glanced at her watch as she headed toward her parked car. She was already late and knew Ruth would be worried.

As often as she'd visited hospitals, Julia could never accustom herself to the antiseptic smell. She rushed down the polished hallway to the wing that housed her grandmother. She hated the thought of Ruth being here, away from her comfortable home and the pictures she loved and kept close to her side.

Ruth had tried repeatedly to prepare Julia for her death, but Julia refused to listen, refused to accept life without her adored grandmother.

Checking in at the nurses' station, Julia was left to wait until Velma Williams, the head nurse, returned.

A striking arrangement of red, blue, yellow and white flowers overfilled an inverted straw hat on a corner of the long counter. Julia admired it as she stood there. A few minutes later, Velma was back and Julia was ushered to Ruth's side.

"Good afternoon," Julia whispered. She couldn't tell if Ruth was sleeping or simply resting her eyes. Her grandmother seemed to be doing more of both lately. There were various tubes and pieces of equipment attached to Ruth's body, monitoring her heart and administering drugs intravenously. Julia looked down on this woman she loved so much and had to force back her growing sense of alarm. It seemed to ring in her ears, announcing that the time was fast approaching when Ruth would no longer be with her.

The older woman's eyes gradually drifted open. "Julia, my dear, I'm so glad you're here. Come, sit with me."

Julia pulled up a chair and sat next to the high hospital bed. "How are you feeling?"

Ruth gestured weakly with her hand. "That's not important now. Tell me about you and Alek. How I've prayed for this day. How I've hoped you'd learn to love again."

"The wedding's on Friday afternoon." Julia half suspected her grandmother would find the timing suspicious, but instead Ruth smiled tenderly and a faraway look came into her tired eyes.

"Friday… It's a good thing you won't have a long engagement, because I doubt I'll last more than a week or two."

"Grandma, please don't say that. You're going to be around for years and years."

The weary smile didn't waver. "I won't see my great-grandchildren."

Julia wanted to argue with her, but she couldn't; there'd never be children for her and Alek because there would never be a real marriage. She suffered a slight twinge of guilt but pushed it aside as a luxury she couldn't afford.

"I'm sorry I'm late but I was trying on wedding dresses," Julia explained, injecting some enthusiasm into her voice. She was mildly surprised at how little effort it required to sound excited about the dress she'd bought at the bridal shop. She described it in detail and was pleased at the way her grandmother's eyes brightened.

"You and Alek will come see me after the ceremony, won't you?"

"Of course," Julia promised.

Ruth motioned toward the nurses' station. "He sent me flowers. He's a very thoughtful boy. Velma carried in the bouquet for me to see. Did you notice them?"

"*Who* sent you flowers?"

"Your Alek. An enchanting arrangement, and such a sweet thing to do. I like him, Julia. You've chosen well, my dear."

Julia was uncomfortable talking about Alek. He'd been foremost in her thoughts all day and she wanted to escape him, escape the memory of his gentle kiss.

"Tell me about your romance. You've been so close-mouthed about it all…yet I knew." Ruth's eyes closed slowly and she sighed. With what seemed to be a good deal of effort she opened her eyes again. "He's a special man, that one. Just hearing about you two gladdens my heart."

"Ah…" Julia hesitated, not sure what to say. "It all happened rather quickly…almost overnight."

"So I gathered." A spark appeared in Ruth's eyes. "Oh, how I adore a love story. Tell me more before I fall back asleep."

"Alek's visa was about to expire." Keeping everything as close to the truth as possible made this much easier.

"His visa," Ruth repeated. "Of course, I'd forgotten."

"He was going to have to return to Russia."

"And you realized you couldn't let that happen, didn't you?"

"I hadn't realized how important he was to me," Julia said, adding drama to her voice. "Jerry did everything he could to persuade the Immigration people to let Alek stay, but nothing he said convinced them. The three of us were talking and suddenly I understood how vital it was to me that Alek remain in the United States. I… don't think I could bear to go on without him." This was a stretch, but Julia knew what a romantic her grandmother was. If she was exaggerating the truth just a little, it was a small price to pay to satisfy Ruth.

"Julia, my sweet child." Her grandmother's delicate hand reached for Julia's and she squeezed her fingers. "I always trusted that in time you'd open your heart to love again. It took a special man like Alek. Be happy, my child. Promise me you won't let go until you've found your joy."

Julia wasn't sure she understood Ruth's words. They made little sense to her. She would have questioned her if Ruth hadn't chosen that moment to slip into a peaceful slumber. For several minutes Julia remained at her grandmother's side, taking in the solace she felt whenever she spent time with Ruth.

"Julia." The sound of her name, said with that soft European accent, caught her attention. She jerked around to find Alek standing in the doorway.

She got up abruptly, resenting his intrusion into these quiet moments. She walked toward the door, not wanting him to interrupt her grandmother's rest.

"What are you doing here?" she asked when they were well into the corridor.

The edge of his mouth lifted in a half smile. "I came to see you. There is much we need to discuss." He tucked her hand in the crook of his elbow and sauntered over to the elevator.

"I left the wedding arrangements in Jerry's hands. He'll look after everything. As far as I can see, there's nothing to discuss."

She saw the anger in him, in the prideful squaring of his shoulders and the way his mouth thinned.

"You want me, Julia, and you need me. I just wonder how long it will take before you realize this."

The arrogance of the man was beyond description. She glared at him. She needed no one, especially a man, and never a husband. She wanted to shout out the words, but a hospital corridor was the last place to do that.

Long seconds passed as they stared into each other's eyes.

"You need me," he said again.

"You're wrong," she returned defiantly. Conrad Industries needed him; she didn't.

Their eyes lingered and it seemed neither of them knew what to say or do next. Jerry had mentioned how proud Alek was, and she could see that colossal ego for herself. He released her arm and turned away.

He was several yards down the hospital corridor before Julia spoke.

"I *don't* need you, Alek," she called after him. She had to say something. They'd quickly make each other miserable if this friction between them continued. If he wouldn't make an effort, then it was up to her.

"So you've already said."

"But I *am* willing to admit we need each other."

Grinning, he turned back. His smile grew as he returned to her side. For a heartbeat, he said nothing. Then he lowered his mouth to hers and kissed her. His touch was as gentle as before. Light as air, it left her wondering if she'd imagined his kiss.

"Why did you do that?" she asked.

His smile was worth waiting for. "Because, my soon-to-be-wife, you deserved it." He brushed the hair away from her face. "For that matter," he said with a roguish grin, "so did I."

Three

The wedding ceremony was a nightmare for Julia. When it came time to repeat her vows, her throat closed up and she could barely speak. Not so with Alek. His voice rang out loud and clear, without the least hesitation.

Love and cherish.

Julia's conscience was screaming. She had no intention of loving Alek. She didn't want to love any man, because love had the power to hurt her, the power to break her. Julia had worked hard to blot it from her life. Love was superfluous, unnecessary, painful when abused, and her heart had yet to recover from her first experience with it.

Signing the final documents was even worse than enduring the ceremony. Her hand trembled as she wrote her name on the marriage certificate. Her eyes glazed with tears as she stared at the official document, all too aware of the lie she was living.

Jerry, her assistant and the minister all seemed unaware of her distress. She didn't know what Alek was thinking. His fingers pressed against the small of her back as though to encourage her. She continued to hold the pen and remained bent over the document long after she'd finished signing her name.

"May your marriage be a long and fruitful one," the minister was saying to Alek. Julia squeezed her eyes shut, drew in a steadying breath and straightened. She dared not look at Alek for fear he could read her thoughts.

Long and fruitful, Julia's mind echoed. A sob welled up inside her and she was afraid she'd burst into tears. This deception was so much more difficult than she'd ever imagined.

"Shall we join the others?" Jerry, who had served as Alek's best man, suggested, gesturing toward the door. Julia was grateful for an excuse to leave the room.

The reception was being held in a large hotel suite across the hall from where the wedding had taken place. Their guests were helping themselves to a wide array of hors d'oeuvres served on silver platters, and crystal flutes of champagne.

Julia was surprised by how many people had come on such short notice. Most were business associates, but several family friends were also in attendance. She had few friends left, allowing the majority of her relationships to lapse after her father's death.

Alek was at her side, smiling and cordially greeting their guests. He placed his arm casually around her shoulders. Julia stiffened at the unwelcome familiarity, but if he noted her uneasiness, he paid no heed.

"Have I told you how beautiful you look?" he whispered close to her ear.

Julia nodded. He hadn't been able to take his eyes off her from the moment she'd arrived in her wedding dress. Oddly, that depressed her, planning to deceive him the way she was. He was expecting more from this marriage than she was going to give him. She should've opted for the plain, simple, unadorned dress instead of the ornate one she'd chosen.

The minute she'd viewed herself before the wedding, she was sorry she'd bought this gown. Even Jerry had seemed dumbstruck when he went to escort her to Alek's side. He'd become especially maudlin with his compliments, which added to her stress. And her guilt.

"Could you *pretend* to love me?" Alek whispered. "Just for these few hours?" His warm breath against her skin sent shivers down her spine. "Smile, my love."

She complied obediently, her expression no doubt looking as stiff as it felt.

"Better," he murmured under his breath.

"How soon can we leave?"

Alek chuckled softly. "I know you're eager for me, but if we left too soon, it would be unseemly."

Julia's face burned with a wild blush, which appeared to amuse Alek even more. "Would you like me to get you a plate?" he offered.

She shook her head. Food held no appeal. "Do *you* want something?" she asked.

He turned to her, his eyes ablaze. "Rest assured, I do, but I'll get my dessert later."

Julia didn't think her knees would support her much longer. From obligation more than desire, she drank a glass of champagne. It must've been more potent than she realized because she felt giddy and light-headed afterward.

It was the dress, she decided. She wanted to change out of the wedding gown because it made her feel things she had no right to feel. With Alek standing at her side, she felt beautiful and wanted and loved when she didn't deserve or want any of it. She'd gone into this marriage for all the wrong reasons. She was uncomfortable, using Alek for her own gain, giving nothing of herself in return.

Until she'd stood before the preacher, marriage had been little more than a concept, an idea she didn't believe in. She hadn't expected a few words mumbled before a man of God to be so powerful. But she'd been wrong. Julia was shaken and uncertain afterward, as if she was mocking important human values.

"Jerry." She reached out to her brother and clasped his arm with both hands. "I've got to get out of here…"

He must have read the desperation in her eyes, because he nodded gravely. Whatever he said to Alek, Julia didn't hear. She assumed her brother would escort her from the room, but it was Alek who slipped his arm around her waist. It was her husband who led her out of the reception.

"Jerry is making our excuses," he explained.

She nodded. "I'm sorry," she whispered as he took her down the hallway to the changing room. "I don't know what happened."

"Are you feeling faint?"

"I'm fine now, thanks." Or she would be, once she was out of this dress and back in her own clothes. And once he removed his arm from her waist… The walls seemed to close in around her. She wished Alek would leave her, but he stayed even when she reached the door leading to the changing room.

"We didn't kiss," Alek whispered. "Not properly."

Julia didn't bother to pretend she didn't know what

he was talking about. When Alek was told to kiss his bride, Julia had made sure he'd merely given her a peck on the cheek. Alek had been disappointed, and Jerry's eyes had revealed his frustration. A passionate kiss would've put the stamp of credibility on their act.

"You're not sick, are you?"

She could have lied, could have offered him countless excuses, but she didn't. "I'm fine," she said, just as she had a minute earlier.

"Then I'll kiss my bride."

Her first instinct was to put him off, to thwart him again, but a kiss seemed like such a simple way to ease her conscience. His touch had always been tender, as if he understood and appreciated her need for gentleness.

"Yes," she agreed breathlessly.

Her back was against the wall and his arms went around her waist. Unsure what to do with her own hands, she splayed them across his chest. He pulled her against him, and for a long moment he held her, as if savoring the feel of her in his arms.

The trembling returned and Julia closed her eyes. She could smell his cologne, feel his heart beat beneath her flattened palms. His breath echoed in her ears and rustled her hair.

His mouth met hers. His touch was light and brief. She tipped her head back and her eyes drifted shut as his mouth brushed hers again. And again. A sigh worked its way through her as his tongue outlined the shape of her mouth. After a series of nibbling kisses, he caught her lower lip between his teeth.

Julia held her breath, unable to respond. She was content to let him be the aggressor, to allow him to touch her and kiss her without fully participating herself.

But her lack of involvement obviously bothered Alek. "Julia," he pleaded, "kiss me back."

Tentatively, shyly, her mouth opened to him and he moaned, then deepened the kiss. His arms tightened their hold and he slanted his mouth over hers. Strange, unwelcome pleasure rippled through her body.

She sighed at the sensations she experienced; she couldn't help it. She felt hot and shaky, as though she'd suffered a near miss, as though she'd stepped off a curb and felt the rush of a car passing by and come within inches of being struck.

Her hands, which had seemed so useless moments before, were buried in his dark hair. Her body, so long untouched, felt about to explode. She moved against him, clinging to him, fighting back tears.

The sound of someone clearing his throat broke the spell. Alek stilled, as did Julia. Slowly, reluctantly, she opened her eyes to find half of the reception guests lined up in the hall watching them.

Jerry stood in the background, smiling broadly. He gave her a thumbs-up, looking ecstatic. If they were hoping to fool their guests, they'd succeeded beyond her brother's expectations.

As though loath to do it, Alek released her. He seemed perturbed by the interruption and muttered something she didn't understand.

"I'll change clothes," she said, hurriedly moving into the room. She was grateful there was a chair. Sinking down onto it, she pressed her hands to her red face and closed her eyes. She felt as if she'd leapt off a precipice in the dark and had no idea of where she'd be landing. A kiss that had begun as a compromise had become something else. She'd been trying to soothe her conscience, but instead had added to her growing list of offenses, leading Alek to believe he should expect more.

Julia took her time changing. Fifteen minutes later she reappeared in a bright red flowered dress she'd found in the back of her closet. These days she dressed mostly in business suits—jackets, straight skirts and plain white blouses. The dress was a leftover from her college days. The design was simple and stylish.

Alek was pacing the hallway anxiously.

"I'm sorry I took so long."

His smile was enthusiastic. He touched her lips, still swollen from his kiss. The color hadn't faded from her cheeks, either; if anything, it had deepened with this fresh appraisal.

"I…promised my grandmother we'd stop in at the hospital after the reception," Julia said nervously. "I'd hate to disappoint her."

"By all means we will see her."

They said their farewells and left the reception. Julia knew the minute they walked into Ruth's hospital room that she'd been waiting for them. Her grandmother's smile was filled with love as she held her hands out to them.

Julia rushed forward and hugged her. She was reminded each and every time she saw her grandmother that Ruth was close to death. She clung to life, not for herself, but for Julia's sake. It hurt her to know Ruth was in pain. Why did those who were good always have to suffer? Why couldn't God spare her grandmother just a few more years? This day, her wedding day, had started a cauldron of emotions churning in her mind. She couldn't bear to think of what her life would be like without her grandmother.

It had been Ruth's kindness that had gotten her through Roger's deception and her father's death. Otherwise, Julia feared she would've ended up in a mental ward.

Other emotions long buried and ignored came to the surface, as well. Kissing Alek had stirred up needs and desires she'd assumed were lost to her.

There were no answers, at least none she felt confident enough to face. Only myriad questions that assailed her on every front. She couldn't trust herself; her power to discern had been sadly lacking once and had cost her and her family dearly. She dared not trust herself a second time.

She was married to a man she didn't love, a man who didn't love her, either. To complicate everything, her grandmother was dying. This was what her life had come down to. A loveless marriage and a desperate loneliness.

When Julia released her grandmother, Ruth looked up and brushed the tears from Julia's cheeks. "You're crying?" she asked softly. "This should be the happiest day of your life."

Alek placed his arm around Julia's waist and helped her into the chair next to the bed. He stood behind her, his hands resting lightly on her shoulders. Julia pressed Ruth's hand to her cheek and held it there. Her grandmother seemed much weaker today.

"I remember when I married Louis," she said with a wistful smile.

Her grandfather had been dead many years now. He was only a vague memory to Julia, who guessed she'd been about seven or eight when he died.

"I was frightened out of my wits."

"Frightened?" Julia didn't understand.

"I wondered if I was doing the right thing. There were very few divorces in those days and if a woman happened to marry the wrong man, she was often sentenced to a miserable life."

"But I thought you'd known him for a long time."

Ruth arched one delicate brow. "A long time?" she repeated. "In a manner of speaking, you're right. But we'd only gone out on a handful of dates before we were married."

"I'd always assumed you knew Grandpa for years."

Ruth's hand stroked Julia's cheek. "It's true that in the early days Louis worked for my father at the paint company my family owned. I'd see him now and then when I dropped in at the office, but those times were rare."

Julia was enthralled. She knew her grandmother had deeply loved her grandfather, but she couldn't remember ever hearing the story of their courtship.

"When did you fall in love?"

"Louis stopped working for my father, and Dad was furious with him. They were both strong-willed men and it seemed they were constantly disagreeing. Louis started his own business in direct competition with my family's." She smiled whimsically. "It was a bold move in those depression years, before the war. He managed to keep his head above water, which infuriated my father even more. I think at that point Dad would've taken pleasure in seeing Louis fail." She paused and closed her eyes for a moment, as though to gather her strength.

"Then the war came and Louis joined the army. Before he left for England he came to the house. I thought he was there to see my father. Can you imagine my surprise when he said I was the one he'd come to see? He told me he was going overseas and he asked if I'd be willing to write him. Naturally I told him I would be, and then he did the strangest thing."

When Ruth didn't immediately continue, Julia prompted her. "What did he do?"

Ruth shook her head. "It was such a little thing and so very sweet, so much like Louis. He took my hand and kissed it."

Her grandmother's gaze fell to her hand, as if she still felt the imprint of his lips.

"As I look back on it," Ruth went on, "I realize that was when I lost my heart to Louis. You see, I don't believe he ever expected to return from the war. He loved me then, he told me much later, and had for a long time, but Louis was afraid Dad would never approve of him as my husband."

"How long was he away?"

"I didn't see him for three years, although I heard from him regularly. I treasured his letters and reread them so often I nearly wore them out. By the time he came home I was so deeply in love with him, nothing else mattered. My family knew how I felt and I feared the worst when Dad insisted on accompanying me to meet Louis's train."

"What happened?"

Ruth's smile was weak, but happy. "Dad offered to merge his business with Louis's. Even though Louis himself had been away, his small company had survived the war. Louis accepted, with the stipulation that both the company and I take on his name." She smiled again. "It was a...unique proposal. My father agreed without much hesitation—and I agreed with none at all. We were married less than a month later."

"What a beautiful story," Julia whispered.

"We had a wonderful life together, better than I dared dream. I'll never stop missing him."

Julia knew her grandmother had taken Louis's death hard. For a long while afterward, she'd closed herself off from life. It was in those bleak years that Julia's father had wisely sent Julia and Jerry to spend the summers with their grandmother.

"You, my children," Ruth continued, turning to Alek, "will have a good life, too. Alek, be gentle with my lamb. Her heart's been bruised, and she can be a bit… prickly, but all she needs is love and patience."

"Grandma!"

Ruth chuckled and gestured with her hand. "Off with you now. You don't want to spend your wedding night with me."

"I love you," Julia murmured as Ruth settled back against the pillows. "Have a good sleep, and I'll call you in the morning."

"It was a privilege to spend this time with you," Alek said. Reaching for her grandmother's hand, he bent down and kissed it. "I would have liked your Louis," he told her. "He was a rare man of honor."

A smile coaxed up the corners of Ruth's mouth. "Indeed he was. When we first married, there was talk, there always seemed to be talk. Some folks said Louis had married me for my connections, for the money I would one day inherit. Few realized the truth. *I* was the fortunate one to be loved by such a man."

Julia looked at Alek, but when their eyes met, she quickly glanced away.

"Now go," Ruth urged. "This is your wedding night."

The words echoed in Julia's ears. Her grandfather

had been a man of honor, but she clearly hadn't inherited his grit or his honesty. She planned to cheat Alek and he was about to learn exactly how much.

Julia had surprised him. Alek had misjudged this woman who was now his wife. For two years he'd studied her, astonished by her tenacity. Jerry had told him little of what had led to the company's financial problems. Ever since his arrival, he'd picked up bits and pieces of what had happened, but no one had explained the events that had brought near ruin. From what he understood, Conrad Industries had come very close to introducing a long-lasting exterior paint with a twenty-five-year guarantee. Jerome Conrad, Jerry and Julia's father, had been a chemist, too, and he'd been personally involved in developing it. The company was on the brink of making one of the most innovative and progressive advances in the industry. This high-tech development was expected to have a dynamic impact on sales and give Conrad Industries a badly needed financial boost. The company had been set for expansion, confident of success. Then a series of mishaps occurred.

This was the part that remained vague to Alek. He'd heard something about a burglary and a defection to a rival company. But by far the worst was a huge fire that had destroyed the lab and the warehouse. Not until much later had they learned the fire was arson.

An employee was suspected. That much he'd been told by Jerry. But there wasn't enough proof to prosecute whoever it had been. Shortly after the fire, Jerry and Julia's father had suffered a heart attack and died. It was then that Julia had taken over the company. They'd struggled for a year, trying to recover lost ground, before Jerry made the arrangements to bring Alek from Russia. Since that time he'd been working hard on implementing his ideas.

"You're very quiet," Julia commented, breaking into his thoughts.

He glanced over at his bride. Her nervousness didn't escape him. He wanted to do whatever was necessary to put her at ease. He'd enjoyed listening to the story of Ruth and Louis Conrad's love. It had touched his heart, reminding him of his own grandparents, long dead. They'd loved each other deeply and he could have asked for no finer heritage. His grandfather had died first and his grandmother had followed less than a year later. His mother claimed her mother-in-law had succumbed to a broken heart.

Julia shifted restlessly in the car. He caught the movement from the corner of his eye and wondered about this woman he'd begun to love. He'd been observing her for two years; he knew her far better than she could possibly grasp. And he'd known the instant Jerry had suggested they marry that he would accept nothing less than total commitment from her. He was not a man who did things by half measures. He looked forward to the time he would sleep with his wife. He'd sensed fire in her, but hadn't realized how hot the flames were until they'd kissed. Really kissed.

No woman had ever affected him as strongly as Julia. The kisses had enhanced his appetite for what was to follow. He would be patient with her. Careful and slow. Although every instinct insisted he take her to his bed now, do away with her fretting and worry so they could enjoy the rest of the evening together. He must be patient, he reminded himself.

"Where would you like to go for dinner?" he asked. He suggested a couple of his favorite restaurants.

"Dinner?" she echoed, as though she hadn't given the matter a second thought. "I...don't know."

"You decide."

"Would you mind if we went to my...our condo?" In one of their few practical conversations, they'd agreed that he'd move into her place; his own apartment had been a furnished rental, so there hadn't been much to bring over—just books, his computer, clothes and a few personal effects. He had a small moving company take care of it and continued to pay rent on the place so his sister, Anna, could eventually move in there.

Alek's nod was eager. She would relax there and—what was the American term—unwind? Yes, she would unwind so that when the time came for them to retreat to the bedroom, she'd be warm with wine and eager for his touch.

"We'll have to send out for something," Julia announced when they reached the high-rise condominium. It was situated in the heart of downtown Seattle on the tenth floor, overlooking Puget Sound. A white-and-green ferry could be seen in the distance. The jagged peaks of the Olympic Mountains rose majestically to the west. The day had been clear and bright, but now the sun was setting, casting a pink glow over the landscape.

"Send out?" he repeated, frowning.

Julia stood in the middle of her modern home and clasped her hands in front of her. "I don't cook much."

"Ah." Now he understood. "I am excellent in the kitchen." In the bedroom, too, but he couldn't say that without embarrassing her. She would learn that soon enough.

"You want to make our dinner?"

"Yes," he answered, pulling his attention from the magnificent view and following her into the kitchen. He liked her home. The living room was long and narrow with windows that extended the full length. The dining room and kitchen were both compact, as if their importance was minimal.

"Would you like a glass of white wine?" Julia asked him.

"Please." While she was busy with the wine, he explored his new home. A narrow hallway led to two bedrooms. The larger was dominated by a king-size bed, covered with a bright blue comforter and what seemed like a hundred small pillows. The scent of flowers, violets he guessed, hung in the air. The second bedroom was much smaller and the closet was filled with boxes. A quick examination revealed Christmas decorations.

He returned to the kitchen and took the wineglass from his wife's hand. Her eyes, so large and dark, appealed to him, but for what he wasn't sure. One thing was certain: Alek knew he couldn't wait much longer to make love to her.

Julia felt like a fox about to be released for the hunt. She would soon be cornered, trapped by her own lies. Alek didn't realize, at least not yet, that she had no intention of sleeping with him. So far he'd been patient and kind, but she couldn't count on his goodwill lasting.

"I found a couple of chicken breasts in the freezer," she told him. She felt as though she was in danger of swallowing her heart. She was pretending for all she was worth, acting the role of devoted wife, when she was anything but. "I'll make a salad."

He was searching through her drawers, stopping when he came across an old cloth dish towel. He tucked it at his waist and continued to survey her cupboards, taking out a series of ingredients.

He'd chopped an onion, a green pepper and several mushrooms by the time she dragged a stool to the counter. Perhaps she'd learn something about cooking from him. She'd seen Alek working in the laboratory. But now he astonished her with the familiar way he moved about her kitchen, as if this was truly his second home.

"When did you learn to cook?"

"As a boy. My mother insisted and I enjoy it."

"Thank her for me."

Alek paused and, glancing her way, smiled. "You can do that yourself someday. I'm doing what I can to arrange for her immigration to the States."

"If…there's anything I can do, please let me know."

He nodded, seemingly pleased by her offer.

Julia drank her wine and refilled both their glasses. Her mind was working at a frantic pace, devising ways of delaying the inevitable moment when he'd learn the truth. Her original plan had been to get him drunk. Two glasses of wine and she was feeling light-headed and a bit tipsy. Alek had consumed the same amount and was completely sober. He wielded a large knife without the slightest hesitation.

Her next thought was to appeal to his sense of honor. A strange tactic, she had to admit, coming from a woman who planned on cheating him out of an intimate relationship. He must recognize that she didn't love him. This was a business arrangement that profited them both; turning it into something personal could ruin everything.

The kiss. She must've been mad to let him kiss her like that. She'd done nothing to resist him. Instead she'd encouraged him, led him to believe she welcomed his touch.

She'd been shaken afterward. It shouldn't have happened. The very fact that she'd permitted him to hold her and touch her in such an intimate manner defeated her own purpose. Anger rose within her, not at Alek, but at herself for having let things go so far. Now he expected more, and she couldn't, wouldn't allow it. She was angry, too, about the enjoyment she'd found in his arms. It was as if she'd been looking for a way to prove herself as a woman, to show him—and everyone else— that she was more feminine than they'd suspected.

Her foolishness had only complicated an already difficult situation.

"More wine?" she asked nervously. The rice was cooking in a covered pot and the chicken was simmering in a delicious-smelling sauce. Alek appeared relaxed and at ease while Julia calculated how many steps it would take to reach the front door.

Alek shook his head. "No more wine for me."

"I'll set the table," she said, slipping down from the stool and moving into the dining room. Soon he'd know. Soon he'd discover what a phony she was. He'd learn that she was a liar and a cheat and a coward.

Her hands were trembling as she set the silverware on the table. She added water glasses, anything to delay returning to the kitchen. To Alek.

He'd filled up their plates when she walked back into the room. Julia didn't know if she could eat a single bite, and she watched transfixed as he carried their meal into the dining room.

"Julia, my love."

"I'm not your love," she told him coolly, leaning back against the kitchen counter.

His grin was slow. Undisturbed. "Not yet, perhaps, but you will be."

She closed her eyes, afraid to imagine what might come next.

"Let us eat," Alek said, taking her unresisting hand and leading her to a chair. With impeccable manners, he held it out for her, then seated himself.

"This is very nice," she said. The smells were heavenly. In other circumstances she would have appreciated his culinary skills.

"My sister is an excellent cook," he said casually. He removed the linen napkin from the table and spread it across his lap. "If you agree, she will prepare our meals once she arrives from Russia. She'll welcome the job and it'll simplify her receiving a visa."

"Of course..." Julia was more than willing to be generous with his family.

"You are nervous?" Alek asked, after several bites. Julia hadn't managed even one taste.

"Yes."

He grinned. "Understandably. Don't worry, I will be gentle with you."

Julia's heart plummeted.

"I admire you, Julia. It isn't any woman who would accept the terms of our marriage. You are brave as well as beautiful. I feel fortunate to have married you."

Four

Julia vaulted to her feet, startling Alek. Her hand clutched the pink linen napkin as though it were a lifeline, and her dark eyes filled with tears.

"Julia?"

"I can't do it! I can't go through with it… You expect me to share a bed and for us to live like a normal married couple, but I just can't do it. I lied…everything's a lie. I'm sorry, Alek, truly sorry."

"You agreed to my terms," he reminded her without rancor. She was pale and trembling and it disturbed him to see her in such emotional torment. He would have liked to take her in his arms and comfort her, but he could see she wouldn't welcome his touch.

"I was overwrought. I… I didn't know what I was doing. Everything happened so fast."

Alek considered her words and slowly shook his head. "You knew."

She retreated a couple of steps. "I've had a change of heart. It's understandable, given the circumstances."

It pained him to see her so distraught, but she'd willingly agreed to his stipulations, and there'd been ample opportunity for her to speak her mind before the wedding. Calmly he pointed this out.

"You didn't have to go through with the ceremony, but you did," he said. "You wanted this marriage, but you refuse to admit it even to yourself." He stared at her, demanding that she relent and recognize her foolishness. They were married, and she was his wife. There was no going back now.

"I… I felt I had no choice. Jerry was convinced that marrying you was the only way to keep you in the country. My grandmother's dying and she likes you, believes in you, and it seemed, I don't know, it just felt like the right thing to do at the time."

"But now it doesn't?" he asked calmly, despite his mounting frustration.

"No," she said emphatically. "It doesn't feel the least bit right."

Alek rubbed his hand over his chin as he contemplated her words. "You Americans have many sayings I do not understand. There is one expression I remember and it seems to fit this situation."

"What's that?"

"Hogwash."

Julia went speechless. Once she'd composed herself, she tilted her head regally and glared at him. Alek suspected she used this cold, haughty regard to intimidate those who dared to differ with her. A mere look was incapable of daunting him or distracting him from his purpose. It was apparent his bride had much to learn about him.

"Have you so little pride," she asked disdainfully, "that you'd hold me to an agreement I made when I was emotionally distraught?"

Alek was impressed with her ability to twist an argument. "Pride," he echoed slowly. "I am a proud man. But what are you, Julia? Have you so little honor that you would renege on an agreement made in good faith and expect me to accept weak excuses?"

Her face reddened and she slumped into her chair.

"I've fulfilled my part of the bargain," he continued. "Is it wrong or unjust to expect you to live up to yours? I think not. You have what you wanted, what you needed. Therefore, shouldn't you satisfy *my* demands?"

She scowled at him and even though an entire room separated them, Alek could feel the heat of her outrage. "You ask too much," she muttered.

"All I ask is that you be my wife—share my life and bear our children."

Tears marked her pale cheeks. "You have every right to be angry, every right to curse me, but I can't be your wife the way you want."

"It's too late to change your mind." His voice was flat and hard. "We are married. You spoke your vows, you signed your name to the document. There is no turning back now. I suggest you forget this foolishness and finish your meal."

"Please try to understand. This isn't easy for me, either. I've been sick with guilt. I don't want to cheat you… I never wanted that."

Alek sighed, his patience shrinking. "You're beginning to sound like a disobedient child."

"You're correct about one thing," she said, gesturing beseechingly with her hands. "I should've said something sooner. I should never have gone through with the ceremony, but it's not too late. I'm saying something now."

"We are married." He sat down at the table and reached for his fork. He refused to give her the satisfaction of thinking her arguments had troubled him.

In abject frustration, Julia threw her hands in the air. "You're impossible!"

"Perhaps," he said readily enough. "But you are my wife and, as you yourself have agreed, you shall remain so."

Without another word she stormed out of the dining room. He heard her in the kitchen banging around pots and pans, but couldn't tell what she was doing. He finished his meal, although his appetite had long since deserted him.

He heard her trying to make a phone call, but whoever she called didn't answer. From his chair he witnessed her frustration when he saw her replace the receiver and lean her forehead against the wall.

His dinner finished, Alek returned to the kitchen to find Julia busily rinsing dishes and placing them in the dishwasher.

She ignored him for several minutes, until he said, "Shall we prepare for bed?"

Julia froze, then turned and stared at him. "Are you crazy?" Each word was spoken slowly, as if he didn't understand English.

"No," he answered thoughtfully. "I am a husband. Yours."

"I'm sorry, Alek," she said, her face pale, her voice shaking. "I know I should've spoken up before the ceremony... I've put in a call to my brother. As soon as possible I'll make whatever arrangements are necessary to have our marriage annulled."

Alek didn't swallow the bait. Jerry Conrad was not

only his friend but an attorney and had sanctioned this marriage with his sister. In fact, he'd encouraged it from the beginning.

Although Jerry hadn't shared his concerns with Alek, he was convinced Julia's brother was worried about her. Whenever Jerry mentioned Julia's name his eyes clouded. After working with her these past two years, Alek understood her brother's anxiety. She was aggressive, domineering and driven. In themselves those weren't negative attributes, especially for a woman in a competitive business, but Alek had noticed something else. Julia Conrad had closed off her life from everything that didn't involve Conrad Industries. Perhaps he was a fool, but Alek saw this woman as a challenge. More than that, he liked Julia and with very little effort could find himself in love with her. Already he admired her and was attracted to her; he longed for the day she'd feel the same about him.

No, Alek reasoned, Jerry wouldn't give in to her dictates. He would be unemotional, reasonable. Alek knew they couldn't count on the same behavior from Julia. Smiling to himself, he decided he rather looked forward to the battle of wills.

Alek had met Jerry years earlier while the young American had traveled across Europe. Together they'd spent a restless day in a train station. Eager to learn what he could of America, Alek had questioned him and found they shared several interests. Alek had liked Jerry. They'd corresponded over the years and Alek had shared his frustration with his country and his work. Jerry had offered Alek employment soon after the fire that had nearly destroyed Conrad Industries. It had taken them almost a year to secure the necessary visa for him to live in the United States.

"Do you understand what I'm saying?" Julia asked. "I'm arranging an annulment."

"Yes, my love."

"I am *not* your love," she cried, sounding close to tears.

"Perhaps not now," he returned confidently, "but you will be soon. Sooner than you realize. Ah, Julia," he said, "we will have such marvelous children..."

Alek knew when her eyes drifted shut that she wasn't envisioning their offspring, but was desperately fighting to hold on to her temper. Once she accepted their marriage, he told himself, she would be a splendid lover. Already he'd experienced the passion that simmered within her. Soon, in her own time, she would come to him—and he'd be waiting.

Alek sauntered back into the living room, turned on the television and sat back to watch the nightly news.

No man had ever infuriated her more. Julia had needed every ounce of courage she'd ever possessed to confront him with the truth. But he'd been so blasé about it, as if he'd expected her to default on their agreement. As if he'd been calmly waiting for her to defy him.

Then to have him casually announce it was too late to change her mind? That was too much! She'd rather rot in jail than make love to such an uncaring, ill-tempered, scheming—

Suddenly she felt tired. If anyone had been scheming, she was the one. Exhaustion permeated her bones, and it was almost more than she could do to finish the dishes. Alek sat in her living room, watching television. Undaunted. Confident. Sure of himself.

"I'm going to bed," she said shakily, praying he wouldn't follow her.

Alek reached for the remote and turned off the television. He was on his feet, trailing her into the master bedroom, before she had time to protest.

"I'm very tired." Her eyes pleaded with him. If she couldn't reason with him, then perhaps she could evoke sympathy. Bottom-of-the-barrel compassion was all she had left.

"I'm tired, as well." He stood at the opposite side of her bed and unfastened the buttons of his shirt.

Julia felt like weeping. "You expect to sleep in here?"

"You are my wife."

"Please." Her voice cracked.

He didn't pause in his movements, tugging the shirt free from his waist.

"I can't sleep with you." Her words were low and barely audible.

He turned back the bed covers. "We are married, Julia, and we will share this room. You needn't worry that I will make any unwelcome…advances. I'm certain that in time you'll come to me. You will, you know, and when you do, I'll be waiting. I can be patient when the prize is of such high value."

The presumptuousness of the man continued to astound her. "I can't…sleep with you," she repeated.

"I am not a monster, Julia, but a man." He stopped and looked at her as if expecting her to argue further.

"I don't understand you," she cried, nearly hysterical. "I've cheated you and lied to you. Why do you still want me? You should be glad to be rid of me."

"You are my wife."

It demanded all of Julia's energy just to hold up her head. This man confused her and she lacked the resources to go on arguing.

He pulled back the sheets and rearranged the pillows on his side of the bed, making certain she understood that he wouldn't be dissuaded.

"I can't think clearly," she said, holding her hands to her cheeks. "I'll sleep in the guest bedroom."

His disappointment was obvious. "You're sure?"

She nodded. "For now."

"As you wish, then."

Listlessly she moved around the foot of the single bed. She'd made a mess of this marriage from the beginning.

"Julia." His voice was softly accented and warmly masculine. Something in the way he said her name gave her pause.

"I'm so sorry," she said before he could speak. She could hear the tears in her voice.

"For what?"

She shrugged. For another failure. For dragging him into a loveless marriage with a cold, unwilling wife. For countless unconfessed sins.

"You've spent today and many others before it fighting yourself. You're weary of the battle, aren't you?"

Julia nodded. He was behind her, moving closer. She should leave now, walk away from him before he started to make sense, before he convinced her there was hope. She couldn't allow it to happen, because ultimately she would disappoint him. Even hurt him.

"I am your husband," he whispered once more as he turned her into his arms. "Let me carry your burdens and lighten your load. I'm here to be your helpmate, your friend, your lover. Let me take care of you, Julia. Let me love you." As he spoke, his mouth was drawing closer and closer to hers, until their breath mingled.

As hard as she tried, Julia couldn't dredge up a single protest when his mouth settled firmly on hers. He kissed her the way a woman dreams a man will kiss her, with a tenderness that touched some long-hidden spark within her.

And then…he altered the kiss, making it hot and fierce. He buried his hands deep in her hair.

Alek sighed and her name spilled from his lips. His voice was filled with need. With unbridled desire.

"Be my wife."

Julia's eyes fluttered open. It took her a second to comprehend what he'd said. When she did, she stared at him, unable to speak. Her heart was pounding, tapping out a dire warning. One she should heed.

"I…need time."

He continued to hold her gaze. "All right."

Tears filled her eyes and she bit her lip. "You're getting the short end of the stick with me, Alek."

"Short end of the stick?"

She smiled softly. "It means you're getting less than you deserve."

"Let me be the judge of that. As I said, in time you'll come to me of your own accord. In time you'll want me as much as I want you."

"There are many things you don't know about me," she said, her words so low he had to strain to hear.

"Tell me."

She shook her head. "Just remember, I warned you."

He released her, maintaining their contact as long

as possible. His hands slid down the full length of her arms and, catching her fingers, he held on to the tips with his own.

"Good night, my wife," he whispered, then turned away. "I shall be lonely without you."

Julia left the room quickly, knowing that if she stayed a moment longer, she'd end up in the bed next to Alek...

Julia found it surprisingly easy to avoid Alek. Their schedules were different and they drove to work in separate cars. She left for the office early, before he awoke. In the afternoons she visited her grandmother, then ate a quiet meal by herself. She was usually preparing for bed about the time Alek returned from the lab.

He was working long, hard hours, getting ready to put his latest research into production. From the weekly reports he sent her, she knew that they were speeding ahead; the marketing and distribution plans for Phoenix Paints were under way. The advertising blitz had yet to be decided, but that was coming. Everything looked promising.

But then, it had looked promising three years ago, too. Yet within the course of a single week she'd lost her father, been betrayed by the man she loved and nearly destroyed a business that had been in the family for four generations.

Julia had learned harsh but valuable lessons about promises. Probably the most painful lessons of her life. She'd come away convinced she could trust only a cherished few. Equally important, she'd learned never, ever to cash in on mere potential. The promise of a check in the mail wasn't money in the bank.

Dear heavens, she mused as she left the office, she

was becoming very philosophical. Perhaps that was what marriage did to a woman.

Marriage.

Even the word sounded strange to her. She was married for better or worse. Married. After her tirade on their wedding night, when she'd pleaded, threatened and tried to reason with Alek, she'd decided he was right. There was no backing out now. They *were* married, for better or worse.

Her decision was prompted by a certain amount of pride. Jerry had made sure the news of their wedding was carried by the local newspapers. The business community and their acquaintances would know about her marriage. It would be acutely embarrassing to seek an annulment so soon after the ceremony.

Mentally she added vanity to her growing list of character defects.

"Julia," Ruth said weakly when she entered the hospital room, "what are you doing here?"

Julia grinned as she leaned forward to kiss her grandmother's pale cheek. "It's good to see you, too."

"Alek will never forgive me."

"Alek is hard at work," she assured Ruth.

"But you're newlyweds."

Julia's gaze skirted past her grandmother's. "He's been so busy lately. I'd rather spend time with you than go home to an empty apartment."

"I worry about you," Ruth said, her voice growing weaker.

"Worry?" Julia repeated. "There's no need. Our schedules are hectic just now. Coming here is the best thing for me… That way, when Alek gets home, I'm calm and relaxed."

"Good. He's such a dear boy. You married well… I so want you to be happy—it's what you deserve. Your season of pain is past now that you have Alek."

Julia wanted to avoid the subject of her husband. "Would you like me to read to you?"

"Please. From the book of Psalms, if you would?"

"Of course." Julia reached for the well-worn Bible and sat in the chair next to her grandmother's bed and began. She read long past the moment Ruth had fallen asleep. Long past the dinner hour. Long past the time she should leave for home.

The night was hot and muggy, the air heavy. Her air-conditioning system must not be working properly because it felt like the hottest night of the year. Even her skimpy, baby-doll pajamas seemed clammy and constricting.

Sleep seemed just beyond her grasp no matter how hard she tried to capture it. The night was still and dark, and she flopped from her side to her back, then onto her side once more, attempting to find the touch of a cool breeze. But there was none.

Another hour passed and she gave up the effort. Getting out of bed, she moved into the living room, standing in front of the window. A few scattered lights flickered from Puget Sound. The last ferry crossing before dawn, she guessed, on its way to Winslow on Bainbridge Island.

The lights from Alki Point gleamed in the distance. Julia had no idea how long she stood there, looking into the still, dark night. Raising her arms high above her head, she stretched, standing on her toes. The thin fabric of her pajama top rustled. Her hair felt damp and heavy and she lifted the long tresses from the back of her neck. She shook her head, sending a spray of hair in a circle around her face.

She heard the briefest of noises behind her and whirled around to see a shadow unfold from the chair. Alek stood. He wore only the bottom half of his pajamas and his hard chest glistened in the muted light.

"Alek," she said breathlessly.

"I couldn't sleep, either," he told her.

"How…long have you been here?" she demanded.

"I wasn't spying on you, if that's what you're insinuating."

"I…you startled me, that's all."

"Come sit with me."

She shook her head again and watched as his jaw tightened at her refusal.

"We're married," he reminded her. "You can't ignore me the rest of your life. We made a bargain, which has yet to be fulfilled."

Why he chose to bring up the subject of their marriage now, Julia didn't know. They'd lived peacefully together for nearly two weeks, barely seeing each other, rarely talking. She'd almost convinced herself they could continue like this forever.

"I don't want to talk about our marriage."

She sensed that his irritation turned to amusement. "No, I don't imagine you do," he said.

"I'm sorry… I didn't mean to snap at you. It's just that I didn't realize you were here."

"Fine. I forgive you. Now sit and we can talk."

Julia hesitated, then decided it would do more harm than good to refuse him. She sank onto the sofa across from him. Holding a decorative pillow to her stomach helped ease her discomfort over her state of undress, although not by much.

"How is your grandmother?"

"About the same. I talked to her doctor this afternoon and he said…" She paused, biting her lip. "He said we shouldn't expect her to return home."

"Is she in pain?"

"Yes, sometimes, although she tries to hide it from me. Listen, do you mind if we don't talk about Ruth, either?"

"Of course not. I didn't mean to bring up a subject that causes you distress."

Julia lowered her eyes. "It's just that…she's so important to me. Ruth's all the family Jerry and I have left."

"Your mother died years ago, didn't she?"

Julia wasn't surprised he knew that, since he and Jerry had been friends since her brother's college days, when they'd met in Europe. "When I was fifteen, and as you probably recall, my father," she added, "died three years ago…shortly after the fire."

Silence stretched between them. Julia's pressure on the pillow increased. Even in the darkened room, she could feel his smoldering gaze move caressingly over her. He wanted her and was growing impatient. Her heart pounded with dread and some other emotion. Regret? Perhaps…yearning?

"Please don't look at me like that," she begged. It seemed as if his eyes were about to devour her. He wanted her to know how much he longed to make love to her. The memory of his kisses returned to haunt her and she tried to dispel the image before it took root in her mind and her heart.

"You're very beautiful."

She'd heard those meaningless words before. Beauty was fleeting and counted for little of real value in life. Being outwardly attractive hadn't made her a better judge of character. It didn't do one iota of good as far as her grandmother's health was concerned. If anything, it had been a curse, because it attracted the wrong kind of man.

"This makes you sad?"

She shrugged. "Beauty means nothing."

"You are wise to recognize that."

"Then why do you mention it?"

"Because you were not beautiful, not in the same way, when we first met. It's only recently that I've come to appreciate that you are a real woman."

A real woman. Julia nearly laughed aloud.

"This is what makes being married to you and not sleeping with you so difficult. Have you reconsidered yet, my love? Come with me, share my bed."

"I...can't, please don't ask me." Her response was immediate. Tossing the pillow aside, she leapt to her feet, needing to escape. "Good night, Alek."

He didn't answer and she didn't look back as she rushed to her room. Her heart was roaring in her ears when she reached the bed. Not for the first time she felt like the fox in an English hunt, and the baying of the hounds was closing in on her.

"Julia."

She nearly fell off the bed when she looked up and found Alek framed in her doorway. Her breath froze in her lungs.

"Someday you won't run from me."

"I wasn't running from you." It was a lie and they both knew it, yet Julia persisted in claiming otherwise.

His smile was more than a little cocky. "Someday you will come to me voluntarily."

She wasn't going to argue with him. He watched her closely in the muted moonlight and she studied him with equal intensity. She suddenly realized her top had inched up and exposed her breasts. Furiously she tugged it down, glaring at him as though he'd purposely arranged the immodest display.

He smiled roguishly at her. "As I said earlier, you are very beautiful." Then he turned and left.

After a sleepless, frustrating night, Julia was in no mood to deal with a long list of complicated problems. Virginia, her middle-aged assistant, looked apologetic when Julia arrived at the office early the next morning.

"Please get my brother on the line when you can," Julia said. Her mind was made up. She wanted out of this farce of a marriage.

"He's already called for you." Virginia hugged a file folder against her chest. "He asked that you call him the moment you got here."

Julia reached for her phone and punched out the extension. Jerry answered on the first ring. "Come down to my office," he said impatiently.

"Now?"

"Right now."

"What's wrong?"

"You'll find out soon enough."

This morning was quickly going from bad to worse, much like her life. She paused, catching herself. Her thoughts hadn't always been this negative. When had it started? The wedding? No, she decided—long before then. Three years before... She wondered why she was so aware of it now.

She rounded the corner that led to the suite of offices her brother occupied on the floor below her own.

"Jerry, what's this all about?" she asked before she noticed Alek. She halted when she saw her husband sitting in one of the visitor's chairs, waiting for her.

"Sit down." Her brother motioned toward Alek.

Julia did as he asked. Jerry paced back and forth behind his desk. "I was contacted this morning by the Immigration people. I knew this would happen, I just didn't expect it to be quite so soon."

"We're being investigated?" Alek murmured.

Jerry nodded. "The two of you are going to have to convince them you're madly in love. Do you think you can do it?"

Julia saw that he focused his gaze on her. "Ah..."

"Yes," Alek responded without hesitation.

"Julia, what about you?"

"Ah..." She'd never been good with pretense.

"She'll convince them." Alek revealed far more confidence in her than she had in herself. "It won't take much effort." He reached for her hand, gripping it in his own. "All we need is a little practice, isn't that right, Julia?"

Five

Only seconds earlier Julia had decided she wanted to end this charade of a marriage, no matter what the price. Just when it seemed that very thing was about to happen, she discovered herself willing to do whatever was necessary to keep their relationship intact.

Counseling. That was what she needed, Julia thought. Intensive counseling. She wasn't an indecisive woman; that would be a death knell for someone in her position. Generally she knew what she wanted and went after it with a determination that left everyone in her wake shaking their heads in wonder.

It was Aleksandr who managed to discomfit and confuse her. It was Alek who made her feel as though she was walking through quicksand.

"Julia?" Jerry turned the full force of his attention on her. "Can you do it?"

Both men were studying her. Could she pretend to be in love with Alek? Pretend her happiness hinged on spending the rest of her life with him? Could she?

"I… I don't know."

"Shall I repeat what's at stake here?" Jerry muttered.

It wasn't necessary; he'd gone over the consequences of their actions when he'd proposed the idea of marrying Alek in the first place. The government did much more than frown upon such unions. There was the possibility of jail time if they weren't able to persuade the Immigration department of their sincerity.

"Julia knows," Alek assured Jerry calmly. "Isn't that right?"

She lowered her eyes. "I'm fully aware of what could happen."

"That's fine and dandy, but can you be convincing enough to satisfy the Immigration people?" Jerry demanded.

She nodded slowly, thoughtfully. It wasn't just a question of being able to pull this off with the finesse required; it also meant lowering her guard, opening her heart to the truth. She was attracted to him, both physically and emotionally. Otherwise she wouldn't have participated in or enjoyed the few times they'd kissed. The most important factor wasn't her ability to fool Immigration, but resurrecting the shield protecting her against the pull she felt toward Alek.

To complicate matters, the attachment she felt was growing stronger every day. She often found herself thinking about him. Hard as it was to admit, Julia had discovered she enjoyed his company and looked forward to the short time they spent together in the evenings.

"You're sure?" Jerry asked, sounding as if he thought she was anything but.

"Positive," she said, chancing a look in Alek's direction. He caught her eye and smiled reassuringly. Taking her hand, he squeezed her fingers.

"We'll do just fine," Alek said to Jerry. "Wait and see. What both of you fail to realize is that Julia and I *did* marry for love."

"Stop pacing," Alek said, more testily than he intended. The Immigration officer was due in fifteen minutes and Julia was understandably nervous. Unable to sit still, she stalked the living room.

"Walking helps take my mind off the interview," Julia snapped back.

The tension between them was thick enough to slice and serve for dinner. That would hurt their case more than anything they said or did. The man or woman doing the interview would sense the strain immediately and count it against them.

"You should know more about me," Julia said, whirling around to face him as if this was a new thought. "The brand of toothpaste I use and stuff like that."

"Don't be ridiculous."

"I'm not… That's exactly the kind of questions he'll ask."

"Julia, my love," he said patiently, "a man doesn't pay attention to such things. Now relax."

"How can you be so calm?" Julia shrugged, raising both hands. "Our future hinges on the outcome of this meeting. There's a very real possibility I could go to jail for involving myself in this…marriage." Her arms seemed to have lost their purpose and fell lifelessly to her sides. "I'm not the only one who has a lot at stake with this. Your mother and sister's plans depend on the outcome, as well. Didn't you mention you've already seen to the necessary paperwork for them?"

"I'm aware of the consequences."

"Then how can you be so *calm?*"

"Very simple, my love." He said this evenly and without emotion as he leaned forward, clasped her around the waist and brought her down into his lap.

Julia struggled at first. "Stop," she said, wriggling against him. "What are you trying to do?"

He let her struggle, but her efforts were weak. His arms were around her and he felt her yielding. Taking advantage of her acquiescence, he brushed his face against her hair. She'd left it down, at his request, and he gathered the length of it in his hands, loving its clean jasmine scent.

"Alek, are you insane?"

He dropped a trail of moist kisses along her throat and shoulder. "That's better," he whispered as her tight muscles relaxed. "Much better."

"I… I don't think we should be doing this."

"What?" he asked as his hand caressed her back in a slow, soothing motion. "This?" He eased her against the chair until her hair spilled over his arm. A sigh escaped her as he pressed his lips to hers.

Julia felt hot, then cold and shaky in his embrace, but no more so than he. They'd kissed a handful of times and each had been a battle for him. His wife had balked at his touch in the beginning, then gradually she'd opened herself to him until he was so needy he ached.

This time the skirmish between them was over even before it started. Julia accepted his kiss with little more than a token protest. Perhaps she was ready for more…

He broke off the kiss and told her how badly he needed her. He pleaded with her as only a man who needs his wife can implore. It wasn't until he saw the confusion in her eyes that he realized he'd spoken in his native tongue. His English was hopeless just then.

Julia's fingers were digging into his shoulders. He felt the rapid beat of her heart and heard the ragged echo of her breath as it rasped in his ear.

The doorbell chimed and Alek would have ignored it if Julia hadn't frozen and then jumped from his lap as though she'd caught fire.

"Oh, my goodness," she cried. Her face was a rich shade of red as she swept back her hair. "The interviewer is here." She stared at him as if he had the magical power to make everything right.

"That would be my guess."

"Alek." Her voice shook as she quickly adjusted her clothes. "I'm scared."

"Don't be. Everything will be fine," he said. He gave her a moment to fuss with her hair before he stood, kissed her lightly on the lips and answered the door.

Although Alek appeared outwardly composed, he was as shaken as Julia. And not because their future hung in the balance. His head reeled with the aftershock of their kissing. A few kisses, he'd thought, to take the edge off their nervousness. In another five minutes, he would've carried her to his bed...

"Hello," Alek said, opening the door to admit a lanky, official-looking gentleman. He wore a crisp business suit and from the tight set of his mouth, Alek guessed he would brook no foolishness. His expression was sharp and unfriendly.

"Patrick O'Dell," he said.

"My name is Alek and this is my wife, Julia," Alek said.

Julia stood on the far side of the room, her smile

fleeting and strained. "Welcome to our home, Mr. O'Dell. Would you care to sit down?"

"Thank you." He moved into the living room and didn't pause to look at the view. Indeed, there might not have been one for all the notice O'Dell took. He sat on the recliner they'd recently vacated and set his briefcase on the coffee table.

Alek walked over to Julia's side and held her hand in his. Together they ventured to the sofa opposite the interviewer and sat down.

Mr. O'Dell removed a file from his briefcase. He scanned the contents, then frowned with clear disapproval. "How did you two meet?"

"Through my brother," Julia said quickly. "He'd met Alek several years earlier while he was in Europe. They corresponded for a number of years and then after the fire…" She hesitated and turned to Alek.

"Jerry offered me a job in this country almost three years ago. I've lived here for the past two."

"Tell me about your work."

Alek answered the questions thoroughly, while minimizing his importance to Conrad Industries. No need to raise suspicions.

"Alek is a gifted biochemist," Julia added with unnecessary enthusiasm. "The company was nearly ruined a few years back following the fire I mentioned. I don't know what would've become of us if it hadn't been for Alek."

Although he smiled, Alek was groaning inwardly. Julia was offering far more information than necessary. He wished now that they'd gone over what they planned to say. Jerry had advised them to do so, but Alek had felt spontaneity would serve them better than a series of practiced responses.

"In other words, you needed Mr. Berinski."

"Yes, very much so." Julia was nothing if not honest.

"Do you continue to need him?" the interviewer pressed.

"No," Alek answered before Julia could.

"I disagree," she returned, looking briefly at Alek. "I find we need him more than ever now. The new line of paints Alek's been working on for the past two years is ready to be marketed. That's only the beginning of the ideas he's developing."

Alek's concern mounted as O'Dell made a notation. Julia really was as bad at pretense as she'd claimed.

"My husband has worked hard on this project. He deserves to reap the fruits of his labors." Fortunately, Julia didn't stumble over the word *husband*. She'd said it a number of times since their marriage and it always seemed to cause her difficulty.

"You give me more credit than I deserve, my dear," he murmured, feeling they'd dug themselves into a pit.

"Nonsense," Julia said, obviously warming to her subject. "Alek is a genius."

Another notation.

Alek squeezed Julia's fingers, willing her to stop speaking, but the more he tried to discourage her, the more she went on.

"If you two held each other in such high esteem, why did you wait until Alek's visa had almost expired before you agreed to marry?"

"Love isn't always planned," Julia answered quickly. "No one completely understands matters of the heart, do they? I know I didn't." She glanced shyly toward Alek.

"I understand why the Immigration department is suspicious of our marriage," Alek added. "We realized you would be when we decided to go ahead and marry. It didn't make any difference."

Another notation, this one made with sharp jagged movements of his pen.

There were several more questions, which they answered as forthrightly as possible. Alek was uncertain of how well they were coming across. He'd rarely heard Julia sound more animated and, to his surprise, sincere. When he'd first learned of the interview, his biggest concern had been Julia, but now he suspected she'd be his strongest asset.

If he was forced to return to Russia, Alek would go, because he had no other choice. He hadn't dwelled on the consequences, refusing to allow any negative suggestions to enter his mind. He realized as they were speaking how much he'd hate to leave Julia.

"I think that answers everything," O'Dell said, closing his file and placing it back in his briefcase.

The unexpectedness of his announcement caught Alek off guard.

"That's all?" Apparently Julia was as astonished as he was. "You don't want to know what brand of toothpaste Alek uses or about his personal habits?"

The official smiled for the first time. "We leave that sort of interrogation for the movies. It's obvious to me that you two care deeply for each other. I wish all my assignments were as easy."

"Will I need to sign anything?" Julia asked.

"No," O'Dell said as he stood. "I'll file my report by the end of the week. I don't believe there's any reason for us to be in further contact with you. I appreciate your agreeing to see me on such short notice."

Alek stood in order to escort Mr. O'Dell to the door. Julia seemed to be in a state of shock. She sat on the sofa, her mouth hanging open, staring up at the official with a baffled, uncertain look.

"Thank you again for your trouble," Patrick O'Dell said when Alek opened the front door.

"Julia and I should be the ones thanking you."

The two men exchanged handshakes. Alek closed the door with relief and leaned against the frame. He slowly expelled his breath.

"Julia." He whispered her name as he returned to the living room. She hadn't moved. "We did it."

She nodded as though she was in a trance.

"You were fantastic."

Her eyes went to him and she blinked. "Me?"

"You were straightforward and honest. At first I was worried. I thought you were giving him far more information than necessary. Then I realized that was what convinced him. You acted as though you had nothing to hide. As if our staying married meant all the world to you. It wasn't anything *I* said or did, it was you."

"Me?" she repeated again, sounding close to tears.

Alek knelt down in front of her and took her hands. "Are you all right?"

Sniffling, she shook her head. The ordeal had been a strain, but he was surprised by her response. Julia wasn't the type of woman to buckle easily. Nor did she weep without provocation. Something was definitely going on.

"What's wrong?" he asked tenderly, resisting the urge to take her in his arms.

Tears filled her eyes and she made an effort to blink
them away. "I think I'll go lie down for a while. I'm
sure I'll be fine in a few minutes."

Alek didn't want her to leave. He was hoping they
could pick up where they'd left off before they were interrupted by O'Dell's arrival. The craving she'd created
in him had yet to be satisfied. He wanted her to share
his bed. She was his wife. They belonged together.

Alek had learned enough about Julia to know that
she'd come to him in her own time, when she was ready
and not before. He prayed he had the patience to wait
her out.

As she lay in her bed, pretending to nap, Julia realized it wasn't until the Immigration official had stood
to leave that she'd recognized how sincere she was in
what she'd told him. She'd answered the questions as
candidly as possible, becoming more fervent the longer
she spoke. It had suddenly struck her that Alek was as
important to her personally as he was to the company.
Perhaps more so. That came as an unexpected shock.

He'd been patient and loving and kind. His kisses
stirred her soul. That sounded fanciful, overdramatic,
but she was at a loss to explain it otherwise.

Heaven help her, she was falling in love with him. It
wasn't supposed to happen this way. She didn't *want* to
love him, didn't want to care about him. After Phoenix
Paints was launched and he'd established his mother and
sister in the country, she wanted Alek out of her life.
That was what she'd planned. Involving her heart would
be both foolish and dangerous. She'd already learned
her lesson when it came to trusting a man. Roger had
taught her well.

"Julia?" His voice was a whisper. She kept her eyes closed, not wanting Alek to know she was awake. Afraid he might want to resume what they'd started…

Her face filled with color at the memory of their kisses. She couldn't believe the liberties Alek had taken with her earlier that afternoon. Worse, liberties she'd encouraged and enjoyed. She would be forever grateful that Mr. O'Dell had arrived when he had.

Julia had eventually drifted off. Because of her nap, she was unable to sleep that evening. Hoping to sidestep any questions from Alek, she'd gone to the hospital to visit Ruth later in the afternoon.

The condo was empty when she returned and Julia guessed Alek had gone to the lab to work. Feeling somewhat guilty, she microwaved her dinner, hoping he'd pick up something for himself while he was out.

He wasn't back by the time she showered and readied for bed. She should've been grateful; instead she found herself waiting for him. It was nearly eleven when she heard the front door open. Light from the kitchen spilled into the hallway outside her bedroom as he rummaged around, apparently looking for dinner.

A second bout of guilt didn't improve her disposition. Knowing next to nothing about cooking should prove beyond a doubt what a terrible wife she was. Another, more domesticated woman would have been knitting by the fireplace, awaiting his return with a delectable meal warming in the oven. Forget that it was summer; this imaginary dutiful wife would have a cozy fire roaring anyway.

Then, when he'd eaten, she'd remove her housecoat and stand before him dressed only in a sheer nightie.

But Alek hadn't married the ideal wife; instead he was stuck with her.

"Julia?"

She was so surprised by the sound of her name that she lifted her head from the pillow.

"I hope I didn't wake you."

"No... I hadn't gone to sleep yet." She sat up in bed and tugged the sheets protectively around her.

His shadow loomed against the opposite wall like... like some kind of fairy-tale monster. But try as she might, Julia couldn't make him into one.

"How's your grandmother?" he asked.

She shrugged hopelessly. It became more apparent with every visit that Ruth wouldn't last much longer. A part of Julia clung to her grandmother and another part struggled to release Ruth from this life and the pain that accompanied it.

"You were at the lab?"

Alek nodded.

"Is it really necessary for you to work so many hours?"

Alek crossed his arms and leaned against the door-jamb. "Work helps me deal with my frustration."

He didn't need to clarify his answer. Julia knew he was referring to the sexual disappointment of their marriage.

When she didn't respond, he sighed and added, "I know why everything went so smoothly with the Immigration official. You, my dear wife, are in love with me."

The audacity of the comment was shocking. "I'm what?"

"In love with me," he repeated.

"You're badly in need of some reality therapy," Julia

said, making her words as scathing as she could. "That's the most ridiculous thing you've ever said."

"Wait, I promise you it'll get better. Much better."

"Much worse, you mean," she said with an exaggerated yawn. "Now if you don't mind, I'd like to get some sleep."

"Later. We need to talk."

"Alek, please, it's nearly midnight."

"You've already admitted you hadn't been to sleep."

"Exactly," she said. "And I need my rest."

"So do I."

"Then leave it until morning," she suggested next.

"You're my wife. How long will it take before you live up to your end of our bargain?"

"I...already explained I need time...to adjust to everything. Why are you doing this?" she cried, furious with him for dragging out a subject she considered closed. "I refuse to be pressured into making love just because you've got an overactive libido."

"Pressured," he echoed, and a deep frown formed. He rubbed his hand over his face, sighing audibly. "I've been waiting for you since our wedding night. You agreed that we'd be married in every sense of the word."

"It's only been a few weeks," she protested.

"Ah, but you love me. You proved it this afternoon. There's no need to wait any longer, Julia. I need you, and you need me." With a knowing smile, he turned and walked away.

The comment irritated her so much she couldn't bear to let it go unanswered. Grabbing her pillow with both hands, she threw it after him. It hit the doorframe with a soft thud that was barely discernible. She knew Alek heard it, however, because he started laughing.

* * *

The following morning, as was her habit, Julia rose early and stood barefoot in the kitchen while she waited for the first cup of coffee to filter into the glass pot. The aroma pervaded the kitchen.

"Morning." Alek spoke groggily from behind her.

Julia's eyes flew open. Normally Alek didn't get up until after she'd left for work. "Morning," she greeted him with little enthusiasm.

"Did you sleep well?"

No. "Fine. How about you?" Her attention remained focused on the coffeepot. She didn't dare turn around to confront her rumpled, groggy husband. Knowing he was only a few feet behind her activated her imagination. His hair was probably unkempt and his eyes drowsy, the way hers were. He'd look sexy and appealing.

"Julia," he whispered, moving forward. He slipped his arms around her waist and nuzzled her neck. "We can't go on like this. We're married. When are you going to recognize that?"

She braced her hands against his, which were joined at her stomach. His lips located the pulse pounding at the side of her neck and he kissed her. Small, soft kisses...

Julia's breath caught in her throat. "Alek, please, don't."

"Stop?" He raised his head as though she couldn't have meant it.

"Yes."

"I couldn't sleep for want of you," he whispered.

Her throat felt as dry as a desert. Speaking was impossible.

"All I could think about was how good you tasted and how much I wanted to hold you and kiss you again," he went on.

The coffee had finished brewing, but Julia couldn't make herself move.

"I know you want me, too. Why do you torture us like this?"

"I...have to get to work." Each syllable was a triumph.

"Let me make love to you," Alek urged, his mouth close to her ear.

"No. We can't. I... I'll be late for work." She didn't wait for him to argue with her, but rushed toward her bedroom. Toward sanity.

By the time Julia reached her office, she was in a terrible mood. She blamed Alek for this. As much as she wished it, she wasn't made of stone. She was flesh and blood. A woman. When he kissed her and touched her she experienced a certain sexual yearning.

It was inevitable. A mere physiological reaction. It meant nothing. He insisted she was in love with him, but Julia knew that was just talk. Sweet talk, with a single purpose. To seduce her.

Julia had been seduced before, by an artful master. In comparison, Alek was so much more honest and, therefore, easier to defend herself against. She refused to give in to his pressure, subtle or otherwise. As for misleading him, she had, but only to a limited degree.

Furious now, she marched into her office, reached for her phone and dialed Jerry's extension. "Can you come up?"

"Yes. Is everything okay?"

"No."

Jerry paused. "I thought things went hunky-dory with the inspector."

"They did, as far as I know. This has to do with Alek."

"I'll be right up," her brother said.

She was pacing her office with precise steps when he arrived. Julia stopped, angry with herself, feeling close to tears and not understanding why.

"What's wrong?" he asked, his concern evident in his eyes.

"I...there's a problem."

"With what?"

"Whom," she corrected. "Aleksandr Berinski."

Jerry frowned, then sighed with resignation. "What's he done?"

"Everything... Listen, I don't want to get into this. Let me make this as plain and simple as I can. I think it's time he moved out of the condo. One of us has to and it's either him or me."

Six

"You want Alek out of your condo?" Jerry repeated.

"You heard me the first time," she said impatiently. "Our marriage has been sanctioned by the government. What reason do we have to continue this charade?"

"Julia…"

She'd heard that tone all too often. "Jerry, I'm not in any mood to argue with you." She walked around her desk and claimed her seat. Reaching for a file from her in-basket, she opened it. "I'll leave the arrangements in your hands."

"Do you plan to talk this over with Alek?"

She hadn't thought of that. "It…won't be necessary. He'll get the picture once he hears from you."

"I won't do it."

Her brother's refusal caught her attention as nothing else could have. "What do you mean, you won't do it?"

"First, I won't have you treating Alek as though he's…some pest you're trying to get rid of."

"It wouldn't be like that," she insisted, realizing even as she spoke that Jerry was right. She couldn't treat Alek this way.

"Secondly," her brother said, "it'd be crazy to throw everything away now. You think that just because you've passed some interview with an Immigration official, you're in the clear. Think again, Julia. That's exactly the kind of thing the government's expecting."

"They won't know."

"Don't count on it. They make it their business to know."

"Jerry, please." She rarely pleaded with her brother. "The man's impossible… I've done my duty. What more do you expect of me?"

"Alek is your husband."

"You're beginning to sound just like him! He frightens me… He makes me feel things I don't want to feel. I'm scared, Jerry, really scared." Close to tears, she covered her mouth, fearing she'd break down.

"I don't know what to do," Jerry said with a sympathetic shrug. "I wish I did, for your sake. Alek's, too."

With nothing left to say, he returned to his own office.

Her mood didn't improve when two hours later Alek unexpectedly showed up. He walked into her office without waiting for her assistant to announce him. Julia happened to be on the phone at the time and she glanced up, irritated by the intrusion. Alek glared at her, and every minute she delayed appeared to infuriate him further.

He began to pace, pausing every other step to turn and scowl in her direction.

Julia finished her conversation as quickly as she could without being rude—and without letting him believe he was intimidating her.

"You wanted something?" she asked calmly as she replaced the receiver.

Anger was etched on his features. "Yes, I do. I understand you spoke to Jerry this morning about one of us moving. I want to know what's going on in that head of yours."

Julia folded her hands on her desk. "It seemed the logical thing to do."

"Why?"

She stood, feeling at a distinct disadvantage sitting. "It makes sense. The only reason we were living together was for show because—"

"We're living together, my dear wife, because we're married."

"In name only."

He muttered something blistering in Russian, and Julia was grateful she couldn't understand him.

"You deny your vows. You abuse my pride by involving your brother. You ask for patience and then stab me in the back."

"I…explained on our wedding day that I need time. I let you know you were being cheated in this marriage. You can't say I didn't warn you." Contacting Jerry had been wrong, she saw now. But she was frightened and growing more so each day. No longer could she ignore the powerful attraction she felt for Alek. No longer could she ignore his touch. He was chipping away at the barrier she'd erected to protect herself from feelings. From love. He was working his way into her life and her heart. She had to do something.

"You are my *wife*," Alek shouted.

Julia closed her eyes at the anger in his voice.

"I'm not a very good one," she whispered.

"We are married, Julia. When will you accept that?" He turned away from her and stalked to the door.

"I…don't know if I can."

At her words, he spun around.

They stood no more than a few feet apart, yet an ocean might have lain between them. He was furious with her and she with him.

"I may never be your wife in the way you want." Julia didn't know what drove her to say that.

And yet, at the same moment, she realized she wanted him. Needed him. And that frightened her half to death.

"You're afraid, aren't you?" he asked as if he could read her thoughts. "Afraid you aren't woman enough to satisfy me. That's what's behind all this, isn't it? That, and the fact that you're afraid to trust another man. But I'm not like the one who hurt you, Julia, whoever he was. I'm not like him at all. I respect you—and I want you. Which, if you're honest, is how you feel about me, too."

Stricken, Julia closed her eyes. It felt as if he'd blinded her with the truth, identified her fears, hurled them at her to explain or reject.

"Julia?"

She sobbed once, the sound nearly hysterical as she backed away from him.

"I didn't mean…" he began.

She stopped him by holding out her arm.

He cursed under his breath and, reaching for her, drew her into his arms. She didn't resist. Without pause he lowered his head and covered her mouth, sealing their lips together in a wild kiss. The craziness increased with each impatient twist of their heads, growing in frenzied desperation.

Her breasts tingled and her body grew hot as his powerful hands held her against him. It was where she wanted to be…

His hands were busy with the zipper at the back of her straight, no-nonsense business skirt. It hissed as he lowered it. Julia made a token protest, which he cut off with a bone-melting kiss.

"I'm through fighting you," he whispered. "Will you stop fighting me?"

He gently brought his mouth back to hers. They were so close Julia felt as if they were drawing in the same breath, as if they required only one heart to beat between them.

Sobbing, she slid her arms around his neck and buried her face, taking deep, uneven breaths. Not understanding her own desperate need, she clung to him as a low cry emerged from her lips. The grief she felt was overwhelming. She was lamenting the wasted years, when she'd closed herself off from life. Ever since her father's death and Roger's betrayal, she'd lived in limbo, rejecting love and laughter. Rejecting and punishing herself.

"Julia," Alek whispered, stroking her hair, "what is it?"

She shook her head, unable to answer.

"Say it," he told her softly, sitting in her chair and taking her with him so she was nestled in his lap. "Tell me you need me. Tell me you want me, too."

She sobbed and with tears streaming down her face, she nodded.

"That's not good enough. I want the words."

"I...need you. Oh, Alek, I'm so scared."

He held her, kissed her gently, reassured her while she rested her head on his shoulder and cried until her tears were spent.

"I don't know why you put up with me," she finally gasped.

"You don't?" he asked, chuckling softly. "I have the feeling you'll figure it out soon enough, my love."

Her intercom hummed and Virginia's voice echoed through the silence. "Your nine-thirty appointment is here."

Her eyes regretfully met Alek's.

"Send whoever it is away," Alek urged.

"I... I can't do that."

"I know," he said, and kissed the tip of her nose. He released her slowly.

Just when Julia was convinced her day couldn't possibly get any more complicated, she received a call from Virginia Mason Hospital. Her grandmother had slipped into a coma.

Jerry was away, so she left a message for him and for Alek, canceled her appointments for the rest of the day and drove directly to the hospital.

Julia realized the instant she walked into her grandmother's room that Ruth's hold on life was tenuous, a slender thread. Her heart was failing, and Julia felt as though her own heart was in jeopardy, too.

In the past few years she'd faced a handful of crises, starting with the fire that had nearly destroyed the business and their family. Her father's death had followed. Immediately afterward she'd realized Roger had used her, had sold out her family. And her.

Ruth, her beloved Ruth, was dying, and Julia was powerless to stop it. She was terrified. For the past months she'd watched helplessly as her grandmother's health deteriorated.

Sitting at Ruth's bedside now, Julia could almost hear the older woman's calming voice. "My death is inevitable—" the unspoken words rang in her head "—but not unwelcome."

Silently Julia pleaded with her grandmother to live just a little longer, to give her time to adjust, to grant her a few days to gather her courage. Even as she spoke, Julia recognized how selfish she was being, thinking of herself, of her own pain. But she couldn't make herself stop praying that God would spare her grandmother.

"You have walked through your pain," the silent voice continued. "The journey has made you wiser and far stronger than you know."

Julia wanted to argue. She didn't feel strong. Not when it seemed Ruth was about to be taken from her. She felt pushed to the limits, looking both ways—toward despair in one direction and hope in the other, toward doubt and faith.

An hour passed as Julia struggled with her grief, refusing to let it overwhelm her. Fear controlled her, the knowledge that if she gave in to her grief, she might never regain her sanity.

"Please," she pleaded aloud, praying Ruth heard her. It was the selfish prayer of a frightened child.

Jerry arrived, pale and shaken. "What happened?"

Julia shrugged. Their grandmother's physician, Dr. Silverman, had been in earlier to explain the medical symptoms and reasons. Most of what he'd said had meant only one thing. Ruth was close to death.

"She's in a coma," Julia answered. "I talked to her doctor earlier. He's surprised she's hung on this long."

Her brother pulled out a chair and sat down next to Julia. "I love this old woman, really love her."

"What are we going to do without her, Jerry?"

Her brother shook his head. "I don't know. We'll make do the way we always have, I suppose."

"I'm going to miss her so much." Julia heard the tears in her voice.

"I know." He reached for Julia's hand and gently squeezed it. "Alek phoned. He'll be here as soon as he can."

Julia instinctively wanted Alek with her. She'd never needed him like this before. That thought produced another regret. Alek was devoted to her and she didn't deserve it. She'd treated him terribly and yet he loved her.

Her grief, fed by her burning tears and broken dreams, was overwhelming. She couldn't sit still; she stood and started pacing, then returned to her chair.

They sat silently for another hour. She did what she could to make her grandmother more comfortable. She held Ruth's hand, read her favorite passages from Scripture, stroked her forehead.

"I have to go." Jerry spoke from behind her.

Understanding, Julia nodded. She loved her brother and knew he was grieving in his own way. She was grateful he was leaving; she preferred this time alone with Ruth.

"When will you go home?" he asked.

"I don't know yet."

The next thing she heard was the sound of the door closing. Being alone was a relief and a burden. Julia recognized the inconsistency of her reactions. Never had she craved Alek's company more, and yet she wanted these hours alone with her grandmother, sensing that it would be the last time they'd be together.

She found it ironic that hope and despair could feel the same to her.

The nurses came in a number of times. One encouraged her to take a break, go have some dinner, but Julia refused. She was afraid to leave, fearing that once she did, her grandmother would quietly release her hold on life.

Leaning her forehead against the side of the hospital bed, Julia must have dozed because the next thing she knew Alek was there.

"How is she?"

"There's been no change."

Alek sat down next to Julia. "Have you had dinner?"

"I'm not hungry."

Alek nodded and when he spoke again it was in his own language, which had a distinct beauty. Whatever he was saying seemed to please her grandmother because Ruth smiled. At first Julia was convinced she'd imagined it, which would've been easy enough to do. But there was no denying the change in Ruth's ashen features.

"It's midnight, my love."

Julia glanced at her watch, sure he was mistaken. She must have slept longer than she'd realized.

"Come," he said, standing behind her, his hands on her shoulders. "I'll drive you home."

She shook her head, unwilling to leave.

"You aren't doing her any good, and you're running yourself down, both physically and mentally."

"You go ahead," she said. "I'll stay a little longer."

She heard the frustration in his sigh. "I'm not leaving without you. You're exhausted."

"I'm afraid to leave her," she whispered brokenly. The time had come for the truth, painful though it was. Julia was surprised she'd chosen to voice it to Alek and not her brother.

"Why?" her husband inquired gently.

She was glad he was standing behind her and couldn't see the tears in her eyes. "If Ruth dies, when she dies, a part of me will go with her." The best part, Julia feared. Something would perish in her own heart. Her faith in God and in herself would be shaken, and she wondered if this time the damage would be beyond repair.

"Do you wish to bind her to this life, this pain?"

"No," Julia answered honestly. Yet she held on to Ruth fiercely.

A part of Julia had died with her father. It had been joy. Trust had vanished afterward when she realized everything he'd told her about Roger was true. She hadn't wanted to believe her father, had argued with him, fought with him. It was while they were shouting at each other that he'd suffered the heart attack that had prematurely claimed his life.

Joy had faded from her soul that afternoon, replaced by guilt. In the years since, she'd made a semicomfortable life for herself. She wasn't happy, nor was she unhappy. She buried herself in her work, the desire to succeed propelling her forward, dictating her actions. Her goal was to undo the damage Roger had done to the company. First she would rebuild Conrad Industries to its former glory and then continue on the course her father had so carefully charted.

She was making progress, not only with the company, but with her life. Encouraged by Ruth, Julia was just beginning to recapture some of the enthusiasm she'd lost. She could laugh occasionally, even joke every now and then.

It had seemed impossible that she'd ever again feel anything but the weight of her sadness. Then, without being aware of the transformation, she realized she was feeling again, and it had started after her marriage to Alek.

Now here she was, trapped in pain and fear, and it was too soon. Much too soon.

"Come." Alek took her by the shoulders.

She followed because she didn't have the strength to resist. Leaning forward, she kissed Ruth's cheek and felt the tears run down her own.

Alek gently guided his wife from the hospital room. He kept his arm around her, wanting to lend her his strength. She would never admit she needed him, never confess she was pleased he'd come to be with her. He'd been at the airport that afternoon, dealing with the Immigration people, working out the final details of his sister's entry into the country. He'd been torn between his duty to his sister and Julia.

Alek found he was weary of this constant battle between them. She fought him at every turn, cheated him out of her love. Yet he'd begun to love her and was more determined than ever to win her heart.

He knew only bits and pieces of the past. Even Jerry seemed reluctant to discuss Julia's relationship with Roger Stanhope.

Whenever his friend mentioned the other man's name, Jerry's mouth tightened and anger flashed in his eyes. Because he was often so involved with his own work, Alek couldn't interact with other staff members as much as he would've liked. Recently he'd made a point of doing so.

Over lunch that afternoon, he'd casually dropped Roger Stanhope's name and was astounded by the abrupt silence that fell over the small gathering.

"If you want to know about Roger, just ask Julia," someone suggested.

It sounded like an accusation, which puzzled Alek. From the little he was able to surmise, Roger had been blamed for the fire, although presumably nothing was proven or he'd be in jail. Questions abounded. The answers, like so much else in his marriage, would come with time.

Julia was silent on the ride from the hospital to their home. Alek led her into the condo and toward the guest bedroom, where she chose to sleep.

She sat on the edge of the bed like a lifeless doll.

"Would you like some help undressing?" he asked her.

She shook her head. "No, thanks."

He left her, but not because he wanted to.

Venturing into the kitchen, he made a pot of tea. Julia needed something hot and sweet. When the tea had finished steeping, he returned to her room and knocked lightly on the door.

"Come in."

She'd changed clothes and was dressed in a sexless pair of cotton pajamas.

"I made tea." He carried in a cup and saucer, and set them on the nightstand by her bed.

She stared at the cup as if she'd never seen anything like it before.

"I don't know if you remember, but I told you yesterday that my sister was arriving this afternoon. I was at the airport meeting Anna and then drove her to my old apartment. That's why I couldn't come to the hospital until late. Anna will be here tomorrow morning."

"Why are you so good to me? I don't deserve it... not after the way I've treated you. Not after the things I've said."

He had no answer for her because the truth would only enhance her distress. He loved her as any husband loved his wife. In time she'd recognize and accept it. But she wasn't ready yet.

Alek peeled back the covers of her bed and fluffed up the pillow. She stood behind him, her breathing labored, as if she was struggling not to weep.

"Alek." His name was a mere whisper. "Would you mind...would you sleep with me tonight? Just this once?"

The desire that invaded his body came as a greater shock than her request. From the first night of their marriage, Alek had been waiting for her to voluntarily invite him to her bed. He hadn't imagined it would happen this way, when she was emotionally distraught.

In the same instant, Alek recognized that she wasn't offering him her body. She was seeking his comfort. It wasn't what he wanted, but it was a small step in the right direction and he'd take whatever Julia was willing to give him.

He reached for her hand, kissed her fingers and then moved to the doorway where he switched off the light. Darkness filled the room. He heard the mattress squeak as she slipped beneath the sheets. Then he walked back to the bed, stripped off his clothes and joined her.

It was the sweetest torture he'd ever known to have Julia move into his waiting arms. She cuddled her soft, feminine body against his, molding herself against him, her satiny smooth leg brushing his. She released one long sigh as her head nestled on his chest and was instantly asleep.

Asleep.

Alek grinned mockingly to himself and wrapped his arm around her shoulders. He listened to the even sound of her breathing and after a few moments, kissed the crown of her head.

So this was to be his lot. Comforter. Not lover or husband, but consoler. His body throbbed with wanting her. Holding her so close, yet unable to really touch her, was the purest form of torment Alek had ever endured.

He didn't sleep and was grateful he hadn't, because Julia stirred suddenly, apparently trapped in a nightmare. She thrashed around until he managed to hold her down.

"No," she sobbed and twisted away from him. Her nails dug into his flesh.

"Julia," he whispered, "wake up. It's just a dream."

She raised her head from the pillow, looked into his eyes and frowned. Rubbing a hand over her face, she looked again as though she expected him to have disappeared.

"It's all right," he whispered soothingly. "I'm here."

He could feel her heart racing. Her eyes met his in the darkness and he saw her confusion. It was on the tip of his tongue to remind her she'd invited him into her bed. But he didn't. Instead he plowed his fingers into the thickness of her hair and brought her mouth to his.

She welcomed his kiss without hesitation, without restraint, moaning. She flattened her palms against his chest, then sighed when they'd finished kissing. A sigh that spoke of satisfaction. And confusion.

His body was on fire, but he didn't press her for more. She snuggled against him and draped her arm around him, nestling back into their original position. Her hand was restless as it leisurely roamed across his chest.

Her face angled toward his, her eyes shining in the dark. Alek couldn't resist kissing her again. He couldn't force himself to draw too far away from her. They were so close, physically and emotionally, he wanted this moment to go on forever.

A soft lullaby came to him. He didn't have much of a singing voice, but this was a song his mother had sung to him as a child when he was troubled. Julia wouldn't understand the words, but they would soothe her spirit as they had his.

After the first verse, she released a long, trembling sigh. A few minutes later, she was sound asleep once more.

Alek followed her shortly afterward.

Julia opened her eyes and felt the unbearable weight of her sadness crushing her. Ruth was dying. She rolled over and, despite her sadness, realized it wasn't grief that was pressing her down, but Alek.

Alek! In a sudden panic, she vainly tried to recall the events from the night before. Oh, no, she'd asked him... asked him to sleep with her. She'd been distraught. She hadn't known what she was doing and now he'd think, he'd assume she wanted him to make love to her...that she'd welcome him to her bed every night.

Scrambling to her feet, she backed away from him, her hand at her breast.

"Julia?"

Her heart leapt into her throat. She'd hoped to slip away without waking him.

"Good morning."

"'Morning," she said shyly.

"Did you sleep well?"

Julia nodded and glanced down as the tears sprang readily to her eyes.

"Julia?" He reached for her hand, pulling her back to the bed. She sat on the edge and he slid his arms around her. Words weren't necessary just then. She was grieving and Alek was there to comfort her. She placed her hands over his and their fingers entwined.

"Thank you," she whispered when she could form the words. She leaned back, relaxing into his warmth. He kissed her hair and she turned abruptly and flung her arms around his neck, holding him for all she was worth.

He spoke to her, and she smiled softly when she realized it was in Russian. He seemed to forget she didn't understand him. It didn't matter. She knew what he was saying from his tone—that he was there, that he loved her.

For the first time, the thought didn't terrify her.

Sometime later, Julia dressed, although she had trouble holding back the tears. She finished before Alek did and wandered into the kitchen, intent on starting a pot of coffee. She stopped short when she caught sight of a woman working in her kitchen.

"Good morning," the woman said, struggling with the language. "I am Anna, Alek's sister."

Seven

"Hello, Anna." Julia had forgotten Alek's sister was coming that morning. "Welcome to America."

"Thank you." Alek's sister was small and thin with brown hair woven into a braid. Her eyes were so like Alek's, it was as if Julia were staring into her husband's own dark gaze. Her smile was warm and friendly and despite this awkward beginning, Julia liked her immediately.

"My English is poor, but I'm studying every day."

"I'm sure you'll do just fine," Julia said, wondering why Anna was staring at her.

"I will cook your breakfast."

"Thank you."

"Eggs and toast?"

"Yes, please," Julia answered and hurried into the bathroom. By the time she entered the kitchen, she understood Anna's concern. There'd been tears in her eyes, and Alek's sister must have assumed they'd been arguing. Julia hoped to find a way to reassure her that wasn't the case.

Her breakfast was on the table. Generally she ate on

the run, usually picking up a container of orange juice and a muffin at the local convenience store on her drive to the office. When Alek had suggested they hire his sister as a housekeeper and cook, Julia had readily agreed. It was a way of helping his family. A way of repaying her debt to him. A way of eating regular meals herself.

It wasn't until she sampled the fluffiest, most delicious scrambled eggs she'd ever tasted that Julia realized Anna was the one doing her and Alek the favor.

She was reading over the morning paper when Alek appeared in the kitchen, smartly dressed. He poured himself a cup of coffee while his sister spoke enthusiastically in Russian.

"English," Julia heard him say. "You must speak English."

"This country is so beautiful."

"Yes," Alek agreed, pulling out the chair across from Julia and sitting down. She ignored him, concentrating on the paper.

"Did you phone the hospital?" Alek asked.

"Yes…there's been no change. I'm going into the office this morning."

"You'll let me know if you hear anything?"

"Of course."

His eyes met hers and he smiled. Julia found herself responding, treasuring this understanding between them, this sense of trust they'd stumbled upon. But it frightened her. When Alek recognized her reserve, he sighed and mumbled something she didn't catch.

Anna responded to him in Russian. Naturally Julia couldn't understand the words, but it sounded very much as if her sister-in-law was upset with him. She offered Julia a sympathetic look as she hurried out the door.

Alek returned his attention to Julia. "She thinks I caused your tears this morning. Suffice it to say, she wasn't pleased with me."

"Did you tell her about Ruth?"

"No. Not yet."

"But—"

Alek leaned forward to place his finger on her lips. "Don't worry about my sister. Or me."

It was a mistake to go into the office; Julia realized that almost immediately. There were several pressing matters that needed to be taken care of before she could spend any more time at the hospital. Appointments to reschedule, work to delegate. Julia resented every minute away from her grandmother. She found herself impatient to get back to the hospital. Her relationship with Alek concerned her, too.

Sitting at her desk, Julia supported her face on her hands. She'd been so sure this marriage would never work. Now she wasn't sure of anything. She needed Alek, and he'd come to her, held her, comforted her. She'd given him plenty of reasons to turn away from her. But when the opportunity came to comfort her, he'd come, willingly, unselfishly.

Each day, Julia felt herself weakening a little more, giving in to the attraction she felt for Alek. Every day he found some small way of dismantling the protective barrier around her heart. He was slowly, methodically, exposing her to the warming rays of the sun.

And yet… Julia wanted to shout that she didn't *need* a man in her life, didn't want a husband. Silently she did, forcing his image from her mind—with only limited success.

It was while she was trying not to think of Alek, to concentrate on the tasks before her, that he casually strolled into her office.

"I thought we should talk," he said, dropping into a chair as if he had every right to be there.

"About what?" She pretended to be absorbed in reading her latest batch of correspondence.

"Last night."

He sounded so flippant, so glib, as if their sleeping in the same bed had all been part of his game plan from the start. She'd conveniently fallen into his scheme without realizing it. His attitude infuriated her.

"It was a mistake," she informed him sharply. "One that won't be repeated."

"I suppose it was too much to hope you'd think otherwise," he said with a beleaguered sigh. "If you don't want to accept the truth, then I'll say it for you. It felt good to hold you in my arms, Julia. I'm here if you need me. I'll always be here for you. If you believe nothing else about me, believe this."

Julia felt her chest tighten as he stood and, without waiting for her to comment, walked out of her office. She didn't understand this man she'd married, and wasn't sure she ever would. She'd rewarded his kindness by cheating him out of the kind of marriage he'd expected, the marriage she'd agreed to. She'd insulted him and hurt his pride. Not once, but time and again.

Julia didn't want to love Alek. Love frightened her more than any other emotion, even pain. She pulled a little more inside herself, blocking Alek from her heart, because it was only then that she felt safe.

Removing the slim gold band from her finger, she stared at it. She put it back on her finger, wondering if she'd *ever* understand Alek, then doubted it was possible when she had yet to understand herself.

She spent nearly two hours clearing her desk and her schedule before she was free to leave for the hospital.

Her heart grew heavy as she walked down the long corridor that led to her grandmother's room. She didn't stop at the nurses' station, didn't ask to talk to Ruth's physician. Instead she went directly to the woman who'd helped her through the most difficult period of her life.

As Julia silently opened the door and stepped inside, she felt tears burn the backs of her eyes. Her grandmother appeared to be asleep. Ruth's face was pale, but she seemed more at peace now, as if the pain had passed.

Tentatively Julia stepped over to her grandmother's bed and took her hand. She held it to her own cheek and pressed it there. Slowly Julia closed her eyes.

As soon as she did, it felt as if Ruth were awake, waiting to speak with her.

"Don't be sad," Ruth seemed to be saying. "I don't want you to grieve for me. I've lived a good, long life. You were my joy. God's special gift to me."

"No, please," Julia pleaded silently. "Don't leave me, please don't leave."

"Julia, my child. You have your whole life ahead of you. Don't cling to the past. Look instead to the future. You have a husband who adores you and children waiting to be born. Your life is just beginning. So much love awaits you, more joy than you can possibly imagine now. Your pain shall reap an abundant harvest of life's treasures. Trust me in this."

"Treasures," Julia whispered. She couldn't look past

the present moment to think about the future. Not when her heart was breaking.

Tears ran unrestrained down her face and she felt her grandmother's presence reaching out to comfort her, a last farewell before she set out on the journey before her.

Julia didn't know how long she stood there, holding on to Ruth's hand. She realized as she looked up at the monitor registering her grandmother's heartbeat that it had gone silent. Ruth had quietly slipped from life into death with no fuss, no ceremony, as if she'd been awaiting Julia's arrival so she could leave peacefully.

Julia had known it would be impossible to prepare herself emotionally for this moment. Ruth's death wasn't a shock; she'd been ill for years. Julia had been aware that each day could be her grandmother's last. She'd accepted the inevitability of Ruth's passing as best she could. But nothing could have prepared her for the grief that slammed against her now. Nothing.

Collapsing into the chair, Julia cried out, the sound a low, anguished wail as she swayed back and forth.

A nurse came, so did a doctor and several other health professionals. Julia didn't move. She couldn't. The sobs racked her shoulders and she hid her face in her hands. And slowly rocked with grief.

Someone led her from the room. She sat in the private area alone, desolate, inconsolable.

Jerry and Alek arrived together. Jerry spoke with the hospital officials while Alek wrapped Julia in his arms and held her against him as she wept until she had no more tears.

She needed him and was past pretending she didn't. Her own strength was depleted. Clinging to Alek, she buried her face in his chest, seeking what solace she could. When her father died, she'd been numb with guilt and grief. The tears hadn't come until much later.

He held her close and she was grateful for his comfort, for his willingness to share her grief.

They seemed to be at the hospital for hours. There were papers to sign and a hundred different decisions to make. Jerry went with her and Alek to the funeral home, where arrangements were made for Ruth's burial.

Julia was surprised by the calm, almost unemotional way she was able to deal with the details of the funeral. The flowers, the music, discussing the program with first the funeral home director and then the family's minister, Pastor Hall.

It was dark by the time they'd finished. Jerry, solemn and downcast, walked out to the parking lot with her and Alek.

"Do you want to come back to the condo with us?" Julia asked, not wanting to leave her brother alone. Unlike her, he'd return to an empty house. Ruth's death had shaken him badly. He didn't express his grief as freely as she had.

Jerry shook his head. "No, thanks."

"Anna has dinner ready and waiting," Alek said.

"I'll pick up something on the way home," he assured them both. "Don't worry about me."

Alek drove through the hilly streets that led to their condominium. "How are you feeling?" he asked, when he opened the front door for her.

"Drained." The emotions seemed to be pressing against her chest. She was mentally and physically exhausted; her fatigue was so great she could barely hold up her head.

Alek guided her into the kitchen. She hadn't eaten

since breakfast, hadn't thought about food even once. The smells were heavenly, but she had no appetite.

He brought two plates from the oven and set them on the table.

"I'm not hungry," she told him. "I'm going to take a bath." She half expected him to argue with her, to insist she needed nourishment. Instead he must have realized she knew what was best for herself right now.

One look in the bathroom mirror confirmed Julia's worst suspicions. Her eyes were red, puffy, and her cheeks were pale, her makeup long since washed away by her tears. She looked much older than her thirty years. About a hundred years older. She looked and felt as if she'd been hit by a freight train.

Ruth was gone, and other than Jerry she was alone in the world. She was grateful for Alek's assistance during this traumatic day, but in time he'd leave and then she'd be alone again.

Running her bathwater, she added a package of peach-scented salts and stepped into the hot, soothing water. She leaned against the back of the tub and closed her eyes, letting the heat of the bath comfort her.

Children waiting to be born.

She didn't know why that phrase edged its way into her mind. There would be no children because there would be no real marriage. She was more determined than ever not to cross that line, especially now, when she was most vulnerable. She'd hurt Alek enough, abused his gentleness, taken advantage of his kindness.

He was standing in the hallway outside the bathroom waiting for her when she finished. "I'm fine, Alek," she said, wanting to reassure him, even if it wasn't true.

"You're exhausted. I turned back the sheets for you."

"Thank you."

He ushered her into the bedroom as if she were a child. In other circumstances, Julia would have resented the way he'd taken control of her life, but not then. She felt only gratitude.

She slid beneath the covers, nestled her head against the pillow and closed her eyes. "Alek," she whispered.

"Yes, my love?"

"Would you sing to me again?"

He complied with a haunting melody in his own language. His voice was clear and strong, and even though she couldn't understand the words, she found it beautiful and soothing. She wanted to ask him the meaning, but her thoughts drifted in another direction. Toward rest. Toward peace.

Julia woke with a start. She didn't know what had jarred her awake. The room was dark, although the hall light offered little illumination. The digital clock on the nightstand informed her it was nearly 1:00 a.m. As her eyes adjusted, she realized Alek was sitting beside her in a chair, his legs stretched out before him and his head cocked at an odd, uncomfortable angle.

"Alek?" she whispered, propping herself up on one elbow.

He stirred immediately and straightened. "Julia?"

"What are you doing here?"

"I didn't want you to be alone."

"I'm fine," she said again.

"Do you want me to sing to you?"

Hot, burning tears filled her eyes at his tenderness, his concern. She shook her head. What she needed was to be held.

"Julia, my love," he whispered, moving from the chair to the edge of the bed. His hand smoothed the hair from her face, his touch as gentle as if she were a child in need of reassurance, which was exactly the way Julia felt.

"Why do you have to be so wonderful?" she sobbed. "Why are you so good to me?"

His lips touched her forehead, but he didn't answer.

"I'm a rotten wife."

He laughed. "You haven't given yourself a chance yet."

"I've treated you terribly. You should hate me."

"Hate you?" He seemed to find her words amusing. "That would be impossible."

"Will you lie down with me? Please?" The words were out before she could censor them. It was a completely selfish request. "I...need you, Alek." She added this last part for honesty's sake, to ease her conscience.

He kissed her, his mouth locating hers unerringly in the near-dark. Although his kiss was light, she knew it was his way of thanking her for admitting the truth.

He stood and stripped off his pants and shirt. Julia lifted the covers and moved over as far as she could in the narrow bed.

Despite sleeping in his embrace the night before, she felt strangely shy now. He put his arm around her shoulders and brought her close. He was warm and real and felt so alive that she trembled when she laid her head on his chest. His heart was pounding strong and steady against her ear.

"Can you sleep now?" he whispered.

"I...think so. What about you?"

"Don't worry about me."

That didn't answer her question, but she didn't press him. "We kissed last night, didn't we?"

He rubbed his chin across her hair. "Yes." She heard the strain in his voice and felt unusually pleased. She tilted her head back so that she was looking into his warm, dark eyes. Only a few inches separated their mouths.

"Would you…mind—" she hesitated and moistened her lips "—kissing me again?"

His breathing stopped abruptly and his eyes narrowed as if he wasn't sure he should trust her. Julia didn't blame him.

Rather than waiting for his permission, she arched toward him until their lips met. Their kiss was sweet and undemanding. She was breathing hard when they finished, but so was he.

He kissed her again, a little deeper, a little more intensely. Then a lot more intensely.

Julia sighed as his mouth left hers, their bottom lips clinging momentarily. "Oh, Alek." She sighed, and a trembling kind of response made its way through her body.

She said his name again, more softly this time. "I want to make love."

She watched him closely and noted the different emotions flashing in his eyes. He wanted her, too; there was no question of that. He wanted her and had from the beginning of their marriage. He'd made certain she knew how much. Yet he hesitated.

His eyes gradually changed and told her another story. They darkened with doubt, which won over the needy, sensual look she'd seen in him seconds earlier.

"Julia." He breathed her name, his tone regretful. "Not now."

"Why not?" She knew she sounded defensive and couldn't help it. He'd demanded she share his bed from the first night of their marriage.

But when she finally agreed to fulfill her part of their bargain, he rejected her. It made no sense. And it angered her.

"I'd feel as if I was taking advantage of you."

"Shouldn't I be the judge of that?" she said irritably.

"Right now, no."

Stunned, she jerked her head away. His fingers came to her face, resting on her cheek, directing her gaze back to his.

"I want you, Julia, don't ever doubt that. But I refuse to put my own needs before yours. You're confused and hurting. There's nothing I'd like more than to—" He stopped. "I'm sure you understand."

She nodded.

He kissed her briefly, then tucked his arm around her and brought her even closer to his side. His lips were in her hair. "When we make love, I don't want there to be any regrets in the morning."

Julia smiled and kissed his bare chest. "No one told me you were so noble."

"No one told me, either," he muttered disparagingly.

The way he said it with a deep, shuddering sigh led her to believe that if anyone had regrets in the morning, it would be her husband.

Content now, she curled up against him and shut her eyes. She'd prefer it if they made love, but being in his arms would satisfy her for now.

Alek envied Julia her ability to sleep. For weeks he'd been waiting for his wife to come to him, to fulfill her wedding vows by her own choice. Yet when she invited him to her bed, held her arms softly around him, he felt compelled to do the honorable thing.

Honor. But at what price? His body throbbed with need. His heart ached with love. No woman had led him on a finer chase. No woman had challenged him as much as his wife. No woman had defied and infuriated him more than Julia.

She'd been hurt and angry at his refusal, then seemed to accept the wisdom of his words. Wisdom, nothing! He was a fool.

Maybe not, he decided after a moment. Perhaps he *had* been wise. Only time would tell.

He felt Julia stir some time later and was surprised to realize it was morning. Slowly he opened his eyes to discover her face staring down at his, studying him. "Good morning," she whispered.

He waited, thinking she might be angry at finding him in bed with her, but she revealed none of the outrage she had the morning before. Still, her eyes were clouded and her grief was evident.

"Did you sleep well?" he asked.

She nodded shyly, her gaze avoiding his. "What about you?"

"As well as can be expected." He stretched his cramped arms and yawned loudly. They were fools, the pair of them. His sister had said as much yesterday morning. They were sleeping in a single bed when there was a perfectly good king-size bed in the other room.

Alek didn't have a single excuse to offer his sister and finally told her to mind her own business. But Anna was right.

"Thank you, Alek," Julia said, climbing out of bed. Her face was turned away from him.

"For what, staying with you?"

"No...well, yes, that, too, but for...you know, not..."

"Making love to you?"

She nodded. Reaching inside her closet, she took out a set of clothes and held them in front of her as if to shield her body from his view. She'd spent most of the night cuddling against him. He'd felt every inch of her creamy smooth skin; there wasn't anything left to hide. It didn't seem right to point that out, however.

"The next few days are going to be very busy. I'll be spending a lot of my time finishing up the funeral arrangements and...and going through Ruth's things, so we probably won't see much of each other for a while."

She didn't need to sound so pleased at the prospect, Alek mused.

By the time he'd showered and dressed, Julia had already left the condominium. His sister was eyeing him critically, clearly displeased about something.

"What's wrong with Julia?" Anna asked in an accusatory voice. "She looks as if she was crying."

Naturally it would be his fault, Alek thought, ignoring his sister's glare.

"Her grandmother died," he explained and he watched as Anna's eyes went soft with sympathy.

"You love this woman."

"She's my wife." He saw now that it was a mistake to have hired his sister. It was obvious that she was going to be what Jerry called "a damned nuisance."

"You did not marry her for love."

"No," he admitted gruffly, resenting this line of

questioning. He wouldn't have tolerated it from anyone else and Anna knew it.

"She knows that you did not love her. This is why
she sleeps in the small bed."

"Thank you, Dear Abby."

"Who?"

"Never mind," Alek said impatiently. He grabbed a
piece of toast from the plate and didn't wait for the rest
of his breakfast. He turned to leave the room.

"Aleksandr," she said sharply, stopping him. "You've
become very American." Her face relaxed into a wide
smile. "I think this is good. You teach me, too, okay?"

"Okay," he said, chuckling.

Sorting through Ruth's possessions proved to be
far more difficult than Julia had expected. Her grandmother's tastes had been simple, but she'd held on to
many things, refusing to discard life's mementos.

Disposing of her clothes was the easiest. Julia boxed
them up and took them to a shelter for the homeless.
It was the little things she found so difficult. A token
from the Seattle World Fair, an empty perfume bottle
that had long since faded. The photographs. She could
never part with the photographs.

Julia had no idea her grandmother had collected so
many snapshots. The comical photos Ruth sent Louis
Conrad while he was away fighting in the Second World
War made her smile.

Julia came across a packet of pictures that caused
her to laugh outright. Her grandmother, so young and
attractive, was poised in a modest-looking swimsuit
in front of a young soldier's photograph. It had to be

Julia's grandfather, but she'd never seen pictures of him at that age.

The whole thing must have been rather risqué for the time. Julia guessed Ruth had been giving Louis a reason to come home. Heaven knew it had worked.

Julia studied the picture and sat for several minutes remembering the love story Ruth had told her. It was sweet and innocent, unlike now when sex so often dominated a relationship.

Except for her marriage, she thought defeatedly. It was difficult to believe she could've been married to Alek this long without making love.

He'd been eager for the physical side of their relationship—until she'd revealed the first signs of wanting him, too. How typical of a man.

"Oh, Alek," she breathed, holding her grandmother's picture. "Will there ever be a way for us?"

In her heart she heard a resounding *yes*. But the voice wasn't her own, nor was it Alek's. It came from Ruth.

The day of the funeral, Julia wore a black dress and an old-fashioned pillbox hat with black netting that fitted over her face.

Julia hadn't slept well the past few nights and the fatigue was beginning to show. She'd made a point of coming home late, knowing Alek would be waiting for her. She'd mumble something about being tired and close her bedroom door, slipping into bed alone.

She'd spent the past two nights wishing Alek was there with her. She cursed her foolish pride for not approaching him. But she was afraid that once she did, she'd ask him to make love to her again, and this time she wouldn't take no for an answer.

The limousine delivered Julia, Jerry and Alek to the Methodist church where Ruth had worshiped for a number of years. Jerry and Alek climbed out first. Alek offered her his hand as Julia stepped out of the car. A small group of mourners had formed on the sidewalk outside the church, awaiting the family's arrival. Julia's gaze quickly scanned the crowd, then stopped abruptly.

There, seeking her eyes, stood Roger Stanhope.

Eight

Julia hesitated, one foot on the curb, the other in the limousine. Crouched as she was, she felt in danger of collapsing. Roger had dared to show up at her grandmother's funeral! The man had no sense of decency, but that didn't come as any surprise.

Although Alek couldn't have known what was happening, he leaned forward, put his arm around her waist and assisted her to an upright position.

His eyes were filled with concern. Julia's heart was beating double time and her head was spinning. She was afraid she might faint.

"I... I need to sit down."

"Of course." With his hand securely around her waist, Alek led her into the church vestibule. A row of wooden pews lined the wall and Alek encouraged her to take a seat.

"What's wrong?" Jerry asked.

Julia couldn't answer. "Water...could you get me a glass of water?"

Jerry hurried away and returned a moment later with

her drink. Other friends were beginning to arrive and after taking a moment to compose herself, Julia stood.

How dare Roger come to her grandmother's funeral! He'd done it to agitate her, and his unscrupulous ploy had worked. Julia had never been so close to passing out. Not even the day her father had— She pushed the thought from her mind, refusing to dwell on anything that had to do with Roger.

Jerry caught sight of their former employee, and his mouth thinned with irritation. "You saw him, didn't you?"

Julia nodded.

"I'll have him thrown out."

"Don't," she said. Roger wasn't worth the effort. "He'll cause a scene. Besides, I think Ruth would've gotten a kick out of it. We tried everything but a subpoena to talk to him after the fire, remember?"

"I'm not likely to forget."

"Who would've believed he'd end up coming to us?"

"Not me," Jerry agreed.

Alek didn't say anything, but Julia was well aware of his presence at her side. She wasn't fooled; he took in every word of the exchange between her and her brother.

"Point out this man to me," Alek said to them both. "I will see to his removal."

Jerry glanced at Julia, looking for her consent. She thought about it a moment, then decided she wouldn't give Roger the satisfaction.

"Don't kid yourself, Julia, he's up to something," Jerry warned.

"I'd be a fool if I didn't know that," she returned testily. She'd been duped by Roger once and it wasn't a mistake she cared to repeat. She knew his methods and wouldn't be taken in a second time.

The three of them had gathered in the back of the church and were unaware of anyone else until Pastor Hall approached them and announced they were ready for the service to begin.

Julia had known this ordeal would leave her emotionally depleted. Several times during the funeral she felt close to tears, but she held them at bay, taking in deep, even breaths. Her fingers were entwined with Alek's and she appreciated more than ever that he was with her. His presence lent her the strength she needed to get through the heartrending experience of saying goodbye to the woman she loved so dearly.

Anna sat nearby, and despite the solemnity of the occasion, Julia thought she saw Jerry cast her several interested glances.

From the church they traveled to the north end of Seattle to the cemetery where Ruth would be buried in the plot next to her beloved Louis.

Julia was surprised by how many people came. The day was bright and clear and the sky a pale shade of blue she'd only seen in the Pacific Northwest.

There were so many lovely bouquets of flowers. The group of mourners gathered under the canopy at the cemetery. Julia, Jerry and Alek were given seats, along with a few of Ruth's more elderly friends. Pastor Hall read from his Bible and the words were familiar ones since Julia had read them so often to Ruth herself.

Her heart felt as if it would shatter into a thousand pieces as the casket was slowly lowered into the ground. Alek must have sensed her distress because he placed his arm around her shoulders. The tears sprang from her eyes and she quietly sobbed her last farewell.

Afterward, the assembly met at Ruth's home. Charles, who'd been with the family for years, had insisted on having it there, although it demanded extra work on his part. The meal was catered, but several friends brought dishes themselves. A wide variety of casseroles, as well as salads, cheeses and sliced meats, were served.

Julia and Jerry stood by the doorway and greeted their visitors, thanking each of them for their love and support. Julia received countless hugs. Anna had felt uncomfortable about being among so many strangers and had left, with Julia's fervent thanks for attending the service.

Various family friends recounted stories involving Ruth and Louis, and before she realized it, Julia found herself smiling. Her grandmother had been a wonderful, generous, warmhearted woman. Julia didn't need others to tell her that, but their comments reaffirmed what she'd always known.

The gathering broke up into small groups of mourners. Every available seat in the living room and formal dining room was taken. Julia assisted Charles in seeing to the guests' comfort.

She was filling coffee cups when Roger spoke from behind her. "Hello, Julia."

It was fortunate that she didn't empty the steaming coffee into someone's lap. Roger had apparently sneaked into the house through the back door, because Jerry would never have allowed him in the front.

"Hello, Roger," she said as unemotionally as she could.

"I'm sorry to hear about your grandmother."

"Thank you." Her words, if not her tone, were civil.

"Julia, Julia," he said with an injured sigh, "isn't it time for us to let bygones be bygones? How often do I have to tell you it was all a horrible mistake? It seems a shame to rehash something that happened so long ago, don't you agree?"

"I'm sure it wasn't a mistake. Now, if you'll excuse me, I have to see to my guests."

Roger surprised her by taking her arm and stopping her. Her gaze flew back to him and she wondered how she could ever have thought herself in love with him.

He was handsome, but his good looks were so transparent that she was shocked she hadn't seen through his guise sooner. She'd learned a good deal about character in the past few years, and that thought, at least, comforted her.

"I suggest you let go of my wife's arm," Alek said. He was angry. Julia could tell by how heavy his accent had become.

Roger looked puzzled, as if he didn't understand.

"And I suggest you do as he says," Julia said.

Roger released her arm. He held up both hands for Alek's inspection. "I heard you were married," he said, continuing to follow her as she filled yet another coffee cup. Alek came after Roger and the three of them paraded across the room.

"Why you chose to marry a Russian is beyond me. I figured you were smarter than to involve yourself with some foreigner."

Julia didn't dignify that comment with a reply. Instead she introduced the two men. "Roger Stanhope, meet Aleksandr Berinski."

"Ah," Roger said sarcastically, "and I thought he was your bodyguard."

"I am," Alek said in a less heavy accent. "Touch my wife again and you'll be sorry. We *foreigners* have effective ways of making our point."

"Alek," Julia admonished with a grin.

Roger seemed to take the threat as some kind of joke. "I'm truly sorry to hear about your grandmother," he went on.

"Thank you." The coffeepot was empty and Julia returned to the kitchen with both Roger and Alek in tow. If it hadn't been such a sad occasion, Julia would've found the antics of the two men funny.

"I'd like to take you to lunch sometime," Roger said, leaning against the kitchen counter as Julia prepared another pot of coffee. "We could talk over old times."

"Great. I'd love it. Do you mind if I bring the arson investigator?"

"Julia won't be having lunch with you," Alek said before Roger could react.

"I'm sorry, Roger, I really am, but my husband is the jealous sort. You've started off on the wrong foot with him as it is. Don't press your luck."

"Julia, sweetheart," Roger said meaningfully, "it's time for us to clear the air."

"The air will be much clearer once you leave," Alek muttered. "Perhaps you would allow me to show you the door?" He advanced one menacing step, then another.

"Ah…" Roger backed up, hands raised. "All right, all right. I'll go."

"I thought you'd see matters my way," Alek said.

Roger cast an ugly look in his direction. He straightened the cuffs of his starched white shirt and wore an injured air as he left the house through the back door.

Julia's gaze followed Roger. "That really wasn't necessary, you know."

"Ah, but it gave me pleasure to send him."

Her smiling eyes met his. "Me, too."

"Tell me about this man. You loved him?"

She felt her amusement drain away. She was surprised no one had ever told Alek about her fateful relationship with Roger. But she'd dealt with enough grief for one day and didn't feel like delving into more.

"Another time?" she asked.

Alek seemed to require a moment to think over his response. "Soon," he told her. "A husband needs to know these things."

She agreed with an unenthusiastic nod.

Alek was leaving the kitchen when she stopped him. "I'll tell you about Roger if you tell me about the women in your life."

This, too, seemed to give him pause. "There's never been anyone but you," he said, then grinned boyishly.

The gathering broke up an hour or so later. Julia insisted on staying to help Charles with the cleanup. Jerry and Alek were helpful, too, stacking folding chairs, straightening the living room and carrying dirty dishes into the kitchen.

By the time Alek unlocked the door to their home, Julia felt drained.

"Sit down," Alek said, "and I'll make you a cup of tea."

"That sounds heavenly." She kicked off her shoes and stretched out her tired legs, resting her feet on the ottoman. Alek joined her a few minutes later, bringing a china cup and saucer.

He sat across from her.

"I don't think I'll ever stop missing her," Julia whispered, after her first sip of tea. Now that she wasn't so busy, the pain of losing Ruth returned full force. "She's left such a large void in my life."

"Give yourself time," Alek said gently.

Julia looked over at her husband and her heart swelled with some emotion she couldn't quite identify. Possibly love. That frightened her half to death, but she sensed that with Alek there was the chance of feeling safe and secure again.

He'd been so good to her through the difficult weeks of Ruth's illness and death, even when she'd given him ample reason to be angry with her.

"When was the last time you ate?" he asked unexpectedly.

Julia shrugged. "I don't remember."

"You didn't have anything this afternoon."

"I didn't?" There'd been so much food, it seemed impossible that she hadn't eaten something.

"No," Alek informed her. "I was watching. You saw to everyone but yourself. I'll make you dinner."

"Alek, please," she said, trailing him into the kitchen. "That isn't necessary."

"It'll be my pleasure." Lifting her by the waist, he sat her effortlessly on the stool next to the kitchen counter. "You can stay and observe," he said. "You might even learn something."

Relaxed now, Julia smiled.

Alek looked at her for a moment. "You don't do that

often enough," he said, leaning toward her and dropping a kiss on her lips.

"Do what?" she asked in surprise.

"Smile."

"There hasn't been much reason to."

"That's about to change, my love."

She leaned her chin on her hands. The sadness she'd carried with her all these weeks seemed to slide off her back. "You know, I think you're right."

Alek, who was beating eggs, looked over at her and grinned. "Anna said something to me the other morning. As her older brother I'm guilty of not listening to my sister as often as I should. This time, I did—and I agree with her."

"I like Anna very much."

"She feels the same way about you. She told me you were wise not to let me make love to you."

Julia lowered her gaze, uncomfortable with the topic.

"When we married I wasn't in love with you," Alek confessed. "You weren't in love with me. This is true?"

Given no option but the truth, Julia nodded.

"My heart tells me differently now." He put the bowl down and moved to her side. With one finger, he raised her chin so her eyes were level with his own. "I love you, Julia, very much."

She bit her trembling lower lip. "Oh, Alek…" Tears blurred her vision until his face swam before her.

"This makes you sad?"

"This terrifies me. I want to love you… I think I already do, but I don't trust myself when it comes to falling in love."

Alek frowned. "Because of this man you saw today?"

"Roger? Yes, because of Roger."

"I am not like him. You know that."

"I do." Logically, intellectually, she understood, but emotionally—that was harder. That was a risk...

Alek slipped his arms around her and Julia was struck not for the first time by the incredible beauty she saw in him. Not merely the physical kind. Oh, he was handsome, but that wasn't what captivated her. She saw the man who'd held and comforted her when her grandmother died. The man who'd sung her to sleep. The man who'd refused to take advantage of her even when she'd asked him to do so.

They stared at each other, and Julia knew the exact moment Alek decided to make love to her. It was the same moment she realized she wanted him to—wanted it more than anything.

His mouth sought hers in a hungry kiss. "I love you," he whispered against her lips.

"I love you, too," she echoed, so lost in his kiss that she couldn't speak anything but the truth. She'd tried to fool herself into believing it wasn't possible to trust a man again. Alek was different; he had to be. If she couldn't trust *him,* there was no hope for her.

He took her by the waist as he lifted her from the stool. Her feet dangling several inches off the floor, he carried her out of the kitchen and into the bedroom, kissing her, nibbling at her lips.

Julia tipped her head back in an effort to gather her scattered wits. Her breath came in short bursts, her lungs empty of air. Feeling seemed more important than breathing. Alek's touch, which was most important of all, brought back to life the desire that had lain dormant in her for years.

He lay with her on the king-size bed, bringing his

mouth to hers, revealing sensual mysteries with his lips and tongue. He was sprawled across her, pinning her to the bed.

"You're so beautiful," he whispered. "You make me crazy."

"Love me," she told him, her arms around his neck. Just as she'd known she would, Julia felt safe with Alek. And she felt sure, of him and of herself.

"I do love you, always." He lowered his mouth to hers again. His kiss was sweet as his hands fiddled with the zipper at the back of her dress. Growing impatient, he rolled her onto her side, turning with her in order to ease it open. He removed the dress, along with her bra and panties.

Then his own clothes came off...

Afterward, neither spoke. Alek kissed her repeatedly and Julia kissed him back, in relief and jubilation. Her season of pain had passed just as her grandmother had claimed it would. She'd found her joy in Alek.

They slept, their arms around each other, their bodies cuddling spoon-fashion. Alek tucked his leg over hers and pressed close to her back.

Julia woke first, hungry and loving. She turned over so that her head was nestled beneath Alek's chin.

"Hmm."

"You awake?"

"I am now," he muttered drowsily.

"I'm hungry. Do you want to order out for dinner?"

Alek grinned. "I was going to cook for us, remember?"

Julia scooted closer, wrapping her arms around his neck, her fingers delving into his thick hair. "I think you should conserve your strength for later," she advised, bringing his mouth down to hers.

Gentle flames flickered over the gas logs in Julia's fireplace while they lounged on the floor, the remains of a boxed pizza resting nearby on the plush, light gray carpeting. Alek had found a bottle of wine and poured them each a glass.

"You're quiet," Alek commented.

Julia leaned back her head and smiled up at him. They couldn't seem to be apart from each other, even for a moment. Not just then. His touch was her reality.

His arms tightened around her. "Any regrets?"

"None."

He kissed the side of her neck. "Me, neither."

"I thought you'd gloat. Our making love is a real feather in your cap, isn't it?"

"I care nothing for feathers. All I want is my wife." He stroked his chin across the top of her head. "Are you still hungry?"

Julia patted her stomach. "Not a bit. Are you?"

"Yes. I'm half-starved."

The odd catch in his voice told her it wasn't food that interested him. He went still, as though he feared her response. Looking up at him, she stared into his eyes and smiled. "I have a feeling I've awakened a monster," she teased.

Alek pressed her down into the thick carpet, his eyes seeking hers. "Do you mind?"

"No," she whispered, untying the sash to her silk robe. "I don't mind at all."

Alek's mouth had just touched hers when the phone rang. He froze and so did Julia.

"Let it ring," she suggested, rubbing her hands over his chest, loving the smooth feel of his skin.

"It could be important." Reluctantly his eyes moved from her to the phone.

"You're probably right," Julia said, although she was far more interested in making love with her husband than talking on the phone.

"I'll get it." He scrambled across the floor and grabbed the receiver. "Hello," he said impatiently.

Julia followed, kneeling beside him. Leaning forward, she caught his earlobe between her teeth.

"Hello, Jerry," he said curtly.

Julia playfully progressed from his ear to his chin, then down the side of his neck.

"Yes, Julia's right here." He seemed winded, as if he were under strain.

"It's for you." He handed her the phone.

Julia took it, her eyes holding his. "Hello, Jerry," she said in a clear, even voice. "You caught me at a bad moment. Would you mind if I called you back in say... half an hour?"

"Ah...sure." Her brother obviously wasn't pleased, but Julia didn't really care.

"Thanks." She hung up the phone. "Now..."

"A bad moment?" Alek repeated, struggling to hide a smile. "Or a good one?"

"Definitely a good one," she said. "At least from my point of view."

"And mine, too..."

Nearly thirty minutes passed before Julia returned her brother's call.

"Hello, Jerry," she said, when he answered the phone. "I'm sorry I couldn't talk earlier."

"What's going on over there, anyway?"

"Sorry. We were busy."

The pause that followed was full of meaning. "Ah. I see. So," he said smugly, "how do you like married life now?"

"I like it just fine." She felt embarrassed to be discussing her love life with her brother even in the vaguest way. "Why are you calling? Is there a problem?"

"Yes, there is." Jerry's voice sharpened. "It's Roger."

Julia groaned inwardly. Would she never be rid of him? "What's he up to now?"

"I told you he was after something when he showed up for the funeral."

"We both know he didn't come out of respect," Julia agreed.

"I got a call from a friend who said he's heard Roger's been asking a lot of questions about Phoenix Paints."

"What did your friend learn?" A cold chill skittered down Julia's spine. Three years ago she'd handed Roger their latest formula—the biggest advance in house paint in over thirty years. A month before Conrad Industries' new line of paints was scheduled to hit the market, their plant burned to the ground. Within a matter of weeks Roger had left the company, and Ideal Paints was marketing Conrad Industries' new product.

Because of the fire, it was impossible to meet the demand for their innovation, while Ideal Paints was capable of delivering paint to every hardware store in the country.

"My friend? He couldn't find out very much."

"Let's double security around the plant," Julia suggested.

"I've already done that."

"Who has Roger contacted?" she asked, pushing the hair from her forehead. They wouldn't allow him to steal from them again.

"I don't know." Jerry sounded equally concerned.

"Should we bring in a private investigator?"

"For what?"

"Tracking phones calls. See if he's getting information from any of our employees. We could have him watched. What do you think?"

"I don't know what to think. This is crazy. It's like a nightmare happening all over again. How soon did Alek say the new product would be ready for marketing?"

"Soon. He's been working a lot of hours."

"I figure we should move ahead as quickly as possible, don't you? I'll see what I can do to schedule a meeting with the marketing folks. The sooner we can get our new paint on the store shelves, the better."

"Okay. Let me know if you hear anything else," Julia said.

"I will," Jerry promised.

They said a few words of farewell and when she replaced the receiver, she sighed.

"What was that all about?" Alek asked.

Julia shook her head, not wanting to explain, because explaining would mean telling him about her relationship with Roger. That was something she wanted to avoid, at least for now.

"These lines," he said, tracing his finger along the creases in her brow, "are because of Roger Stanhope, aren't they?"

Julia nodded.

"That's what I thought. Tell me about him, Julia. It's time I knew."

Nine

"Julia," Alek urged when she didn't immediately respond.

"Roger was just a man I once knew and trusted... several years ago. He proved he wasn't trustworthy. Can we leave it at that?"

"You loved him?"

Admitting it hurt her pride. Mixed in with all the regrets and the guilt was shame. Her only crime had been loving a man who didn't deserve it. A man who'd used her and shocked her with his betrayal, so much so that she'd refused to believe he was responsible for what had happened until her father had literally shoved the evidence at her. Even then she'd made excuses for him, unable to accept the truth. Her father had become so exasperated with her that he'd... Julia turned her thoughts from that fateful day when her life had become a living nightmare.

"Yes, I loved him," she answered finally. "It was a mistake. A very bad one."

"*What* was your mistake?" Alek probed gently.

"It's too complicated. But rest assured, I learned my lesson."

"And what was that?"

"That…love sometimes hurts."

Alek studied her for a moment, but what he was hoping to see, Julia could only speculate.

"Love doesn't always bring pain," he said. "My love will prove otherwise." He kissed her with a compassion that brought tears to her eyes. She managed to blink them back and offer him a look of gratitude.

"Come," he said softly, lifting her into his arms. "It's time for bed."

At dawn Alek was suddenly awake. Moonlight waltzed across the bedroom walls and the room was silent.

A chime rang the hour from the anniversary clock Julia kept on top of her bookcase. It was only 5:00 a.m. and he *should* be exhausted. But he was drained, sated, happy. His wife slept contentedly at his side, her slim body curled against his. He kissed her cheek, grateful Julia was married to him.

He'd wanted to ask her more about Stanhope, but he could see the raw anguish the man's name brought to her eyes, and even satisfying his curiosity wasn't worth causing her additional pain.

Alek knew very little of this man, but what he did know, he didn't like. He'd seen the way Roger had reached for Julia, placing his hand on her arm as though he had a right to touch her, to make demands. Alek didn't like the way the other man had looked at her, either, with a leer, as if he could have her with no more than a few persuasive words.

Alek hadn't thought of himself as jealous, but the

quiet rage he'd felt when he found Roger Stanhope pestering Julia couldn't be denied.

The man was a weakling. Stanhope relied on his sleek good looks, his flashy smile and compelling personality instead of intelligence, honest work and business acumen.

Alek wasn't fooled. Roger Stanhope was an enemy. Not only of Julia's, but Jerry's, as well. Julia hadn't explained the telephone conversation she'd had with her brother, even when he'd asked.

Although she'd tried to make light of Jerry's call, Alek had caught snatches of the conversation, enough to know she was worried. She'd been unable to disguise her distress. Stanhope wasn't worth one iota of anxiety. As Julia's husband, it was up to Alek to make sure that the man who'd betrayed her and her family wouldn't be allowed to do so again.

Alek was gone when Julia woke and she instantly experienced a surge of disappointment. One look at the clock explained Alek's absence. The last time she'd slept past ten had been as a teenager.

Nevertheless, she missed him. A slow smile spread over her lips. She'd married quite a man. Obviously he worked with as much energy and enthusiasm as he made love.

She climbed out of bed and threw on her robe. Since it was Saturday, and her week had been hellish, she intended to relax. There would be problems enough to deal with on Monday morning. The desire to rush into her office today was nonexistent.

She was knotting the belt on her pink silk robe as

she wandered into the kitchen. Anna was there, busily whipping up something delicious, no doubt.

"Good morning, Anna."

"Good morning." Alek's sister stopped what she was doing and brought Julia a cup of coffee.

Being waited on was a luxury that would soon spoil her. "I'll take care of myself," Julia told her, not unkindly. "You go back to whatever you're doing." She walked over to the counter and on closer examination saw that the contents of Anna's bowl resembled cookie dough. A sample confirmed her guess. Oatmeal raisin, she thought.

"Yum."

Anna grinned at the compliment. "Alek asked me to bake them this morning for your picnic."

Julia paused halfway across the kitchen floor. "Our picnic?"

"Yes, he left a note asking me to pack a basket of food. He gave me a long list of everything he wants."

"Where is he?" Julia asked, adding cream to her coffee. "Do you know?"

Anna shook her head as she resumed stirring the thick batter. "No. He had some errand. He doesn't tell me much. I'm only his sister."

"He doesn't tell me much, either," Julia added with a short laugh. "I'm only his wife."

Anna giggled. "He should be back soon. He said you were very tired and wanted to be sure you slept as long as you needed. I'm very sorry about your grandmother."

"Thank you—I'm sorry, too," Julia said, breathing in deeply at the fresh stab of pain she felt at the mention of Ruth's death. That pain would be with her for a long while. Losing her grandmother had left a wide, gaping hole in her heart. Alek's love had helped her begin to heal, but she would always miss Ruth.

Sitting down at the table with the morning paper, Julia tried to focus her attention on the headlines. Soon the words blurred and ran together. The tears came as an unwelcome surprise, and she bent her head, hoping Anna wouldn't notice.

The sound of the front door opening announced Alek's return. Julia hurriedly wiped the tears from her cheeks and smiled up at him. She hadn't fooled him, she realized, but it didn't matter. He strolled over to her, his eyes full of love, and kissed her deeply.

Julia had trouble not losing herself in his kiss. It would have been so easy to let it lead to something more…

Alek glanced impatiently over his shoulder at his sister. "I'll give her the rest of the day off," he whispered.

"Don't be silly."

The hunger in his eyes told her how serious he was. He raised her effortlessly from her chair, sat down and held her in his lap.

"You slept late?" he questioned, smoothing the hair away from her face.

"Very late. You should've gotten me up."

"I was tempted. Tomorrow I will have no qualms about waking you."

"Really?" she asked, loving him so much it felt as if she could hardly contain it. She saw Anna watching them and could tell that Alek's sister was pleased at their closeness. "We're going on a picnic?"

"Yes," Alek said, his face brightening.

"Where?"

"That's a surprise. Bring a sweater, an extra set of

clothes and a…" He hesitated, as if searching for a word, something he rarely did. "A kite."

"Kite…as in a flying-in-the-wind kite?"

He nodded enthusiastically.

"Alek," she said, studying him, "Are you taking me to the ocean?"

"Yes, my love, the ocean. And," he added, "we're leaving our cell phones and BlackBerries behind."

Julia had no problem with that directive.

Within fifteen minutes they were on their way. Anna's basket was tucked away in the backseat, along with an extra set of clothes for each of them, several beach towels, a blanket—and no fewer than five different kites, all of which Alek had bought while he was out.

He drove to Ocean Shores. The sun shone brightly and the surf pounded the sand with a roar that echoed toward them. The scent of salt stung the air. Seagulls soared overhead, looking for an opportune meal. There were plenty of people, but this was nothing like the crowded beaches along the Oregon and California coasts.

Alek parked the car and found them an ideal spot to spread out their blanket and bask in the sunshine. Julia removed her shoes and ran barefoot in the warm sand, chasing after him.

"This is *perfect*," she cried, throwing out her arms. "I love it."

Alek returned to the car for their picnic basket and the kites and joined her on the blanket. He looked more relaxed than she could ever remember seeing him. He sank down beside her and stretched out with a contented sigh.

The wind buffeted them and a minute later, Alek

moved, positioning himself behind her. He wrapped his arms around her and inhaled slowly, drawing the salty air into his lungs. Julia did the same, breathing in the fresh clean scent of the sea.

"It's so peaceful here," she murmured. There were a number of activities going on around them, including horseback riding, kite flying, a football-throwing contest, even a couple of volleyball games, but none of those distracted her from the serenity she experienced.

"I thought you'd feel this way." He kissed the side of her neck.

Julia relaxed against his strength, letting him absorb her weight.

"My mother often brought Anna and me to the Black Sea after our father was killed."

Julia knew shockingly little about her husband's life before he came to the United States. "How old were you when he died?"

"Ten. Anna was seven. It was 1986."

"How did he die?"

It seemed an eternity passed before Alek spoke, and when he did his voice was low. "He was murdered. I don't think we will ever know the real reason. They came, the soldiers, in the middle of the night. We were all asleep. I woke to my mother's screams but by the time I got past the soldier guarding the door, my father was already dead."

"Oh, Alek." Julia's throat tightened with the effort to hold back tears.

"We learned from someone who risked his life to tell us that the KGB suspected my father of some illegal activity—we never heard the details. It made no sense to us since my father was a loyal Communist. Like me, he worked as a chemist."

"Oh, Alek. How terrible for all of you."

"Yes," he agreed, "and it nearly destroyed my mother. If it hadn't been for Anna and me, I believe my mother would have died, too. Not at the soldiers' hands, but from grief."

"What happened afterward?"

"My mother had to support us. Both Anna and I did everything we could to help, but it was difficult. Because I was a good student, I was given the opportunity to attend university. It was there that I met my first Americans. I couldn't believe the freedom and prosperity those students told me about. I've always been good with languages—Anna, too. Soon afterward, I started learning English. After I met Jerry, he sent me books and CDs. He was my link to America."

"Were you surprised when he asked you to come and work for Conrad Industries?"

"Yes."

"Did Jerry ever tell you about his beautiful younger sister?" Julia prodded.

"In passing."

"Were you curious about me?"

"No."

She poked him in the ribs and was rewarded with a mock cry of pain.

"I'm more curious now," he said, laughing.

"Good."

His hand edged beneath her blouse.

"Alek!"

"I'm just wondering how fast I can make you want me."

"Fast enough. Now, stop. We're on a public beach."

He sighed as though her words had wounded him. "Maybe we should get a hotel room."

"We could have done that in Seattle. Since we're at the beach and the day is gorgeous, let's enjoy ourselves."

"Julia," Alek said sternly, "trust me, we would enjoy ourselves in a hotel room, too."

Smiling, she leaned back her head to look at him. "No one told me you were a sex fiend."

"You do this to me, Julia, only you."

"I promise I'll satisfy your, uh, carnal appetite," she assured him with a grin. "And I'm a woman of my word."

"I must not be so selfish," Alek said, and the teasing quality was gone from his voice. "I didn't bring you here to make love, I brought you here to heal. After my father was killed, my mother made weekly trips to the beach with Anna and me. It was a time of solace for us, and it helped us heal. I hoped it would help you, too."

"It does," Julia said, looking out at the pounding surf.

"You must forgive my greed for you."

"Only if you forgive my greed for you." The lovemaking was so new, they were eager to learn everything they could about each other, eager to give and to receive. Julia didn't fool herself into believing this kind of desire could continue. If it did, they might both die of sheer exhaustion.

"I want you to relax in my arms," Alek said, "and close your eyes." He waited a moment. "Are they closed?"

She nodded. The sounds that came at her were intense. The ocean as it slapped against the shore, the cry of the birds and the roar of scooters as they shot past her, kicking up the sand. The smells, carried on the wind, were pungent.

"Now open your eyes."

Julia obeyed and was overwhelmed by the richness of the colors around her. The sky was blue with huge puffy clouds. The water was a sparkling green that left a thin, white, frothy trail on the sand. Every color was vibrant, every detail. Julia's breath caught in her throat at the beauty before her.

"Oh, Alek, it's so lovely."

"My mother did that with Anna and me, but I think she was doing it for herself, too. She wanted us to see that life could be good, if we looked around at the world instead of within ourselves."

Julia knew that was what she'd been doing these past few years, looking at the darkness and the short-comings within herself. Under such intense scrutiny, her faults had seemed glaring. It was little wonder that she'd been so miserable.

"Alek," she said, with her discovery, "thank you, thank you so much."

They kissed, and it was as if his love was absolution for all that had gone before and all that would come later. She turned in his embrace and slipped her arms around his neck. When they'd finished kissing, they simply held each other.

Alek knew his relationship with Julia had changed that afternoon by the ocean. Things between them were different now. More open, more trusting. They'd had fun, too—childish, uncomplicated fun—something neither of them had done in years. They'd flown kites, run through the surf, eaten Anna's sandwiches and cookies, feeding each other bites.

Sunday evening, the day after their venture to the

beach, Alek needed to run down to the lab. When he told Julia, she offered to go with him, as if even an hour apart was more than she could bear.

Her willingness had taken him by surprise.

"You're sure?" he asked.

"Of course. It'll do me good to get out."

They listened to classical music on the way across town. Security had been increased at the plant, with extra guards posted; Alek gave them a friendly nod. Julia went with him into his office. He found the notes he needed and brought them home.

"Would you like some coffee?" she asked once they'd returned.

"Please." Her desire to indulge him with small pleasures was something of a surprise, too, a pleasant one.

While he read over his calculations, Julia was content to sit at his side, absorbed in a novel. He couldn't remember a time when she'd voluntarily sat still. Her body always seemed to be filled with nervous energy. That was gone from her now and in its place had come a restfulness.

"I'm not looking forward to work in the morning," she said when Alek was finished. Leaning against him, she stretched her legs out along the sofa and heaved a giant sigh. "These past few days have been so wonderful. I don't feel ready to deal with the office again."

"Will you always work, Julia?"

"I...don't know. I hadn't thought about it. I suppose I will until after the children are born at any rate, but even then I'll still be involved in the management of the company."

"Then you wouldn't mind if we had a family."

"No, of course I wouldn't mind. Did you think I would?"

"I wasn't sure."

"Then rest assured, Mr. Berinski, I want your children."

Alek felt his heart expand with eagerness. "So you'd like a family," he said. "Could we work on this project soon?"

"How soon?" she whispered.

He fiddled with the buttons of her shirt. "Now," he said, aware of the husky sound of his voice.

Julia sighed that womanly sigh he'd come to recognize as a signal of her eagerness for him. "I think we might be able to arrange that."

"Julia, my love," Alek said with a groan, "I'm afraid I'll never get enough of you. What have you done to me? Are you a witch who's cast some spell over me?"

Julia laughed. "If anyone's cast a spell over anyone, it's you over me. I'm lonely without you. If we can't be together, I feel lost and empty. I never thought I could love again, certainly not like this, and you've shown me the way."

"Julia." He rasped her name and, folding her over his arm, bent forward to cover her soft reaching mouth with his. The kiss revealed their need for each other. He heard Julia's book fall off the sofa and hit the floor, but neither cared. His hands were busy with her shirt and once it was open, she twisted around to face him.

"I vote for the bed this time."

"The bed," he said mockingly. "Where's your sense of adventure?"

Julia laughed softly. "It was used up in the bathtub

this morning. Did you know it took me twenty minutes to clean the water off the floor?"

He carried her into their bedroom, kissing her all the while.

Afterward, they lay on the bed. Julia was sprawled across him. Every now and then she kissed him, or he kissed her. Alek had never known such contentment in his life. It frightened him. Happiness had always been fleeting, and he wasn't sure he could trust what he'd found with Julia. His hold on her tightened and he closed his eyes and discovered he couldn't imagine what his life would be like without her now. Bleak and empty, he decided.

When Jerry had first suggested this marriage, Alek had set his terms. He wasn't a believer in the staying power of love. It had always seemed temporary to him, ephemeral, and it came at the expense of everything else. Alek couldn't claim he'd never been in love before. There'd been a handful of brief relationships over the years, but each time he'd grown bored and restless. He was a disappointment to his mother, who was hoping he and Anna would provide her with grandchildren to spoil.

How perceptive his sister was to realize he hadn't loved Julia in the beginning. He hadn't expected to ever truly love her. He'd offered her his loyalty and his devotion, but had held his heart in reserve. She had it now, though, in her palm. His heart. His very life.

Julia lay across her husband's body and sighed deeply, completely and utterly content. She'd never known a time like this with a man. A time of peace and discovery. His talk of children had unleashed long-buried dreams.

They hadn't bothered to use protection. Not even once. They each seemed to pretend it didn't matter, that what would be would be.

Pregnant.

She said the word in her mind as though it was foreign to her, and in many ways it was. A few weeks ago she would've sworn it was impossible; after all, she didn't intend to sleep with her husband. *That* had certainly changed, and now, thoughts of a family filled her mind and her heart. Perhaps it was because she'd so recently lost Ruth and because one of the last things her grandmother had said was about children "waiting to be born."

After so many years of pain, Julia hardly knew how to deal with happiness. In some ways she was afraid to trust that it would last. She'd been happy with Roger—and then everything had blown up in her face. The crushing pain of his deception would never leave her, but she'd lost the desire to punish him. Conrad Industries' success would be revenge enough. There might not have been sufficient evidence to charge him, but people in the business suspected him. They talked. That meant he wasn't likely to be hired by any other company once he left Ideal Paints—or they fired him. After what had happened, no one else would trust him. Without realizing what he was doing, he'd painted himself in a corner. She smiled at her own pun.

"Something amuses you?" Alek asked, apparently having felt her smile.

"Yes...and no."

"That sounds rather vague to me."

"Rest," she urged.

"Why?" he challenged. "Do you have something… physical in mind?"

Julia grinned again. "If I don't, I'm sure you do. Now hush, I'm trying to sleep."

"Then I suggest you stop making those little movements."

Julia hadn't been conscious of moving. "Sorry."

He clamped his hands on her hips. "Don't be. I'm not."

Julia resumed her daydream. A baby would turn her world upside down. She'd never been very domestic. If her child-rearing skills were on the level of her cooking skills, then she—

"Now you're frowning." Alek murmured. "What's wrong?"

"I… I was just thinking I might not be a very good mother. I don't know anything about babies. I might really botch this."

He took her head between his hands and brought her mouth to his. "You're going to be a wonderful mother. We'll learn about this together when the time comes. Agreed?"

Julia sighed loudly. "You're right. As a logical, practical businessperson I know it, but as a woman, I'm not so sure."

"Listen, woman, you're making it impossible to nap. As far as I can tell, there's only one way to keep you quiet." With his arms around her waist, he turned her onto her back and nuzzled her neck until Julia cried out and promised to do whatever he said.

Monday morning, Julia arrived at the office before eight. Virginia, her assistant, appeared a few minutes after she did, looking flustered.

"I'm sorry, I didn't realize you were planning to be here quite so early. If I had, I would've come in before eight myself. I'll get your coffee right away."

"Don't worry about it," Julia said, reaching for the stack of mail in her in-basket. Her desk was neatly organized, and she was grateful Virginia had taken the time to lighten her load.

"I read over the mail and your emails and answered everything I could," Virginia said. "I hope that's okay."

"Of course. I'm grateful for your help."

Virginia hurried out to the lunchroom, returning a few minutes later with a steaming cup of coffee. "I'm sorry but there doesn't seem to be any cream. I'll send out for some."

"I can live without cream," Julia said absently, turning on her computer. "Would you ask my brother to drop in when it's convenient? And please contact my husband and see if he could meet me for lunch." She'd left while he was in the shower and had forgotten to leave him a note. "I meant to ask—" She stopped, realizing she probably already had a luncheon appointment. "That is, if I'm not tied up."

"You were scheduled to meet with Mr. Casey, but I wasn't sure if you'd feel up to dealing with him your first day back. I took the liberty of rescheduling the luncheon for Tuesday."

Virginia knew Doug Casey, their outside counsel, was one of her least favorite people, and she smiled her appreciation. "Thanks."

"I'll get right back to you," Virginia said. True to her word, she returned a few minutes later. "Your brother will be down shortly and your husband suggests you meet at noon at Freeway Park."

"Great." She turned back to her computer and didn't hear Virginia leave her office.

Jerry hurried into her office. "I'm worried about Stanhope," he said immediately. "I think he's up to something. I've got a private investigator following him. If he makes contact with any of our people, we'll know about it."

Julia rolled a pen between her palms. "I can't believe any of our employees would sell us out, can you?"

Jerry tensed. "After what happened last time, who's to tell?"

"Let me know the second you hear anything."

"I will. The investigator's going to make regular reports."

Her brother left, and Julia was involved with a large stack of correspondence when she noted the time. She stopped in the middle of a dictation.

Virginia raised her head, anticipating Julia's next move.

"We'll continue this after lunch," she said, standing and reaching for her purse. "I won't be back until after one. Cover for me if need be."

"Of course." Virginia was on her feet, too, and Julia felt her scrutiny.

"Is something wrong?" she asked the older woman.

"No," Virginia said with a shy smile. "Something's very right."

"Oh?" Julia didn't understand.

"I don't think I've ever seen you look happier."

Ten

Freeway Park was one of Seattle's many innovative ideas. A large grassy area built over a freeway. Green ivy spilled down the concrete banks, reaching toward the road far below.

At noon, many Seattle office workers converged on the park to enjoy their lunch in the opulent sunshine. Each summer the city offered a series of free concerts. Julia didn't know if there was one scheduled for that afternoon, but nothing could have made her day any more perfect than meeting her husband.

She saw Alek from across the grass and started toward him. He'd obviously seen her at the same time because he grinned broadly and moved in her direction.

"Did you bring anything for lunch?" he asked, after they kissed briefly.

Eating was something Julia often failed to think about. "Oh, no, I forgot."

"I thought as much. Luckily you have a husband who knows his wife. Come, let's find a place to sit down."

"What'd you buy?" she asked, pointing at the white sack in his hand.

"Fish and chips. Do you approve?"

"Sounds great." She *was* hungry, she realized, which had become a rarity. Generally she ate because it was necessary, not for any real enjoyment. Anna was sure to change that. Alek's sister cooked tempting breakfasts and left delicious three-and four-course dinners ready to be served when they got home. By the end of the year, Julia predicted she'd gain weight—from all the wonderful food…and because by then she'd likely be pregnant. The thought produced a deep sense of excitement.

Alek found a spot for them on a park bench. He set the white bag between them and lifted out an order of fish-and-chips packed in a cardboard container.

"Are you trying to fatten me up?" she teased.

His eyes twinkled. "You know me almost as well as I know you."

"Indeed I do." She laughed.

"But the question is," Alek said, eyeing her speculatively, "do you like me?"

It was an effort to pull her gaze away from his magnetic eyes. "More each day," she answered honestly.

An electric moment passed before Alek spoke. "You won't be working late tonight, will you?"

"No. Will you?"

He shook his head. "I plan to be home at five-fifteen."

"That early?" She usually didn't leave the office until after six.

"I'll be lucky to last that long," he whispered.

There was no missing his meaning. Julia's body went into overdrive. She'd never thought of herself as a highly sexual person, but in that instant she knew she had to do *something* to appease the overwhelming urge she had to make love with her husband.

"Alek...would you mind kissing me?"

He blinked, then bent his head, meaning only to brush her lips, she suspected, but that wouldn't be enough to satisfy her. Not anymore. She touched his lips with her tongue, teasing and taunting him.

A deep moan came from low within his throat, which aroused her as nothing ever had before. The kiss deepened and deepened until they were completely lost in each other.

She wrenched her mouth from his, gasping. "Five-fifteen," she said when she could manage to speak.

"I'll be there."

Jerry was waiting in her office when Julia returned from lunch. Without greeting her, he announced, "Roger's made contact with someone from the lab."

Julia was stunned into speechlessness. "How do you know?" she asked when she could. There was a cold, sinking feeling in her stomach.

"Rich Peck."

"Who's Rich Peck?"

Jerry spun around and glared at her. "The private eye I hired. Rich traced the phone numbers that came into Roger's home for the past several days."

"How did he do that?"

"Julia," Jerry said, clearly exasperated with her, "that isn't important right now. What *is* important is that someone from Conrad Industries contacted Roger. They used the phone from the lab."

"But...who?"

"That's the point. It could've been any number of

people. The phone's used by nearly everyone on staff. What I'm saying is that we've got a traitor on our hands."

Julia found that hard to believe. Almost everyone who was employed at the lab had been with them three years earlier. Their dislike of Roger was well-known. After the fire it had taken months to rebuild, and Julia had tried to keep as many employees on the payroll as possible during that time, in order not to lose her trained and loyal help. There were at least twenty who'd been with Conrad Industries fifteen years or longer. The strain on the budget crippled the company financially. And nearly every employee had hung on, counting on the promise of reimbursement once Julia could get the company back on its feet.

Julia appreciated their sacrifice. And their trust. Her father had recently died, and to say she was inexperienced would've been an understatement. The company was on the verge of bankruptcy. It was one of the bleakest times in Julia's life and in the company's history.

Ruth's faith in her to pull the company out of financial disaster had helped Julia survive that grim period.

The idea that someone working in the lab was selling her out now—it seemed impossible. She refused to believe it. Refused to accept it.

"What do you think we should do?" Jerry asked.

Julia walked over to the window and stared down at the street ten floors below. Cars and people looked miniature and seemed to be moving in slow motion. It was as if she was staring at another world that had no connection to her own.

"Nothing," she said after a moment. "We do nothing."

"But…"

"What *can* we do?" she demanded impatiently. "All we have is the knowledge that someone contacted Roger. Should we haul every employee in for questioning by Peck, hoping his expertise at grilling fifty-year-old men and women will flush out whoever wants to betray us?"

"We could have Alek scout around and—"

"No," she said quickly, interrupting him. "Alek is as much a suspect as anyone else."

"Don't be ridiculous! Alek's poured his whole life into this project. You don't think *he'd* betray us."

"No, I don't," she agreed readily enough. "But that doesn't change the facts. Roger had every reason to hope Conrad Industries would prosper, too, and look what he did."

"But Alek…"

"Alek is a suspect, like everyone else. I warn you, Jerry, don't say a word to him. Not a single word."

Her brother stared at her. "He's your husband. You don't even trust your own husband?"

"You're right," she admitted. "I don't. You can thank Roger for that. I wouldn't trust my own mother after the lesson Roger taught me. If you think I'm coldhearted, then fine. I'd rather have you think poorly of me than hand over the fate of this company to a man who could destroy us."

Making love to his wife was probably the most fabulous sensation Alek had ever experienced. Perhaps it was because she'd withheld herself from him for so long that he treasured the prize so highly. Julia was open, honest and genuine.

Alek had never lost control of himself with another woman, but he had with Julia. She was fast becoming as necessary to him as the air he breathed. He wanted her, and that need was growing at an alarming rate.

Every time they were intimate, she gave him a little more of herself. A little more of her trust. A little more of her heart and soul.

He glanced at his watch and frowned. It was well past the time they'd agreed to meet. Knowing Julia, she'd probably got caught up in her work and let the time slip away from her.

He waited another ten minutes before calling her office. Her assistant answered.

"This is Alek. Has Julia left the office yet?"

"No." Virginia sounded surprised. "She's still here. Would you like me to connect you?"

"Please." He waited a moment before Julia came on the line.

"Hello," she said absently. Alek could picture her sitting behind her desk with her reading glasses at the end of her nose.

"Do you know what time it is?"

"Five-forty. Why?"

"We had an appointment, remember?" He lowered his voice. "I've got a deck of cards and—"

"A deck of cards?"

He wasn't sure what he heard in her voice, but it wasn't amusement. It troubled him, but he didn't have time to analyze it just then. "Yes, I recently heard about this American card game that I want to play with you."

"A *card* game?"

"Strip poker. Sounds like fun. I've got everything ready. How much longer are you going to be?"

"Oh, Alek, listen, I'm really sorry, but I could be at

the office another hour or more. Everything from last week is piled up on my desk. I really shouldn't leave."

"I understand." He didn't like it, but he understood. "My game can wait, and it looks like I'll have to, as well." He was hoping for a little sympathy, or at least a sigh of regret, but he received neither.

Julia was keeping something from him. He heard it in her voice, felt it as clearly as if it were a tangible thing.

Julia didn't arrive home until nearly nine. It would be too much to ask that Alek *not* be there waiting for her. She didn't know how she was going to look him in the eye.

A headache had been building from the moment Jerry had left her office. Everything in her told her Alek would be the last person who'd sell them out. It would make it much easier to believe in him if she hadn't so staunchly defended Roger to her father. She'd been wrong once and it had nearly cost her sanity.

Alek greeted her at the door. Without a word he drew her into his arms and hugged her. She was swallowed in his embrace, surrounded by his love, and she soaked it up, needing it so badly.

"Tell me what's troubling you," he said.

She had no choice but to sidestep the question. "What makes you think anything's wrong?"

"I'm your husband. I know you," he said, echoing his comment from that afternoon. But then he'd been teasing; now his statement sounded like the simple truth.

"I've got a terrible headache."

He studied her as if he wasn't sure he should believe her, although it was true enough. Her temples throbbed and she was exhausted. "Did you have dinner?" she asked, wanting to turn the subject away from herself.

"No, I waited for you. Are you ready?"

Her appetite was nil. "I'm not very hungry. If you don't mind, I'd like a bath." She left him without giving him a chance to respond.

The hot water was soothing and a full thirty minutes passed before she could bring herself to leave the tub. She dressed for bed, craving the oblivion of sleep. But Alek was waiting for her when she finished. He seemed to anticipate her every need, which increased her guilt.

He followed her into the bedroom. "Would you like me to rub your temples?" he asked, sitting on the edge of the bed.

"You'd do that?"

He seemed surprised by her question. "Of course. There's nothing I wouldn't do for you."

"Oh, Alek," she moaned.

"Come," he said, sitting on their bed, his back against the headboard, his legs stretched out. "Rest your head on me and I'll massage your forehead. Would you like me to sing to you again?" He reached for the light at the side of the bed and turned it off.

"Please." The meaning of the words he was singing was beyond her, but she loved the deep, melodic sound of his voice. As he sang, his nimble fingers gently soothed the throbbing pain in her head. She was sleepy when he finished. Lifting her head from his lap, he began to leave her. It was then that Julia realized how much she wanted him to stay.

"Don't go," she pleaded softly. "Come to bed with me."

"For a few minutes," he agreed with obvious reluctance. He undressed in the dark and slipped beneath the sheets, then gathered her in his arms.

Alek held her for a long time and she savored these moments of closeness as the warmth of his love stole over her. Alek alleviated the feelings of abandonment and loss she'd felt since Roger's betrayal, since her father's death and now her grandmother's. He loved her as no man ever had.

Julia was restless. She didn't understand why she couldn't sit still. Then again, she could. It was only natural to be nervous, considering the phone call she'd received earlier that morning. It had been a week since Jerry had hired Rich Peck and now Rich had phoned wanting to give them his first weekly report. Since Jerry was out for the afternoon, Julia had agreed to meet with the investigator herself.

Virginia announced his arrival and Peck entered her office. He was tall and wiry, and much younger than she'd expected. Perhaps thirty, if that.

"Hello," he said, stepping forward and shaking her hand.

"Please sit down," Julia invited.

He took the chair on the other side of her desk. "This Stanhope fellow is an interesting character," he began. "I've been tailing him for nearly a week. I managed to get photos of just about everyone he's met. My guess is that whoever's leaking information to him is a woman. Once you get a look at the photographs you'll understand why. He's quite the ladies' man."

This wasn't news to Julia.

Rich brought out a folder thick with photographs,

reached for a small pad and flipped through the first couple of pages.

"He had several business lunches, as best as I can tell. Although we've got a twenty-four-hour tail on him, there are certain periods of time we can't account for."

"I see. Do you think he knows he's being followed?"

Rich snickered. "The guy hasn't got a clue. He's way too arrogant. He lives on the edge, too. I talked to his landlady and learned he's two months behind on his rent. It's happened before. His credit rating's so full of holes he couldn't get a loan if his life depended on it."

"What about his position with Ideal Paints? Is that secure?"

"Who knows? From what I've been able to find out, he doesn't have many friends. He seems to get along all right on the job. As for what he does with his money, that isn't hard to figure out. The guy goes out with a different woman every night. He seems to get his kicks showing off what a stud he is."

This, too, didn't come as any surprise to Julia. Roger liked to refer to himself as a "party animal."

"Go ahead and look through those photos and see if there's anyone you recognize. Take your time. I've got them stacked according to the day of the week. Thursday of this week is on top. He left his apartment about ten. He seemed to be in a hurry and got to his office around ten-fifteen. He didn't leave again until four, and then came out a side entrance. My tail noted that some girl came out the front of the building directly afterward and seemed to be looking for someone. Our guess is that he was escaping her.

"He waited around ten or fifteen minutes and then left. He went home, changed his clothes and was out again by six. He picked up some chick and they went to dinner. He spent the night with her."

That, too, was typical.

"Wednesday..." Rich continued as Julia flipped through the photographs. "Again he was late to the office. He arrived about ten and left again at eleven-thirty. He drove to Henshaw's, that fancy restaurant on Lake Union."

Julia nodded; she knew it well. An eternity earlier it had been one of their favorite places. The food was delicious and the ambience luxurious but not overpowering.

"Whoever he was supposed to meet was waiting for him outside. I assume this was a business lunch. The guy he was meeting was angry about something. The two of them exchanged words outside the restaurant. We got several excellent photos. It looked for a moment like they were going to have a fistfight. Frankly, Stanhope was smart to avoid this one. The guy would've pulverized him in seconds."

Julia flipped to the next series of pictures. Her gaze fell on Alek's angry face and she gasped.

Rich's attention reverted from the tablet to her. "You recognize him?"

Julia felt as if she was going to vomit.

"Ms. Conrad?"

She nodded.

"An employee?"

Once again she nodded. "Yes," she managed. "An employee. You can leave the rest of the photographs here and I'll go through them later. You've done an excellent job, Mr. Peck." She stood and ushered him to the door. "Jerry will be in touch with you sometime later this afternoon. I believe you've solved our mystery."

"Always glad to be of service."

"Thank you again."

Julia collapsed against the door the instant it was closed. Her stomach twisted into a knot of pain. This *couldn't* be happening. This couldn't be real. She felt nauseous and made a dash to her wastepaper basket, where she threw up her lunch. She was kneeling on the floor, her trembling hands holding her hair away from her face, when Virginia walked into the office.

"Oh, dear! Are you all right?"

Julia nodded.

"Let me help you," Virginia said. With her hand under Julia's elbow, she raised her to her feet. "You need to lie down."

"Could…would you see if you could find my brother for me?"

"You don't want me to call your husband?"

"No," she said forcefully, "get Jerry. Have him come as soon as he can… Tell him it's an emergency."

Her legs were unstable and she slumped into her chair. In the past three years Julia had received a number of lessons in pain. Roger had been her first teacher, but his tactics paled when compared to Alek's. It would've been easier to bear if Alek had aimed a gun at her heart and pulled the trigger.

It took her brother twenty minutes to reach her office; he must've been in the middle of something important when Virginia called. As she waited she gazed sightlessly at her desk. She should be sobbing hysterically; instead, she found herself as calm and cool as if the man who'd been betraying her and her brother was barely more than an acquaintance.

Jerry rushed into her office, apparently having run

at least part of the way, because his face was red and he was breathless.

"Virginia said it was an emergency."

"I… I was being a bit dramatic."

"Not according to Virginia. She wanted to know if she should phone for an ambulance. You're pale, but otherwise you look fine."

"I'm not, and you won't be, either, once you take a look at these." She handed him the series of three photographs.

The blotchy redness faded from Jerry's face and he blanched as he studied Rich Peck's photographs.

"Alek?" he breathed in disbelief.

"It appears so."

"There's got to be some explanation!"

"I'm sure there is." There always was. Something that would sound logical and persuasive. She'd been through this before and knew all there was to know about betrayals of trust. When she'd confronted Roger, he'd worn a hurt, incredulous look of shock and dismay. He'd angrily declared his innocence, told her it was all a misunderstanding that he'd be able to clear up in a matter of minutes, given the opportunity. Because she loved him so desperately and because she wanted to believe him so badly, she'd listened. In the end it all seemed credible to her and she'd defended him because she loved and trusted him. She loved and trusted Alek, too, but she'd been wrong before, so very wrong, and it had cost her and her family dearly.

"What are you going to do?" Jerry asked in a whisper. He hadn't recovered yet. He continued to stare at the photographs as though the pictures themselves would announce the truth if he studied them long enough.

"I don't know," she said unevenly.

"You aren't going to fire him, are you?"

"I don't know yet."

"Julia, for the love of heaven, Alek's your *husband*."

"I don't know what I'm going to do," she repeated. "I just don't know."

Jerry rubbed a hand over his face and inhaled deeply. "We should confront him, give him the opportunity to explain. It's possible that he's got a very good reason for meeting Roger. One that has nothing to do with Phoenix Paints."

"Jerry, you were ten before you stopped believing in Santa Claus. Remember? There's only one reason Alek would contact Roger and we both know it."

"That doesn't make any sense," he argued. "Alek has more reason for Phoenix Paints to succeed than anyone. His career hinges on the success of our new line. Why would he deliberately sabotage himself? He spent years researching these developments." His eyes pleaded with her.

"If you're looking to me for answers, I don't have any. Why do any of us do the things we do? My guess is that he's out for revenge."

"Revenge? Alek? Why? We've been good to him, good to his family, and he's been good to us. He doesn't have any score to settle."

"Dad was good to Roger, too, remember? He was the one who gave Roger his first job. Dad hired him directly out of college when he could've taken on someone with far more experience. If we're looking for reasons Alek would never do this, we'd be putting blindfolds over our own eyes."

Jerry watched her for several minutes. "I'm going to talk to him."

Julia folded her arms around her waist and nodded.

"Do you want to come with me?"

"No! I couldn't bear it. Not again." She squeezed her eyes shut and her body swayed with the pain. "I can't believe this is happening."

"I can't believe it is, either."

"Why do I continually fall for the wrong kind of man? There must be something wrong with me."

Jerry walked to her window and stared out. His shoulders moved in a deep sigh. "We're overreacting."

"Maybe," Julia agreed. "But I have that ache in the pit of my stomach again. The last time it was there was when Dad forced me to face the truth about Roger."

"The least we can do is listen to his explanation."

Julia shook her head. "You listen, I…can't." She didn't want to be there when Alek made his excuses. She'd let her brother handle this because she was incapable of dealing with it.

Jerry's eyes narrowed. "It's been a long time since I've seen you so…detached."

"Let me guess," she returned sarcastically. "Could it have been following my breakup with Roger?"

"This is different. You're married to Alek."

"That means it's a little more involved, a little more complicated than before, but it's not really so different. Until…this is resolved it would be better if Alek didn't come into work. Tell him that for me."

"Julia…"

"Tell him, Jerry, because I can't. Please." Her voice cracked. "It's just until this is settled. Alek will understand."

."But you aren't going to listen to his explanation?"

"No. You listen to what he has to say, but don't argue his case with me. I tried that with Dad, remember? I was so certain Roger was an innocent victim of circumstances."

Her brother looked older, as though he'd suddenly aged ten years. Julia understood. She felt old herself. And sick. Her stomach felt decidedly queasy.

Jerry left and her stomach pitched again. Automatically she reached for the wastepaper basket.

Julia left the office an hour later, her cell phone turned off. She wasn't sure where she intended to go, but she knew she couldn't stay at work any longer. She started walking with no destination in mind and ended up at the Pike Place Market. People were bustling about and, not wanting to be in a crowd, she headed for the waterfront. Not the tourist areas, but much farther down where the large cruise vessels docked.

She walked for hours, trying to sort through her emotions, and eventually gave up. She was in too much pain to think clearly.

She didn't cry. Not once. She figured this numbness was her body's protective device.

It was well past dark and she'd wandered into an unsafe area of town. She finally realized she had to make her way home.

When she reached her building, the security man looked surprised to find her arriving so late. He greeted her warmly and held open the heavy glass door for her.

The elevator ride up to her apartment seemed to take forever, but it wasn't long enough. Soon she'd face her husband.

She'd barely gotten her key into the lock when the door was wrenched open. Alek loomed above her like a bad dream.

Eleven

She saw the same signs in Alek that she'd seen in Roger. The indignation. The hurt, angry look that she could believe such a terrible thing of him. As if *she* were the betrayer. As if she were the guilty one.

Roger had turned the tables on her with such finesse she didn't realize what was happening until too late. Julia studied her husband and if she didn't know better would've believed with all her heart that he'd never betray her.

"Where have you been?" Alek demanded. "I've been worried sick."

"I went for a walk."

"For five hours?"

She moved past him. "I should've phoned. I'm sorry, but I needed to think."

Alek followed her. "Why didn't you come to me yourself? Instead you sent Jerry." His voice revealed his pain. "I don't deny talking to Roger Stanhope, but at least give me the chance to explain why."

"You *can't* deny seeing him since we have the evidence," she responded lifelessly. "You called him, too, from the lab. We know about that, as well."

If he was surprised, he didn't show it. "I called him because I wanted him to stay away from you. He wouldn't listen. Our meeting at Henshaw's was an accident, he was arriving just as I was leaving. He taunted me, said he could have you back anytime he wanted. He said other things, too, but I don't care to repeat them. Ask the man you hired to take photographs what happened that day. Stanhope and I nearly got into a fistfight."

Julia desperately wanted to believe that he was telling the truth about his motives. Her heart yearned to trust him. But this was like an old tape being played back again and the memories it brought to the surface were too compelling to ignore.

"That man Stanhope is slime. I won't have him anywhere near you," Alek said heatedly. "If you want to condemn me for protecting you, then you may. But I would rather rip out my own heart than hurt you."

He was saying everything Julia longed to hear. She pressed her hands to her head, not knowing what to do. "I have to think."

He nodded, seeming to accept that, but he was hurt and she felt his pain as strongly as her own. Rather than continue a discussion that would cause them both grief, she showered and dressed for bed.

Alek appeared in the doorway to the guest bedroom when she'd finished. "Anna left you some dinner."

"I'm not hungry."

"You're too thin already. Eat."

"Alek, please, I'm exhausted."

"Eat," he insisted.

Julia's appetite was gone. She'd thrown up her lunch and hadn't eaten since. Unwilling to argue with him, she went into the kitchen, took the foil-covered dinner plate warming in the oven and sat down at the table.

His sister had cooked veal cutlets, small red potatoes and what looked like a purple cabbage stir-fry. Even after sitting in the oven for hours, the food was delicious. Julia intended to sample only a few bites to appease Alek and then dump the rest in the garbage disposal, but she ended up eating a respectable amount of food. When she'd finished, she rinsed off her plate and retired to the guest room. Alone.

In the morning, Julia woke to the sound of Anna and Alek talking in the kitchen. They were speaking in Russian and it was apparent that Anna was upset.

Donning her robe, Julia wandered in and poured herself a cup of coffee. Anna eyed her with open hostility.

"My brother would not do this thing," she said forcefully.

"Anna," Alek barked. "Enough."

"He loves you. How can you think he would ever hurt you? He is a man of honor."

"It isn't as simple as it seems," Julia said in her own defense. Anna didn't understand, and she didn't expect her to.

Alek said something sharp and cold in Russian, but that didn't stop Anna from turning to Julia once more. "You do not know my brother. Otherwise you wouldn't believe he could do this terrible thing."

Alek reprimanded his sister harshly. Julia didn't need to understand Russian to know what he was saying.

Anna responded by yanking the apron from her

waist, throwing it on the kitchen counter and storming out of the apartment.

"I apologize for my sister's behavior," Alek said after she'd left. He was so formal, so stiff and proud. He hesitated, as if trying to find the words to express himself. "There is a meeting with the marketing people this afternoon. It is a very important discussion. I need to be there to answer questions. If you'd rather I wasn't, I'll see if someone can take my place."

Julia felt incapable of making any decision, even a straightforward one like this.

"I suggest you attend it, too," he said. "If you feel I am doing or saying anything that would hurt Conrad Industries, then you can stop me. I suggest Jerry be there, as well."

"Alek, please try to understand how awkward this is."

"Come to the meeting," he urged.

"All right," Julia agreed reluctantly.

He told her the time and place, and afterward they were silent. Julia thought with a kind of sad whimsy that she could hear the sound of their heartache, like the loud ticking of a clock. She was sure Alek heard it, too. After a few minutes, he left the condo.

Rarely had Julia ever felt more alone. Her thoughts depressed her. She dressed, determined to act as if life was normal until they resolved this problem.

It wasn't until she was at the office that she made a clear decision, her first sensible one since this whole nightmare began.

She pulled the phonebook out of her desk drawer, swallowed hard, praying she could pull this off, and then, with a bravado she didn't feel, dialed Roger Stanhope's number.

"Mr. Stanhope's office," came the efficient reply.

"This is Julia Conrad for Mr. Stanhope."

"One moment, please."

A short time passed before Roger's smooth voice came over the wire. "Julia, what a pleasant surprise."

"I understand you met with my husband." Preliminary greetings were unnecessary.

"So you heard about that?"

"Alek told me. I'm calling you for your own protection. Alek meant what he said about you staying away from me. If you value your neck, I advise you not to try contacting me again." Her heart was in her throat, pounding so loudly she was sure he must be able to hear it.

"I think there must be some misunderstanding," Roger said in an incredulous tone. "I did meet with your husband. Actually, he's the one who contacted me, but your name didn't enter into the conversation. He wanted to talk to me about Phoenix Paints. He was hoping the two of us could strike some kind of deal. Naturally Ideal Paints is very interested."

"Good try, Roger, but it won't work."

He laughed that slightly demented laugh of his, as though she'd said something hilarious.

"I guess we'll just have to wait and see, won't we?" he added sarcastically.

Julia hung up the phone.

She sat there for several minutes with her hand on the receiver. When she found the strength, she stood, walked out of her office and directly past her assistant's desk.

"Ms. Conrad, are you feeling all right? You're terribly pale again."

Julia shrugged. "I'll be fine," she said, more brusquely than she'd intended.

"Have you thought about seeing a doctor?"

Julia didn't know any physician who specialized in treating broken hearts. Virginia frowned at her, waiting for a reply. "No, I don't…need one."

"I think you do. I'm going to make an appointment for you and ask for the first available opening. We can't have you walking around looking as if you're going to faint at any moment."

Julia barely heard her. She walked farther into the hallway to the elevator and rode down to her brother's office.

Jerry stood when she walked in. "Julia! Sit down. You look like you're about to keel over."

If her brother was commenting on her appearance, she must resemble yesterday's oatmeal. "I'm fine," she lied.

"Do you need a glass of water?"

She shook her head. She hadn't come to discuss her health.

"I'm getting you one anyway. You look dreadful."

Julia pinched her lips together to bite back a cutting commentary, and didn't succeed. "How nice of you to say so."

Jerry chuckled and left his office, returning with a paper cup of water. He insisted Julia drink it, which she did. To her surprise she felt better afterward. But then, it was probably impossible to feel any worse…

"I imagine you're here to find out what Alek said,"

Jerry murmured. "He claims he confronted Roger and told him to leave you alone. I wish I'd done it myself."

"I talked to Roger myself."

Jerry froze and his eyes narrowed suspiciously. "You talked to Roger?"

"This morning."

"What did he say?" Jerry demanded. "Never mind, I can guess." He started pacing then as if holding still was more than he could manage. "Naturally he wasn't going to tell you what Alek actually said. What did you expect him to say, anyway? That he was shaking in his boots with fear? How could you do anything so stupid?"

"I…"

"I thought you were smarter than that!"

"Roger claims Alek tried to strike a deal with our strongest competitor," Julia said, trying hard to control her temper.

"I don't believe that for a minute."

Neither did Julia, not really, but she was so desperately afraid. She needed Jerry to confirm her belief in Alek, needed the reassurance that she wasn't making the same tragic mistake a second time.

"Don't you realize you're playing directly into Roger's hands? This is exactly what he was hoping would happen. He *wants* you to distrust Alek. You certainly made his day."

"I…hadn't thought of it like that," Julia admitted reluctantly. She was a fool not to leave the detective work to Rich Peck.

"You contacted Roger even knowing the kind of man he is, and expected him to tell the truth. You've done some stupid things in your time, Julia, but this one takes the cake."

Julia bristled. "The cake came three years ago, Jerry," she reminded him. "Complete with frosting, don't you remember? That was when I trusted Roger, when I believed in love and loyalty."

"You believe Alek, don't you?"

"Yes…" She did, and yet she had no confidence in her own judgment.

Jerry's eyes narrowed. "Then why'd you contact Roger?"

"Because I hoped… I don't know, I thought he might let something slip."

"He did that, all right, another pile of doubts for you to deal with." He rammed his hand through his hair. "Why on earth would you do anything so asinine?"

"I wish you'd quit saying that."

"It's true. Now are you going to believe in Alek or aren't you?"

With all her heart, she *wanted* to trust her husband, but she'd been badly hurt before. She'd zealously defended Roger, even when faced with overwhelming proof of his betrayal. Her faith in him had nearly destroyed her family.

"I take it you didn't fire him, then?" she asked.

"No. I won't, either. If you want him out of here, then you're going to have to do it yourself. I believe him, Julia, even if you don't."

"Jerry, please, try and understand. This is like waking up to my worst nightmare. Don't you think I *want* to believe him? So much that it's killing me."

"I can see that." He sighed. "Just leave it for now, Julia. Time will tell if he's being honest with us or not. For the record, I'm sure he is."

"I can't let the fate of the company ride on your instinct

and your friendship with him. I can't take that kind of risk. I have no choice but to ask for his resignation."

Jerry's fists clenched at his side. "You can't do that."

"I'm the president of this company, I can do as I please." She didn't want to get hard-nosed about this, but her first obligation was to protect their family business. Jerry was silent as he absorbed her words. "So you're going to pull rank on me."

"I didn't mean it like that. The last thing we need to do now is argue with each other."

"If you ask Alek to go…"

"Jerry, please, I have to, don't you see?"

"If you ask for Alek's resignation," he started again, "you'll receive mine, as well."

Julia felt as if her own brother had kicked her in the stomach. "It's funny," she said unemotionally, "I remember saying those very same words to Dad three years ago. I believed Roger, remember?"

"A week," Jerry said. "We'll know more in another week. All I ask is that you give him the opportunity to prove himself."

"As I recall, I said something along those lines to Dad, too."

"Alek isn't Roger," Jerry said angrily. "What's it going to take to convince you of that?"

"I know he's not," she said vehemently. "Maybe it would be best if I was the one who resigned."

"Don't be ridiculous. Just give this time. If Alek sold us out, then there's nothing we can do about it now. The deed's done. It isn't going to hurt us any to sit on our doubts for the next few days. Promise me you'll do that."

"All right," Julia said. "One week, but then it's over, Jerry. Unless there's incontrovertible proof that Alek's telling the truth. If not, he goes and I can return to running this company the way it's supposed to be run."

Jerry's smile was fleeting. "I promise you, it's going to be different this time."

She stood to leave, then recalled her conversation with her husband that morning. "Alek mentioned an important meeting with marketing this afternoon." She gave Jerry the particulars. "He said he'd like us both to be there. Can you make it?"

Jerry nodded. "With a bit of juggling. You're going, too?"

"Yes," she said, but she wasn't looking forward to it.

Alek waited for Julia and Jerry to arrive. He watched the door anxiously, glancing repeatedly at his watch. Jerry was the first to show up; he walked into the conference room and took the chair next to Alek. Apart from them, the room was still empty.

"You talked to her?" Alek didn't need to explain who he meant.

Jerry nodded. "I've never seen her like this. It's tearing her apart."

"It hasn't been easy on any of us. I wish I knew how to clear my name. Julia would barely listen to me. It's as though she's blocked out everything and everyone, including me."

"It would be a lot easier if she were a man," Jerry muttered.

Alek arched his brows and laughed for the first time in days. "No, it wouldn't."

"Yeah, it would. I hate to stereotype, but maybe then she'd listen to reason. Sometimes I forget my sister is a woman—she clouds the issues with emotion."

Personally Alek had no trouble remembering Julia
was female. "Not all women have been betrayed the
way she was," he said. "I understand her fears, but at
the same time I want her to believe what I say because
she loves me and knows me well enough to realize I'd
never do anything to hurt either of you. Until she does,
there's nothing I can do."

"I don't know what Julia believes anymore and she
doesn't either," Jerry said after a moment. "I talked her
into giving the matter a week."

"A week," Alek repeated. "Nothing can happen in
that short a time. The paint won't reach the market for
another two to three weeks at the earliest."

"Unfortunately, there's more than that to consider
from her point of view," Jerry said.

"She's miserable," Alek added. "She doesn't eat
properly, she's working herself to death and she's sleeping poorly." In truth he wasn't in much better shape
himself.

He loved Julia, but he couldn't force her to trust him,
he couldn't demand that she believe him. She would
have to come to those conclusions herself. In the mean-
time he was left feeling helpless and hopeless and, worst
of all, defenseless. She was judging him solely on her
experience with another man, one who'd hurt and betrayed her.

"I thought Stanhope was out of our lives once and
for all," Jerry was saying. "I should've figured he'd be
back since we're on the brink of a major product break-
through. We should've been prepared."

"No one could have known."

"I should have," Jerry said, his lips thinning with an-
noyance. "Only this time Roger knows he doesn't have

a chance of stealing anything, so he's undermining our trust in each other."

The marketing people rushed in with their displays. Most of what they'd be reviewing was geared toward television and radio advertising. The magazine ads had been done a month earlier and would be coming out in the latest issues of fifteen major publications.

The advertising executive glanced at his watch. Alek sighed. Jerry did, too. Everyone in the room was waiting for Julia.

"Virginia, please, I have a meeting with marketing."

"But I've got Dr. Feldon's office on the line. If you could wait just a few minutes."

Julia looked pointedly at her watch while her assistant haggled for the first opening in Dr. Feldon's already full appointment schedule.

"That'll be fine, I'll make sure she's there. Thank you for your help."

"Well?" Julia said when Virginia hung up.

"Five o'clock. The doctor's agreed to squeeze you in then."

Julia nodded. She wished now that she'd put her foot down about this appointment issue. A doctor wasn't going to be able to tell her anything she didn't already know. She was suffering from stress, which, given her circumstances, was understandable.

"You won't forget now, will you?" Virginia called after her as Julia headed for the elevator.

"No, I'll be there. Thank you for your trouble."

"You do what Dr. Feldon says, you hear? We can't have you getting sick every afternoon."

Julia grinned. The never-married Virginia was beginning to sound like a mother. "I'll see you in the morning," Julia said. "Why don't you take an early afternoon?" she suggested. "You deserve it for putting up with me."

Her assistant looked mildly surprised, then nodded. "Thank you, I will."

Every head turned when a breathless Julia burst into the conference room. "Sorry I'm late," she muttered, sitting in the chair closest to the door.

The marketing director smiled benignly and walked over to a television set that had been brought in for the demonstration. "I thought we'd start with the media blitz scheduled to air a week from this Thursday," he said as he inserted a DVD.

Julia couldn't help being aware of Alek. His eyes were on her from the moment she'd entered the room. She expected to feel his anger; instead she felt his love. Tears clogged her throat. It would've been less painful if she'd found him with another woman than to learn he'd been talking to Roger, no matter what his reason.

"Our ad agency tested this twenty-second commercial and is very pleased with its effectiveness."

The figure of a man and a woman came onto the screen. The husband was on a ladder painting the side of a house. The woman was working on the lawn below, painting a patio table with four matching chairs. Two children played serenely on a swing set in the background. The music was a classical piece she recognized but couldn't immediately name. The announcer's well-modulated voice came on but Julia couldn't hear what he was saying.

The room started to spin. The light fixtures faded in and out as though someone was controlling a dimmer switch. She thought she heard a woman cry out but even that seemed to be coming from far away.

When she regained consciousness, Julia found herself on the floor. She blinked up at the ceiling. Alek was crouched over her, his arm supporting the back of her neck. His eyes were filled with anxiety.

"What happened?" she asked.

"You fainted," Jerry said. He was kneeling beside her, holding her hand, patting it gently. "I'll say this for you, Julia, you certainly know how to get a man's heart going. You keeled right over."

"Where is everyone?"

"We had them leave. Alek and I will review the commercials later."

"I don't understand it," she said, struggling into a sitting position. "One moment I was perfectly fine and the next thing I knew, the room started whirling."

"I'll get her some water," Jerry said.

He left the room and Alek slid his arm behind her back, helped her into an upright sitting position and held her against his chest. She braced her hands against his ribs, intent on pushing herself free.

"No," he said, kissing her temple. "You can mistrust and hate me later, but for right now let me hold you."

"That's the problem," she whispered. "I believe you."

"Right now, we won't speak of this again. You've worked yourself into a state of collapse."

"I don't know what happened here, but I'm sure it's nothing important. I've just been overstressed, that's all."

Jerry returned with the water. "Why is it I'm always getting you water?" he joked, handing her a paper cup.

"You'd think I'd gone to college to be a water boy instead of an attorney."

"I'm sorry," she said, pressing her hand to the side of her head. "I didn't mean to create such a commotion."

"Should we take her back to her office?" Jerry asked, looking at Alek.

"No, I'll take her home."

"If you don't mind, I prefer to make my own decisions," Julia stiffly informed them both. They made it sound as if she were a piece of furniture they couldn't decide where to place.

Leaning against the back of a chair, she stood. She felt a bit unstable, but that dizziness quickly passed. "I'm fine. You two go about your business and I'll go about mine."

"Julia, for heaven's sakes, would you listen to common sense? You just fainted," Jerry informed her, as if she hadn't figured it out yet.

"I know that."

"Let Alek take you home."

"No."

"I think she'd feel more comfortable if you took her," Alek suggested.

"I *fainted,*" she told both men, "I didn't have a lobotomy. Let me assure you, I'm perfectly capable of making my own decisions, and I'm not leaving my office until I'm finished with what I need to do."

"Some of those decisions should be questioned," Jerry snapped.

"Jerry."

"Shut up, Alek, this is between me and my sister. She's an emotional and physical wreck because of this mess and to complicate matters she decides to play detective herself."

"I don't understand."

"Jerry, could we discuss this another time?" Julia asked pointedly.

"No. Alek has a right to know. Tell him."

"Julia?" Alek turned to face her. "What's Jerry talking about?"

She flashed her brother a scathing look. "It's nothing."

"Fine, I'll tell him. Julia had the bright idea of calling Roger Stanhope herself and playing this crazy game with him. She said she knew about the meeting between the two of you."

Alek's gaze narrowed. "And what did Stanhope say?"

"You can well imagine."

"I didn't believe Roger," Julia said. "I never did." Jerry was right, contacting Roger hadn't been the smartest thing she'd ever done, but she was desperate.

"What my sister failed to remember is that Roger isn't stupid. She was fishing for information and he knew it, so he made up this ridiculous story about you trying to strike a deal with Ideal Paints."

Alek released a one-word expletive.

"It's driving her crazy," Jerry continued. "She looked terrible when she came to see me this morning."

Julia watched her husband. He was distancing himself from her, physically and emotionally, freezing her out.

"She must make her own decision and I must make mine." Without another word, Alek turned and left the conference room.

"I wish you hadn't said anything to him about my talk with Roger."

"Why not? He had a right to know."

Her lack of faith—and the fact that she'd acted on it—had hurt Alek. She'd seen it in his eyes and in the way he'd stiffened and moved away from her. Covering her face with her hands, Julia slowly exhaled.

"I have to go," she whispered. "I'll talk to you tomorrow."

Julia's head was pounding as she walked out of the conference room. She checked the time, wanting to know how long she had before her appointment with Dr. Feldon. The physician had been treating her family for the past fifteen years and knew Julia well.

She arrived at his office at one minute past five and was ushered directly into the exam room. His nurse asked her a series of questions.

"Basically, I've been under a lot of stress lately," Julia explained. "This afternoon the craziest thing happened. I fainted. Me! I can't believe it."

After taking her temperature and her blood pressure, Dr. Feldon's nurse asked for a urine sample.

Minutes later, she was joined by Dr. Feldon. His hair was grayer than the last time she'd seen him and he was a little thicker around the waist.

"Julia, it's good to see you, although I wish it were under different circumstances. Now tell me what the problem is."

The tears came as a surprise and an acute embarrassment. "I... I'm just not myself lately. There's been so much happening with the company and I've been so stressed, and today I fainted right in the middle of a marketing meeting. I gave my husband and my brother quite a scare."

"Yes, I heard you got married. Congratulations."

She smiled weakly in response.

Dr. Feldon reached for a tissue and pressed it into her hand. "How are you feeling now?"

She had to stop and think about it. "A little woozy."

"And emotional?"

She nodded, paused, then blew her nose.

"I'd say this is all normal, my dear. Most pregnant women experience these symptoms."

Twelve

"Pregnant?" Julia repeated in a shocked whisper. "You mean all this, the nausea and the fainting spell, is because I'm going to have a baby?"

"No, I think the stress you've talked about is complicating the symptoms."

"But I don't have morning sickness."

"A good many women don't. Some have what you might call afternoon sickness instead. My guess is that you're one of those."

"I should've realized..." Julia began, wondering why she hadn't recognized her condition herself.

"As you probably know I stopped delivering babies several years back. I can recommend an excellent obstetrician. I'll have my receptionist make an appointment for you, if you'd like. Her name is Dr. Lois Brandt and my patients who've had babies delivered by her have been very pleased."

"Yes, that would be fine." Julia was both excited and surprised, although heaven knew she had no right to be. "How...far along do you think I am?"

Dr. Feldon chuckled. "My estimate is about two weeks."

She nodded, knowing it couldn't be much more than that, astonished, too, that her pregnancy could be detected so early.

"I'm going to prescribe prenatal vitamins and have you start watching your diet. According to those ridiculous charts the insurance companies put out, you're about five pounds underweight. Don't skip meals, and make an effort to eat from the major food groups every day. Plenty of fresh fruit and vegetables," he emphasized.

Smiling, Julia nodded. Dr. Feldon made it sound as if she were pregnant with a rabbit instead of a baby.

She left the office a few minutes later, her step lighter. *A baby.* She was going to have a baby. Alek would—

Alek.

Her thoughts came to a skidding halt. This complicated everything tenfold. There was far more at stake now than before. There was far more involved. They'd introduced a tiny being into the equation.

Julia's steps slowed. She wasn't sure what to do or say to him, if anything. At least, not yet. He had a right to know, but Julia wasn't convinced now was the time to tell him.

She returned to her condominium and let herself in. Two steps into the entry, she nearly stumbled over a large leather suitcase.

She heard movement in the master bedroom and walked down the hallway leading to it. Alek stood inside the walk-in closet, carefully removing his clothes from their hangers. Another large leather suitcase yawned open on top of the bed.

"Alek? What are you doing?"

He continued his work without looking at her. "It should be obvious."

"You're moving out," she whispered and the truth hit her like a slap of icy rain. Alek was leaving.

"I knew you'd figure it out sooner or later." He walked over to his suitcase and carefully folded his shirts and placed them inside.

"Where will you be living?"

"I don't know yet. I don't believe there's any reason for us to stay in touch after I move out."

"What about at the office? I mean—"

"As of four-thirty this afternoon I am no longer an employee of Conrad Industries."

Julia's heart froze at what his words implied. "I see… You're going to work for Ideal Paints."

He whirled around to face her. "No, Julia, I am not going to work for the competition. I know it means nothing to you, but the Berinski word of honor is all I have to offer you as proof. On the grave of my father, I swear I would never do anything to hurt you or Jerry. That includes betraying you to Ideal Paints or any other of your competitors." He spun back around and resumed his task, his movements abrupt and hurried as if he was eager to be on his way. Julia didn't want him to leave, but she couldn't ask him to stay, either.

"Why now?" she asked, sitting on the edge of the bed. She wasn't sure her shaky legs would support her. She felt as if she was about to burst into tears, which would have embarrassed them both.

"I'd hoped that given time you'd see the truth, but I no longer believe that's possible."

"Why not?"

"If you believe Stanhope's word over mine, then I have to accept that you're not capable of recognizing the truth when you hear it."

Julia had no argument to give him, although her doubts and fears were beginning to mount. "Do you want a divorce?"

He went still for a moment, as if the question required some consideration. "That's up to you. I told you once that my religion forbids it."

Julia relaxed a little, but not much.

"I can't live with you, Julia, and I can't see ever living with you again."

"It wasn't so bad, was it?" she said, looking for something, anything, to bring them back together, to force him to acknowledge his love for her. She was tempted to tell him her news, but if he stayed, she wanted it to be because he loved her and not because she'd trapped him.

"No, Julia, living with you wasn't bad—if you don't mind a porcupine for a wife."

She sucked in her breath at the pain his words caused.

His shoulders sagged and he exhaled sharply. "I shouldn't have said that. I apologize."

"I've hurt you, too."

He didn't respond, but she knew she *had* hurt him. He was intent on his packing and refused to look up. He closed the suitcase, then dragged it from the bed and carried it into the other room, setting it beside the first one.

"If you forget anything, where would you like me to

send it?" she asked, hoping to appear helpful when she was actually looking for a means of staying in contact.

He frowned, then said, "Give it to Anna. She'll know where I am." He paused. "I trust you're willing to let her go on working here? Until she gets another job? She hopes to be hired as a translator soon."

She nodded. "Yes. Of course. But... I think you might be acting a bit hastily, don't you? Why don't you give it some thought?" This was as far as she was willing to go. She wouldn't ask him to stay, wouldn't plead with him or make an issue of his going. Those choices were his.

"There's nothing to think about," he told her stiffly. "Goodbye, Julia." He added something softly in Russian, then opened the door, reached for his suitcases and walked out of the condominium. And her life.

Julia stood for a moment, so stunned and feeling so bereft that she couldn't move. Or breathe. Or think. Those abilities returned slowly. Taking small, deliberate steps, she walked into the living room, collapsing onto the white leather sofa.

She'd had the most dreadful day. Within the space of a few hours, she'd fainted, learned she was pregnant and been abandoned by her husband. The prospects for the future didn't look bright. Except for the baby...

The phone rang fifteen minutes later and Julia grabbed it, thinking, praying, it was Alek. "Hello," she answered quickly.

"Julia, have you seen Alek? You've got to talk some sense into him! I just got back to my office and found his letter of resignation. What do you know about this? Listen, don't answer that, just put him on the line. I'll convince him he's overreacting."

"I can't," she said, biting her lower lip. "I really wish I could, but... Alek's not living here anymore."

"What do you mean?"

"He moved out. He was packing when I got home."

"Why didn't you stop him?"

"How?"

"Oh, I don't know," Jerry said with heavy sarcasm. "Maybe you could've told him you believe in him and trust him. You might've thanked him for working two long years on the project that's going to take this company's profit line right off the page. You could even have told him you love him and didn't want him to go."

Julia, who was crying softly by then, sniffled. "Yeah, I guess I could."

"Do you believe him now?"

"I...don't know. I think I do, because not trusting him hurts too much."

Jerry swore under his breath, then sighed loudly. "You've got a really bad sense of timing. Did anyone ever tell you that?"

"No," she said, wiping the tears from her cheek.

"Go to him, Julia," Jerry advised, "before it's too late."

"It's already too late," she whispered. "I don't know where he is and he didn't want to tell me."

The following morning, Julia was waiting for her sister-in-law. "Good morning, Anna," she said when the woman arrived.

Alek's sister frowned and didn't respond. She walked over to the broom closet, took out her apron and tied it around her waist, all the while ignoring Julia.

"I guess you heard that Alek moved out?" Julia asked, following her.

Still Anna didn't acknowledge her. She opened the refrigerator and removed a carton of eggs.

"Do you know where he is?"

"Of course. He is my brother."

"Would you mind telling me?"

"So you can hurt him more? So you can think terrible things of him? So you can insult his honor? No, I will not tell you anything about my brother."

"I love him," Julia whispered. "I've just been so afraid. You see, three years ago I loved a man who betrayed my family and me. I believed him when I shouldn't have. I defended him, and my father and I got into a terrible argument and my father...while we were fighting he suffered a heart attack. He died and I felt so incredibly guilty. I blamed myself." Anna had turned to face Julia, her face white and emotionless. "Can you understand why it was so difficult for me to believe Alek? Can you see why I'm skeptical after all the things that have happened?" Tears were very close to the surface, but she held them back, crumpling a tissue in her hand until it was a small wad.

"My brother would never betray you."

"I know that. In a way, I've always known that."

"Alek isn't this other man."

"I realize that, too, but...because of my experience with this...other man, I made a mistake and gave Alek reason to believe I doubted him." She stopped, because arguing her case with Alek's sister wasn't going to help.

She dressed for work with no enthusiasm. In another ten days, Phoenix Paints would be on sale to the public. Conrad Industries had developed a whole new kind of paint, several kinds, in fact, thanks to her father's dream and Alek's genius. Somehow it all seemed empty now. The purpose that had driven her all these years meant nothing without Alek at her side.

Jerry was waiting in her office. "Did you find out where he's staying?"

Julia shook her head. "His sister wouldn't tell me. I don't blame her. If our positions were reversed, I wouldn't tell her, either."

"I'll get Rich on it right away."

"No," she said quietly. "Leave Alek his pride. I've robbed him of everything else." She walked around her desk and sat down. Reaching for her desk calendar, she flipped the pages ahead eight months. "I'm going to need some extensive time off soon."

"We all need a vacation, Julia."

"This is going to be more than a two-week vacation, Jerry. I'll need maternity leave."

Alek sat at a table in the library, where he came to spend part of every day. He'd moved into another small furnished apartment, near Anna's, and came here to read—and primarily to escape his own four walls. Books were his comfort, his consolation.

Perhaps that was his problem. He knew more about books than people. He had badly bungled his marriage. It'd been over a week since he'd seen Julia. Two weeks since he'd moved out of their condominium—*her* condominium, he corrected.

He'd seen her interviewed on a local television station the day Phoenix Paints hit the market. She'd looked pale and so beautiful he hadn't been able to take his eyes off the television screen. Long after her face vanished from view, he'd continued to stare at the television, not even seeing.

She'd answered the reporter's questions, explained her father's vision for the paint industry and how Alek had seen it to fruition. Alek had been surprised that she'd mentioned his name, credited him with the innovations. Paints that changed color, paints developed for easy removal, paints that were guaranteed to last into the next generation.

Alek thought long and hard about what she'd said, wondering if she was trying to tell him something. If she was, he'd missed it. He was worried about her; she looked drained, but jubilant. Jerry was with her and had responded to some of the questions.

Alek closed the book he was reading. He relied on Anna for information about Julia, but his sister had grown stubborn, refusing to give him the detailed answers he sought. She seemed to think that if he was so curious, he should talk to Julia himself.

Alek considered her suggestion. He'd left because he couldn't tolerate her mistrust.

His gaze fell onto his swollen, bruised knuckles and he flexed his hand. Standing, he returned the book to the shelf and picked up his jacket. It was raining outside, a cold, persistent drizzle. His hair was drenched by the time he'd gone a single block.

It was while he was passing a large parked van that he glanced at the side mirror—and caught the reflection of a man in a beige raincoat behind him. He'd seen this same man in the library. Alek wondered. It would be foolish to believe he was being followed. Then again, he'd lived in a country where it wasn't uncommon for citizens to disappear and never be heard from again.

He stepped into an alley and waited. The man casually strolled past and continued down the walkway. Alek expelled his breath, thinking he'd become fanciful. Then again, it wouldn't be beneath Stanhope to hire someone to injure him.

No, he decided, Stanhope was just the type to have someone else do his dirty work for him.

Alek walked for several blocks until he reached the Seattle waterfront, which had become one of his favorite places. The fish and chips were excellent and there was a covered eating space along the pier. It was late afternoon, and he hadn't eaten since breakfast, so he purchased a double order and carried it onto the farthest end of the dock. Here he could look out over the water; he enjoyed viewing the nautical activity on Puget Sound. He claimed a picnic table and sat down to enjoy his dinner.

He was lost in thought, apparently, because he didn't notice the man in the raincoat until he was directly in front of him.

"I guess I'd better sit down and introduce myself," the man said. He held out his hand. "Rich Peck."

Alek stood and they exchanged handshakes. "Hello. Alek Berinski."

"You figured out I was following you, didn't you?" Uninvited, Peck sat down at the table, across from Alek.

Alek shrugged. "I had my suspicions."

"Huh," Peck muttered, "I must be getting sloppy."

"There was a reason you've been tracking my movements?"

Peck grinned, that cocky grin Alek often saw in American men. "There generally is a reason. And it usually involves someone paying me. Rather handsomely, I might add."

Alek looked at him, confused. "Are you saying Roger Stanhope paid you to follow me?"

"Stanhope? Don't bet on it. The man hasn't got two dimes to rub together. Oh, by the way, I heard about your little skirmish with him. Provoking him into taking the first swing was smart. I heard he tried to hit you from behind. The man's a sleaze. Are you pressing assault charges against him?"

"No, I decided I'd punished him enough. I know one thing for sure. He'll stay out of Julia's life now. He knows what will happen to him if he doesn't."

"Listen, Stanhope's got more problems than you know," Peck went on to say. "He'll be happy to stay away from anything to do with Conrad Industries for the next fifteen years. If he lives that long, which I personally doubt. He borrowed money from the wrong kind of people, if you know what I mean."

"You know a lot about this…slimeball." That was an American expression Alek found particularly fitting.

Peck shrugged. "I was paid to learn what I could. The guy's an open book. You, on the other hand, weren't so easy to track down. Your sister wouldn't tell me a thing. She pretended she didn't understand English."

"Who hired you to follow me?" Alek was growing bored with this detailed speech.

"Sorry, but that's privileged information."

"Julia?" His heart pounded hard with excitement.

"Nope. My lips are sealed. But I can tell you it *isn't* her. She doesn't know anything about this, although what I'm supposed to tell you concerns her."

Alek was beginning to think he didn't like Peck as much as he initially had. "Then tell me."

Peck arched his brows at Alek's less than patient tone. "First, let me ask you a couple of questions."

"I don't have time for this." Alek surged to his feet and stalked away. He half expected Peck to follow him, but when the investigator didn't get up, he slowed his pace.

Alek had gone a block before he recognized his mistake. His impatience had cost him what he'd wanted most, information about Julia. He turned back, walking at a fast clip. He need not have worried; Peck was sitting at the table, enjoying the fish-and-chips dinner Alek had hastily left behind.

Alek stood over him and Peck licked his fingers. "I thought you might have a change of heart."

"Tell me."

"No problem. There's something Jerry thought you'd like to know about his sister. She's going to be a mother. If I understand correctly, that means you're about to become a daddy."

Alek felt as if he'd had his legs knocked out from under him. He literally slumped onto the picnic table. "When?"

"Don't know. But I don't think she's very far along. A month, maybe two."

"Have you seen her? Is she healthy?"

Peck shrugged. "The last time I did, she was a little green around the gills."

Another crazy American idiom, one that made no sense to him at all. "Green gills? What does that mean?"

"You know, a little under the weather."

Alek's confusion increased. "Say it in plain English, please."

"Okay, okay. She's sick every afternoon. Jerry says

it's like watching Old Faithful. About three-fifteen her assistant leads her to the ladies' room so she can lose her lunch. It's perfectly normal from what I understand. Not that I know much about pregnant women."

Alek felt as if someone were sitting on his chest and the weight kept increasing. A baby. *His* baby. Julia was going to have his baby.

He stood up again, frowning. He had a right to know, and the news shouldn't have come from his brother-in-law, either. Julia should have told him herself.

A low, burning anger simmered in his blood. He was angry, angrier than he'd been in a long time, and he wasn't about to let this go.

"You tell Jerry something for me," Alek muttered.

"Sure."

He paused. He didn't have any cause to be angry with Jerry. His friend had taken the initiative and sent Peck to tell him what he should've been told from the beginning—by Julia. And he himself had been avoiding Jerry, at least for now—*because* of Julia.

"You wanted me to pass something along to Jerry?" Peck pressed.

"Yeah," Alek said, feeling the beginnings of a smile. "Tell him I think he's going to make a very good uncle."

Julia took another bite of her celery stalk, then set it back on the plate. Her attention wavered from her book for only an instant while she reached for a slice of apple.

The manual, one she'd recently picked up at a bookstore, described the stages of pregnancy week by exciting week. She kept the book hidden from Anna and brought it out in the evenings. By the time Junior was ready to be born, she'd practically have the whole three hundred pages memorized.

She called the baby Junior, although she didn't know yet if it was a boy or a girl. Funny, only a couple of weeks ago she hadn't even known she was pregnant, and now it seemed as though the baby had always been a part of her.

At night, she slept with her hand on her stomach. She talked to Junior, carrying on lengthy conversations with her unborn child.

Jerry and Virginia had become ridiculously vigilant. Julia swore her assistant suffered more from her bouts of afternoon sickness than Julia did herself. And Jerry. She smiled as she thought about her brother and how solicitous he'd become. He was constantly asking after her health. He'd even gone so far as to contact Dr. Feldon about her daily bouts of afternoon sickness.

She had been to see Dr. Brandt and liked the young, attractive woman very much. Thanks to her and the pregnancy book she'd recommended, Julia understood far better the changes that were taking place within her body.

She tried not to think about Alek, tried not to dwell on how much she missed him. Or the mistakes she'd made in her brief marriage. Sooner or later she'd have to get in touch with him. She needed to tell him about the baby. And to thank him. Phoenix Paints had taken the market by storm. A national television network had called today wanting to do a news piece on the ideas behind the innovative paints.

She owed Alek so much and she'd treated him so poorly.

She hadn't asked Anna his whereabouts since that

first morning. His sister didn't volunteer any information about Alek even when Julia asked. Julia didn't think Anna had forgiven her yet for hurting her brother.

She pressed her hand to her stomach and whispered, "Your daddy is a wonderful man, Junior. He's going to love you so much."

She took another bite of the celery stalk and turned the page of her text. Labor and delivery. She'd read this chapter first, the same night she'd bought the book, wanting to learn everything she could on the subject.

When she did deliver Junior, she hoped Alek would be there to coach her. From what she'd seen of Jerry, he wouldn't last ten minutes in a delivery room. And Virginia wouldn't be able to take watching her in pain, Julia was convinced of that.

When she'd finished her snack, Julia moved into the living room to exercise. She turned on the television and inserted the low-impact prenatal aerobics DVD. Ten minutes later she was huffing and puffing and sweating enough to dampen the gray T-shirt she wore.

"I hope you appreciate this," she told the baby.

After a full thirty minutes, she went into the kitchen, got a glass from the cupboard and gulped down some water. After that, she grabbed a pencil and marked the schedule posted on the refrigerator. Anna thought it was a diet sheet and it was. Sort of. Julia listed the food she ate, plus her water intake. Eight glasses a day, no excuses.

That was another interesting aspect of her condition. Her life was now ruled by how long it would take her to reach a bathroom. She'd considered having one installed in her office because it was so disruptive to hurry down the hall every hour, and sometimes more often. The eight glasses of water didn't help matters.

She was feeling better, though, and for that Julia was grateful. The first couple of weeks after Alek had moved out she'd felt as if she were living in a nightmare. She did what needed to be done, performed her duties, ate, worked and slept, but did it all with a low-grade sense of dejection—and with an air of expectancy. She couldn't seem to let go of the idea that Alek would come into her office one day the way he used to. It was the hope of seeing him again, of telling him about the baby, that had kept her going. That and, of course, her happiness about the baby.

The doorbell rang and Julia ripped the sweatband from her forehead. It was probably Jerry, who'd taken to checking up on her in the evenings.

But it wasn't. When she opened the door, Alek stood before her, looking more furious than she'd ever seen him.

Thirteen

"Alek." Julia couldn't say anything more. He looked wonderful, while she must have resembled a towel that had been sitting at the bottom of the dirty-clothes hamper.

"I just heard you're pregnant. Is that true?" His eyes were hard as granite. He was furious with her and didn't bother to disguise it.

"It's true."

"You might have told me. I played an important role in this event."

"Yes, I know, it's just that…" She realized she'd left him standing in the hallway outside the condo. Opening the door wider, she said, "Come inside, please."

"You weren't going to tell me about the baby?" He was frowning.

"Of course I intended to tell you!"

"When?"

"Would you care to sit down?"

"No, just answer the question."

Julia ignored the demand in his voice. "Would you like something to drink?"

"Just answer the question!"

"There's no reason to yell. I was going to tell you, how could I not? This baby is as much a part of you as of me. How could I keep something this important from you?" She hoped that would appease him.

"That's my question exactly." Alek's hands were knotted into fists at his sides. Julia wanted to think that meant he was restraining himself from holding her—not simply expressing his frustration.

She started to walk into the kitchen. He hesitated, then followed her. She poured a glass of water for him and then one for herself and set them down on the kitchen table.

"Anna knew?"

"No. I couldn't tell her. I was afraid she'd say something to you." Her explanation didn't satisfy him; if anything, his scowl darkened.

Julia pulled out a chair and sat. Alek did, too. Avoiding his probing eyes, she lowered her gaze to her water glass. "I'm drinking two quarts of water every day now. Eight full glasses... I'm keeping track of my intake on that sheet on the fridge."

"The baby needs water?"

"In a manner of speaking, I guess, but actually it's me the doctor's concerned about."

"Why is the doctor concerned?"

She hadn't said this to alarm Alek. It was just conversation, a way to ease the tension between them. "I'm perfectly healthy, Alek. Don't look so worried."

"Then why is your doctor concerned?"

"That's her job. She keeps a close eye on my health and the baby's. So far I'm having a perfectly normal pregnancy. That's what my doctor says. So does the book." She reached across the table for the manual she'd read from cover to cover three times over. "Junior's doing just great."

"Junior?"

"That's what I call him...or her."

The anger had faded and in its place Julia saw a love and devotion so deep it wounded her. To think she'd abused that love and mistrusted his word. Her throat grew thick. Tears filled her eyes.

"Julia."

She looked away. "Don't worry, it's all part of this pregnancy thing. I'm very emotional. The other night I started crying over a TV ad." She didn't tell him it was the one for Phoenix Paints. The tears had come because she'd realized how much she missed her husband.

Alek passed her his handkerchief.

"Thanks." She dabbed her eyes. "Look on page fifty-three. It explains why a woman's more likely to cry when she's pregnant."

Alek flipped through the pages until he found the one she'd mentioned. He scanned the text and nodded.

"How have you been feeling?"

She shrugged. "All right, I guess. I don't get sick in the mornings the way most women do. I usually get nauseous around three-thirty in the afternoon. I don't know why I bother with lunch since it comes right back up again."

"Have you had any other problems?"

"No," she was quick to assure him. "Actually, I've been feeling great. And the nausea should be over soon." She smiled. "You'll be proud of me. I've been eating well, with lots of fresh fruit and vegetables." She stopped when she noticed the way he was staring at her. "Is something wrong?"

Alek's eyes left hers and he shook his head. "Never mind."

"No, tell me, please."

He hesitated and Julia felt a jolt of fear. She'd read about this, in the very book that rested on the table between her and Alek. Some men were turned off by their wives during pregnancy.

"You are more beautiful than ever," Alek whispered.

Julia bit her lower lip and a sigh trembled through her.

"That disappoints you?"

"I'm not beautiful, Alek. Judging by the way Jerry and my assistant are constantly fussing over me, I must look awful."

Emotion produced a second quivering sigh. "I've missed you so much," she admitted. "I wanted to tell you about the baby right away... I learned I was pregnant the afternoon you moved out. I came home from the doctor's office to find you packing."

"And you didn't tell me then?" he bellowed.

"Would it have changed anything if I *had* told you?" she asked calmly.

"Yes," he answered, then lowered his gaze. "I don't know."

"I'd hurt you and was hurting so badly myself. If I'd told you about Junior then, I was afraid it might sound like blackmail."

"You realize now that I would never betray you?"

"I knew it then, I always knew it...in my heart. I just did a poor job of showing you. I couldn't get past my own fears." A tear ran from the corner of her eye. "No words can ever express how sorry I am for the pain I caused you. When we got married, I didn't expect to fall in love with you. I'd steeled myself against it. I'd been in love once before and, as you know, the experience cost me and others dearly.

"A green-card marriage seemed workable. I was determined not to involve my heart, but day after day you treated me with love and affection, chipping away at my defenses no matter how much I fortified them.

"When Ruth died... I don't think I would've survived that time without you. Your comfort and love meant the world to me. I'll always treasure our day at the beach."

She stopped to catch her breath and to keep her voice from cracking. "This much is a fact—I love you, Alek, and I'm deeply sorry for the pain I caused you. I swear I'll never doubt you again." Tears fell unheeded from her eyes.

"Don't cry, Julia."

She noticed he didn't call her *my love* the way he so often had in the past. Covering her face with her hands, she wiped away the moisture, expelled a sigh and forced herself to smile. "I know it's a lot to ask, but could you ever find it in your heart to forgive me for contacting Roger?"

"If you can forgive me for letting my pride stand in the way."

"Your pride? Oh, Alek, I trampled over it a hundred times, and still you loved me. I didn't know how to deal with love and I made so many mistakes."

"I made my own mistakes."

"I asked Anna about you countless times, but she refuses to talk about you. I don't think she's forgiven me for hurting you."

"Ah, my sister," Alek said slowly. "She played the same game with me. I asked her about you so often, she finally told me that if I was so curious, I should go ask you myself."

"She was right, you know. Neither of us had any business putting her in the middle, pumping her for information about the other."

"I agree. But I still don't like it that you didn't tell me about our baby."

Julia thought her heart would melt at the tender way he said *baby*. Alek was going to be a wonderful father. She hadn't gone into this marriage with any great expectations; she hadn't thought she'd be married long, despite her undeniable attraction to him. Falling in love with Alek had come as a delightful surprise.

His gentleness, his patience, his comfort had seen her through that bleak time surrounding Ruth's final days and the dark weeks that followed. Without him, she would have become lost and tormented. How wise of Ruth to recognize the type of man Alek was. To recognize that he would become her compass, guiding her toward happiness.

"I would've eventually found a way of getting in touch with you," Julia said. "Soon, too... I don't know how much longer I would've been able to keep this baby to myself." She stopped talking, realizing Alek had come to her because he'd learned of her condition. Slowly she raised her eyes to his. "Who told you I was pregnant?"

If Jerry had known where Alek was all this time, she'd have a few words to say to him.

"Does it matter?"

"Yes."

"All right, if you must know, a private detective told me."

"You hired a detective to—"

"No, Jerry was the one who did the hiring. A man

named Peck. Your brother thought it was my right to know about the baby."

It didn't escape Julia's notice that he still hadn't referred to her as his love.

"I see," she said. "And now that you know, what do you expect to happen?"

He frowned. "That depends on several matters."

"Yes?" she pressed when he didn't elaborate. "What sort of matters?"

"I'll expect to be a major part of our child's life."

Julia nodded in full agreement; she was hoping he'd be a major part of her life, too. "I'd like that. Is there anything else?" she asked when he didn't continue.

Alek seemed to need time to think over his response. "I'd very much like to be your husband," he finally said, "to live with you and love you and perhaps have another child. Would this be agreeable to you?"

She threw her arms around his neck with such fervor that she nearly toppled the chair he was sitting on.

"Be careful, my love..."

"Say that again." She choked out the words through her tears. "Call me your love. Oh, Alek, I've missed hearing that so much. Wait, kiss me first." She had so many requests he obviously didn't know which one to comply with first. It didn't take him long, though, to direct her mouth to his.

"My love."

"Oh, Alek."

"Julia."

Their names were trapped between two hungry mouths. Between two eagerly beating hearts.

Their mouths strained toward each other. Julia felt the emotion rise within her. She'd missed him so much, more than she dared to admit even to herself. He was speaking to her in Russian, short snatches of words between frantic kisses.

She tightened her arms around his neck.

He surprised her by standing and carrying her into the bedroom. "You are so romantic," she told him, languishing in his arms.

"I plan to get a whole lot more romantic in about thirty seconds." His intentions were clear as he lovingly placed her on the bed.

"Oh, good… Hurry, Alek, I've needed you so much."

He stripped while she watched him, marveling at his maleness and his readiness for her. Sitting up, Julia struggled out of her T-shirt and tossed it aside. Her tennis shoes came next. "I really should shower," she commented as the spandex pants flew in the opposite direction.

"No time now," Alek said. "Later, we'll shower together."

"But I just finished a workout."

"And you're about to start another," he said.

Long minutes later, they were exhausted, panting in each other's arms, their bodies linked, their hands and hearts entwined.

"I love you, Alek."

"You are my love," he returned as their bodies thrilled, excited and satisfied each other.

Julia slept in her husband's arms afterward, her head on his chest. When she stirred into wakefulness, she found his hand pressed against her abdomen and heard him communicating in whispers to his child. Since he was speaking Russian, she could only speculate on what he was saying.

He noticed her looking at him and smiled shyly. "I told him to be good to his mother."

"Him?"

"A daughter would please me just as well." He smiled. "Someday a young man will come to me and thank me for having fathered such a beautiful daughter. Wait, and you'll see that I'm right."

"Someday a young woman will come to me and tell me our son is totally awesome, or whatever expression is popular at the time." She wrinkled her nose. "They change every few years, you realize."

"I sometimes go crazy with the things you Americans say. Your strange idioms and slang—they're constantly changing."

"Don't worry, you'll catch on. I'll help you."

"Awesome," he said with a mischievous grin.

They showered and Julia dressed in a thick terry-cloth robe and padded barefoot into the kitchen. "I don't know about you, but I'm starved."

Alek grinned again. "I see your appetite has increased."

It was true. "I suppose it has." She opened the refrigerator and took out a container of ice cream and served them both large bowls.

"Should we call Jerry?" Julia asked. "We seem to owe him a great deal."

"No, I don't want to share you with anyone just yet. Tomorrow will be soon enough. We'll invite him and Anna," he said, and Julia nodded delightedly.

They sat in the living room, cuddled against each other, eating their ice cream. "The late news is on," Julia commented. "Okay with you if I turn it on?"

"Of course." He took the empty bowl and set it aside.

Then he brought her back against him. His roving hands distracted Julia from her intention and she gasped at the sensation that shot through her.

"I keep up with current events as much as I can," she said, trying to get her mind *off* the subject at hand. "I missed the earlier newscast because I had a doctor's appointment."

Alek's eyes widened with concern.

"It was the dentist, don't worry." She leaned forward to pick up the remote control. The screen flared to life just as the sportscaster began the latest update on the Mariners. It was heavenly to sit quietly with Alek's arms around her.

"I will take our son to baseball games," Alek announced, "and the library."

"I hope you intend to take your daughter and your wife while you're at it."

"Whoever wishes to go," he said, as though their family was already complete and they were making ordinary, everyday plans.

Julia smiled to herself.

After the sports news, they watched the five-day weather forecast. "I hope it rains every day," Alek whispered close to her ear. "That way I can keep you in the apartment, or better yet, in our bed."

"I've got news for you," Julia whispered, kissing his lips, still cold from the ice cream. "You don't need an excuse to take me to bed. In case you haven't noticed, I'm crazy about you."

"I noticed," he said with a satisfied smile. "And I approve."

Soon they were kissing again. They would have continued, Julia was certain, if the newscaster hadn't returned to announce the breaking news stories of the day.

"Ideal Paints, a national paint manufacturer based here in Seattle, has declared bankruptcy. As many as three hundred jobs have been lost."

Julia was stunned. "I knew they were having financial difficulties," she said, breaking away from Alek. "But I didn't realize it was that serious."

"They couldn't hope to compete with Conrad Industries any longer," Alek told her. "Stanhope hurt them, but it took them three years to feel the effects. Their whole developmental program came to a halt after he sold them the formula for guaranteed twenty-five-year paint. They had the latest advance without having gone through the learning process, without the trial and error that comes with any major progress. It set them back."

Julia had never thought of it in those terms. What she did remember was something Ruth had told her years earlier, when revenge and justice had ranked high on her list. Her grandmother had insisted time had a way of correcting injustices, and she'd been right.

"I wonder what'll happen to Roger," she said absently, almost feeling sorry for him.

"He's finished in the business world," Alek said calmly. "It's a well-known fact he sold out Conrad Industries. No company's going to risk hiring an employee with questionable loyalty and ethics. He'll be lucky to find any kind of job."

"Everything's come full circle," Julia said, leaning into her husband's strength. He wrapped his arms around her waist and she pressed her hands over his. "Everything I lost has been returned to me a hundred-fold."

Alek kissed her neck. "Same for me."

"I didn't know it was possible to be this happy. Only a few years ago I felt as if my whole life was over, and now it seems to get better every day." Leaning back, she reached upward for her husband's kiss.

* * * * *

BRIDE WANTED

For Eric, Kurt, Neal and Clay Macomber—
the other Macombers. Love, Aunt Debbie.

Prologue

"Let me see if I've got this right," the man behind the desk asked Chase Goodman. He spoke around the cigar in his mouth. "You want to rent a billboard and advertise for a wife."

Chase wasn't about to let a potbellied cynic talk him out of the idea. He had exactly three weeks to find himself a bride before he returned to Alaska, and that didn't leave time for a lot of romantic nonsense. This was the most direct route he could think of for getting himself a wife. He was thirty-three, relatively good-looking and lonesome as heck. He'd spent his last winter alone.

Okay, he was willing to admit, his idea was unorthodox, but he was on a tight schedule. He intended to wine and dine the right woman, sweep her off her feet, but he had to meet her first. Although Seattle was full of eligible women, he wasn't fool enough to believe more than a few would want to leave the comforts of city life for the frozen north. The way Chase figured it, best to lay his cards on the table, wait and see what kind of response he got. He also figured this would get noticed by women who wouldn't necessarily look at newspaper ads or internet dating sites.

"You heard me," Chase said stiffly.

"You want the billboard to read BRIDE WANTED?" The fat cigar moved as if by magic from one side of his mouth to the other.

"Yes, with the phone number I gave you. The answering service will be screening the calls."

"You considered what sort of women are going to be responding to that advertisement?"

Chase simply nodded. He'd given plenty of thought to that question. He knew what to expect. But there was bound to be one who'd strike his fancy, and if everything went as he hoped, he'd strike her fancy, too. That was what he was looking for, that one in a thousand.

He was well aware that it wasn't the best plan. If he had more time to get to know a woman, he could prove he'd be a good husband and, God willing, a father. He wasn't like a lot of men who could blithely say the things a woman wanted to hear. He needed help and the billboard would make his intentions clear from the first.

"I'll have my men on it tomorrow morning."

"Great," Chase said and grinned.

The wheels were in motion. All he had to do was sit back and wait for his bride to come to him.

One

Lesley Campbell glared at the calendar. The last Saturday in June was to have been her wedding day. Only she wasn't going to be a bride. The wedding dress hanging in the back of her closet would eventually yellow with age, unworn and neglected. Given Seattle's damp climate, the lovely silk-and-lace gown would probably mildew, as well.

Enough self-pity, Lesley decided, and with her natural flair for drama, she squared her shoulders. She wasn't going to let a little thing like a broken engagement get her down. Even losing money on the deposits for the hall and everything else didn't matter. Not really. Her life was full. She had good friends—really good friends. Surely one of them would realize the significance of today and call her. Jo Ann wouldn't forget this was to have been her wedding day and neither would Lori. Lesley couldn't ask for two better friends than her fellow teachers, Jo Ann and Lori. Both would have been her bridesmaids. They'd remember; no doubt they were planning something special to console her. Something unexpected. Something to chase away the blues and make her laugh.

Her mother and stepfather were traveling and probably wouldn't think of it, but that was okay. Her friends would.

The hollow feeling in the pit of her stomach seemed to yawn wider; closing her eyes, Lesley breathed in deeply until the pressure lessened. She refused to give Tony the power to hurt her. The fact that they still worked together was difficult to say the least. Thank heaven, school had been dismissed for the summer the week before and she had three months to regroup and recuperate.

Lesley opened her refrigerator and looked inside, hoping some appetizing little treat would magically appear. The same shriveled head of lettuce, two overripe tomatoes and a soft-looking zucchini stared back at her. Just as well; she didn't have much of an appetite anyway.

Men—who needed them? Lesley shut the refrigerator door. Not her. She refused to become vulnerable to any man ever again.

Several of her friends had tested their matchmaking skills on her in the past few months, but Lesley's attitude was jaded. Whose wouldn't be?

The man she loved, the man she'd dedicated five years of her life to, had announced six months before their wedding that he needed more time. *More time.* Lesley had been incredulous. They'd dated their last year of college, gone through student teaching together. They even worked at the same elementary school, saw each other on a daily basis and then, out of the blue, Tony had insisted he needed more time.

It wasn't until a week later that Lesley discovered *more time* meant he'd fallen head over heels in love with the new first-grade teacher. Within three weeks of meeting April Packard, Tony had broken his engagement to Lesley. If that wasn't bad enough, Tony and April were married a month later, following a whirlwind courtship. Since she was under contract and her savings slim, Lesley couldn't just leave the school; she'd been forced to endure the sight of the happy couple every day since. Every school day, anyhow.

She worked hard at not being bitter, at pretending it was all for the best. If Tony was going to fall in love with another woman, then it was better to have discovered this penchant of his *before* the wedding. She'd heard that over and over from her friends. In fact, she'd heard all the platitudes, tried to believe them, tried to console herself with them.

Except they didn't help.

She hurt. Some nights she wrestled with the loneliness until dawn; the feeling of abandonment nearly suffocated her. It didn't help to realize how happy Tony and April were.

He'd tried to make it up to Lesley. He'd wanted her to assuage his guilt. Because they worked in such close proximity, there was nothing she could do but repeat the platitudes others had given her. For the last months of school, she'd had to make believe a broken heart didn't matter.

But it did.

The last time she'd felt this empty inside had been as a six-year-old child, when her father had arranged for the family to fly to Disneyland in California. Lesley had been excited for weeks. It would've been her first trip in an airplane, her first time away from Washington State. Then, three days before the vacation was to begin, her father had packed his bags and left. He'd gone without warning, without a word of farewell to her, apparently without regret, taking the money they'd saved for the family trip.

Her mother was so trapped in her shock and anger that she hadn't been able to comfort Lesley, who'd felt guilty without knowing why.

As an adult she chose to forgive her father and accept that he was a weak man, the same way she'd decided to absolve Tony of the pain he'd caused her. It would do no good to harbor a grudge or to feed her own discontent.

Although it was easy to acknowledge this on a conscious level, it took more than logic to convince her heart. Twenty-one years had passed since that fateful summer, but the feelings were as painful and as complex now as they'd been to the little girl who missed her daddy.

When neither Jo Ann nor Lori had phoned by noon, her mood sank even lower. Maybe they were thinking she'd forgotten what day it was, Lesley reasoned. Or maybe they didn't feel they should drag up the whole ugly affair. But all Lesley wanted was to do something fun, something that would make her forget how isolated she felt.

Jo Ann wasn't home, so Lesley left an upbeat message. The significance of the day seemed to have slipped past Lori, as well, who was all starry-eyed over a man she'd recently started dating.

"Any chance you can get away for a movie tonight?" Lesley asked.

Lori hemmed and hawed. "Not tonight. Larry's been out of town for the last couple of days and he'll be back this evening. He mentioned dinner. Can we make it later in the week?"

"Sure," Lesley said, as though it didn't matter one way or the other. Far be it from her to remind her best friends that she was suffering the agonies of the jilted. "Have fun."

There must have been some telltale inflection in her voice because Lori picked up on it immediately. "Lesley, are you all right?"

"Of course." It was always *of course*. Always some flippant remark that discounted her unhappiness. "We'll get together later in the week."

They chatted for a few more minutes. When they'd finished, Lesley knew it was up to her to make the best of the day. She couldn't rely on her friends, nor should she.

She mulled over that realization, trying to decide what to do. Attending a movie alone held no appeal, nor did treating herself to dinner in a fancy restaurant. She sighed, swallowing the pain as she so often had before. She was sick of pretending it didn't hurt, tired of being cheerful and glib when her heart was breaking.

A day such as this one called for drastic measures. Nothing got more drastic than a quart of chocolate-chip cookie-dough ice cream and a rented movie.

Lesley's spirits rose. It was perfect. Drowning her sorrows in decadence made up for all that pretended indifference. Men! Who needed them? Not her, Lesley told herself again. Not her.

She reached for her purse and was out the door, filled with purpose.

It was while she was at a stoplight that Lesley saw the billboard. BRIDE WANTED. PHONE 555-1213. At first she was amused. A man advertising for a wife? On a billboard? She'd never heard anything so ridiculous in her life. The guy was either a lunatic or a moron. Probably both. Then again, she reasoned, she wasn't exactly sympathetic to the males of the species these days. She'd been done wrong and she wasn't going to smile and forget it! No, sir. Those days were past.

Still smiling at the billboard, Lesley parked her car at the grocery store lot and headed toward the entrance. Colorful bedding plants, small rosebushes and rhododendrons were sold in the front of the store, and she toyed with the idea of buying more geraniums for her porch planter box.

She noticed the man pacing the front of the automatic glass doors almost immediately. He seemed agitated and impatient, apparently waiting for someone. Thinking nothing more of it, she focused her attention on the hanging baskets of bright pink fuchsia, musing how nice they'd look on her porch.

"Excuse me," the man said when she approached. "Would you happen to have the time?"

"Sure," she said, raising her arm to glance at her watch.

Without warning, the man grabbed her purse, jerking it from her forearm so fast that for a moment Lesley stood frozen with shock and disbelief. She'd just been mugged. By the time she recovered, he'd sprinted halfway across the lot.

"Help! Thief!" she screamed as loudly as she could. Knowing better than to wait for someone to rescue her, she took off at a dead run, chasing the mugger.

He was fast, she'd say that for him, but Lesley hadn't danced her way through all those aerobics classes for nothing. She might not be an Olympic hopeful, but she could hold her own.

The mugger was almost at the street, ready to turn the corner, when another man flew past her. She didn't get a good look at him, other than that he was big and tall and wore a plaid shirt and blue jeans.

"He's got my purse," she shouted after him. Knowing she'd never catch the perpetrator herself, her only chance was the second man. She slowed to a trot in an effort to catch her breath.

To her relief, the second man caught the thief and tackled him to the ground. Lesley's heart leapt to her throat as the pair rolled and briefly struggled. She reached them a moment later, not knowing what to expect. Her rescuer was holding the thief down, and as Lesley watched, he easily retrieved her purse.

"I believe this belongs to you," her rescuer said, handing her the bag.

The mugger kicked for all he was worth, which in Lesley's eyes wasn't much. He was cursing, too, and doing a far more effective job of that.

"That's no way to talk in front of a lady," her hero said calmly, turning the thief onto his stomach and pressing his knee into the middle of his back. The man on the ground groaned and shut up.

A police siren blared in the background.

"Who called the police?" Lesley asked, looking around until she saw a businessman holding a cell phone. "Thanks," she shouted and waved.

The black-and-white patrol car pulled into the parking

lot. A patrolman stepped out. "Can either of you tell me what's going on here?" he asked.

"That man," Lesley said indignantly, pointing to the thief sprawled on the asphalt, "grabbed my purse and took off running. And that man," she said, pointing to the other guy, "caught him."

"Chase Goodman," her white knight said. He stood up, but kept his foot pressed against the thief's back as he nodded formally.

Lesley clutched her handbag to her breast, astonished at how close she'd come to losing everything. Her keys were in her purse, along with her identification, checkbook, money and credit cards. Had she lost all her ID, it would've been a nightmare to replace. Nor would she have felt safe knowing someone had the keys to her home and her car, along with her address. The thought chilled her to the bone.

There seemed to be a hundred questions that needed answering before the police officer escorted the mugger to the station.

"I'm very grateful," Lesley said, studying the man who'd rescued her purse. He was tall—well over six feet—and big. She was surprised anyone that massive could move with such speed. At first glance she guessed he was a bodybuilder, but on closer inspection she decided he wasn't the type who spent his time in a gym. He had a rugged, outdoorsy look that Lesley found strongly appealing. A big, gentle "bear" of a man. A gym would've felt confining to someone like Chase. Adding to his attractiveness were dark brown eyes and a friendly smile.

"My pleasure, Miss…"

"Lesley Campbell. I go by Ms." She paused. "How did you know I'm not married?"

"No ring."

Her thumb absently moved over the groove in her finger where Tony's engagement ring had once been and she nodded. He wasn't wearing one, either.

"Do you do this sort of thing for a living?"

"Excuse me?" Chase smiled at her, looking a bit confused.

"Run after crooks, I mean," Lesley said. "Are you an off-duty policeman or something?"

"No, I work on the Alaska pipeline. I'm visiting Seattle for the next few weeks."

"That explains it," she said.

"Explains what?"

She hadn't realized he'd heard her. "What I was thinking about you. That you're an open-air kind of person." She felt mildly surprised that she'd read him so well. Generally she didn't consider herself especially perceptive.

Her insight appeared to please him because he smiled again. "Would you like to know what I was thinking about you?"

"Sure." She probably shouldn't be so curious, but it wouldn't do any harm.

"You run well, with agility and grace, and you're the first woman I've met in a long while who doesn't have to throw back her head to look up at me."

"That's true enough." Lesley understood what it meant to be tall. She was five-eleven herself and had been the tallest girl in her high school class. Her height had been a curse and yet, in some ways, her greatest asset. Her teachers assumed that because she was taller she should be more mature, smarter, a leader, so she'd been burdened with those expectations; at the same time, she now realized, they'd been a blessing. She *had* learned to be both tactful and authoritative, which served her well as a teacher. However, buying clothes had always been a problem when she was a teenager, along with attracting boys. It was only when she entered her twenties that she decided to be proud of who and what she was. Once she refused to apologize for her height, she seemed to attract the opposite sex. Shortly after that, she'd met Tony. It had never bothered her that he was an inch shorter than she was, nor had it seemed to trouble him.

She and Chase were walking back toward the grocery store. "You're a runner?"

"Heavens, no," Lesley answered, although she was flattered by the assumption.

As they were standing under the hanging fuchsia baskets, Lesley realized they had no reason to continue their discussion. "I'd like to thank you for your help," she said, opening her purse and taking out her wallet.

He placed his hand on hers, his touch gentle but insistent. "I won't take your money."

"I'd never have caught him without you. It's the least I can do."

"I did what anyone would have done."

"Hardly," Lesley countered. The lot had been full of people and no one else had chased the mugger. No one else had been willing to get involved. She'd received plenty of sympathetic looks, but no one other than Chase had helped her.

"If you want to thank me, how about a cup of coffee?"

Lesley's gaze went to the café, situated next to the grocery store in the strip mall. She'd just been mugged, and having coffee with a stranger didn't seem to be an especially brilliant idea.

"I can understand your hesitation, but I assure you I'm harmless."

"All right," Lesley found herself agreeing. Chase smiled and his brown eyes fairly sparkled. She'd hardly ever met a man with more expressive eyes.

When they took a table by the window, the waitress immediately brought menus and rhymed off the specials of the day.

"I'll just have coffee," Lesley said.

"What kind of pie do you have?" Chase wanted to know.

The waitress listed several varieties in a monotone as if she said the same words no less than five hundred times a day.

"Give me a piece of the apple pie and a cup of coffee."

"I'll take a slice of that pie, too," Lesley said. "I shouldn't," she muttered to Chase when the waitress left, "but I'm going to indulge myself." She'd forgo the gourmet ice cream in favor of the pie; later she'd drown her blues in a 1990s Meg Ryan movie, where love seemed to work out right and everything fell neatly into place just before THE END scrolled onto the screen. If ever there was a time she needed to believe in fairy tales, it was today.

"Sure you should," Chase said.

"I know," Lesley said, straightening and looking out the window as she thought about the reason she was pampering herself. To her embarrassment, tears flooded her eyes. She managed to blink them back but not before Chase noticed.

"Is something wrong?"

"Delayed shock, I guess," she said, hoping that sounded logical, and that he'd accept it without further inquiry. Funny, she could go weeks without dwelling on the pain and then the minute school was out and Tony and April weren't around anymore, she started weeping.

"It's just that today was supposed to have been my wedding day," she blurted out. Lesley didn't know what had made her announce this humiliation to a complete stranger.

"What happened?" Chase asked softly. His hand reached for hers, his fingers folding around hers in a comforting way.

"Oh, what usually happens in these situations. Tony met someone else and…well, I guess it was just one of those things. The two of them clicked, and after a whirlwind courtship, they got married. They both seem happy. It's just that…" Her voice faltered and she left the rest unsaid.

The waitress delivered the pie and coffee and, grateful for the interruption, Lesley reached for her purse and took out a tissue. "My friends forgot that today was the day Tony and I'd chosen for the wedding." She sighed. "In retrospect, I don't know if I miss him as much as I miss the idea of the wedding. You know, starting off our marriage with this beautiful celebration, this perfect day…"

He nodded. "And?"

"And I guess I became so involved in getting ready for the wedding that I didn't realize how unhappy and restless Tony had become. When he asked for time to think about everything, I was shocked. I should've known then that something was really wrong, that it wasn't just pre-wedding jitters. As it turned out, it was good old-fashioned guilt. He'd met April— Oh, we all work at the same elementary school," she explained.

"Teachers?"

Lesley nodded. "Anyway, he was attracted to April, and she was attracted to him, and the whole thing got out of control... I'm sure you get the picture."

"Yes, I do. It seems to me that your friend's a fool."

Lesley laughed, but it sounded more like a hiccup. "We're still friends, or at least he tries to be my friend. I don't know what I feel—not anymore. It all happened months ago, but it still hurts and I can't seem to put it behind me."

"It's only human that you should feel hurt and betrayed, especially today."

"Yes, I know, but it's much more than that. Tony felt terrible and with all of us working together, well, that just makes it more difficult. I asked the school district for a transfer but when Tony heard about it, he asked me not to. He didn't think I should disrupt my life and why can't we still be friends, blah, blah, blah. The problem is he feels so guilty."

"As well he should."

"I knew I was making a mistake, but I withdrew the request." Lesley wasn't sure why she was discussing her broken engagement, especially with a stranger. It felt better to speak of it somehow, to lift some of the weight of her unhappiness.

Lesley lowered her eyes and took a deep breath. "Listen, I'm sorry to burden you with this," she said in a calmer tone.

"No, you needed to talk and I'm honored that you told me. I mean that. Have you been seeing anyone since?"

"No." Lesley sliced off a bite of her pie. "Lately I find myself feeling cynical about relationships. I'm almost convinced love, marriage and all that simply aren't worth the effort—although I would like children someday," she added thoughtfully.

"Cynical, huh? Does that mean you don't date at all? Not *ever?*"

"I don't date and I don't intend to for a long time. I'm not feeling very sympathetic toward men, either. On the way to the store just now, I saw the most ridiculous billboard. Some guy's advertising for a bride, and instead of feeling sorry for him, I laughed."

"Why would you feel sorry for the guy?" Chase asked. He'd already finished his pie and was cradling the ceramic mug of coffee with both hands.

"Think about it. What kind of man advertises for a wife? One who's old and ugly and desperate, right?"

"What makes you say that?"

"If he can't find a wife any other way, there must be something wrong with him. If that isn't cause for sympathy, I don't know what is."

"You think the women who respond will be old and ugly, as well?" Chase asked, frowning. "And desperate?"

"Heavens, I wouldn't know. I don't understand men. I've tried, but I seem to be missing something. Tony was the only man I ever considered marrying and...well, I've already told you what happened to *that* relationship."

"In other words, you'd never think of dating a man who advertised for a wife?" Chase asked.

"Never," she assured him emphatically. "But my guess is that he'll get plenty of takers."

"The old coot's probably lonely and looking for a little female companionship," Chase supplied.

"Exactly," she agreed, smiling as she mentally envisioned the man who was so desperate he'd advertise for a wife. "Like I said, I couldn't even feel a little empathy for the guy. That's how cynical I am now."

"Yes, you told me you laughed." He paused. "You think other women will laugh, too?"

Lesley shrugged. "I don't know. Perhaps." Women like herself, maybe. The jaded and emotionally crippled ones.

"How long will you be in town?" she asked, deciding to change the subject. This conversation was becoming uncomfortable—and it wasn't revealing her in the best light.

"Another two and a half weeks. I can't take city living much longer than that. The noise gets to me."

"You've been to Seattle before?"

"I come every year about this time. I generally visit the Pacific Northwest but I'm partial to San Francisco, too. By the end of my vacation I'm more than ready to return to the tundra."

"I've heard Alaska is very beautiful," Lesley said conversationally.

"There's a peace there, an untouched beauty that never fails to reach me. I've lived there all my life and it still fascinates me."

Lesley was mesmerized by his words and the serenity she sensed in him. "What town are you from?"

"It's a little place in the northern part of the state called Twin Creeks. I doubt you've heard of it. I won't kid you—the winters are harsh, and there isn't a lot to do for entertainment. By mid-December daylight's counted in minutes, not hours. By contrast, the sun's out well past midnight at this time of the year."

"Other than your job, how do you occupy yourself in the dead of winter?" It fascinated her that someone would actually choose to live in such an extreme environment.

"Read and study mostly. I do a bit of writing now and then."

"I guess you've got all the peace and quiet you need for that."

"I do," he said. "In fact, sometimes a little too much..."

They'd both finished their pie and coffee and the waitress returned to offer refills. Lesley didn't entirely understand his comment, and let it pass. This was probably the reason he came to Seattle every year, to kick up his heels and party. Yet he didn't look like the party type. His idea of the urban wild life was probably drinking beer in a hot tub, Lesley thought, smiling to herself.

"What's funny?"

Lesley instantly felt guilty. She was being more condescending than she'd realized. Chase was a gentleman who'd kindly stepped in to help when all those around her had chosen to ignore her plight.

"Thank you again," Lesley said, reaching for the tab.

"No," Chase told her, removing the slip from her fingers, "thank *you* for the pleasure of your company."

"Please, picking up the cost of your pie and coffee is such a little thing to do to thank you for what you did. Don't deny me that."

He nodded, giving it back to her. "On one condition."

Lesley left a tip on the table, then walked over to the cash register and paid the bill before Chase could change his mind—and before he could set his condition.

"What's that?" she asked, dropping the change in her coin purse.

"That you have dinner with me."

Her first inclination was to refuse. She wasn't interested in dating and hadn't been in months. She'd told him as much. She wasn't ready to get involved in a relationship, not even with a man who was a tourist and who'd be out of her life in a few weeks. Besides, he was a stranger. Other than his name and a few other details, what did she know about him?

He must have seen the doubt in her eyes.

"You choose the time and place and I'll meet you there," he suggested. "You're wise to be cautious."

Still she hesitated.

"I promise I won't stand you up the way Todd did."

"Tony," she corrected. "And that's not exactly—" She stopped, amused and frustrated that she found herself wanting to defend Tony.

"One dinner," Chase added. "All right?"

Lesley sighed, feeling herself weakening. If she declined, she'd be stuck watching Meg Ryan and Tom Hanks in her sweats in front of the TV—and probably gobbling ice cream straight from the container, despite the pie she'd just had. The image wasn't a pretty one.

"All right," she said, with a decisiveness she didn't feel. "Six o'clock, at Salty's at Redondo Beach."

"I'll make reservations."

"No," she said quickly. "Not Salty's." That had been her and Tony's restaurant. "Let's try the Seattle waterfront. I'll meet you in front of the aquarium at six and we can find someplace to eat around there."

His smile touched his eyes as he nodded. "I'll be there."

Two

Chase Goodman stepped out of the shower and reached for a towel. He'd turned on the television and was standing in the bathroom doorway listening to snippets of news while he dried his hair.

He dressed in slacks and a crisp blue shirt, hoping Lesley didn't expect him to wear a tie. Gray slacks and a decent dress shirt was as good as he got. A regular tie felt like a hangman's noose and he'd look silly in a bow tie. He didn't usually worry about what a woman thought of his appearance, but he liked Lesley.

That was the problem. He liked her, *really* liked her. The hollow feeling hadn't left his stomach since the moment they'd parted. It was the kind of sensation a man gets when he knows something's about to happen, something important. Something good.

He liked that she was tall and not the least bit apologetic about it. He preferred a woman he didn't have to worry about hurting every time he held her. His size intimidated a lot of women, but obviously not Lesley. She had grit, too; it wasn't every woman who'd race after a mugger.

Objectively, he supposed, Lesley wasn't stunningly beautiful nor did she have perfect features. Her face was a little too square, and her hair a dusty blond. Not quite brown and not quite fair, but somewhere in between. Maybe it wasn't the conventional pale blond most guys went for, but it reminded him of the color of the midnight sun at dusk.

Her eyes appealed to him, too. He couldn't remember seeing a darker shade of brown, almost as dark as his own.

Chase was physically attracted to Lesley and the strength of that attraction took him by surprise. It confused and unsettled him. He'd come to Seattle to find himself a wife, had gone about it in a direct and straightforward manner. You couldn't get more direct than renting a billboard! And yet he'd met Lesley by complete chance. Not only that, his billboard clearly hadn't impressed her, he thought wryly.

Nonetheless, he wanted to develop a relationship with Lesley, but he was worried. Lesley was vulnerable and hurting just now. If he romanced her, even convinced her to marry him, he'd never be certain he hadn't taken advantage of her and her battered heart. Even worse, she might feel he had. Regardless, nothing could dampen his anticipation of their evening together. That was all he wanted. One evening, and then he'd be better able to judge. Afterward he could decide what he was going to do. If anything.

Sitting on the edge of the bed, Chase reached for the TV remote and turned up the volume, hoping the newscaster would take his mind off the woman who attracted him so strongly. Not that it was likely. Not with that swift emotional kick he'd felt the minute he saw her.

* * *

"Hiya, doll," Daisy Sullivan said, letting herself into Lesley's place after knocking a couple of times. "I'm not interrupting anything, am I?" Daisy lived in the house adjacent to Lesley's rental and had become one of her best friends.

"Sit down," Lesley said, aiming an earring toward her left ear. "Do you want some iced tea?"

"Sure, but I'll get it." Lesley watched as her neighbor walked into the kitchen and took two glasses from the cupboard. She poured them each some tea from the pitcher in the fridge. "I'm glad to see you're going out," Daisy said, handing Lesley one of them. "I don't think it's a good idea for you to spend this evening alone."

Lesley felt warmed at this evidence that someone had remembered today's significance. "The date slipped by Jo Ann and Lori."

"So what are you doing? Taking yourself out to dinner?" Daisy was nothing if not direct. Her neighbor didn't have time to waste being subtle. She attended computer classes during the day and worked weekends as a cocktail waitress. Lesley admired her friend for taking control of her life, for getting out of a rotten marriage and struggling to do what was right for herself and her two boys.

Her neighbor was a little rough around the edges, maybe a little *too* honest and direct, but she was one heck of a friend. Besides school and a job, she was a good mom to Kevin and Eric. Daisy's mother watched the boys during the daytime now that school was out, but it wasn't an ideal situation. The boys, seven and eight, were a handful. A teenage girl from the neighborhood filled in on the nights Daisy worked; Lesley occasionally helped out, as well.

"How does this dress look?" Lesley asked, ignoring Daisy's question. She twirled to give Daisy a look at the simple blue-and-white-patterned dress. The skirt flared out at the knees as she spun around.

"New?" Daisy asked, helping herself to a few seedless red grapes from the fruit bowl on the table. She held one delicately between manicured nails and popped it into her mouth.

"Relatively new," Lesley said, glancing away. "I've got a date."

"A *real* date?"

"Yes, I met him this afternoon. I was mugged and Chase—that's his name—caught the thief for me."

"In other words, Chase chased him."

"Exactly." She smiled at Daisy's small joke.

"You sure you can trust this guy?"

Lesley took a moment to analyze what she knew about Chase Goodman. Her impression was of strength, eyes that smiled, a gentle, fun-loving spirit. He was six-four, possibly taller, his chest was wide and his shoulders were broad. Despite his size, he ran with efficiency and speed. Her overall impression of Chase was of total, unequivocal masculinity. The type of man who worked hard, lived hard and loved hard.

Her cheeks flushed with color at the thought of Chase in bed...

"I can trust him," Lesley answered. It was herself she needed to question. If she was still in love with Tony, she shouldn't be attracted to Chase, but she was. She barely knew the man, yet she felt completely safe with him, completely at ease. She must, otherwise she wouldn't have blurted out the humiliating details of her broken engagement. She'd never done that with anyone else.

"I'm meeting Chase at the Seattle aquarium at six," Lesley elaborated.

"Hmm. Sounds like he might be hero material," Daisy said, reaching for another cluster of grapes after she stood. "I've got to get dinner on for the boys. Let me know how everything goes, will you? I'll be up late studying, so if the light's on, let yourself in."

"I will," Lesley promised.

"Have fun," Daisy said on her way out the door.

That was something Lesley intended to do.

At 6:10, Lesley was standing outside the waterfront aquarium waiting. She checked her watch every fifteen seconds until she saw Chase coming toward her, walking down the hill, his steps hurried. When he saw her, he raised his hand and waved.

Relief flooded through Lesley. The restless sensation in the pit of her stomach subsided and her doubts fled.

"Sorry I'm late," he said, after dashing across the busy intersection. "I had a problem finding a place to park."

"It doesn't matter," Lesley said, and it didn't now that he was here. Now that he was grinning at her in a way she found irresistible.

He smiled down at her and said in a low, caressing voice, "You look nice."

"Thank you. You do, too."

"Are you hungry?" he asked.

"A little. How about you?" Pedestrian traffic was heavy and by tacit agreement, they moved to a small fountain and sat on a park bench. She didn't explain that her appetite had been practically nonexistent ever since she'd lost Tony.

"Some, but I've never been to the waterfront before," Chase said. "Would you mind if we played tourist for a while?"

"I'd like it. Every year I make a point of bringing my class down here. They love the aquarium and the fact that some of the world's largest octopuses live in Elliott Bay. The kids are fascinated by them."

They stood and Chase reached for her hand, entwining their fingers. It felt oddly comfortable to be linked to him. They began to walk, their progress slowed by the crowds.

"Other than the aquarium, my kids' favorite stop is Pier 54," she said.

"What's on Pier 54?"

"A long row of tourist shops. Or in other words, one of the world's largest collections of junk and tacky souvenirs."

"Sounds interesting."

"To third-graders it's heaven. Imagine what their parents think when the children come home carrying a plastic shrunken head with *Seattle* stamped across it. I shouldn't be so flippant—it's not all like that. There's some interesting Northwest Indian and Eskimo art on display, if you want to walk there."

"Sure. Isn't that the ferry terminal?" he asked, pointing toward a large structure beyond the souvenir shops.

"Yes. The Washington State Ferries terminal. Did you know we have the largest ferry system in the world? If you're looking for a little peace and some beautiful scenery, hop on a ferry. For a while after Tony told me about April, I used to come down here and take the Winslow ferry over to Bainbridge Island. There's something about being on the water that soothed me."

"Would you take a ferry with me sometime?" Chase asked.

"I'd like that very much," she replied. His hand squeezed hers and she congratulated herself on how even she managed to keep her voice. Countless times over the past few months she'd ridden the ferry, sat with a cup of coffee or stood on the deck. She wasn't sure exactly what it was about being on the water that she found so peaceful, but it helped more than anything else.

They walked along the pier and in and out of several of the tourist shops, chatting as they went. It'd been a long time since Lesley had laughed so easily or so often and it felt wonderful.

As they strolled past the ferry terminal, Lesley asked, "Have you been to Pioneer Square? There's a fabulous restaurant close by if Italian food interests you."

"Great!"

"I'll tell you all about Pioneer Square while we eat, then," Lesley said, leading the way. The restaurant was busy, but they were seated after a ten-minute wait.

No sooner were they handed menus than a basket of warm bread appeared, along with a relish tray, overflowing with fresh vegetables and a variety of black and green olives.

"Pioneer Square is actually the oldest part of Seattle," Lesley explained, somewhat conscious of sounding like a teacher in front of her class—or maybe a tour guide. "It was originally an Indian village, and later a rowdy frontier settlement and gold rush town."

"What's all the business about mail-order brides?"

Chase asked while dipping a thick slice of the bread in olive oil and balsamic vinegar.

"You heard about that?"

"I wouldn't have if it hadn't been for a TV documentary I saw. I only caught the end of it, though."

"The brides are a historical fact. Back in the 1860s, Seattle had a severe shortage of women. To solve the problem, a well-intentioned gentleman by the name of Asa Mercer traveled East and recruited a number of New England women to come to Seattle. These weren't ladies of the night, either, but enterprising souls who were well-educated, cultured and refined. The ideal type of woman to settle the wild frontier."

"What would Asa Mercer have said to induce these women to give up the comforts of civilization? How'd he get them to agree to travel to the Wild West?" Chase asked, setting aside his bread and focusing his full attention on her.

"It might surprise you to know he didn't have the least bit of difficulty convincing these women. First, there was a real shortage of marriageable men due to the Civil War. Many of these women were facing spinsterhood. Asa Mercer's proposition might well have been their only chance of finding a husband."

"I see."

Lesley didn't understand his frown. "What's wrong?"

"Nothing," he was quick to assure her. "Go on, tell me what happened."

"The first women landed at the waterfront on May 16, 1864. I remember the day because May 16 is my birthday. Seattle was a riproaring town and I imagine these women must've wondered what they were letting themselves in for. But it didn't take them long to settle in and bring touches of civilization to Seattle. They did such a good job that two years later a second group of brides was imported."

"They all got married, then?"

"All but one," Lesley told him. "Lizzie Ordway. Eventually she became the superintendent of public schools and a women's activist. It was because of her and other women like her that Washington State granted women the right to vote a full ten years ahead of the constitutional amendment."

"Now you're the one who's frowning," Chase commented.

"I was just thinking that... I don't know," she said, feeling foolish.

"What were you thinking?" Chase asked gently.

She didn't want to say it, didn't want to voice the fears that gnawed at her. That she was afraid she'd end up like Lizzie, unmarried and alone. These few details were all Lesley knew about the woman's life. She wondered if Lizzie had found fulfillment in the women's suffrage movement. If she'd found contentment as a spinster, when her friends had married one by one until she was the only one left. The only one who hadn't been able to find a husband.

"Lesley?" Chase prompted.

"It's nothing," Lesley said, forcing herself to smile.

The waiter came just then, to Lesley's relief, and they ordered. Their dinner was wonderful, but she'd expected nothing less from this restaurant.

Afterward, they caught the streetcar and returned to the waterfront. On the short ride, Lesley regaled Chase with the history of the vintage streetcars, which had been brought from Australia.

"This is Tasmanian mahogany?" Chase repeated.

"And white ash."

"I'm impressed by how well you know Seattle's history," Chase said when they climbed off the streetcar.

"I'm a teacher, remember?"

Chase grinned and it was a sexy, make-your-knees-weak sort of smile. "I was just wondering why they didn't have anyone as beautiful as you when I was in school. I only ever seemed to have stereotypical old-maid teachers."

Lesley laughed, although his words struck close to home. Too close for comfort.

"How about taking that ferry ride?" Chase suggested next.

"Sure." Lesley was game as long as it meant their evening wouldn't end. She didn't want it to be over so soon, especially since she'd done most of the talking. There were a number of questions she wanted to ask Chase about Alaska. Normally Lesley didn't dominate a conversation this way, but Chase had seemed genuinely interested.

As luck would have it, the Winslow Ferry was docked and they walked right on. While Lesley found them a table, Chase ordered two lattes.

He slid into the seat across from her and handed her the paper cup. Lesley carefully pried open the lid.

"I've been doing all the talking," she said, leaning back. "What can you tell me about Alaska?"

"Plenty," he murmured. "Did you know Alaska has the westernmost and easternmost spots in the country?"

"No," Lesley admitted, squinting while she tried to figure out how that was possible. She guessed it had to do with the sweep of islands that stretched nearly to the Asian coastline.

"We've got incredible mountains, too. Seventeen of the twenty highest mountains in the entire United States are in Alaska."

"I love mountains. When we're finished with our drinks, let's stand out on the deck. I want to show you the Olympics. They're so beautiful with their jagged peaks, especially at this time of night, just before the sun sets."

A short while later they went onto the windswept deck and walked over to the railing. The sun touched the snowcapped peaks, and a pale pink sky, filled with splashes of gold, spilled across the skyline.

"It's a beautiful night," Lesley said, holding on to the railing. The scent of the water was fresh and stimulating. The wind blew wildly around her, disarranging her hair. She tried several times to anchor it behind her ears, but the force of the wind was too strong.

Chase stood behind her in an effort to block the gusts. He slipped his arms around her shoulders and rested his jaw against the top of her head.

Lesley felt warm and protected in the shelter of his arms. There was a feeling of exquisite peace about being in this place with this man, on this day. This stranger had helped her more in the few hours they'd been together than all the wisdom and counsel her family and friends had issued in months.

"Let him go," Chase whispered close to her ear.

A thousand times Lesley had tried to do exactly that. More often than she cared to count, more often than she wanted to remember. It wasn't only her day-to-day life that was interwoven with Tony's, but her future, as well.

Everything had been centered on their lives together. She couldn't walk into her home and not be confronted by memories of their five-year courtship.

The bookcases in her living room had been purchased with Tony. They'd picked out the sofa and love seat together, and a hundred other things, as well. Even her wardrobe had been bought with him in mind. The dress she was wearing this evening had been purchased to wear to a special dinner she and Tony had shared.

"I want to go back in now," she said stiffly, and wondered if Chase could hear her or if he'd chosen to ignore her request. "It's getting chilly."

He released her with obvious reluctance, and in other circumstances his hesitation would have thrilled her. But not now, not when it felt as if her heart were melting inside her and she was fighting back a fresh stab of pain.

"I'm sorry," she said when they returned to their seats.

"Don't be," Chase said gently. "I shouldn't have pressured you."

Lesley struggled for the words to explain, but she could find none. Some days her grief was like a room filled with musty shadows and darker corners. Other days it was like a long, winding path full of ruts. The worst part of traveling this road was that she'd been so alone, so lost and afraid.

The ferry docked at Winslow and they walked off and waited in the terminal before boarding again. Neither seemed in the mood to talk, but it was a peaceful kind of silence. Lesley felt no compulsion to fill it with mindless conversation and apparently neither did Chase.

By the time they arrived back at the Seattle waterfront, the sun had set. Chase held her hand as they took the walkway down to street level, his mind in turmoil. He should never have asked Lesley to let go of the man she loved. It had been a mistake to pressure her, one he had no intention of repeating.

"Where are we going?" she asked as he led her down the pier. The crowds remained thick, the traffic along the sidewalk heavy even at this time of night. The scents of fried fish and the sea mingled.

"Down there," he said, pointing to a length of deserted pier.

It was a testament to her trust that she didn't seem at all nervous. "There's nothing down there."

"I know. I'm going to kiss you, Lesley, and I prefer to do it without half of Seattle watching me."

"Aren't you taking a lot for granted?" she asked, more amused than offended.

"Perhaps." But that didn't stop him.

Not giving her the opportunity to argue, he brought her with him and paused only when he was assured of their privacy. Without another word, he turned her toward him. He took her hands and guided her arms upward and around his neck. He felt a moment of hesitation, but it was quickly gone.

He circled her waist with his arms and pulled her to him. At the feel of her body next to his, Chase sighed, marveling when Lesley did, too. Hers was a little sigh. One that said she wasn't sure she was doing the right thing.

He smelled her faint flowery scent. It was a sensual moment, their bodies pressed against each other. It was a spiritual moment, as well, as though they were two lost souls reaching toward each other.

For long minutes, they simply held each other. Chase

had never been with a woman like this. It wasn't desire that prompted him to take her into his arms, but something far stronger. Something he couldn't put words to or identify on a conscious level.

He longed to protect Lesley, shield her from more pain, and at the same time he was looking to her to end *his* loneliness.

Chase waged a debate on what to do next—kiss her as he'd claimed he would or hold her against him, comfort her and then release her.

He couldn't not kiss her. Not when she felt so good in his arms.

Slowly he lowered his head, giving her ample opportunity to turn away from him. His heart felt as if it would burst wide open when she closed her eyes and brought her mouth to his.

Chase wanted this kiss, wanted it more intensely than he could remember wanting anything. That scared him and he brushed his lips briefly over hers. It was a light kiss, the kind of kiss a woman gives a man when she's teasing him. The kind a man gives a woman when he's trying to avoid kissing her.

Or when he's afraid he wants her too much.

He should've known it wouldn't be enough to satisfy either of them. Lesley blinked uncertainly and he tried again, this time nibbling at her slightly parted lips.

This wasn't enough, either. If anything, it created a need for more. Much more.

The third time he kissed her, he opened his mouth and as the kiss deepened, Chase realized he'd made another mistake. The hollow feeling in his stomach returned—the feeling that fate was about to knock him for a loop.

Sensation after sensation rippled through him and his sigh was replaced with a groan. Not a groan of need or desire, but of awakening. He felt both excited and terrified. Strangely certain and yet confused.

Lesley groaned, too, and tightened her hold on him. She'd felt it, too. She must have.

His hands bracketed her face as he lifted his head. This wasn't what he expected or wanted. He'd feared this would happen, that he'd be hungry for her, so hungry it demanded every ounce of strength he possessed not to kiss her again.

They drew apart as if they were both aware they'd reached the limit, that continuing meant they'd go further than either of them was prepared to deal with just then. Their bottom lips clung and they pressed their foreheads together.

"I..." He couldn't think of any words that adequately conveyed his feelings.

Lesley closed her eyes and he eased his lips closer to hers.

"I want to see you again," Chase said once he'd found his voice, once he knew he could speak without making a fool of himself.

"Yes" came her breathless reply.

"A movie?" That was the first thing that came to his mind, although it was singularly unimaginative.

"When?"

"Tomorrow." Waiting longer than a few hours would have been a test of his patience.

"Okay. What time?"

He didn't know. It seemed a bit presumptuous to suggest a matinee, but waiting any longer than noon to see her again seemed impossible.

"I'll give you my phone number," she said. "And my cell."

"I'll call you in the morning and we can talk then."

"Yes," she agreed.

"I'll walk you to your car."

He didn't dare take hold of her hand or touch her. He'd never felt this way with a woman, as if he'd lose control simply brushing her lips with his. All she needed to do was to sigh that soft womanly sigh that said she wanted him and it would've been all over, right then and there.

They didn't need to walk far. Lesley had parked in a slot beneath the viaduct across the street from the aquarium. He lingered outside her door.

"Thank you," she whispered, not looking at him.

"Dinner was my pleasure."

"I didn't mean for dinner." She looked at him then and raised her hand, holding it against his face. Softly, unexpectedly, she pressed her mouth to his.

"I...don't know if I would've made it through this day without you."

He wanted to argue with that. She was strong, far stronger than she gave herself credit for.

"I'm glad I could help," he said finally, when he could think of no way to describe the strength he saw in her without making it sound trite. He wished he could reassure her that the man she loved had been a fool to let her go, but she didn't want to hear that, either. Those were the words he knew others had said to her, the counsel she'd been given by family and friends.

"I'll wait to hear from you," she said, unlocking her car door.

He'd be waiting, too, until a respectable amount of time had elapsed so he could phone her.

"Thank you again," she said, silently communicating far more than thanks. She closed the door and started the engine. Chase stepped aside as she pulled out of the parking space and stood there until her car had disappeared into the night. Then he walked to his own.

Three

The phone in his room rang at eight the next morning. Chase had been up for hours, had eaten breakfast and leisurely read the paper. After years of rising early, he'd never learned to sleep past six.

The phone rang a second time. It couldn't possibly be Lesley—he hadn't mentioned the name of his hotel— yet he couldn't help hoping.

"Hello," he answered crisply.

"Mr. Goodman, this is the answering service." The woman sounded impatient and more than a little frazzled.

"Someone responded to the ad," Chase guessed. He'd nearly forgotten about the billboard.

"Someone!" the woman burst out. "We've had nearly five hundred calls in the last twenty-four hours, including inquiries from two television stations, the *Seattle Times* and four radio stations. Our staff isn't equipped to deal with this kind of response."

"Five hundred calls." Chase was shocked. He'd never dreamed his advertisement would receive such an overwhelming response.

"Our operators have been bombarded with inquiries, Mr. Goodman."

"How can I possibly answer so many calls?" The mere thought of being expected to contact that many women on his own was overwhelming.

"I suggest you hire someone to weed through the replies. I'm sorry, but I don't think any of us dreamed there'd be such an unmanageable number."

"You!" Chase was astonished himself. "I'll make arrangements this morning."

"We'd appreciate it if you'd come and collect the messages as soon as possible."

"I'll be there directly," Chase promised.

Five hundred responses, he mused after he'd replaced the receiver. It seemed incredible. Absurd. Unbelievable. He'd never guessed there were that many women who'd even consider such a thing. And according to the answering service, the calls hadn't stopped, either. There were more coming in every minute.

He reached for his car keys and was ready to leave when a knock sounded at the door. When he opened it, he discovered a newswoman and a man with a camera on the other side.

"You're Chase Goodman?" the woman asked. She was slight and pretty and he recognized her from the newscast the night before. She was a TV reporter, and although he couldn't remember her name, her face was familiar.

"I'm Chase Goodman," he answered, eyeing the man with the camera. "What can I do for you?"

"The same Chase Goodman who rented the billboard off Denny Way?"

"Yes."

She smiled then. "I'm Becky Bright from KYGN-TV and this is Steve Dalton, my cameraman. Would you mind if I asked you a few questions? I promise we won't take much of your time."

Chase couldn't see any harm in that, but he didn't like the idea of someone sticking a camera in his face. He hesitated, then decided, "I suppose that would be all right."

"Great." The reporter walked into his hotel room, pulled out a chair and instructed Chase to sit down. He did, but he didn't take his eye off the cameraman. A series of bright lights nearly blinded him.

"Sorry," Becky said apologetically. "I should've warned you about the glare. Now, tell me, Mr. Goodman, what prompted you to advertise for a wife?"

Chase held up his hand to shield his eyes. "Ah... I'm from Alaska."

"Alaska," she repeated, reaching for his arm and moving it away from his face.

"I'm only going to be in town a few weeks, so I wanted to make the most of my time," he elaborated, squinting. "I'm looking for a wife, and it seemed like a good idea to be as direct and straightforward as I could. I didn't want any misunderstanding about my intentions."

"Have you had any responses?"

Chase shook his head, still incredulous. "I just got off the phone with the answering service and they've been flooded with calls. They said there've been over five hundred."

"That surprises you?"

"Sure does. I figured I'd be lucky to find a handful of women willing to move to Alaska. I live outside Prudhoe Bay."

"The women who've applied know this?"

"Yes. I left the pertinent details with the answering service as a sort of screening technique. Only those who were willing to accept my conditions were to leave their names and phone numbers."

"And five hundred have done that?"

"Apparently so. I was on my way to the agency just now."

"How do you intend to interview five hundred or more women?"

Chase rubbed the side of his jaw. This situation was quickly getting out of hand. "I'm hoping to hire an assistant as soon as I can. This whole thing has gone *much* further than I expected."

"If you were to speak to the women who've answered your ad, what would you say?"

Chase didn't think well on his feet, especially when he was cornered by a fast-talking reporter and a cameraman who seemed intent on blinding him. "I guess I'd ask them to be patient. I promise to respond to every call, but it might take me a few days."

"Will you be holding interviews yourself?"

Chase hadn't thought this far ahead. His original idea had been to meet every applicant for dinner, so they could get to know each other in a nonthreatening, casual atmosphere, and then proceed, depending on how they felt about him and how he felt about them. All of that had changed now. "I suppose I'll be meeting them personally," he muttered reluctantly. "A lot of them, anyway."

Becky stood and the lights dimmed. "It's been a

pleasure talking to you, Mr. Goodman. We'll be running this on the noon news and later on the five o'clock edition, if you're interested in seeing yourself on television."

"So soon?"

"We might even do a follow-up report after you've selected your bride, but I'll have to wait until I talk that over with my producer. We'd appreciate an exclusive. Can we count on you for that?"

"Ah…sure."

"Great." She beamed him a game-show-host smile.

"Before you go," Chase said, gathering his wits, "how'd you know where to find me?" He'd purposely made arrangements with the answering service to avoid this very thing.

"Easy," Becky said, sticking her pad and pen inside her purse. "I contacted the billboard company. They told me where to reach you."

Chase opened the door for the two, feeling very much like an idiot. He should never have agreed to the interview. They'd caught him off guard, before he realized what he was doing. If anything, this meeting was likely to generate additional calls and he already had more than he knew how to deal with.

Chase slumped onto the bed. He'd tried to be honest and fair. He wanted a wife. For thirty-three years he'd been content to live and work alone, waiting until he could offer a woman a decent life. He was finished with that.

The shortage of women in Alaska was well-known, especially in the far north. When Lesley had told him the details about those Seattle brides back in the 1860s, he felt a certain kinship with Asa Mercer and the desperate, lonely men who'd put up the money for such a venture.

Lesley had told him Mercer hadn't had much difficulty convincing women to move west. That had surprised him, but not as much as the response his own ad had generated.

Lesley.

He'd meant to tell her about the billboard that first afternoon. But then she'd mentioned it herself and implied that anyone who'd advertise for a wife was crazy and pathetic. He'd been afraid she'd never agree to their dinner if she'd known he was that man.

He reached for the phone, intending to call her right then to explain. He fumbled for her phone number inside his wallet and unfolded it, placing it on the nightstand. After punching the first four numbers in quick succession, he changed his mind and hung up. This sort of thing was best said face-to-face. He only hoped she'd be more inclined to think well of him now that she knew him better.

He'd wait until a decent hour and contact her, he decided. His one hope was that she wouldn't watch the noon news.

Lesley woke happy. At least she thought this feeling was happiness. All she knew was that she'd slept through the entire night and when morning came, the dark cloud of despair that had hung over her the past few months had lifted. Her heart felt lighter, her head clearer, her spirit whole.

She wasn't falling in love with Chase. Not by a long shot. But he'd helped her look past the pain she'd been walking under; he'd eased her toward the sun's warmth.

With Chase she'd laughed again and for that alone she'd always be grateful.

She showered and twisted her hair into a French braid, then brewed a pot of coffee. While reading the paper, she decided to bake chocolate-chip cookies. Eric and Kevin, Daisy's two boys, would be thrilled.

Chase might enjoy them, too.

She smiled as she held the coffee cup in front of her lips, her elbows braced on the kitchen table. No point in kidding herself. She was baking those cookies for him. Later she'd suggest an outing to Paradise on Mount Rainier.

True, Eric and Kevin would appreciate their share, but it was Chase she was hoping to impress. Chase she was looking forward to hearing from again. Chase who dominated her thoughts all morning.

The cookies were cooling on the counter when Daisy let herself in.

"Say, what's going on here?" she asked, helping herself to a cookie.

"I don't know. I felt the urge to bake this morning."

Daisy pulled out a chair. "It's the nesting instinct. Mark my words, sweetie, those ol' hormones are kicking in."

Lesley paused, her hand holding a spatula that held a cookie. "I beg your pardon?"

"You're how old now? Twenty-five, twenty-six?"

"Twenty-seven."

"A lot of your friends are engaged or married. You've probably got girlfriends with kids."

"Yes," Lesley admitted, agreeably enough, "but that doesn't mean anything."

"Who are you trying to fool? Not me! As far as I'm

concerned, marriage and a family were the big attraction with Tony. He was never your type and we both know it. What you were looking forward to was settling down, getting pregnant and doing the mother thing."

"We agreed not to discuss Tony, remember?" Lesley reminded her neighbor stiffly. Her former fiancé was a subject she chose to avoid whenever possible with her friends, especially with Daisy, who'd insisted from the first that Tony was all wrong for her.

"*You* agreed we wouldn't," Daisy muttered, chewing the cookie, "but I'll respect your wishes as long as you fill me in on your date last night."

Lesley smiled. "Ah, yes, my date."

"You must've gotten back late. I didn't go into work at the bar yesterday because I had to study and I wasn't through until after midnight and I didn't hear you come home."

Lesley hadn't stopped to chat with Daisy, fearing that sharing her experience would somehow diminish it. She'd gone to bed almost immediately, wanting to mull over her time with Chase, put some perspective on it, luxuriate in the memory of their kisses.

She'd intended to think about all that. Instead, she'd fallen asleep almost immediately. Even now she wasn't sure how to interpret their evening together.

"Did you have a good time?" Daisy asked.

"Wonderful. We walked along the waterfront, and then went to dinner." She didn't mention the ferry ride. She couldn't. It was too special to share even with Daisy.

She didn't know what, exactly, had happened between them, only that something had. Whatever it was, she'd allowed it. Had participated in it, and in the end couldn't deny him or herself the pleasure of those kisses.

No one had ever kissed her the way Chase had, gently, with such infinite care, such tenderness. He'd kissed her the way a woman dreams of being kissed, dreams of being held. Trying to explain that was beyond Lesley. She had no idea where to even begin.

Daisy yawned with great exaggeration. "Sounds like a boring date if you ask me."

"Maybe, but I've never had two men fight over me with switchblades the way you did."

"Both of 'em were staggering drunk. Besides, I had no interest in dating either one. After being married to Brent for five years, why would I want to involve myself with another biker wannabe? Charlie had the police there so fast my head spun. Good thing, too."

Personally, Lesley believed Charlie the bartender had a crush on Daisy, but she'd never said as much. He was a nice guy and he looked out for her neighbor, but in Lesley's opinion, his feelings were more than just friendship for a fellow employee.

"Don't sidetrack me," Daisy insisted. "We were talking about you and Chase. That's his name, isn't it?"

Lesley nodded. "There's not much more to say. I already told you I had a nice time."

"I believe you described it as *wonderful*. You seeing him again?"

"We're going to a movie…at least I think we are. He mentioned it last night, but we didn't discuss the time. And he didn't say anything about it when he phoned a few minutes ago."

"So he's already called again?"

Lesley tried not to show how pleased she was. Chase had seemed distracted, but there was no disguising the warmth in his voice. She hoped he'd tell her whatever was troubling him when he picked her up that evening. He'd asked for her address and Lesley had no qualms about giving it to him.

"What's this?" Daisy asked, reaching across the table to a stack of mail and pulling out a catalog.

"A knitting catalog," Lesley said, putting the cookie sheets in her sink to cool.

"When did you start knitting?" Daisy asked, slowly flipping through the pages.

"A couple of months ago."

"Aha! The nesting instinct strikes again."

"Don't be ridiculous," Lesley said impatiently. She walked onto her back porch, retrieved an empty coffee can and filled it with cookies. "Here," she said, thrusting the can toward her smart-mouthed neighbor. "For Eric and Kevin."

Chuckling, Daisy stood and reached for the cookies. "I can take a hint. You don't want me talking about Tony *and* you don't want me saying anything about your hormones. It's downright difficult to carry on a conversation with you, girl."

After shooing Daisy out the door, Lesley made herself a sandwich and turned on the local noon news. She was chewing away when the billboard she'd seen earlier that week came on the screen.

Her interest was piqued, and she put her sandwich back on the plate.

The camera left the billboard to focus on the reporter who was standing below it. Lesley liked Becky Bright and the offbeat stories she reported. It was a compliment to her professionalism, as far as Lesley was concerned, that Becky Bright could cover the billboard story and keep a straight face.

"This morning I talked with the man who's so ear-
nestly seeking a wife," Becky announced. "Chase
Goodman agreed to an interview and…"

Chase Goodman.

Lesley didn't hear a word after that. His face appeared on the screen and he squinted into the camera and said he only had a limited time in Seattle and
wanted to be as straightforward as he could.

Straightforward. He'd misled *her*. Talk about being
unethical; why, he'd…he'd kissed her. He'd held her in
his arms and… Mortified, she raised her hands to her
face. She'd so desperately wanted to believe in Chase,
but he was like all the other men she'd known. He was
just like her father, who'd cruelly deceived her. Just like
Tony, who'd broken her heart. Never again would she
make herself vulnerable. Never again would she be so
naive as to trust a man.

Never again.

"Your next appointment is waiting," Sandra Zielger,
the attractive middle-aged woman Chase had hired that
morning, announced. He'd been interviewing women
all afternoon.

The first one who'd come was a pleasant woman a
few years his senior who worked as an executive assistant for a big manufacturing company. She was congenial, well-educated and professional. When Chase
asked her why she wanted to marry him and move to
Alaska, she said she was ready to "get out of the rat
race" and take life at a more leisurely pace. She'd been
divorced twice, with no children. After ten minutes with
her, Chase knew a relationship between them wouldn't

work. He wasn't comfortable with her the way he was with Lesley.

The second interview turned out to be with a female plumber who'd been working in construction. She'd been out of work for three months and was looking for a change of scene. The first thing she asked was whether he wanted to sleep with her to sample the goods before making his decision. Even before he collected his wits enough to respond, she'd unbuttoned her blouse, claiming she didn't mind a little kinky sex if that interested him, but she wasn't overly fond of whips and chains. By the time he'd ushered her out the door, Chase felt shaken.

He wasn't sure what he'd expected when he'd placed the ad, but it wasn't this. He was looking for a woman with a generous heart, one with pluck and spirit. A woman with depth and sensitivity. A woman like... Lesley.

He rubbed the back of his neck, closed his eyes and sighed.

He tried phoning Lesley just to calm his nerves, but she wasn't home. He didn't leave a message.

By four, Chase had talked with so many women that their names and faces and stories had all started to blend together. Not a single one had strongly appealed to him. He couldn't meet with these women and not compare them to Lesley. They seemed shallow by contrast, frivolous and, in some cases, reckless. There were a couple he might've liked under other circumstances, and he'd kept their names and phone numbers, but not a single woman to compare to the one he'd met yesterday, quite by chance.

He glanced at his watch and knew he wasn't up to

interviewing another woman. The suite he'd rented at the hotel was packed with applicants. Word had gotten out that he was in the process of talking to prospective brides and they were coming in off the street now. Sandra Zielger seemed to have her hands full, and seeing that, Chase intervened, escorting the husband-seeking women from the room with promises of another day.

"I've never seen anything like this," Sandra said, pushing her hair away from her face with both hands. "You should've brought some of your bachelor friends with you."

Chase closed his eyes and expelled a weary sigh. "How many women did we see?"

"Twenty."

"That's all?" He felt the panic rise. He'd spent nearly an entire day meeting with women, and he'd hardly made a dent in the crowd.

"I take it you're finished for the day?" Sandra asked.

Chase nodded. He needed space to breathe and time to reflect. What he *really* needed was Lesley. He hadn't stopped thinking about her all day, or the kisses they'd shared. Nor could he forget how she'd felt in his arms. He wanted to hold her again, and soon.

He was halfway out the door when Sandra said, "You're not leaving, are you?"

"You mean I can't?"

"Well, it's just that there are a number of phone messages that need to be returned."

"Who from?"

"The radio stations, for one. Another TV station."

"Forget them. That last thing I need now is more publicity."

Sandra grinned. "I've had several interesting jobs

working for Temp Help over the years, but I've got to tell you, this is the most unusual. I wish you luck, young man."

"Thanks," Chase answered. He had the distinct feeling he was going to need it.

Lesley had been filled with nervous energy from the moment she'd seen Becky Bright stand beneath that ridiculous billboard and say Chase's name. None of her usual methods for relieving tension had worked.

She'd gone shopping and fifteen minutes later left the store. She was too mad to appreciate a fifty-percent-off sale. That was an anger so out of the ordinary it surprised even her.

A long soak in the tub hadn't helped, either. By the time she'd finished, she'd sloshed water all over the floor and had spilled her favorite liquid bubble bath.

Even a fitness DVD didn't help, but then she'd stopped five minutes into the exercises and turned it off. If she was going to do anything aerobic, Lesley decided, she'd prefer to work in her yard.

She weeded the front flower beds and was watering the bright red geraniums with her hose when Daisy walked out of her town house in a pair of shorts and a Mariners T-shirt.

"You upset about something, honey?" she called, crossing the driveway that divided their properties.

"What makes you ask that?" Lesley returned in a completely reasonable voice. The fact that Daisy could easily see how upset she was fueled her already short temper.

"Could be 'cause you're nearly drowning those poor flowers. They need to be watered like a gentle rainfall—"

she made sprinkling motions with her hands "—and not with hurricane force."

"Oh," Lesley murmured, realizing her neighbor was right.

"The boys thank you for the cookies."

"Tell them I've got a jarful they're welcome to, as well."

"I thought you baked those cookies for Chase."

"I never said that." Lesley was sure she hadn't.

"Of course you did, maybe not in words, but it was obvious. You like this guy and you aren't going to fool me about *that*. All I can say is great. It's about time you got over that no-good jerk."

"Chase isn't any better," Lesley said, continuing with her watering efforts, now concentrating on her lawn.

"What makes you say that?"

"You know that billboard off Denny Way that's causing all the commotion?" Lesley asked.

"The one where the guy's advertising for a bride?" It must have clicked in Daisy's mind all at once because she snapped her fingers and pointed at Lesley. "That's *Chase*?"

"The very one."

"And that's bad?"

"The man's insane," Lesley muttered.

"You didn't think so earlier in the day. Fact is, you were as happy as I've seen you in ages."

"That was before I knew. He goes on TV and says the reason he decided on the billboard was so he could be—and I quote—direct and straightforward. He wasn't either one with me."

"You've got to trust your instincts," Daisy advised, "and you had a wonderful time with him last night."

Now Lesley had heard everything. "Trust my instincts? I was engaged to a man who wasn't even in love with me and I didn't figure it out until half the school knew, including the student body." It still mortified her to remember the strange, sympathetic looks she'd gotten from her peers weeks prior to her broken engagement.

"Quit blaming yourself for that," Daisy said, placing her hands on her hips. "You didn't suspect Tony because you *shouldn't* have suspected him. Believe me, honey, you got the better end of that deal. Mark my words. Two or three years down the road, he's going to start looking around again. It's a pattern with certain men. I've seen it before."

"Tony's not like that," Lesley insisted. Even after all this time she couldn't keep from defending him. She still wasn't over him, still wasn't over the loss of her dreams and the future she'd envisioned. She *wanted* to forget him, but it was hard. The first ray of hope had been Chase, and now that hope was dashed by his deception.

"It seems to me there's more to Chase than meets the eye," Daisy said thoughtfully. "You have to admit he's innovative."

"The man rented a billboard and advertised for a wife," Lesley cried. "That's not innovation, it's stupidity."

Daisy went on, undaunted. "He shows initiative, too."

"How can you defend him when you haven't even met him?"

"You're right, of course," Daisy agreed, "but there's something about him I like. He can't be so bad, otherwise you'd never have gone out with him."

"That was before I knew what he really was like."

"The guy's obviously got money. Did you ever stop to think about that? Billboards don't come cheap."

"Money's never interested me."

"It doesn't unless you need it," Daisy answered with a hint of sarcasm. "Another thing…"

"You mean there's *more?*"

"There's always more. This guy is serious. He isn't going to string you along the way you-know-who did. Good grief, you were with the-guy-you-don't-want-me-to-mention *how* many years?"

"Five."

"That's what I thought. Well, let me tell you, there's an advantage in knowing what a guy wants from you. Chase doesn't have a hidden agenda."

"Everything you say is true, but it doesn't discount the fact that he deceived me."

"Just a minute." Daisy frowned at her. "Didn't you tell me Chase ran after the guy who stole your purse? It isn't every man who'd get involved in something like that, you know. Did you ever stop to think that mugger might've had a gun?"

Lesley had raced after him herself and that possibility had completely escaped her. Apparently it had escaped Chase, too.

"It isn't every man who's willing to put his life on the line in order to help another human being," Daisy continued.

"If the mugger had owned a gun, he would have used it to get my purse," Lesley said. That had just occurred to her. Now she was free once again to be furious with Chase. She didn't want to think of him as a hero, even if he'd gotten her purse back for her. The action had been instinctive, she told herself, and nothing more.

"I'm offering you some advice," Daisy said.

"Are you going to give it to me whether I want it or not?"

"Probably."

"Then fire away."

"Don't be so quick to judge Chase. He sounds like the decent sort to me, and more of a man than—"

"I thought we weren't going to discuss Tony again."

Daisy shook her head as if saddened by Lesley's lack of insight into men. Her eyes brightened as she looked toward the road. "What type of car did you say Chase drives?"

"I didn't. Why?"

"Because a great-looking guy just pulled up in a red car."

Lesley whirled around to see Chase climbing out of it. His smile was tentative as his eyes fell on her watering the lawn.

"I haven't come at a bad time, have I?" he called from the driveway.

Four

"Hey," Daisy whispered as Chase approached, "this guy is gorgeous. You don't happen to remember the phone number on that billboard, do you? I think *I'll* apply."

Lesley cast her neighbor a scalding look.

Daisy laughed, obviously considering herself amusing.

"I take it you saw the noon news," Chase said cautiously.

"You mean the story about your crazy billboard? Yes, I saw it."

Chase took a couple of steps toward her. "Are you going to squirt me with that hose?"

"I should." She figured it was a credit to her upbringing that she didn't.

Angry shouts burst from Daisy's house and Eric chased Kevin out the front door. Lesley's neighbor hollered for the two boys to stop fighting. It soon became obvious that she was needed to untangle her sons.

"Darn," Daisy said, "and I was hoping to hear this." She stepped forward and shook hands with Chase. "I'm

Lesley's neighbor, Daisy Sullivan. Be patient with her. She'll come around."

"Daisy!" It irritated Lesley to no end that her friend was siding with Chase and, worse, offering him advice on how to handle her.

"I'll talk to you later," Daisy said as she hurried over to her own house.

"I would've said something yesterday," Chase told her, keeping a safe distance between them. "But you mentioned having seen the billboard yourself, remember?"

Lesley lowered her eyes. She'd more than mentioned the billboard, she'd offered a detailed opinion of the mental state of the man who'd paid for it, never guessing it was Chase.

"You could have told me later, after dinner," she reminded him. "That would have been the fair thing to do."

Chase advanced one step. "You're right, I should have, but it completely slipped my mind. I got so caught up in being with you that I forgot. I realize that's a poor excuse, but it's the truth."

Lesley felt herself weakening. She'd enjoyed their evening together, too. That was what hurt so much now. For the first time in months she'd been able to put aside the pain of Tony's betrayal and have fun. Playing the role of tour guide and showing Chase the city she loved had been more than a pleasant distraction, it had freed her. But after she'd seen the noon news, all those reawakened emotions felt like a sham. Instead of anticipation, she'd suffered regret.

"I was hoping you'd agree to see me again," Chase

said enticingly. "I've been meeting with women all day and I haven't met a single one I like as much as you."

"Of course you like me the best," Lesley said indignantly. "Only a crazy woman would answer that ad."

Chase buried his hands in his pants pockets. "That's what you said when you mentioned the ad, remember? You had me wondering, but, Lesley, you're wrong. I've spent hours meeting with them, and that isn't the case. Most have been pleasant and sincere."

"Then you should be dating *them*." Her minuscule lawn was well past the point of being watered, but she persisted, drenching it. If she continued, it'd soon be swampland.

"You're probably right. I should be getting to know them better. But I'd rather spend my free time with you. Will you have dinner with me tonight?"

The temptation was strong, but Lesley refused to give in to it. "I...don't think so."

"Why not?"

"Something's come up unexpectedly."

"What?"

"I forgot I was meeting a friend."

"That's not very original, Lesley. Try again."

"Don't do this," she pleaded.

"Where would you like to eat?"

"I said I couldn't."

"Any restaurant in town—you name it."

Lesley hadn't expected him to persevere. But she could be equally stubborn. A rejection had already formed in her mind, when Chase removed the hose from her hand, putting it down. He took her by the shoulders and turned her to face him. She might've been able to send him away if he hadn't touched her, but the moment he did, Lesley realized it was too late.

She knew the exact second she surrendered; it was the same second she knew he was going to kiss her and how badly she wanted him to.

His palms framed her face and he took her mouth greedily. Not only did Lesley allow the kiss, but she assisted him. Her hands splayed across his chest and she leaned closer. His kiss was hungry and demanding, and she clenched her fists in the fabric of his shirt as she battled against the sensations and feelings that came to life inside her. By the time it ended, Lesley knew she'd lost.

"Do you believe in fate?" he whispered.

"I… I don't think so."

"I didn't until I met you."

"Stop, Chase. Please…" She was fighting him for all she was worth and losing more ground every second he held her.

"Dinner. That's all I ask. One last time together and if you decide afterward that you don't want to see me again, I'll accept that."

"Promise?"

"Cross my heart and hope to die."

Despite her indecision, Lesley had to laugh. That sounded like something the kids next door would say.

"Now, where would you like to eat? Anyplace in town, just name it."

"Ah…"

"The Space Needle? Canlis? Il Bistro?"

Lesley could suggest a better way of testing a man's character than sitting across from him in some fancy restaurant with a bevy of attentive waiters seeing to their every need.

"I'd like to eat at Bobby's Burgers and then play a game of golf."

Chase's eyes widened. "Golf?"

"You heard me."

"Lesley, I don't know if you realize this, but there isn't a golf course within eight hundred miles of Twin Creeks. I've never played the game."

"You'll pick it up fast, I'm sure. Anyway, those are my conditions. Take them or leave them."

Chase groaned. "All right, if you want to see me make a fool of myself."

Miniature golf. That was what Lesley had in mind.

She'd left him worrying all the way through their hamburgers before they drove to the golf course and he learned the truth. It was a just punishment, he decided, for what he'd put her through.

He'd suspected Lesley would be good at it and she was, soundly defeating him on the first nine holes. But as she'd said, he was a fast learner, rallying on the last nine. When they added up their scores, Lesley won by three strokes.

"I can't remember the last time I laughed so much," she said over a glass of iced tea. They were relaxing on the patio under a pink-and-orange-striped umbrella, surrounded by children and a handful of adults. "You're a good sport, Chase."

"Does that surprise you?"

She hesitated. "A little. Men don't like to lose, especially to a woman."

"That's not true in all situations, just some."

"Name one." Her challenge was there, bold and unmistakable.

"When it comes to a woman deciding between two men," he said thoughtfully. "Naturally, I can't speak for all men, but there's one thing that bothers me more than anything."

"And that's?"

"When I'm forced to compete with another man for a woman's affection."

Lesley grew quiet after that, and Chase hoped he hadn't offended her with his honesty. He couldn't apologize for speaking the truth.

"Tell me about the women you saw today," she said unexpectedly, sounding almost cheerful. He caught the gleam in her eye and realized she was prepared to hear horror stories.

"I was really surprised by some," he began.

"Oh? Were they that awful?"

"No." He shook his head. "Not at all—there were some classy women in the group, with good educations. One of the first few I interviewed had her master's degree."

"What prompted *her* to respond to your ad?" The self-satisfied look disappeared, replaced by one of genuine curiosity.

Chase had wondered about that himself. "I asked about her motives right off. Don't get me wrong—Twin Creeks is a nice, civilized town, but it's a long way from shopping centers, large libraries and cultural events. Granted, we have TV and the internet, but you aren't ever going to see any Broadway shows performed there. I explained all that to Christine."

"And she still wanted to marry you?"

Chase nodded. "At least she said she did. She explained that she's in her late thirties and has a successful career. But now she realizes how badly she wants a husband and family. She claimed every guy she's dated in the last few years is emotionally scarred from a break-up or a divorce."

"Having reentered the dating scene myself, I'm beginning to see how true that is."

"Christine is mainly interested in starting a family," Chase concluded.

"How do you feel about children?" She propped her elbows on the table and rested her chin in her palms as she studied him.

"I want a family, but I'd prefer to wait a year or two, to give my wife the opportunity to know me better and for me to know her. In my view, it's important to be sure the marriage is going to last before we bring a child into the equation."

"That's an intelligent way of looking at it."

Lesley went silent again and he saw pain in her eyes and wondered at the cause. He was about to question her when she spoke again.

"Other than Christine, is there another woman who made an impression on you?"

"Several. A female plumber who let me know she doesn't, uh, mind kinky sex."

The look that came over Lesley was very prim and proper. "I see."

"And Bunny, who has four children under the age of six."

"Oh, my goodness."

"She was looking for someone to help her raise her

kids and was honest about it. Her ex-husband abandoned them nine months ago."

"The creep."

Chase agreed with her. "I don't understand how a man can walk away from his responsibilities like that. What he did to Bunny is bad enough, but to leave those beautiful children…"

"She brought them?"

"No, I asked to see a picture. They're cute as could be. I felt sorry for her." He didn't mention that he'd given her enough money to fill her gas tank so she could get home and paid for a week's worth of groceries. She hadn't asked, but he could tell she was in dire financial straits.

"You aren't interested in a woman with excess baggage?" she asked, almost flippantly. Though he'd only known Lesley a short time, he already knew it wasn't like her to be so offhand. He suspected something else was bothering her.

"Bunny's a good woman who didn't deserve to be treated so badly by the man she'd loved and trusted. The divorce was final less than a week ago. Bunny, and the children, too, need more love and help than I could give them. To answer your question, no, I don't object to marrying a woman with children."

Lesley was silent for a long time after that. "My dad left us," she finally said in a small voice.

Chase chose his words carefully, not knowing how to comment or if he should. "It must have been very hard."

"I was only six and we were going to Disneyland. Mom had worked a second job in order to save extra money for the trip. Dad took the money when he left."

"Oh, Lesley, I'm sorry."

The look in her eyes became distant, as if she were that six-year-old child, reliving the nightmare of being abandoned by her father all over again.

"I know I shouldn't have blamed myself. I didn't drive my father away, but for years I was convinced that if I'd been the son he wanted, he'd never have left."

"Have you had any contact with him since?"

"He called when I was fifteen and wanted to see me."

"Did you?"

She nodded. "After being so bitterly hurt, I didn't have a lot of hope for our meeting. It's funny the things a child will remember about someone. I always thought of my dad as big and strong and invincible. When we met again nine years later, I realized he was weak and selfish. We had lunch together and he told me I could order anything I wanted. I remember I asked for the most expensive thing on the menu even though I didn't like steak. I barely touched the steak sandwich and took it home for our dog. I made sure he knew he'd paid top dollar to feed our collie, too."

"What made him contact you after all those years?"

Lesley sighed. "He seemed to want me to absolve him from his guilt. He told me how hard his life had been when he was married to my mother and had a child—me—with all the responsibilities that entails. He claimed he'd married too young, that they'd both made mistakes. He said he couldn't handle the pressures of constantly being in debt and never having money to do the kinds of things he wanted to do.

"That's when I learned the truth. My dad walked out on my mother and me because he wanted to race sports cars. Imagine, driving a sports car meaning more to him than his wife and daughter.

"You might think badly of me, but I wouldn't give him the forgiveness he was seeking—not then. It wasn't until later, in my early twenties, when I learned he'd died of cancer, that I was able to find it in my heart to forgive him."

"I don't know how any fifteen-year-old could have forgiven someone who'd wounded her so deeply," Chase said, reaching for her hand. She gripped his fingers with surprising strength and intuitively Chase knew she didn't often share this painful part of her childhood.

She offered him a brief smile and picked up her drink.

"Did your mother ever remarry?"

"Yes," Lesley answered, "to a wonderful man who's perfect for her. You'd have to meet my mother to understand. She has a tendency to be something of a curmudgeon. It took her a long time to find the courage to commit herself to another relationship.

"I was out of high school before she married Ken, although they'd dated for years. She never told me this, but my guess is that Ken said either they marry or end the relationship. I don't think he would've followed through on the threat, but it worked.

"He and Mom are both retired. They live on a small ranch in Montana now and really love it."

"They sound happy."

"They'd like a couple of grandkids to spoil someday but—" Lesley stopped abruptly and her face turned a soft shade of pink.

"But what?" he inquired.

"Oh, nothing." She shrugged, looking decidedly uncomfortable. "It's just something Daisy said to me this afternoon. And…she might be right." Her voice faded.

"Right about what?"

"Nothing," she said quickly.

Whatever the subject, it was obvious that Lesley wasn't going to discuss it with him.

"Will you be meeting more women tomorrow?" Lesley asked.

Chase nodded with little enthusiasm. "I should never have agreed to that news story. The phones have been ringing off the hook ever since. There's no way I could possibly interview eight hundred women in two weeks' time."

"Eight hundred!"

Lesley sounded as shocked as he'd been when he'd heard the original number of five hundred. Since the story had aired, three hundred additional calls had poured in.

"That's…incredible."

"Just remember, I haven't met a single one I like better than you."

Lesley laughed. "You've already heard my answer to that."

"I don't have much time in Seattle, Lesley. Less than three weeks. I need to make some decisions soon. If you'd be willing to marry me, I'd promise to be a good husband to you."

"Hold it!" she said, raising both hands. "Back up. I'm not in the market for a husband. Not now and possibly never again. Men have done some real damage to my heart, starting with my father and most recently Tony. I don't need a man in my life."

"True, but do you *want* one?"

She hesitated. "I don't know."

"It's something to think about, then, isn't it?"

"Not right now," she answered, her voice insistent. "I don't want to consider anything but having fun. That's my goal for this summer. I want to put the past behind me and get on with life in a positive way."

"I do, too," Chase assured her, and it was true in a more profound way than she probably realized.

"I baked cookies this morning," she said. "It was the first time in months I've wanted to bake anything."

"I don't suppose you saved any for me?"

Lesley smiled as if she knew something he didn't. "There's a full cookie jar reserved for you." She suddenly recalled that she'd said Kevin and Eric could have them. She'd have to compromise. "Well, half a cookie jar," she amended.

Chase couldn't remember the last time he'd tasted home-baked cookies. "This calls for a picnic, don't you think?"

"Paradise."

He frowned. "Do I have to wait that long to try these cookies of yours?"

"No, silly. Paradise is in the national park on Mount Rainier. There's a lodge there and several trails and fields of wildflowers so abundant, they'll take your breath away."

"Sounds like Alaska."

"It's one of my favorite places in the world."

"Let's go, then. We'll leave first thing in the morning."

"You can't," she said, with a superior look.

"Why can't I?"

"Because you'll be interviewing a prospective wife. Eight hundred prospective wives to be exact."

Chase cursed under his breath and Lesley burst out

laughing. Only then did Chase see any amusement in his predicament. What she didn't seem to understand, and what he was going to have to prove, was that he'd willingly leave all eight hundred prospects behind in order to spend time with *her*.

The sun had barely peeked over the horizon when Chase arrived. Lesley had been up for an hour, packing their lunch and preparing for their day. Her hiking boots and a sweater were in a knapsack by the door and the picnic basket was loaded and ready for Chase to carry to his rental car.

"'Morning," she greeted him.

"'Morning," Chase returned, leaning forward to kiss her.

The kiss seemed instinctive on both their parts. A kiss, Lesley noticed, that was exchanged without doubt or hesitation.

Suddenly their smiles faded and her lungs emptied of air. It wasn't supposed to happen like this. She was inches, seconds, from walking into his arms before she caught herself.

Chase, however, felt no such restraint and reached for her, pulling her toward him. Even with her mind crying no, she waited impatiently for his mouth to touch hers.

His lips were gentle, as if he were aware of her feelings.

"I love it when you do that," he whispered, kissing her neck.

"Do what?" she asked, sighing deeply.

He groaned. "You just did it again. That sigh. It tells me so much more than you'd ever be willing to say."

"Don't be ridiculous." She tried to ease away from

him, but felt his breath warm and moist against her throat—and couldn't move. His fingers loosened the top button of her blouse.

"I… I don't think this is a good idea," Lesley murmured as he backed her against the door. He braced his hands on either side of her head, his eyes gazing into hers.

"I don't want you to *think*. I want you to feel." He kissed her then with the same wicked sweetness that had broken her resolve seconds before. She sighed, the same sigh he'd mentioned earlier, and regretted it immediately.

"Lesley, I don't know what to do." He leaned his forehead against hers.

"Kiss me again." She held his face with her hands, buried her fingers in the thickness of his hair and directed his lips back to hers. By the time they drew apart, both were panting and breathless.

For a moment neither of them said anything. "I think you might be right," he finally said with reluctance. "This isn't such a good idea, after all. One taste of you would never be enough. I'm greedy, Lesley. I want it all. It's better not to start what we can't finish."

He reached for the picnic basket and took it outside. Lesley felt weak and shaken. She wouldn't have believed it possible for any man to evoke such an intense reaction with a few kisses.

Her knees were trembling as she grabbed her knapsack and purse and followed him out the door. Chase stored her things beside the picnic basket in the trunk. He helped her into the passenger seat and got into the car a moment later, waiting until she'd adjusted her seat belt before he started the engine.

Neither of them had much to say on the long drive

to Paradise. Lesley had planned to play the role of tour guide as she had previously, pointing out interesting facts along the way, but changed her mind. She was going to mention that Mount Rainier National Park was one of the first parks ever established—in 1899. But it wasn't important to tell him that, not if it meant disturbing the peaceful silence they shared.

Lesley loved Mount Rainier and the way it stood guard over the Pacific Northwest. The view of the mountain from Seattle was often breathtaking. Her appreciation increased even more when she saw the look in Chase's eyes as they drove the twisting road through the forest-thick area. He surprised her with his knowledge of trees.

"Everyone recognizes a Douglas fir when they see one, don't they?" he teased.

"No."

They stopped at a campsite and took a break. When Lesley returned from using the facilities, she saw Chase wandering through the mossy, fern-draped valley. She joined him, feeling a sense of closeness and solemnity with Chase, as though they were standing on holy ground. The trees surrounding them were tall and massive, the forest a lush green. Breathing deeply, Lesley felt the fullness of beauty standing there with him. The air was sharp, clean, vibrant with the scent of evergreens.

Chase took her hand and entwined his fingers with hers. "Are you ready?" he asked.

Lesley nodded, uncertain what she was agreeing to, and for once in her life not caring.

They got back in the car and in companionable silence traveled the rest of the way to Paradise. Since they hadn't eaten breakfast, Chase suggested they have their picnic, which they did. He finished the chocolate chip cookies she'd brought for him, praising them lavishly.

Afterward, Lesley put on her boots and they walked the trails through the open, subalpine meadowlands, which were shedding their cold blankets of snow.

"You know what I love most here? The flowers, their color, the way they fight through the cold and stand proudly against the hillside as if to say they've accomplished something important," Lesley said as they climbed up the steep path.

"The flowers respond the way most of us do, don't you think?" Chase asked.

"How's that?"

"They respond to *life*. To the power and force of life. I feel it here and you do, too. It's like standing on a boulder and looking out over the world and saying, 'Here I am. I've done it.'"

"And what exactly *have* you done, Chase Goodman?"

He chuckled. "I haven't figured it out yet, but this feeling is too good to waste."

She laughed. "I know what you mean."

They hiked for a couple of hours, and ascended as far as the tree line. The beauty of the hills and valleys was unending, spilling out before them like an Impressionist painting, in vibrant hues of purple, rose and white.

After their hike, they explored the visitor center, then headed back to the car.

Lesley was exhausted. The day had been full and exciting. Over the years, she'd visited Paradise countless times and had always enjoyed herself, but not the way she had today with Chase. With him, she'd experienced a spiritual wonder, a feeling of joy, a new connection with nature. She couldn't think of a logical way to explain it any more than she could say why his kisses affected her so strongly.

When they arrived back in Seattle, Eric and Kevin, Daisy's two boys, ran out to the car to greet them.

"Hi, Lesley," Eric, the oldest boy, said, eyeing Chase.

"Hello, boys. This is Chase."

Chase cordially shook hands with the youngsters. "Howdy, boys."

"You're sure big. Even bigger 'n Lesley."

Lesley wasn't sure if that was a compliment or not.

"We came to see if you had any cookies left."

"Mom said you might have some more," Kevin chimed in.

"Yup, I saved some for you."

"But don't forget she made them for me," Chase said. "You boys should make sure I'm willing to share the loot before you ask Lesley."

"She used to make them for us. So we've got dibs."

"You gonna share or not?" Kevin asked, hands on his hips, implying a showdown if necessary.

Chase rubbed the side of his jaw as if giving the matter consideration.

"Those boys bothering you?" Daisy shouted from the front door.

"We just want our share of Lesley's cookies before Chase eats 'em all."

"I'll buy you cookies," Daisy promised, throwing an apologetic look at Lesley. For her part, Lesley was enjoying this exchange, especially the way Chase interacted with the two boys. Tony had treated Daisy's sons as pests and shooed them away whenever they came around. Although he worked with children, he had little rapport with them outside the classroom.

"We don't want any *store-bought* cookies," Eric argued.

"Don't try and bake any, either, Mom, not after last time." He looked at Lesley, and whispered, "Even my friend's dog wouldn't eat them."

Lesley smothered a giggle.

"Will you or won't you give us some cookies?" Eric demanded of Chase.

Chase himself was having trouble not smiling. "I guess I don't have much choice. You two have a prior claim and any judge in the land would take that into account."

"Does that mean he will or he won't?" Kevin asked his brother.

"He will," Eric answered. "I think."

"But only if you help us unload the car," Chase said, giving them both a few things to haul inside.

Lesley emptied the cookie jar, setting aside a handful for Chase, and doled out the boys' well-earned reward. While Chase was dealing with the picnic basket, she absently checked her answering machine.

"Lesley, it's Tony. I've been doing a lot of thinking lately and thought we should get together to talk. April's out of town this week visiting her mother, so give me a call as soon as you can."

Lesley felt as if someone had just hit her. Instinctively her hands went to her stomach, and she stood frozen in a desperate effort to catch her breath.

She turned slowly around, not knowing what to do, and discovered Chase standing there, staring at her.

Five

"Well," Chase said, studying Lesley closely. "Are you going to call him?"

"No."

"You're sure?"

He seemed to doubt Lesley and that upset her, possibly because she *wasn't* sure. Part of her wanted to speak to Tony. School had been out for more than a week now and she was starved for the sight of him. Admitting her weakness, even to herself, demanded rigorous, painful honesty. Tony was married, and it sickened her that she felt this way.

"I'm sure," she snapped, then added, "although it's none of your business."

He nodded, his eyes guarded as though he wanted to believe her but wasn't convinced he should. "Are you going to invite me in for a cup of coffee?"

Lesley stared at him, not knowing what to say. She needed privacy in order to analyze her feelings, but at the same time, she didn't want Chase to leave, because once he did, she'd be forced to confront her weakness for Tony.

Eric came into the kitchen, munching loudly on a cookie. "Lesley's the best cook I ever met," he announced, looking proud to be her neighbor. His jeans had large rips in the knees and his T-shirt was badly stained, but his cheerful expression was infectious.

"A better cook than Mom," Kevin agreed, rubbing his forearm over his mouth to remove any crumbs.

"Even Dr. Seuss is a better cook than Mom. Remember the time she made us green eggs and ham for breakfast? Except they weren't supposed to be." Both boys laughed and grabbed another cookie.

"Say, you two ever been fishing?" Chase asked unexpectedly.

"Nope." They gazed up at Chase with wide, eager eyes.

"I was planning to ask Lesley to go fishing tomorrow and I thought it might be fun if you two came along. You think you could talk your mom into letting you join us?"

"I'll ask," Eric said, racing from the kitchen.

"I want to ask," Kevin shouted, running after his brother.

Lesley made a pot of coffee. She wasn't gullible; she knew exactly why Chase had included the boys. He wanted to see her again and knew she wouldn't refuse him if it meant disappointing her ragamuffin neighbors. She said as much when she brought two mugs of coffee to the table.

"What would you do if I said I couldn't go with you?" she asked, sitting across from him.

The healing calm she'd experienced earlier with Chase on Mount Rainier had been shattered by Tony's call. She hadn't realized how frail that newfound peace had been or how easily it could be destroyed. She hated the fact that Tony continued to wield such power over her, especially when she felt she'd made strides in letting go of her love for him.

"The boys and I'd miss you," Chase said after a moment, "but I'd never disappoint those two. Every boy should go fishing at some point in his life. I'd like it if you'd come, but I'll understand if you'd prefer to stay home." He sipped his coffee and seemed to be waiting for a response from her.

"Would it be all right if I let you know in the morning?"

"Of course."

The front door flew open and Eric and Kevin shot into the room like bullets, breathless with excitement. "Mom said we could go! But she needs to know how much money we need and what we should bring."

"Tell her you don't need a dime and all you have to bring is an extra set of clothes."

"What time?"

"Six sounds good."

"In the *morning?*" Kevin's eyes rounded with dismay. "We don't usually get up before nine."

"You want to catch trout, don't you?"

"Sure, but…"

"We'll be ready," Eric said, elbowing his brother in the ribs. "Isn't that right, Kevin?"

"Ow. Yeah, we'll be ready."

"Good. Then I'll see you boys bright and early tomorrow morning." Chase ushered them to the door, while Lesley sat at the table, hiding her amusement.

When Chase returned, he surprised her by taking one last sip of his coffee and carrying the mug to her sink. He came back to the table, placed his hand on her shoulder and kissed her cheek. "I'll talk to you later."

"You're leaving?" Suddenly it became vital that he stay because once he left, she feared the temptation to return Tony's call would be too strong to control, too easy to rationalize. Standing abruptly, she folded her arms and stared up at him, struggling with herself.

"You don't want me to go?"

She shrugged and finally admitted the truth. "I…want you to help me understand why Tony would phone me out of the blue like this. I want you to help me figure out what I should do, but more importantly, I need you to remind me how wrong it would be to call him. I can't—won't—betray my own principles."

"Sorry," Chase said, sounding genuinely regretful. "Those are things you've got to figure out on your own."

"But…"

"I'll give you a call in the morning."

"Aren't you going to kiss me?"

He hesitated and desire was clear on his face. "I'd like nothing better, but I don't think I should."

"Why not?" She moved closer, so close she could feel his breath against her face, so close that all she needed to do was ease forward and her lips would meet his.

"I don't think it'd be a good idea just now." His voice was low.

"I *need* you to kiss me," she said, pressing her palms against his shirt and waiting.

"I wish…" she continued.

His breathing was erratic, but so was her own.

"What do you wish?" His mouth wandered to her neck and she sighed at the feel of his lips against her skin. She angled her head back, revealing her eagerness for his touch.

"You already know what I want," she whispered.

He planted slow kisses on her throat, pausing to moisten the hollow with the tip of his tongue. Shivers of awareness rippled down her arms.

Her mouth sought his and he kissed her, his lips soft and undemanding. She slipped her arms around his neck and nestled into his arms, needing the security of his touch to ground her in reality.

When he kissed her again, she moaned, lifting her hand to the back of his head, urging him closer. "Oh, Chase," she breathed once the kiss had ended.

He raised his head and touched her forehead with his lips. "A man could get used to hearing a woman say his name like that."

"Oh." Her response sounded inane, but conversation was beyond her.

"Marry me, Lesley."

She risked a glance at his face and felt emotion well up in her throat. Blinking rapidly, she managed to hold the tears at bay.

"All right," he said. "We'll do this your way, in increments. Will you join the boys and me in the morning?"

Lesley nodded.

"I was hoping you would." He kissed the tip of her nose. "I have to leave now. Trust me, I'd much rather stay, but I can't and we both know why."

Lesley did know.

It wasn't fair to use Chase as a shield against Tony. She would have to stand alone, make her own decisions, and Chase understood that more clearly than she had herself.

"I'll see you at six in the morning," he whispered, and released her. As if he couldn't wait that long to kiss her again, he lowered his mouth to hers, kissed her longingly, then slowly turned away.

The sound of the front door closing followed seconds later, and Lesley stood in the middle of her kitchen with the phone just inches away.

"A trout can sure put up a big fight," Eric said with a satisfied look in his brother's direction after he'd caught his first fish.

The four of them were standing on the banks of Green River, their lines dangling in the water. Through pure luck, Eric had managed to catch the first trout. While Chase helped the boy remove the squirming fish from the line and rebait his hook, Lesley whispered reassurances to Kevin.

"Don't worry, you'll snag one, too."

"But what if I don't?" Kevin asked, hanging his head. "Eric *always* gets everything first just 'cause he's older. It isn't fair. It just isn't fair."

No sooner were the words out of his mouth than his line dipped with such force that he nearly lost his fishing rod. His triumphant gaze flew to Lesley. "I've got one!"

Chase immediately went over to the younger boy, coaxing him as he had Eric, tutoring him until the boy had reeled in the trout and Chase was able to take the good-size fish from the hook.

"Is mine bigger than Eric's?" Kevin demanded.

"You'll have to check that for yourself."

"Yup, mine's bigger," Kevin announced a moment later with a smug look.

Lesley found the younger boy's conviction amusing, but said nothing. To prove his point, Kevin held up both fish and asked Lesley to judge, but it was impossible to tell.

They spent most of the morning fishing, until both boys had reached their limit. Although Chase had brought Lesley a fishing rod, she didn't do much fishing herself. Twice she got a fish on the line, but both times she let the boys reel them in for her. Chase did the same, letting the boys experience the thrill.

By eleven o'clock, all four were famished.

"Let's have trout for lunch," Chase suggested.

"I thought Lesley made sandwiches," Kevin said, eyeing the fish suspiciously. "I don't like fish, unless it's fish and chips, and then I'll eat it."

"That's because you've never had anyone cook trout the way the Indians do." Chase explained a method of slow cooking, wrapping the fish in leaves and mud and burying them in the coals, which had even Lesley's mouth watering in anticipation. He also explained the importance of never allowing the fish they'd caught to go to waste. The boys nodded solemnly as if they understood the wisdom of his words. By then, Lesley guessed, they both thought Chase walked on water.

"I'm going to need your help," he said, instructing the boys to gather kindling for the fire. "Then you can help me clean the trout."

"You won't need me for this, will you?" Lesley asked hopefully.

"Women are afraid of guts," Eric explained for Chase's benefit.

"Is that so?"

"They go all weird over that kind of stuff. Mom's

the same way. One time, the neighbor's cat, a black one named Midnight...you know Midnight, don't you, Lesley?"

She nodded.

"Midnight brought a dead bird into the yard and Mom started going all weird and yelling. We thought someone was trying to murder her."

"I thought Dad was back," Eric inserted, and Chase's eyes connected briefly with Lesley's and for an instant fire leapt into his eyes.

"Anyway, Mom asked Kevin and me to bury it. I don't think she's ever forgiven Midnight, either. She gives him mean looks whenever he comes to visit and shoos him away."

While the boys were discussing a woman's aversion to the sight of blood, Lesley brought out the plastic tablecloth and spread it over a picnic table close to where they'd parked the car.

"That's another thing," Eric said knowingly, motioning toward her. "A woman wants to make everything fancy. Real men don't eat on a tablecloth. Kevin and I never would if it wasn't for Mom and Lesley."

"Don't forget Grandma," Kevin said.

"Right, and Grandma, too."

"Those feminine touches can be nice, though," Chase told the boys. "I live in a big log cabin up in Alaska and it gets mighty lonesome during the winters. Last January I would've done just about anything to have a pretty face smiling at me across the dinner table, even if it meant having to eat on a tablecloth. I wouldn't have cared if she'd spread out ten of them. It would've been a small price to pay for her company."

"You mean you *wanted* a woman with you?" Eric sounded surprised.

"Men like having women around?" Kevin asked.

"Of course," Chase returned casually.

"My dad doesn't feel like that. He said he was glad to be rid of us. He said lots of mean things that made Mom cry and he hit her sometimes, too."

Chase crouched down in front of Eric and Kevin and talked to them for several minutes. She couldn't hear everything he said, because she was making trips back and forth to the car, but she knew whatever it was had an impact on the boys. She was touched when the three of them hugged.

After a while, the fire Chase had built had burned down to hot coals. The boys and Chase wrapped the cleaned fish in a bed of leaves and packed them in mud before burying them in the dirt, which they covered with the hot coals.

"While we're waiting," Chase suggested, "we'll try those sandwiches Lesley packed and go exploring."

"Great." After collecting their sandwiches, both boys eagerly accompanied Chase on a nearby trail. Lesley chose to stay behind. Trekking into the woods, chasing after those two, was beyond her. She got a lounge chair she'd packed, opened it and gratefully sank down on it.

She must have dozed off because she woke with both boys staring down at her, studying her as if she were a specimen under a microscope.

"She's awake," Eric cried.

"Let's eat," Kevin said. "I'm starved."

Lesley had the plastic plates and plastic silverware set out on the table, along with a large bag of potato chips, veggies and a cake she'd baked the night before.

Chase dug up the fish, scraped away the dried mud and peeled back the leaves. The tantalizing aroma of the trout took Lesley by surprise. Until then she hadn't thought she was hungry.

They ate until they were stuffed, until they couldn't force down another morsel. Chase and the boys conscientiously packed up the garbage and loaded the vehicle after Lesley had wrapped the leftovers—not that there were many.

Eric and Kevin fell asleep in the backseat on the ride home.

"They really enjoyed themselves," Lesley whispered. "They'll remember this day all their lives. It was very sweet of you to invite them along."

She watched as his gaze briefly moved to his rearview mirror and he glanced at the boys. "I'd like to meet their father in a dark alley someday. I have no tolerance for a man who hits a woman."

"He has a drinking problem," Lesley said.

"Is that an excuse?"

"No, just an explanation."

"The man should be punished for telling his sons he's glad to be rid of them. What kind of father would say such a thing?"

He didn't seem to expect an answer, which was just as well since Lesley didn't have one.

Daisy was back from her computer classes by the time they arrived at the house. The boys woke up when Chase cut the engine. As soon as they realized they were home, they darted out of the car and into the house, talking excitedly about their adventures.

Daisy came out of the house with her sons and ordered them to help unload the car for Lesley, which they did willingly.

Lesley had been neighbors and friends with Daisy for three years. She'd watched this no-nonsense woman make some hard decisions in that time, but never once had she seen her friend cry. There were tears in Daisy's eyes now.

"Thank you," she said to Chase in a tremulous voice.

"No problem. I was happy to have them with us. You're raising two fine boys there, Daisy. You should be proud of them."

"Oh, darn." She held an index finger under each eye. "You're going to have me bawling here in a minute. I just wanted to thank you both."

"Daisy?" Lesley asked gently. "Is everything all right?"

"Of course everything's all right. A woman can shed a few tears now and then, can't she?"

"Sure, but…"

"I know. I'm making a fool of myself. It's just that I appreciate what you did for my boys. I've never seen them so excited and so happy." Lesley wasn't expecting to be hugged, but Daisy reached for her, nearly squeezing the breath from her lungs. "I want to thank you for being my friend," she murmured, wiping her hand under her nose. Then she returned to her house.

Eric and Kevin were off, eager to relate their escapades to their neighborhood friends.

Chase followed Lesley into the kitchen. He helped her unload the picnic basket, then stopped abruptly, looking over at her.

"Is something the matter?" she asked.

"It looks like you've got a message on your answering machine."

Lesley's heart felt frozen in her chest. Trying to be nonchalant about it, she walked over and pushed the playback button. This time, Tony's voice didn't rip through her like the blade of a knife. In fact, hearing him again so soon felt anticlimactic.

"Lesley, it's Tony. When you didn't return my call, I stopped by the house. You weren't home. I need to talk to you. Call me soon. Please."

Lesley looked at Chase, wishing she could read his thoughts, wishing she could gauge her own. His eyes were darker than she'd ever seen them and his jaw was stiff.

"Are you going to contact him?"

She wasn't any more confident than she'd been earlier. "I don't know."

"I see."

"You want to remind me he's a married man, don't you?" she cried. "I know that, Chase. I have no idea why he's calling or what he wants from me."

"Get real, Lesley. You know exactly what he wants. Didn't he say April's out of town?"

"Tony's not like that." Again, she didn't understand why she felt the need to defend him. She'd done it so often that it came naturally to her, she supposed. Although, she did have to wonder if Tony might be unfaithful to April, as he'd been to her.

"You know him better than I do," Chase admitted grudgingly. "I've got to get back," he said, as though he couldn't get away from her fast enough.

"Are you interviewing more...applicants?" she asked

him on the way to the door, making conversation, not wanting their day to end on a sour note.

"Yes," he said briskly. "Several."

His answer surprised her. "When?"

"I talked to some last night and I have more scheduled for later this afternoon and evening."

"You'll call me?" she asked, trailing after him.

He hesitated, not looking at her. An eternity seemed to pass before he nodded. "All right," he said curtly.

Lesley longed to reassure him; that was what Chase was waiting for her to do. To promise him she wouldn't call Tony. But she couldn't tell him that. She hadn't decided yet. She remembered what he'd said about not wanting to compete with another man for a woman's affections. What Chase didn't understand was that she'd never try to play one man against another.

"I'll look forward to hearing from you," she said. To her own ears she sounded oddly formal. She stood on the other side of the screen door, watching him walk away from her. She had the craziest feeling that he was taking a piece of her heart with him.

She waited until his car was gone before she breathed again. She told herself she couldn't possibly know a man for such a short while and adequately judge her feelings. She was attracted to him, but any other woman with two eyes in her head would be, too.

Then there was Tony. She'd loved him for so long she didn't know how to stop. He'd been an integral part of her life and without him her world felt empty and meaningless.

Lesley walked back into her kitchen and listened to the message again. She thought about phoning Lori and asking for advice, but decided against it. Lori had said she'd get back to her later, and she hadn't yet.

Daisy was the more logical choice, although her feelings about Tony were well-known. Lesley found her neighbor in the backyard, wearing a bikini, soaking up the sun on a chaise longue while propping an aluminum shield under her chin. Amused, Lesley stood by the fence and studied her.

"Where in heaven's name did you get *that?*" Lesley asked.

"Don't get excited. It's one of those microwave pizza boxes the boys like, with those silver linings. I figured I'd put it to good use now that they're finished with the pizza."

"Honestly, Daisy, you crack me up."

"I've only got so much time to get any sun. I've got to make the most of it."

"I know, I know."

"Where'd Chase take off to?"

Lesley looked away. "He had to get back to his hotel. Did I tell you eight hundred women responded to his billboard?"

Daisy's eyes were closed. "Seems to me it's a shame you're not one of them. What's the matter, Lesley, is it beneath your dignity?"

"Yes," she snapped.

Daisy's sigh revealed how exasperated she was with Lesley. "That's too bad, sweetie, because that man's worth ten Tonys."

Lesley's fingers closed around the top of the fence. "It's funny that you should mention Tony because he's been calling me."

"What does that poor excuse of a man have to say for himself?"

"He claims he needs to talk to me."

"I'll just bet."

"He left two messages and Chase was here both times when I listened to them."

Daisy shook her head. "Chase isn't the type to stand still for that nonsense. Did he set you straight?"

"Daisy! I don't need a man to tell me what to do and I resent you even suggesting such a thing." She remembered, a little guiltily, that she *had* asked Chase to help her sort out her feelings for Tony as well as her moral obligations.

"You're right, of course. Neither of us truly needs a man for *anything*. I don't and you've proved you don't, either. But you know, having one around can be a real comfort at times."

"I don't know what to do," Lesley said, worrying her lower lip.

"About Chase and all those women?"

She was astonished by the way Daisy always brought the conversation back to Chase. "No! About Tony calling me."

"You've been miserable because that slimeball dumped you," Daisy went on with barely a pause. "I find it ironic that when you meet up with a really decent guy, Tony comes sniffin' around. Does this guy have radar or what?"

Lesley smiled. "I doubt it."

"He couldn't tolerate the thought of you with another man, you know."

"Don't be ridiculous! He didn't want me, Daisy. You seem to be forgetting that."

"Of course he wants you. For Tony it's a matter of pride to keep two women in love with him. Don't kid yourself. His ego eats it up."

"He's married."

Daisy snorted. "When has that ever stopped a man?"

"I'm sure you're wrong." Here she was defending him *again* although she didn't even know what he wanted from her.

"Listen, sweetie, you might have a college degree, but when it comes to men, you're as naive as those kids you teach. Why do you think Tony didn't want you transferring to another school? He wants to keep his eye on you. Trust me, the minute you show any interest in another man, he'll be there like stink on—"

"I get the picture, Daisy."

"Fine, but do you get the message?"

Lesley gnawed at her lip. "I think so."

Daisy lowered the aluminum shield. She turned her head to look at Lesley. "You're afraid, aren't you? Afraid of what'll happen if you call Tony back."

Lesley nodded.

"Are you still in love with that jerk?"

Once more she nodded.

"Oh, Lesley, you idiot. You don't need him, not when you've got someone like Chase. He's crazy about you, but he isn't stupid. He's not going to ram his head against a brick wall, and who could blame him? Not me."

"I hardly know Chase."

"What more do you *need* to know?"

"Daisy, he's looking for a wife."

"So what?" her neighbor asked impatiently.

"I'm not in love with Chase."

"Do you like him?"

"Of course I do. Otherwise I wouldn't continue to see him."

"What are you expecting, sweetie? This guy is manna from heaven. If you want to spend the rest of your life mooning over Tony, feel free. As far as I'm concerned, that guy's going to do his best to make you miserable for as long as he can."

"Chase is from Alaska," Lesley argued.

"So? You don't have any family here. There's nothing holding you back other than Tony, is there? Is a married man worth all that grief, Lesley?"

"No." How small her voice sounded, how uncertain.

"Do you want to lose Chase?"

"I don't know..."

"You don't *know*? Sometimes I want to clobber you, Lesley. Where do you think you'd ever find another man as good as Chase? But if that doesn't concern you, then far be it from me to point out the obvious." She swung her legs from the chaise longue. "If you want my advice, I'd say go for it and marry the guy. I doubt that you'll be sorry."

Lesley wished she could be as sure of that, but she wasn't. She wasn't even sure how she was going to get through another night without calling Tony.

Six

Chase forced himself to relax. He wasn't being fair to the women he'd interviewed. He tried, heaven knew he'd tried, to concentrate on what they'd said, but it hadn't worked, not in a single case. And this had been going on for several days.

He'd ask a question, listen intently for the first minute or two, and then his mind would drift. What irritated him most was the subject that dominated his thoughts so completely.

Lesley.

She was in love with Tony, although she was struggling to hide it. Not from him, but from herself. All the signs were there.

If he had more time, he might have a chance with Lesley. But he didn't. Even if he could afford a couple of months to court her, it might not be enough.

The best thing, the only thing, he could do was accept that whatever they'd so briefly had was over, cut his losses and do what he could to make up for wasted time.

"That's the last of them for this evening," Sandra

said, letting herself into the room. The door clicked softly behind her.

"Good." He was exhausted to the bone.

"I've got appointments starting first thing tomorrow morning. Are you sure you're up to this?"

He nodded, although he wasn't sure of anything. He could hardly keep the faces and the stories straight.

Sandra hesitated. "Has anyone caught your fancy yet?"

Chase chuckled, not because he found her question amusing, but because he was susceptible to one of the most basic human flaws—wanting what he couldn't have. He wanted Lesley. "The woman I'd like to marry is in love with someone else and won't marry me."

"Isn't that the way it generally works?" Sandra offered sympathetically.

"It must," he said, stretching out his legs and crossing them at the ankles. He wasn't accustomed to so much sitting and was getting restless. The city was beginning to wear on him, too, and the thought of his cabin on the tundra became more appealing by the minute.

"Is there one woman who's stuck out in your mind?" He motioned for Sandra to sit down and she did, taking the chair across from him.

"A couple," she said. "Do you remember Anna Lincoln and LaDonna Ransom?"

Chase didn't, not immediately. "Describe them to me."

"LaDonna's that petite blonde you saw yesterday evening, the one who's working in the King County Assessor's office."

Try as he might, Chase couldn't recall the woman, not when there'd been so many. There'd been several blondes, and countless faces and little that made one stand out over another.

"But I hesitate to recommend her. She's a fragile little thing, and I don't know how well she'd adjust to winters that far north. Seattle's climate is temperate and nothing like what you experience. But...she was sweet, and I think you'd grow to love her, given the opportunity."

"What about Anna Lincoln?"

"We chatted for a bit before the interview and she seemed to be a nice girl. Ambitious, too. Of course there was the one drawback." Sandra shrugged. "She's not very pretty, at least not when you compare her to a lot of the other women who've applied."

"Beauty doesn't count for much as far as I'm concerned. I'm not exactly a movie star myself, you know."

Sandra must have felt obliged to argue with him because she made something of a fuss, contradicting him. By the time she'd finished, she had him sounding like he should consider running for Mr. Universe.

"At any rate, I liked Anna and I think she'd suit you. If you want I'll get her file."

"Please."

Sandra left and returned a couple of minutes later with the file. Chase was reading it over when she said good-night. He waved absently as he scanned the application and his few notes. There wasn't a picture enclosed, which might have jogged his memory. The details she'd written down about herself described at least twenty other women he'd interviewed in the past few days.

He set the file aside and relaxed, leaning back in his chair, wondering if Anna's lips were as soft and pliable as Lesley's, or if she fit in his arms as though she'd been made for him. Probably not. No use trying to fool himself.

He reread the information and, exhaling sharply with defeat, set aside the file. At the rate things were going, he'd return to Twin Creeks without the bride he'd come to find.

"Lori?" Lesley was so excited to find her friend at home that her voice rose unnaturally high.

"Lesley? Hi."

"Hi, yourself. I've been waiting to hear from you. We were going to get together this week, remember?"

"We were? Oh, right, I did say I'd call you, didn't I? I'm sorry, I haven't had a chance. Oh, Les, you'll never guess what happened. Larry asked me to marry him!" She let out a scream that sounded as though she were being strangled.

"Lori!"

"I know, I've got to stop doing that, but every time I think of Larry and me together, I get so excited I can hardly stand it."

"You haven't been dating him that long, have you?"

"Long enough. I'm crazy about this guy, Lesley, and for once in my life I've found a man who feels the same way about me."

"Congratulations!" Lesley put as much punch into the word as she could. She *was* thrilled for Lori, and wished her fellow teacher and Larry every happiness. But in the same breath, in the same heartbeat, she was so jealous she wanted to weep.

Truth demanded a price and being honest with herself had taken its toll on Lesley all week. First, she'd been forced to admit she still loved Tony, despite all her efforts to put him out of her life. It was hopeless, useless and masochistic. She didn't need Daisy to tell her she was setting herself up for heartache. Not when she could see it herself.

Despite the temptation, she hadn't returned Tony's calls. However, it wasn't her sense of honor that had prompted her forbearance, nor had it been her sense of right and wrong.

Good old-fashioned fear was what kept her away from the phone. Fear of what she might do if Tony admitted he'd made a mistake and wanted her back in his life. Fear of what she might become if he came to her, claiming he loved her, needed her.

On the heels of this painful insight came the news of Lori's engagement. Now she and Jo Ann were the only two single women left at the school. And Jo Ann didn't count, not technically.

Jo Ann had separated from her husband a year earlier and she'd taken back her maiden name. But recently they'd been talking. It wouldn't surprise Lesley if the two of them decided to make another go of their marriage.

Now Lori was engaged.

"Larry wants a short engagement, which is fine with me," she was saying. "I'd like it if we could have the wedding before school starts this fall, and he's agreed. You'll be one of my bridesmaids, won't you?"

"I'd be honored." That would make six times now that Lesley had stood up for friends. What was that old saying? Always a bridesmaid, never a bride. It certainly applied in her case.

In the fall she'd be returning to the same school, the

same classroom, the one directly down from Tony's. April's class was on the other side of the building. They'd all return, enthusiastic about the new school year, eager to get started after the long break.

Tony would glance at her with that special look in his eyes and she wouldn't be able to glance away. He'd know in a heartbeat that she still loved him, and worse, so would April and everyone else on staff. That humiliation far outweighed the likelihood of being the only unmarried faculty member.

Lesley knew she never should've let Tony talk her out of transferring to another school. Perhaps she'd asked for another assignment just so he'd beg her to stay; she didn't know anymore, didn't trust herself or her motives.

"Larry talked to my dad and formally asked for my hand in marriage," Lori was saying when Lesley pulled her thoughts back to her friend. "He's so traditional and sweet. It's funny, Les, but when it's right, it's right, and you know it in your gut. It wouldn't have mattered if we'd dated three months or three years."

"Hadn't you met Larry a while ago?"

"Yeah. Apparently. He's a friend of my brother's, but I don't *remember* meeting him until this spring, although he claims I did. He pretends to be insulted that I've forgotten."

Lesley smiled. Lori's happiness sang through the wire like a melodious love song, full of spirit and joy. They spoke for a few minutes longer, of getting together with three of Lori's other friends and choosing the dresses, but it was all rather vague.

Jealous. That was how Lesley felt. Jealous of one of her best friends. She hated admitting it, but there was no other way to explain the hard knot in her stomach.

It wasn't that she wished Lori and Larry anything but the best.

But her feelings were wrapped around memories of the past, of standing alone, helpless and lost. Abandoned.

When she finished talking to Lori, Lesley called a florist friend and had a congratulatory bouquet sent to Lori and Larry with her warmest wishes.

Housework, Lesley decided. That was what a woman did when she suffered from guilt. It was either that or bury herself in a gallon of gourmet ice cream. She stripped her bed, stuffed the sheets in the washer and was hanging them on the line when Eric and Kevin found her.

"Is Chase coming over today?" Eric wanted to know.

"He didn't say," she answered as noncommittally as she could. She didn't want to disappoint them, or encourage them, either.

"Can you call him and ask?"

Lesley shoved a clothespin onto a sheet, anchoring it. "I don't have his phone number," she said, realizing it for the first time.

"He'll be calling you, won't he?"

"I…don't know." She'd asked him to and he'd said he would, but that wasn't any guarantee. He'd been annoyed with her when they parted, convinced she'd contact Tony despite her shaky reassurance otherwise.

Chase was an intelligent and sensitive man; he knew better than to involve himself in a dead-end relationship. It wouldn't surprise her if he never contacted her again.

The thought struck her hard and fast. The pain it produced shocked her. She hadn't realized how much she'd come to treasure their brief time together.

"What do you *mean* you don't know if he'll call you again?" Eric demanded. "You *have* to see him again because Kevin and me wrote him a letter to thank him for taking us fishing."

"Mom made us," Kevin volunteered. His front tooth was missing and Lesley noticed its absence for the first time.

She caught the younger boy by the chin and angled his head toward the light, although he squirmed. "Kevin, you lost your tooth. When did this happen?"

"Last night."

"Congratulations," she said, releasing him. "Did you leave it out for the Tooth Fairy?"

The boy rolled his eyes. "I don't believe in that silly stuff anymore and neither does Eric."

"What do you expect when they've got me for a mother?" Daisy said, stepping out the back porch, her hands on her hips. "I never did believe in feeding kids all that garbage about Santa Claus and the Easter bunny. Life's hard enough without their own mother filling their heads with that kind of nonsense."

"We get gifts and candy and other stuff," Kevin felt obliged to inform Lesley, "but we know who gave them to us. Mom gave me a dollar for the tooth."

"He already spent it, too, on gum and candy."

"I shared, didn't I?"

"Boys, why don't you run along," Daisy said.

"What about the letter?"

"Give it to Lesley and let her worry about it." With that, her neighbor returned to the house.

What Lesley had told the boys about not knowing Chase's phone number was a half-truth. There was always the number on the billboard. If she hadn't heard from him by that evening, she'd leave a message for him through the answering service, although she doubted it would ever reach him.

After a polite knock, Sandra let herself into Chase's makeshift office in the suite he'd rented. He'd interviewed ten more women that morning and was scheduled to meet another fifteen that afternoon and evening.

He hadn't talked to or seen Lesley in two days and the temptation to call her or even drive over to see her was gaining momentum. He was trying, really trying, to meet a woman he liked as much as Lesley. Thus far he hadn't succeeded. Hadn't come anywhere *close* to succeeding.

"Does the name Lesley Campbell mean anything to you?" Sandra asked unexpectedly.

Chase straightened as a chill shot through him. "Yes, why?"

"She left a message with the answering service. Apparently she explained that she wasn't responding to your billboard ad. She wanted it understood that the two of you know each other."

"She left a message?"

"Yes." Sandra handed him the pink slip. "I thought it might be a trick. Some of the applicants have tried various methods to get your attention."

Chase didn't need to be reminded of that. Flowers arrived almost daily, along with elaborately wrapped presents. A few of the gifts had shocked him. He hadn't accepted any of them. The floral bouquets he had delivered to a nearby nursing home and the gifts were dispensed with quickly. He left their disposal in Sandra's capable hands.

One woman, a day earlier, had shown up in full winter garb, carrying a long-barreled shotgun as though that would prove she was ready, willing and able to withstand the harsh winters of the Arctic. He wasn't sure what the gun was meant to signify.

Chase supposed she'd rented the outfit from a costume store. She resembled Daniel Boone more than she did a prospective wife. Chase had lost patience with her and sent her on her way.

He glanced down at the message slip in his hand and tried to decide what to do. Returning Lesley's call could just prolong the inevitable. He wondered if she'd spoken to Tony and what had come of their conversation. The minute he learned she had, it would be over for them. Possibly it was already over.

Objectivity was beyond him at this point. As far as he was concerned, Tony was bad news. All the man represented for Lesley was heartache and grief. If she wasn't smart enough to figure that out for herself, then he couldn't help her.

He waited until Sandra had left the room before he called Lesley. She answered on the second ring. The sound of her voice produced an empty, achy feeling that surprised him; he'd been unaware she had such power to hurt him. He had no one to blame but himself. If Lesley hurt him, it was because *he'd* allowed it.

"It's Chase."

"Chase…" she said breathlessly. "Thank you for returning my call. I wasn't sure you'd get my message."

"How are you?" He'd never been a brilliant conversationalist, but he was generally more adept than this.

"Fine. How about you?"

"Busy."

"Yeah, me, too."

Silence. Chase didn't know if he should break it by saying something or wait for her to do it. They hadn't fought, hadn't spoken so much as a cross word to each other. He couldn't even say they'd disagreed, but there was a gap between them that had appeared after Tony's first call and widened with the second one.

"Eric and Kevin were asking about you," Lesley said before the silence threatened to go on forever. "I didn't know what to tell them."

"I see."

"They wrote you a letter and asked me to give it to you."

"That was thoughtful. They're good kids," he said carefully.

The ball was in her court. If she wanted to see him, she was going to have to ask.

"I could mail it."

His back straightened. "Fine." He rattled off his address and was about to make an excuse to get off the phone when she spoke again.

"I'd rather you came for it yourself."

Finally. Chase hoped she couldn't hear his sigh of relief. "When?"

"Whenever it's convenient for you." She sounded unsure of herself, as though she already regretted the invitation.

"If you want, you could leave it on your porch and I could pick it up sometime."

"No." Her objection came fast enough to lend him hope. "Tomorrow," she suggested. "Or tonight, whichever you prefer."

"I'll have to check my schedule." He didn't know

why he felt it was necessary to continue this pretense but he felt obliged to do so.

"I can wait."

He pressed the receiver to his chest and silently counted to ten, feeling like the biggest fool who'd ever roamed the earth.

"This afternoon looks like it would be the best. Say an hour?"

"That would be fine. I'll look for you then."

Chase waited until he heard the click of the receiver before he tossed the phone in the air and deftly caught it with one hand behind his back. "Hot damn," he shouted loudly enough to send Sandra running into the room.

"Is everything all right?"

"Everything, my dear Sandra, is just fine." He waltzed her across the room, planting a kiss on her cheek before hurrying out of the suite.

For the second time, Lesley fluffed up the decorator pillows at the end of her sofa. Holding one to her stomach, she exhaled slowly, praying she was doing the right thing.

The doorbell chimed and she must have leapt a good five inches off the ground. It was early, too early for Chase. She opened the door to find Daisy standing on the other side.

"He's coming?"

"Yes, how'd you know?"

Daisy laughed. "You wouldn't dress up like that for me."

"It's too much, isn't it?" She'd carefully gone through her wardrobe, choosing beige silk pants, a cream-colored top and a soft coral blazer. Her silver earrings were crescent-shaped and the pendant dangling from her gold chain was a gold-edged magnifying glass.

"You look fabulous, darling," Daisy commented in a lazy drawl. "Just fab-u-lous."

"Am I being too obvious?"

"Honey, compared to me, you're extremely subtle. Just be yourself and you'll do fine." She walked around the coffee table and eyed the cheese-and-cracker tray.

"What do you think?"

Daisy shrugged. "It's a nice touch."

"I've got wine cooling in the kitchen. I don't look too eager, do I?"

"No."

"You're sure?" Lesley had never been less certain of anything. Her nerves were shattered, her composure crumbling and her self-confidence was at its lowest ebb.

"There must be something in the air," Daisy said, reaching for a cracker. She was about to dip it in the nut-rolled cheddar cheese ball when Lesley slapped her hand.

"That's for Chase."

"Okay, okay." But Daisy ate the cracker anyway. "Didn't you tell me your friend Lori is getting married?" she asked.

"Yes."

Daisy relaxed on the sofa and crossed her legs, swinging one foot dangerously close to the cheese. "You'll never guess who's been calling."

"Who?"

"Charlie Glenn. He asked me out on a date. Charlie and me? He shocked me so bad I said yes without even thinking. It's been so long since someone who wasn't half bombed asked me out that I didn't know what to say."

"I've thought for weeks that Charlie's interested in you."

Daisy flapped her hand at Lesley. "Get outta here!"

"I'm serious," Lesley insisted.

"Well, that's why I think there must be something in the air. First you meet Chase, then Lori and Larry decide to tie the knot and then Charlie asks me out."

Lesley smiled. Since her divorce, Daisy had sworn off men. To the best of Lesley's knowledge, her neighbor hadn't dated since she'd separated from her ex.

"Where's Charlie taking you?"

"Taking *us*. He included the boys. We're going to Wild Waves. Eric and Kevin are ecstatic. Did you know Charlie's been married before? I didn't, and it came as a total shock to me. He never mentioned he had a kid, either. His son's a couple of years older than Eric and he wants the five of us to get together."

"I think that's wonderful."

"Yeah, I guess I do, too, but you know, I'm a little surprised. I'd never thought about Charlie in a romantic way, but I'm beginning to think I might be able to. I'm not rushing into anything, mind you, and neither is he. We've both been burned and neither of us is willing to walk through fire a second time." Daisy grabbed a second cracker. "Here I am jabbering away as though Charlie asked me to marry him or something. It's just a date. I have to keep telling myself that."

"I think Charlie's great."

"He's got a soft spot where his heart's supposed to be."

Lesley recalled how the bartender had given her a drink on the house the night Tony broke their engagement. She'd walked the streets for hours and finally landed in the cocktail lounge where Daisy worked weekends as a waitress and Charlie tended bar. Because she hadn't eaten and so rarely drank hard liquor, one stiff whiskey had Lesley feeling more than a little inebriated. Charlie had half carried her to Daisy's car, she remembered. His touch was gentle and his words soothing, although for the life of her she couldn't recall a word he'd said.

"Let me know what happens," Daisy said, uncrossing her legs and bounding off the sofa. She walked to the door and opened it, then turned around. "You're *sure* you know what you're doing?"

"No!" she cried. She wasn't sure of anything at the moment except the knot in her stomach.

"I'll do my best to keep the boys out of your hair but they're anxious to see Chase again. He certainly made an impression on those two," she said with a smile. She left, closing the door quietly behind her.

Lesley didn't blame them. Chase had treated them with compassion and kindness; not only that, he knew how to entertain them.

The phone rang then, and Lesley glared at it. She let the answering machine take the calls most of the time now, since there was always a chance the caller could be Tony. She needed to invest in call display, she told herself. It had been pure luck that she'd picked up when Chase phoned. Her reaction had been instinctive, but she was pleased she'd answered because the caller had been Chase.

The phone rang again and the machine automatically went on after the third ring. Whoever was calling didn't listen to her message and disconnected.

A moment later, she heard the doorbell. It had to be

Chase. She inhaled a calming breath, squared her shoulders and crossed the room.

With a smile firmly in place, she opened the door.

"Hello, Lesley."

"Hello," she said, stepping aside for Chase to enter. "Come in, please."

He hadn't taken his eyes off her, which was both reassuring and disconcerting.

"I'm glad you could come."

"Thank you for inviting me."

How stiff they were with each other, how awkward, like polite strangers. "Sit down," she said, gesturing toward the sofa.

Chase took a seat and looked appreciatively at the cheese and crackers.

"Would you like a drink?" she asked. "I have a bottle of pinot grigio, if you'd care for that. There's a pot of coffee, too, if you'd prefer something hot."

"Wine would be nice."

"I thought so, too," she said eagerly, smiling. She moved into the kitchen, and Chase followed her.

"Do you need any help opening the wine?"

"No, I'm fine, thanks." A smaller, daintier woman might have trouble removing a cork, but she was perfectly capable of handling it. He watched her expertly open the bottle and fill two wineglasses.

"You mentioned the boys' letter," Chase said. Their thank-you note had been an excuse to contact him and they both knew it.

"I'll get it for you," she said, leaving him briefly while she retrieved the note. "They really are grateful for the time you spent with them."

He read it over, grinning, and handed it to her to

read. Eric had written the short but enthusiastic message, and Kevin had decorated the handmade card with different colored fish in odd shapes and sizes.

"So," Lesley said, leading the way back into the living room. "How's it going?"

"Okay." He sat next to her on the sofa. "How about you?"

"Same."

Chase studied her. "Are you going to tell me what Tony wanted or are you going to make me guess?"

"I don't know," she answered, sipping her wine. She hoped he didn't detect the slight shake in her hand.

"You don't know if you're going to tell me or if you're going to make me guess?"

She shook her head. "No. I don't know what he wanted. I didn't return his call."

This seemed to surprise Chase. "Why didn't you?"

Lesley raised one shoulder in a shrug. "I couldn't see that it would do either of us any good."

"You were afraid to, weren't you?"

"Yes," she admitted in a husky murmur. "I was afraid."

"Is that why you contacted me?"

"Yes." He wanted his proverbial pound of flesh, she realized, and at the same moment knew she'd give it to him. "But I don't love you, Chase."

"It's a bit difficult to care for someone like me when your heart belongs to another man." After a significant pause, he added, "A married man."

He made it sound so cold, so…ugly.

"He wasn't married when I fell in love with him," she said, defending herself.

"He is now."

"I don't need you to remind me of that," she cried, raising her voice for the first time.

"Good," he said brusquely.

"How are the interviews going?" she asked, hoping to make light conversation and gain the information she needed.

"All right." He set the wineglass aside as if preparing to leave.

"Would you be willing to look at another application?"

"Probably not." He stood and shoved his hands deep in his pants pockets. "I've got more than I can deal with now. Are you going to recommend a friend of yours?"

"No." Lesley closed her eyes and forced herself to continue. "I was hoping you'd consider marrying me."

Seven

"You?" Chase repeated slowly, unsure he'd heard her correctly. It seemed too good to be true, something he dared not believe.

"Yes." Lesley was standing now, too, her steady gaze nearly level with his own. She studied him as closely as he was studying her. "I'd be willing to marry you."

"Why?" Fool that he was, he had to ask, although he was confident he knew her answer. He wondered if she'd be honest enough to admit it.

"I like you very much," she said, obviously choosing her words with care. "And it's clear that there's a physical attraction between us. I don't usually respond to a man the way I have to you."

He gave her no reassurances nor did he discourage her. She seemed nervous, understandably so. "Those are the only reasons?" he pressed.

"No." She was irritated with him now and he felt relieved. The more emotion she revealed the better. "I don't want to live in Seattle any longer."

She'd disappointed him. "If that's all you want, isn't marrying a man you don't love a little drastic? All you need to do is apply for a teaching position elsewhere. I'm not up on these things, but I seem to remember hearing that teachers were in high demand in a number of states. Try Montana. That's where your mother's living, isn't it?"

"I don't want to move to Montana. I'd rather be in Alaska with you."

"You still haven't answered my question."

"You're going to make me say it, aren't you? You'd like to see me humiliate myself, but I'm not going to. Now, do you want to marry me or not?"

There'd never been a single doubt in Chase's mind. He knew exactly what he wanted and he had from the beginning. He wanted Lesley. He'd always wanted Lesley, and that wasn't going to change.

"It's Tony, isn't it?" he said, as unemotionally as he could. Funny, he'd never met the man but he despised him for what he'd done to Lesley and for the way he was treating his wife. "You're afraid he has the power to reduce you to something you find abhorrent. He wants you, doesn't he? But he's married and that means you'd be his mistress and you're scared out of your wits that you'll do it because you love him."

"Yes. Yes!" Angry tears glistened in her eyes and her hands were clenched into tight fists at her sides.

"You think marrying me and moving to Alaska is the answer to all your problems."

"Yes," she cried again. "I've never lied to you, Chase, not even when it would've been convenient. You know exactly what you're getting with me."

"Yes, I do," he answered softly.

"Well?" she asked with an indignant tilt of her chin. "Are you going to marry me or not?"

"Is this a take-it-or-leave-it proposition?"

"Yes."

"All right," he said, walking away from her. "We'll be married Wednesday evening."

"Next week!" She sounded as if that was impossible. Unthinkable. "I can't put together a wedding in that amount of time. My mother and Ken are traveling in their trailer this summer and—"

"Do you want them at the ceremony?" he interrupted.

"Yes, but...not if it means ruining their vacation."

"Then we won't tell them until they're home." If Lesley was looking for solutions, he'd willingly supply them.

"I'd like to try calling them. And I want to invite a few friends and have a small reception."

"Fine with me. The hotel can arrange whatever you want with twenty-four hours' notice. We'll talk to them on Monday." Chase didn't intend to give her any more time than that or she might well talk herself out of it.

"What about the invitations?"

"Well, there's always email."

"No, I want real invitations."

"I'll have a messenger service hand deliver them."

"But they'll need to be printed, and...oh, Chase, there are so many things to do. I have a dress, but I don't know if you'd want me to wear it since I bought it for another man, but it's so beautiful and—no, I couldn't possibly wear it, and that means I'll have to buy another one. But it took me weeks to find the *first* one."

Chase held his breath until his chest ached with the effort. "It seems to me you're looking for excuses."

"I'm not! I swear I'm not. It's just that..."

"Be very sure, Lesley, because once we say those vows we're married, and I take that very seriously. I assume you do, too."

She nodded slowly. "What about all my things? What will I do with them? I can't cram everything I own in a couple of suitcases."

"Pack what you want and I'll have the rest shipped. You won't need the furniture, so either sell it or give it away—whatever you want."

She took a deep breath. "Okay."

"We'll need to apply for the wedding license tomorrow morning. I'll be here by ten to pick you up," he said.

She nodded again and he started for the door.

"Chase."

He turned around, impatient now and not understanding why. Lesley had agreed to marry him, which was more than he'd expected. "Yes?"

"Would you mind kissing me?" Her voice was small and uncertain. He purposely hadn't made this easy on her for the simple reason that he wanted her to know her own mind. To be satisfied that marriage to him was the right decision. He would've liked to kiss her, and use their mutual attraction to convince her, but he couldn't. That would have felt unethical to him.

He saw that Lesley had taken several steps toward him; the least he could do was meet her halfway. She needed reassurance and he should have given it to her long before now.

He walked back to her, held her face in his hands and kissed her. The kiss deepened and deepened until Chase's control teetered precariously.

He'd forgotten exactly how good she felt in his arms. It shouldn't be like this. His experience might not have been as extensive as that of some men, but with other women he'd always been composed and in control. His response to Lesley worried him. The fact that he found her so desirable was important, but that he could so easily lose his head over her was a negative.

Lesley exhaled, that soft womanly sigh that drove him to distraction. He lifted his mouth from hers and concentrated on the nape of her neck, scattering kisses there while struggling with his own composure.

"Thank you," she whispered. The beauty of her words and the sweetness of her mouth were fatal to his control.

"This will be a real marriage, Lesley," he warned.

"I realize that." She sounded slightly offended, but Chase refused to leave any room for doubt.

"Good. I'll pick you up tomorrow morning, then."

Lesley nodded and Chase felt a sense of victory, hollow though it was. She'd agreed to marry him, but for none of the reasons he would've liked. She was running away from a painful situation that could only bring her heartache.

He was the lesser of two evils.

Not the most solid foundation for a marriage. But time and patience and love were the mortar that would strengthen it.

"You're getting married!" Lori and Jo Ann repeated together in stunned disbelief.

"I didn't offer to buy you lunch in a fancy restaurant for nothing," Lesley commented brightly, forking up a slice of chicken in her chicken-and-spinach salad. "What are you two doing Wednesday evening?"

"Ah...nothing," Lori murmured.

"Not a thing," Jo Ann said.

"Great, I'd like you both to stand up for me at my wedding. Chase and I are—"

"Chase?" Jo Ann broke in. "Who on earth is Chase?"

"I didn't know you were dating anyone," Lori said, sounding more surprised than upset.

Neither of her friends had touched their seafood salads. They sat like mannequins, staring at Lesley as if she'd announced she was an escaped convict.

"Chase Goodman," Lesley repeated casually between bites. "That's the man I'm marrying."

Lori, small and fawnlike, with large dark eyes, gnawed on her lower lip. "Why does that name sound familiar? Do I know him?"

"I doubt it. Chase's from Alaska."

"Alaska." Jo Ann said the name of the state in a low voice, as if trying to remember something. She picked up her fork. "Speaking of Alaska... Did either of you see the news story last week about this guy who came down from Alaska and advertised for a—" She stopped, her eyes widening. She made a few odd sounds, but nothing that resembled intelligible words.

"You're marrying the guy who advertised for a wife?" Lori looked from Lesley to Jo Ann and back again.

"Lesley, have you lost your mind?" Jo Ann finally sputtered.

"Maybe." She wasn't going to argue with her two best friends. A week earlier she'd thought the whole idea of marrying a stranger was crazy. She'd said as much to Chase, belittled the women who'd applied, even made derogatory remarks about the type of man who'd defy convention in such an outlandish manner.

One week later, she'd agreed to be his bride.

"You *will* be my bridesmaids, won't you?"

"Of course, but—"

"No buts. The wedding's on Wednesday. I don't have time for arguments, and please, don't try to talk me out of this because you can't. Chase and I are leaving for our honeymoon after the wedding." She smiled. "The location's a surprise. After that, we're heading to Twin Creeks, where Chase lives. He has to be on the job in eight days and that doesn't leave us much time."

"Pinch me," Lori said to Jo Ann, "because this doesn't seem real. We're not actually hearing this, are we? Lesley, this isn't like you."

Jo Ann shook her head and added, "It's because of Tony, isn't it? You're far too sensible to do something like this otherwise."

"I wasn't going to say anything." Lori looked down, rearranging the salt and pepper shakers on the cream-colored tablecloth. "But... Tony phoned me. He's worried about you, Les. He said he's been trying to get in touch with you, but you weren't returning his calls."

"Tony's been calling you?" Jo Ann sounded outraged. "Does April know about this?"

"She's out of town."

"That creep!"

"I knew when he married April that it wouldn't last," Lori said with a hint of self-righteousness.

Lesley laughed, grateful for her friends' loyalty. "You suspected it wouldn't last because Tony wasn't marrying me. If he had, you would both have been singing his praises."

"I'm beginning to think Daisy might be right about him," Jo Ann said, stabbing her fork into some crabmeat. "How could she see through him so quickly? The three of us work with the guy nine months out of the year and we have to be hit over the head before it dawns on us that Tony isn't playing fair."

"What did you tell Tony about me?" Lesley inquired casually, although her interest was anything but casual.

"Nothing much, just that I'd talked to you recently and you sounded happy.

"He seemed surprised to hear that and said he was afraid you were depressed and avoiding people. He acted concerned and guilty about the way he'd hurt you. I…"

"Yes?" Lesley prompted.

"I felt sorry for him by the time we hung up."

"*Sorry* for him?" Jo Ann asked, incredulous. "Why would you feel sorry for Tony? He's the one who broke Lesley's heart and married someone else."

Lori shrugged, looking mildly guilty herself. "He didn't actually say so, but I had the feeling he regrets marrying April." Lori paused, frowning. "She's never been very friendly toward the three of us, has she?"

"Who can blame her for being unfriendly?" Lesley was the first one to defend April.

"Tony made her situation impossible at school," Lori agreed. "We did our best to make her feel welcome, but we'd all worked with Lesley and April knew that. She attended hardly any faculty functions after the wedding. I'll bet she's really a nice person, and we'd find that out if she ever gave anyone the chance to know her."

"She gave Tony plenty of chances," Jo Ann muttered, unwilling even now to forget the upheaval the new first-grade teacher had brought into their lives.

"You haven't talked to Tony yourself?" Lori asked, ignoring Jo Ann's pettiness. For that, Lesley was grateful.

"Not since school got out." She felt good about resisting the temptation to phone him, but it had exacted a high emotional price. "I won't, either," she said, her resolve growing stronger.

Jo Ann nodded vigorously. Lori looked uncertain.

"Aren't you curious about what he wants?"

"Come on, Lori. What do you *think* Tony wants?" Jo Ann asked.

Lori studied her for a disbelieving moment. "You don't really believe that, do you?"

"Lori, wake up!" Jo Ann said sarcastically and snapped her fingers. "When a married man phones another woman—his ex-fiancée, no less—while his wife's out of town, there's only one reason."

"I hate to think Tony would do that."

Lesley felt the same way, but she couldn't allow her tenderness for Tony to mislead her.

"Stop." Jo Ann raised both hands. "We've strayed from the real subject here and that's Lesley's wedding."

"'Lesley's wedding,'" Lori echoed, sending a dismayed glance at Jo Ann. "Are you in love with Chase?" she asked.

"No." Lesley refused to be anything but honest with her friends. When she'd told her mother and Ken she'd stretched the truth, subtly of course, but she'd never be able to fool her friends. Her mother was another story; she believed Lesley was in love because that was what she wanted to believe.

Lori's jaw fell open. "You don't even love him."

"I've only known the man for a little more than one week. It's a bit difficult to develop a deep, emotional attachment in that length of time."

"You're willing to marry him anyway," Jo Ann

murmured thoughtfully. "That tells me a lot. He's obviously got something going for him."

"He's good with kids, and he's kind. And brave," she said, remembering his pursuit of her mugger. Those were only three of Chase's character traits that appealed to her. Honesty was another.

"What's he look like?" Lori was eager to know.

"Kind of like you'd expect someone from Alaska to look. He's tall and muscular and his eyes are a lovely deep brown. He's a comfortable sort of person to be with, entertaining and funny. When he laughs it comes from his belly."

"You're marrying a man because of the way he laughs?"

It sounded absurd, but in part she was. Chase had a wonderful sense of humor and Lesley found that quality important in any relationship, but vital in a marriage.

"You really like this guy, don't you?"

Lesley nodded. It surprised her how much she did.

"Would you guys have time to shop with me this afternoon?" Lesley asked, ending her introspection. She hadn't said a word about the way Chase kissed. He should win awards for his style. She'd never known a man could arouse such a heated reaction with a few kisses.

"You're going through with this, aren't you?" Even now Lori didn't quite seem to believe it.

"Yes, I am." She turned to Jo Ann, expecting an argument, unsought advice or words of caution.

"I almost envy you," Jo Ann remarked instead. "This is going to be an incredible adventure. You'll email us and let us know what happens, won't you?"

Lesley laughed, astonished when she felt tears gather

in her eyes. Through all the pain and difficulties of the past year, she'd been blessed with truly good friends.

"I wonder what Alaska will be like," Lori said dreamily. "Do you think Twin Creeks will have a friendly moose wandering through town like in the opening of that old TV show?"

"Hi," Lesley said, letting herself into the house. Chase had spent the afternoon at her rented home, supervising the packers so her personal things would be ready for shipping.

He tossed aside the magazine he was reading and smiled up at her with that roguish gleam in his eyes. Her heart reacted with a surprising surge of warmth.

"How'd your meeting with your friends go?" Chase asked.

"Really well." It was ridiculous to be shy with him now.

"They didn't try to talk you out of the wedding?"

Lesley grinned as she sat down on the sofa that would soon belong to Daisy and her boys. "I'll admit they were shocked, but once I told them what a fabulous kisser you are, they were green with envy."

"You aren't going to change your mind, are you?"

Lori and Jo Ann had asked her that question, too, and she gave him the same answer. "No. Are you worried?"

"Yes." His voice was gruff and he reached for her, kissing her hungrily.

Lesley could find no will to resist him. He'd only kissed her once since she'd agreed to be his wife and she needed his touch, longed for it. She leaned forward and braced her hand against his chest. The strong, even feel of his pulse reassured her that he enjoyed their kisses as much as she did. At least she wasn't alone in this.

Chase took hold of her waist and pulled her closer. His kiss was slow, deep and thorough. And not nearly enough.

Chase started to pull away and she protested. "No…"

His mouth came back to hers once more. By the time Chase pulled away from her, she was weak and dizzy and breathless.

"Lesley, listen," he whispered, pressing his forehead to hers.

"No," she whispered back. "Just hold me for a few minutes. Please." She didn't want to talk, not then, nor was she interested in thinking because if she analyzed what she was doing, she might change her mind, after all.

All Lesley wanted was to *feel*. When she was in Chase's arms she could feel again. For months she'd been trapped in a kind of numbness. Sometimes the pain surged up to inundate her but most of the time she'd felt nothing. No laughter. No tears. Just a lethargy that sapped away her energy and destroyed her dreams.

Then she'd met Chase and suddenly she was laughing again, dreaming again. Whenever he kissed her, a cascade of feelings flooded her body—and her heart. She needed to experience that excitement, those emotions.

For reasons of his own, Chase needed her, too. She would reciprocate generously and without reserve because she wanted him as badly as he wanted her.

As she luxuriated in the shelter of his arms, he buried his face in her neck, his breathing heavy.

Then, without warning, he broke away from her, leaving her breathless. Stunned. Before she could analyze what was happening, he was on his feet and moving toward the door. "I have to go."

"Go? But why?"

He paused, his back to her. "Because if I stay we're going to end up in bed."

"You...you don't want to be with me?"

Chase didn't answer. Although Lesley thought she knew why he'd resisted the temptation to make love to her, she still felt hurt. She suspected that he feared she might not go through with the marriage. His lack of trust offended her, and his rejection was more than insulting, it was painful in a way that echoed past anguish. She'd lowered her guard, offered him everything she had to give and he was walking away from her. The six-year-old child whose father had abandoned her was back, chanting her fears.

"Go, then," she said furiously, trying to silence the sounds of grief only she could hear.

He paused at the front door, his shoulders slumped forward. "I can't leave you now."

"Sure you can."

He turned back and walked over to the sofa, sitting down next to her. He pulled her into his arms, disregarding her token objections, and held her. She let him, although the little girl in her wanted to push him away, hurt him for hurting her. But the womanly part of her needed his comfort.

As Chase kissed the crown of her head, she sighed and nestled in his arms.

"You tempt me, Lesley Campbell, more than any woman I've ever known," he whispered.

"You tempt me, too."

She felt his smile and was glad he was there with her.

"Becky Bright, the reporter who did that interview with me, phoned earlier this afternoon," he told her.

"How come?"

"She wants to do an interview with the two of us right after the wedding. Do you mind?"

"I suppose not. Do you?"

"I do, but it's the only way I can think of to stop the phone calls. According to the answering service, they're still coming in."

"Still?"

"I had the billboard taken down and asked Sandra to cancel all the remaining appointments, but there are more women phoning now than ever. I'm sure some called before and were discouraged when they didn't hear back right away. Several were phoning to see if I'd made a decision and others wanted to know it if was too late."

"It's certainly been an…interesting experiment, hasn't it?" she said.

"Yes, but it isn't one I care to repeat."

Lesley jabbed him with her elbow. "I should hope not!"

Chase laughed, slid his arms around her waist and nuzzled her neck. "I'm going to have my hands full with one wife."

"What about the applicants you've already seen?"

"I had Sandra write up a form letter and send it out to everyone, including them."

"To eight hundred women."

Lesley felt his smile against her skin. "Not exactly."

"What do you mean?"

"I got eight hundred calls, yes—well, maybe a thousand in total if we add the recent ones—but not all of them were from women who wanted to be my wife. I found that at least a hundred were from mothers planning to introduce me to their daughters."

Lesley stared at him. "I hope you're joking."

"I'm not. And there were more crank calls than I care to mention."

"So," Lesley said, feeling a bit cocky. "When you come right down to it, exactly how many serious applications did you receive?"

"One."

"One? But you said... I heard on the news—"

"Yours was the only one I took seriously."

His words were sweet and soft and precisely what she needed. She rewarded him by throwing her arms around his neck and directing his mouth to hers. Their kisses were slow and lazy and pleasurable.

Chase wasn't ready to leave for another hour. He needed to finish up some last-minute details with the answering service and the billboard company. After that, she lingered with him on the front porch for ten minutes, neither of them eager to separate even for a few hours.

"I'll be back soon," he promised. "Where would you like to have dinner?"

Lesley smiled. "Are you in the mood for another hamburger and a rematch at the golf course?"

"You're on."

Lesley stood on the porch until his car was out of sight. She glanced at her watch and realized that in twenty-four hours they'd be married.

The house felt empty without Chase. In fact, not just her house but her whole life felt different now that she was marrying him.

She showered and changed clothes, and was packing her suitcase when the doorbell chimed. Her steps were eager as she ran across the living room. Chase could come in without the formality of waiting for her to answer the door. She should have said as much.

Her smile bright, she opened the door.

"Hello, Lesley."

Her heart, which had seemed light only seconds before, plummeted like a deadweight to the pit of her stomach.

"Hello, Tony."

Eight

"Lesley, oh, Lesley." Tony's hands reached for hers, gripping them tightly. "You don't have any idea how good it is to see you again. I've been desperate to talk to you. Why didn't you return my calls?"

The immediate attraction was there, the way it had always been. That shouldn't have surprised her, but it did. Lesley had hoped that when she saw Tony again, she wouldn't experience this terrible need.

She jerked her hands free.

"Lesley." Tony's eyes widened with hurt disbelief.

"I didn't return your calls for a reason. We don't have anything to discuss."

"That's where you're wrong. Lesley, my love—"

"I'm not your love."

"But you are," he said in a hurt-little-boy manner. "You'll always be my love…you always have been."

"You're married to April." He obviously needed to be reminded of that, and so did she. The strength of her love for him, despite his marital status, was nearly overwhelming. All the feelings she'd struggled to vanquish threatened her now.

"I know... I know." He sounded sad and uncertain, a combination that never failed to touch her heart. Part of her longed to invite him into her home and listen to his troubles, but she dared not and knew it.

"I'm making a new life for myself," she insisted, steeling herself against the pleading in his eyes. "I've given notice to the school and to my landlord."

"A new life? One without me?"

"Yes. Please, Tony, just leave." She stepped back, intending to close the door, but he placed his foot over the threshold, blocking her attempt.

"I can't," he said. "Not until I've talked to you."

"Tony, please." This was so much harder than she'd imagined it would be. He must have sensed that because he edged closer.

"Tony." Her voice shook with the force of her desperation. "We have nothing to say to each other."

"Lesley."

Chase's voice sounded like an angel's harp. She was so grateful he'd arrived that she nearly burst into tears.

"Chase," she said, breaking away from Tony and rushing forward. She must have appeared desperate, but she didn't care. Chase was her one link to sanity and she held on to him with both hands.

"What's going on here?" Tony demanded. "Who is this man?"

"Actually, I was about to ask you the same thing," Chase said stiffly.

"I'm Tony Field."

Lesley felt Chase stiffen as soon as he recognized the name. He reacted by placing his arm possessively around Lesley's shoulders and pulling her closer to his side.

"Who *is* this man?" Tony asked again.

Lesley opened her mouth to explain, but before she could utter a single word, Chase spoke.

"Lesley and I are going to be married."

"Married?" Tony laughed as if he'd just heard a good joke. "You can't be serious."

"We're dead serious," Chase responded.

"Lesley?" Tony looked at her, clearly expecting her to deny it.

"It's true," she said with as much conviction as she could manage.

"That's ridiculous. You've never mentioned anyone named Chase and I know for a fact that you weren't dating him before school was out. Isn't this rather sudden?"

"Not in the least," Chase said as if they'd been involved for years.

"Lesley?"

"There's a lot you don't know about my fiancée," Chase said, smiling down at her.

It was all Lesley could do not to tell them both to stop playing these ridiculous games. Tony regarded her with a tormented expression, as though *he* was the loyal one and she'd betrayed him. Chase wasn't any better. The full plumage of his male pride was fanned out in opulent display.

"You can't possibly be marrying this man," Tony said, ignoring Chase and concentrating on her instead.

"I already said I was." She hated the way her voice quavered. Chase didn't seem pleased with the lack of enthusiasm in her trembling response, but that couldn't be helped.

"The ceremony's tomorrow evening," Chase added.

"Lesley, you don't love this man," Tony continued, his gaze burning into hers.

"You don't know that," Chase challenged.

"I do know it. Lesley loves *me*. Tell him, sweetheart. You'd be doing us both a grave disservice if you didn't tell him the truth."

Lesley could see no reason to confess the obvious. "I'm marrying Chase."

"But you love me," Tony insisted, his voice agitated. She noticed that he clenched his fists at his sides as if his temper was about to explode. He'd fight for her if necessary, he seemed to be saying.

"You're already married," Chase told Tony with evident delight.

Tony turned to Lesley once more, ignoring Chase. "Marrying April was a mistake. That's what I've been trying to tell you. If only you'd returned my calls... I love you, Lesley. I have for years. I don't know what came over me... I can see now that April and I were never right for each other. I've been miserable without you."

"You don't need to listen to this," Chase hissed in her ear. He tried to steer her past Tony and toward the front door, but she was rooted to the spot and unable to move.

"You've got to listen," Tony pleaded, "before you ruin both our lives."

"Where's April now?" Chase asked.

"She left me."

"You're lying." Chase's voice was tight with barely restrained anger. "You said she was visiting her mother for a week."

"She phoned and told me she's not coming back. She knows I love Lesley and she can't live with that anymore. It's a blessing to us all."

"If you believe him," Chase said to Lesley, "there's a bridge in Brooklyn you might be interested in buying."

"I'm telling you the truth," Tony insisted. "I should never have married April. It was a mistake on both our parts. April knows how I feel about you. She's always known. I can't go on pretending anymore. April can't, either. That's why she went to visit her mother and why she's decided not to come back."

"I'm marrying Chase." Her voice wavered, but not her certainty. She couldn't trust Tony, couldn't believe him. Chase was right about that. He'd lied to her before, and the experience had taught her painful but valuable lessons.

"Lesley, don't," Tony cried. "I'm pleading with you. Don't do something you'll regret the rest of our lives. I made a terrible mistake. Don't compound it by making another."

"She doesn't believe you any more than I do," Chase said calmly.

"The least you can do is have the decency to give us some privacy," Tony shouted, frustrated and short-tempered.

"Not on your life."

"You're afraid, aren't you?" Tony shouted. "Because Lesley loves me and you know it. You think if you can keep her from listening to me, she'll go through with the wedding, but you're wrong. She doesn't need you, not when she's got me."

"But she *hasn't* got you. In case you've forgotten, I'll remind you again—you're married."

As he was talking, Tony stepped closer to Chase, his stance challenging.

Chase dropped his arm from Lesley's shoulders and

moved toward Tony. The two men were practically chest to chest. It wouldn't take much for the situation to erupt into a brawl.

"Stop it, both of you!" Lesley yelled. She was surprised none of the neighbors were out yet to watch the show. "This is ridiculous."

"You love me," Tony said. "You can't marry this... this barbarian."

"Just watch her," Chase returned with a wide smile.

"I'm not doing *anything* until both of you stop behaving like six-year-olds," Lesley said. "I can't believe either one of you would resort to this childish behavior."

"I'll divorce April," Tony promised. "I swear by everything I hold dear that I'll get her out of my life."

"I'd think a husband would hold his *wife* dear," Chase said. "Apparently that isn't so. Your vows meant nothing the first time. What makes you so sure they'll mean any more on a second go-round?"

"I'm trying to be as civil as I can," Tony muttered, "but if you want to fight this out, fine."

"Anytime," Chase said, grinning broadly as if he welcomed the confrontation, "anyplace."

"Fine."

They were chest to chest once more.

Lesley managed to wedge herself between them and braced a hand against each of their chests. "I think you should go," she said to Tony. It was useless to try to discuss anything now. She wanted to believe him, but Chase was right. The first message Tony had left claimed that April was away for a week visiting her mother. He hadn't said a word about his marriage being a mistake or that he still cared for her.

"I'm not leaving you, not when you're making the

biggest mistake of your life," Tony told her. "I already said I'd divorce April. What more do you want me to do? The marriage was a mistake from the first! What else can I do? Tell me, Lesley, tell me and I'll do whatever it takes to make amends to you."

"I believe the lady asked you to leave," Chase said with the same easy grace. "That's all she wants from you. Get out of her life."

"No."

"It'll give me a good deal of pleasure to assist you."

The next thing she knew, Chase had grabbed Tony's arm and steered him toward his parked car.

Lesley stood on the porch, her teeth sinking into her lower lip as she watched the unpleasant scene. She was furious and didn't know who with—Chase or Tony. Both had behaved like children fighting on the playground. Neither of them had shown any maturity in dealing with an awkward situation.

The two men exchanged a few words at Tony's vehicle and it looked for a moment as if a fistfight was about to erupt. In the end, Tony climbed inside his car and drove away.

Lesley was pacing her living room when Chase entered the house. "How *could* you?" she demanded.

"How could I what? Treat lover boy the way he deserved, you mean?"

"You weren't any better than he was! I expected more from you, Chase. The least you could've done was…was be civil about the whole thing. Instead you acted like a jealous lover." She continued pacing. Her anger had created an energy within her that couldn't be ignored.

"Did you want to talk to him alone?"

"No."

"Then what *did* you expect me to do?"

"I don't know," she said. "Something different than strong-arming him."

"You sound like you wanted to invite him in for tea and then sit around discussing this like civilized adults."

"Yes!" she cried. "That would've been better than a shouting match on my front porch. The two of you behaved as though I was a prize baseball card you both wanted. Tony had traded me away and now he wants me back and you weren't about to see that happen."

Chase went still. "Is that what *you* wanted?" he asked. "To be handed back to Tony?"

"No, of course it isn't!"

"He can't stand the thought of losing you."

"He's the one who ended the relationship, not me. It's over, Chase."

Chase walked to the window and stared outside. He didn't speak for a long time and seemed to be weighing his thoughts.

"You...you told me once that you had a problem with a woman playing one man against another," she said. "I'm not doing that, Chase. I wouldn't. You're the man I'm marrying, not Tony."

"You love him," Chase said, turning to face her, "although he doesn't deserve your devotion. You could have lied to me about your feelings, but you haven't and I'm grateful."

"I don't trust Tony," she said, "but I trust you."

"You might not trust him, but you *want* to believe him, don't you?"

"I... I don't know. It doesn't matter if I do, does it? I've already agreed to marry you, and I'm not backing out." She refused to do to Chase what Tony had done to her. She wouldn't push him aside in favor of Tony's promises. Chase was right; Tony had always been a sore loser, no matter what the stakes.

Chase said nothing for several minutes. "The choice is yours," he finally said, "and I'll abide by whatever you decide. I want you, Lesley. Don't misunderstand me. I'm surprised by how much I desire you. If you agree to marry me, I promise you I'll do my best to be a good husband."

"You make it sound like I haven't made up my mind. I've already told you—and Tony—that I have. I'm going through with the wedding."

"It isn't too late to call it off."

"Why would I do that?" she asked, forcing a laugh.

"Because you're in love with Tony," Chase answered with dark, sober eyes focused on her. "Think about this very carefully," he advised and walked to her door.

"You're leaving?" She was afraid Tony would return and she didn't know what she'd do if Chase wasn't there to buffer his effect on her.

"Will you call me in the morning?" he asked. He didn't need to explain what he expected to hear. That was obvious. If she was willing to go through with the ceremony, she needed to let him know.

"I can tell you that right now," she said, folding her hands in an effort to keep from reaching for him.

"You might feel differently later."

"I won't. I promise you I won't." The desperate quality of her voice was all the answer he seemed to need.

He came over to her, placed his hands on her shoulders and drew her into his arms. "I shouldn't touch you, but I can't make myself leave without kissing you goodbye. Forgive me for that, Lesley." His last words were whispered as he lowered his mouth to hers. The kiss was filled with a longing and a hunger that left her breathless and yearning for more.

He expelled his breath, then turned and walked away.

Lesley watched him go and had the feeling she might never see him again.

Her knees were trembling and she sank onto the sofa and hid her face in her hands.

He'd lost her, Chase told himself as he unlocked the door to his hotel suite. He could've taken the advantage and run with it. At first he thought he'd do exactly that. Tony wasn't right for Lesley—anyone could see it.

Okay, he believed it so strongly because he wanted her for himself. Maybe the jerk *was* good for Lesley, although Chase couldn't see it.

Chase suspected Tony would string her along for years. He'd promise to divorce April but there'd be complications. There were always complications in cases like this, and Lesley would be completely disheartened by the time Tony was free. If he ever followed through on his promises. Chase knew exactly whose interests Tony was serving, and those were his own.

Tony might have some genuine affection for Lesley, but he didn't really love her. He couldn't possibly, otherwise he'd never put her through this agony.

Then again, Chase's own intentions weren't exactly pure, either. He needed a wife and he wanted Lesley. It didn't matter to him that she was in love with another man; all that mattered was her willingness to marry him and live with him in Alaska.

If there was a law against selfishness, he'd be swinging by his neck, right next to Tony.

So he'd done the only thing he could and still live with himself in the weeks to come. This business of being honorable was hard, much harder than he'd realized.

He'd given Lesley both the freedom and the privacy to make whatever choice she wanted. He wouldn't stand in her way, judge or condemn her if she decided not to go through with their marriage.

He was about to lose the wife he wanted, and nobility didn't offer much compensation.

All he had to do was wait until she'd made up her mind. He had the distinct feeling that this was going to be a long night.

"It shouldn't be this hard," Lesley wailed to her no-nonsense neighbor.

"You're right. It shouldn't," Daisy agreed. She stood next to Lesley's refrigerator, one hand on her hip. "Look at it this way. You could let Chase go back to Alaska alone and spend the next year or two being lied to, manipulated and emotionally abused by a jerk. Or," she added with a lazy smile, "you could marry a terrific man who adores you."

"Chase doesn't adore me."

"Maybe not, but he *is* crazy about you."

"I'm not even sure that's true."

"Haven't you got eyes in your head?" Daisy asked sarcastically. "He chose you out of hundreds of women."

"Not exactly..."

"Listen, if you want to argue with someone, let me bring in the boys. They're much better at it than either of us. I don't have time to play silly games with you.

I'm calling this the way I see it. If you want to mess up your life, that's your choice."

"I don't," Lesley insisted.

"Then why don't you phone Chase? You said he was waiting to hear from you."

"I know, but…"

"Is there always going to be a *but* with you?" Daisy demanded impatiently. "Now, call the man before I get really mad."

Smiling, Lesley reached for the phone. She prayed she was doing the right thing. After wrestling all night with the decision, she got up and tearfully called Daisy, sobbing out her sorry tale. Daisy, who was already late for her classes, had listened intently. She seemed to know exactly what Lesley should do. She made it all sound so straightforward, so easy. It should've been, but it wasn't, even now with the phone pressed to her ear.

"Hello."

"Chase, it's Lesley. I'm sorry to phone so early, but I thought you'd want to know as soon as possible."

There was a slight hesitation before he spoke. "It would simplify matters."

"I…want to go through with the marriage this evening."

"You're sure?"

He had to ask. Why couldn't he just have left it alone? "Yes, I'm sure." Her voice shook as if she was on the verge of tears.

Daisy took the receiver from her hand. "She knows what she's doing, Chase. Now don't you worry, I'll have her to the church on time." Whatever Chase said made Daisy laugh. After a couple of minutes, she replaced the receiver. "You going to make it through the day without changing your mind?"

"I...don't have any choice, do I?"

"None. If you stand that man up at the altar, I'm going to murder you and marry him myself. The boys would be thrilled."

Lesley laughed. "All right. I'll see you back here at four. Don't be late, Daisy, I'm going to need all the support I can get."

"What if Tony calls you?"

"He probably will, but fortunately I don't plan on being here. I've got a million things to do and I don't intend to waste a single moment on Tony Field."

"Good." Daisy beamed her a bright smile and was out the door a moment later.

Being nervous came as a surprise to Chase. He'd expected to stand before the preacher he'd hired and repeat his vows without a qualm. He had no doubts, no regrets about making Lesley his bride. Just nerves.

When she and her close friends, including Daisy and sons, arrived at the hotel for the simple wedding ceremony, Chase hadn't been able to take his eyes off her. He'd never seen a more beautiful woman. He'd rented a tuxedo, although what had prompted that was beyond his comprehension. The tie felt like it was strangling him and the cummerbund reminded him of the time he'd broken his ribs. He knew Lesley would be pleased, though, and when she smiled at him, he was glad he'd made the effort.

She'd chosen a soft peach dress, overlaid with white lace. She didn't wear a veil but a pretty pearl headpiece with white silk flowers. The bouquet of white baby roses was clutched in her hands.

Lesley had tried to call her mother and stepfather, wherever they were, but their cell phone wasn't on. Apparently that was typical. Chase reassured her again that they'd tell them later, perhaps arrange to see them in the fall. He, too, was without family—he'd told her only that his parents had died, nothing more—so their guests were mostly Lesley's friends.

It was all rather informal. She introduced Chase to Lori and Jo Ann and a number of others, and he shook hands with each one. Minutes later, it was time for the ceremony.

They stood with everyone gathered around them in the middle of the room. The minister said a few words about marriage and its significance, then asked them to repeat their vows.

It was at that moment that Chase fully comprehended what was happening between Lesley and him. He pledged before God that he would love Lesley and meet her needs, both physical and emotional.

The responsibility weighed on his mind. He'd given Lesley time to weigh the decision before agreeing to be his bride, never dreaming *he* needed to think about it, as well.

He looked at Lesley as she said her vows. Her steady gaze met his and her voice was strong and clear, without hesitation. When it came time, he slipped the gold band on her finger. He noticed tears brightening her eyes, but her smile reassured him. He could only hope these were tears of joy and not regret.

When he received permission to kiss his bride, Chase gently took her in his arms and kissed her. With everyone watching them, he made sure it was a short but intense kiss. A kiss that went on longer than he'd planned…

Lesley's eyes were laughing when they broke apart. "You'll pay for that later, Chase Goodman," she promised in a fervent whisper.

Chase could hardly wait.

There was enough food to feed twice as many people as their fifty or so guests. He wasn't sure how many would be there, so he'd had the hotel staff handle everything. Lesley had given him the names of her friends and he'd invited several people, as well, including Sandra and her husband.

Becky Bright was there, along with her cameraman. Lesley was wonderful during the interview, answering Becky's questions without a hint of nervousness. He suspected it was because of her training as a teacher. Personally he was grateful she'd dealt with the reporter because he was at a loss for words.

He'd considered the ceremony itself a mere formality, something that was necessary, a legal requirement, and that was all.

Now he wasn't so sure.

The vows had gotten to him. He hadn't truly taken the seriousness of his commitment to heart until he realized that these promises were more, much more, than a few mumbled words. They were *vows,* a soul-deep contract made between Lesley and himself. A contract that affected every single part of his life.

"I've never seen a more beautiful bride," he told her while they were going through the buffet line. They hadn't had a moment alone all evening. His heart was crammed full with all the things he wanted to say to her, and couldn't.

"I've never seen a handsomer groom," she whispered back and when she looked at him, her eyes softened.

Chase filled his plate. "I meant what I said." He knew that sounded melodramatic and a little trite, but he couldn't keep it to himself any longer.

"About what?" Lesley added a cherry tomato to her plate.

"The vows. I wasn't just repeating a bunch of meaningless phrases, I meant them, Lesley. I'm going to do everything in my power to be the right kind of husband to you."

She didn't look at him, didn't move, and he wondered, briefly, if he'd frightened her with his intensity, or perhaps shocked her. "Lesley?"

"I'm sorry," she whispered brokenly, staring down at the bowl of pasta salad.

"I shouldn't have told you that." She was suffering from pangs of guilt, he reasoned. The ceremony obviously hadn't affected her the way it had him.

"No... Oh, Chase, that was the most beautiful thing you could've said." She raised her eyes to his and he saw she was struggling to hold back tears. "I meant it, too, every word. I'm eager to show you how good a wife I intend to be."

Until the moment Lesley had walked into the hotel that afternoon, Chase wasn't entirely convinced she'd show up for the wedding. All day he'd tried to brace himself in case she didn't. Now she was his wife, and there was no turning back for either of them.

"Where are you going for your honeymoon?" Daisy

asked, filling her plate on the opposite side of the buffet table. "I meant to ask."

"Victoria," Chase answered. He hadn't said anything to Lesley, wanting to surprise her. That didn't seem important now.

"Victoria," she repeated. "Oh, Chase, what a wonderful idea."

"I don't imagine you're going to do much sightseeing, though," Daisy added with a suggestive chuckle.

"Daisy!" Lesley said as she blushed becomingly.

Their honeymoon. The words floated through his mind. Not knowing if Lesley would even be there for the wedding, he'd put off all thoughts as to what would follow.

He'd wanted to make love with Lesley almost from the moment they'd met. But he was determined not to enter into the physical side of their relationship until they were both prepared to deal with it. To accept the emotional repercussions of that aspect of their lives— of their life together. He didn't know about Lesley, but he was more than ready. He only hoped she was, too.

Their guests didn't seem in any hurry to leave. The champagne flowed freely, but Chase drank only a small amount. He needed a clear head.

They left, under a spray of rice and birdseed. He placed Lesley's suitcase in the back of his rental car and ran around to the front of the vehicle.

"Ready?" he asked, smiling over at his wife. *His wife.* The word still felt awkward in his mind. Awkward, but very right. He'd accomplished what he'd set out to do. He'd gotten himself a bride.

The one bride he'd wanted above all.

Nine

"The honeymoon suite," Lesley whispered as the bellman carried in their suitcases. "You booked us the honeymoon suite?"

Chase gave the bellman a generous tip and let him out the door. "Why are you so surprised? We're on our honeymoon, aren't we?"

"Yes, but, oh, I don't know…" She walked around the room and ran her hand over the plush bedspread on the king-size bed. "Oh, Chase, look," she said after she'd walked into the bathroom. "The tub's huge."

"Imagine wasting all that water," he teased, enjoying her excitement.

"They left champagne and chocolates, too."

"I'll file a complaint. How are any two people supposed to survive on that? A man needs real food."

"There's always room service."

"Right," he said, laughing. "I forgot about that."

"Oh, Chase, this is so lovely." She seemed shy about touching him, stopping just short of his arms. He was a bit embarrassed himself, although he didn't understand why. Lesley was his wife and he was her husband.

"I… I think I'll unpack," she said, reaching for her suitcase.

"Good idea." There was definitely something wrong with him. Lesley should be in his arms by now, begging him to make love to her. Instead, they were standing back to back emptying their suitcases, as though they had every intention of wearing all those clothes.

"Are you hungry?" he asked, just to make conversation.

"No, but if you want to order something, go ahead."

"I'm fine." No, he wasn't. His temperature was rising by the minute.

"I think I'll take a bath," she said next.

"Good idea." He realized after he spoke that she might find his enthusiasm a bit insulting, but by the time he thought to say something she was in the bathroom.

The sound of running water filled the suite. He noted that she'd left the door ajar, but he wasn't certain she'd done it on purpose.

Focusing his attention on unpacking, Chase opened and closed several drawers, but his mind wasn't on putting his clothes in any order. It was on Lesley in the other room.

Lesley removing her clothes.

Lesley stepping naked into the big tub.

Lesley sighing that soft, womanly sigh of hers as she slipped into the steaming water.

The image was so powerful that Chase sagged onto the edge of the bed. He didn't know what was the matter with him. They were married, and he was acting like a choirboy.

"Would you like me to wash your back?" he asked.

"Please."

Chase's spirits lifted. That sounded encouraging. He smoothed back his hair and rolled up his sleeves before advancing into the bathroom.

Lesley was exactly as he'd pictured her. She was lying in the tub, surrounded by frothy bubbles.

The scent of blooming roses wafted up to him, and her pink toes were perched against the far end. The welcome he saw in her eyes made his heart beat so furiously that for a moment he couldn't breathe.

He cleared his throat. "How's the water?" he asked, shoving his hands in his pants pockets.

"It's perfect."

"I see you've added a bunch of women's stuff to that water."

"Women's stuff?"

"Bubble bath or whatever."

"Do you mind?"

"Not in the least." It was driving him slowly insane, but that didn't bother him nearly as much as the view he had of her body. She raised one knee and the bubbles slid down her leg in a slow, tantalizing pattern.

Her leg was pink from the steamy water and for the life of him, he couldn't stop staring at it. For the life of him he couldn't stop thinking about that same leg wrapped around his waist…

"The, uh, water looks inviting." His tongue nearly stuck to the roof of his mouth, he was so excited.

"Would you care to join me?"

His heart was doing that crazy pounding again. "You sure? I mean…" Darned if he knew *what* he meant. "Should I bring the champagne and chocolates?"

"Just the champagne. Let's save the chocolates for later."

He nearly stumbled out of the room in his eagerness to get her what she wanted. He opened the bottle and the popping sound echoed like a small explosion. His hands trembled as he poured them each a flute of champagne. He carried them into the other room, then handed her the glass and sipped from his own, badly needing the temporary courage it offered. Then he realized Lesley hadn't tasted hers.

"I'll wait until you're in the bath with me," she explained.

"Oh." That was when it occurred to him that he'd need to undress. He did his best not to be self-conscious, but didn't know how well he succeeded. He wasn't normally shy, but he'd lived alone for a lot of years and when he undressed there usually wasn't someone watching his every move.

He stepped into the tub and she moved forward to make room for him. He eased himself into the hot water, positioning himself behind her. She was slippery in his embrace and he tucked his arms around her waist and brought her up against him. He brushed his mouth over her hair and relaxed, closing his eyes.

"You feel good," he whispered. That had to be the understatement of the century.

Lesley had gone still and so had he. It was as though they'd both lost the need to breathe. He cupped her breasts and she sighed as if this was what she'd been waiting for, as if she wondered what had taken him so long.

Darned if he knew.

He smiled, not with amusement, but with male pride and satisfaction.

"You feel like silk," he whispered, rubbing his hand

down her smooth abdomen. She turned her head toward him, inviting his kiss.

Chase didn't disappoint her. He bent forward and kissed her slowly, seducing her mouth with his own. Soon he didn't know who was seducing whom. They were both breathless by the time he lifted his head.

They kissed again, the urgency of their need centered on their mouths as she buckled beneath him, gasping and moaning.

Chase broke off the kiss. In one swift motion he stood, taking her with him. Water sloshed over the sides of the tub, but Chase hardly noticed. He carried Lesley to the bed and placed her on it, not caring if they were soaking wet or that they'd left a watery trail.

When the loving was over, he rested his forehead against hers, his breath uneven. He could find no words to explain what had happened. No experience had ever been this intense. No woman had ever satisfied him so completely or brought him to the point of no return the way Lesley had.

Whatever was between them, be it commitment or love or something he couldn't define, it was out of his control.

Everything with Lesley was beyond his experience. Everything with her was going to be brand-new.

Butchart Gardens was breathtakingly beautiful. Chase and Lesley spent their first morning as husband and wife walking hand in hand along the meandering paths, over the footbridges and through the secret corners of the gardens. Lesley couldn't remember ever seeing any place as beautiful, with a profusion of so many varieties of flowers that she soon lost count.

By the time they stopped for lunch, Lesley was famished. Chase was, too, gauging by the amount of food he ordered.

"I've got to build my strength up," he told her.

Lesley didn't know she was still capable of blushing, not after the wondrous night they'd spent. She hadn't known it was possible for any two people to make love so fervently or so frequently. Just when she was convinced she'd never survive another burst of pleasure, he'd convince her that she could. And she did.

"You're blushing." Chase sounded shocked.

"Thank you for calling attention to it," she chided. "If one of us is blushing, it should be you."

"Me?"

She leaned across the table, not wanting anyone to overhear. "After last night," she whispered heatedly.

"What about last night?" His voice boomed like a cannon shot, or so it seemed to Lesley.

"You know," she said, sorry now for having introduced the subject.

"No, I don't. You'd better tell me."

"You're...a superman."

He grinned and wiggled his eyebrows suggestively.

"Chase!"

"As soon as we finish lunch, let's go back to the hotel."

"We've only seen half of the gardens," she protested, but not too strenuously.

"We'll come back tomorrow."

"It's the middle of the afternoon."

"So?"

"It's…early." The excuse was token at best. She couldn't fool him, nor could she fool herself. She wanted him as badly as he wanted her. It was crazy, outrageous, wonderful.

"Don't look at me like that," Chase said with a groan.

She gave herself a mental shake. "Like what?"

"Like you can't wait a minute longer."

She lowered her eyes, embarrassed. "I don't think I can."

He swore under his breath, stood abruptly and slapped some bills down on the table. "Come on," he said, "let's get out of here."

"We came on the tour bus, remember?"

"We'll get a taxi back."

"Chase—" she laughed "—that'll cost a fortune."

"I don't care what it costs. If we don't leave now we could be arrested. There are laws against people doing in public what I intend to do with you."

Lesley was sure her face turned five shades of red as they hurried out of Butchart Gardens. They located a taxi, and the second after Chase gave the driver the name of their hotel, he pulled her into his arms. His kiss was wet and wild and thorough. Thorough enough to hold them until they got back to the hotel.

Chase paid the driver and they raced hand in hand into the hotel and through the lobby, not stopping until they reached their room.

Chase's fingers shook when he inserted the key and Lesley's heart was touched by his eagerness.

"This is the most insane thing I've ever done in my life," she said, trying not to laugh.

The door swung open and Chase drew her inside, closing the door and backing her against it.

"I was going to go berserk if I couldn't touch you the way I wanted," he whispered, kissing her with a hunger that echoed her own.

"Chase..." She wasn't sure what she wanted, only *that* she wanted.

Apparently he knew, because he scooped her into his arms and carried her to the bed.

An hour later, Lesley smiled to herself and buried her face in her husband's neck. With Chase she'd never be alone again. With Chase she felt whole, complete. Was this an illusion? She wasn't sure.

But right now she needed the feel of him, needed the reality of this man, this moment. She pressed her hands to his face and with tears she couldn't explain blurring her vision, she looked up at him.

"Thank you," she whispered.

He kissed her, his touch gentle.

"What's happening to us?" she asked, thinking he could help her understand.

"What do you mean?"

"Is this just good sex or is it more?"

"More," was his immediate response.

"Do I love you?" It obviously wasn't the question he'd expected her to ask, which was fine since it astonished even her.

"I don't know."

"Are you in love with me?"

His brow creased as if that required serious consideration. "I know I've never felt like this about any woman. What's happening between us, this physical thing, is as much of a surprise to me as it is you." He leaned forward and kissed the tip of her nose.

"I'm glad you decided to marry me," Chase continued, "although if this goes on much longer, I may be dead within a year."

Lesley laughed and, wrapping her arms around his neck, lifted her head just enough to kiss him.

"You're pure magic," he whispered against her lips.

"Me?"

He grinned.

She answered him with a grin of her own. "I don't know about you, but I'm starving."

Chase nuzzled her nose with his. "Let's not take any chances this time and order room service. It's ridiculous to pay for meals I never have a chance to eat."

After a leisurely lunch, they played tourist for the rest of the day, but didn't wander far from the hotel. They'd learned their lesson. They had high tea at the Empress Hotel, toured the museum, explored the undersea gardens.

They crammed as much as they could into the afternoon and returned, exhausted, to their hotel early that evening.

"Where do you want to go for dinner?" Chase asked.

"Dinner?" Lesley repeated. "I'm still full from lunch. And tea."

"Okay, then, what do you want to do?"

"Soak in a long, hot bath and take a nap. You kept me up half the night, remember?"

"A bath?" His eyes widened. "Really?"

Despite her exhaustion, Lesley smiled. "Later," she said and kissed him sweetly. "Give me an hour or two to regroup, okay?"

His face fell in mock disappointment.

"Come on," she said, holding her hand out to him. "You can nap with me, if you promise to sleep." She yawned loudly and pulled back the covers. The bath would come later. Right now it would only bring temptation for them both.

"I hoped we'd be in bed by five o'clock," Chase muttered, "but I never thought it would be to sleep. Some honeymoon this is turning out to be."

"Some honeymoon," Lesley agreed, smiling. She laid her head against the thick feather pillow and closed her eyes. Within seconds she could feel herself drift off.

The phone beside the bed rang, startling her badly. Before she could assimilate what was happening, Chase grabbed the receiver.

"Hello," he answered gruffly. Whoever was calling made him laugh. He placed his hand over the mouthpiece as he handed Lesley the phone. "It's Daisy."

"Daisy?" Lesley said, surprised to hear from her neighbor. "Hi."

"Trust me, I wouldn't be calling you at the hotel if it wasn't necessary."

"Don't worry. You weren't interrupting anything."

"Wanna bet?" Chase said loudly enough to be heard at the other end.

"Listen, Lesley, this isn't my idea of a fun call, but I figured you'd better know. Tony's been pestering me for information about you and Chase."

Lesley sat up in bed. "You didn't tell him anything, did you?"

"No, but the movers arrived while he was here and I saw him talking to the driver. He might've been able to get information out of him."

"I doubt it," she said, gnawing on her lower lip. "Those men are professionals. They know better than to give out information about their clients."

"That segment about you and Chase on television tonight didn't help. Tony phoned two seconds after the piece aired."

Lesley groaned. She'd forgotten about that.

"What's wrong?" Chase asked.

"Nothing," she whispered.

"Daisy didn't call for no reason," he argued.

"I'll explain later," she said, although it wasn't a task she relished.

"It's Tony, isn't it?"

"Chase, please."

"All right, all right," he grumbled, but he wasn't happy and didn't bother to disguise it. He climbed out of bed and reached for his clothes, dressing with an urgency she didn't understand.

"Okay, I'm back," she told Daisy.

"Tony's looking to make trouble."

"I guess I shouldn't be surprised."

"I don't know why I'm so worried," Daisy muttered. "It isn't like he could do anything. You're already married."

"Well, what do you think he's going to do?"

She noticed Daisy's hesitation. "I don't know, but I wanted to warn you."

"Thanks," Lesley said, genuinely grateful. Tony seemed light-years away. Only a couple of days earlier she'd been convinced she loved him. That wasn't true anymore. Any feeling she still had was a memory, a ghost of the love she'd once felt.

"So?" Daisy said, her voice dipping suggestively. "How's the honeymoon?"

Lesley closed her eyes and sagged against the velvet headboard. "Wonderful."

"Are you two having fun with each other?"

"Daisy!"

"I meant sightseeing and all."

"I know *exactly* what you meant."

"Then why are you trying to be coy?"

"All right, if you must know, we're having a very good time. There—are you satisfied?"

"Hardly. I've got to tell you, Lesley, I could be jealous. It's been so long since I've been with a man, I feel like a virgin all over again."

Lesley laughed. "If Tony gives you any more trouble, let me know and I'll get a restraining order."

"You'd do that?" Daisy sounded relieved.

"In a heartbeat."

Chase stood on the other side of the room, his back to her. Lesley watched him for a moment and said to her neighbor, "Listen, we'll talk as soon as we get back."

"Which is when?"

"Day after tomorrow, but we'll be flying up to Alaska almost immediately. You have my cell number. Keep in touch, okay?"

"I will," Daisy promised and ended the conversation.

Lesley replaced the receiver. Her hand still on the phone, she mentally composed what she was going to say to Chase.

"So it *was* Tony," he commented, turning back to her.

"Yes. He's making a pest of himself." Chase's hands were in his pockets and he looked unsure. Of her and their marriage. It seemed a bit soon to be having doubts, and she said as much.

"He wants you."

"I know, but I married *you*." Her words didn't seem to reassure him. He stood there apparently deep in thought.

Kneeling on the bed, Lesley murmured, "I feel like having those chocolates and a hot bath. How about you?"

That got his attention. His eyes locked with hers and she started laughing. "Come here," she said, holding her arms out to Chase. "It's time you understood that neither of us has anything to fear from Tony. I've made my decision and chosen to be your wife. A jealous ex-fiancé doesn't stand a chance."

Chase remained where he was, as if he didn't quite believe her.

Lesley got up from the bed and was halfway across the room before she realized she was nearly naked. It didn't bother her—she was proud of her body. Chase had made her feel that way. She was focused on the man in front of her, not on herself.

Rising onto her toes, she kissed him lightly.

"Lesley..."

"Shhh."

He stood perfectly still and, with his eyes closed, allowed her to continue kissing him. When she was satisfied with his lips, she kissed the underside of his jaw, moving her mouth down his neck, then up to his ear. After what seemed like the longest moment of her life, he threaded his fingers through her hair and raised her face to his.

"I want you to be very sure."

"I am," she whispered. "I am sure."

He looked into her eyes. "A hot bath and chocolate sounds like an excellent suggestion," he said.

Lesley smiled contentedly. Marriage was far better than she'd ever imagined.

"Where are we going?" Lesley asked. They'd left Victoria that afternoon and had traveled down the Kitsap

Peninsula, boarding the ferry from Bremerton to Seattle. Lesley had assumed they'd be heading directly back to her house. If so, Chase was taking an interesting route.

"There's something I want you to see."

She glanced at her watch and swallowed her impatience. They'd gotten a later start than they'd expected. Their morning had begun with a hot bath. At least the water had initially been hot, but by the time they finished, it had cooled considerably. Because their schedule was off, they'd been forced to wait for a later ferry.

Their flight to Alaska was leaving early the next morning, and Lesley had a hundred details she needed to take care of before then.

"There," Chase said, pulling into an asphalt parking lot.

"Where?" She didn't see anything.

"The billboard," he said.

Looking up, she saw the original billboard Chase had used to advertise for a wife. The sign had been changed and now read, in huge black letters, THANK YOU, LESLEY, FOR SHARING MY LIFE.

"Well?" he asked, waiting for her to respond.

"I… Oh, Chase, that's so sweet and so romantic. I think I'm going to cry." She was struggling to hold back the tears.

"I want to make you happy, Lesley, for the rest of our lives." He brought her into his arms and kissed her.

Happiness frightened her. Every time she was truly content, truly at peace, something would go wrong, her happiness ruined. The first time it happened, she was a child. A six-year-old. She'd never been happier than the week before they were supposed to leave for

Disneyland. Not only had the trip been canceled, but she'd lost her father.

She'd been excited about her wedding to Tony, planning the event, shopping for her wedding dress, choosing her clothes. But he'd broken their engagement, plunging her into depression and then numbness.

Lesley was happy now, and she couldn't help wondering what it would cost her this time.

Ten

Lesley's hand reached for Chase's as the airplane circled Fairbanks, Alaska, before descending. She'd found the view of Alaska's Mount McKinley, in Denali National Park, awe-inspiring. After living in Seattle, between the Cascade and Olympic mountain ranges, she thought being impressed by Denali was saying something. The tallest peak in North America rose from the land far below, crowned by a halo of clouds.

"Is it *all* so beautiful?" she asked as the plane made its final approach.

"There's beauty in every part of Alaska," Chase told her, "but some of it's more difficult to see. More subtle."

"I'm going to love Twin Creeks," she said, knowing it would be impossible not to, if the area was anything like the landscape she'd seen from the plane.

Chase's fingers tightened around hers. "I hope you do."

They landed and were met by a tall, burly man with a beard so thick it hid most of his face. Beneath his wool cap, she caught a glimpse of twinkling blue eyes.

"Pete Stone," Chase said casually, placing his arm around Lesley's shoulders. "This is Lesley."

"You done it? You actually done it?" Pete asked, briefly removing his wool cap and scratching his head. His hair was shoulder-length and as thick as his beard. "You got yourself a wife?"

"How do you do?" Lesley said formally, holding out her hand. "I'm Lesley Goodman." Pete ignored her proffered hand and reached for her instead, hauling her against him and hugging her so tightly, he lifted her three feet off the ground. Lesley wasn't offended so much as surprised. She cast a pleading glance at her husband, who didn't look any too pleased with this unexpected turn of events.

"Pete," Chase said stiffly. "Put her down. Lesley's not accustomed to being manhandled."

"You jealous?" Pete said, slowly releasing her. His grin would've been impossible to see beneath the mask of his beard, but his eyes sparkled with delight. "That tells me you care about this little slip of a girl."

Being nearly six feet tall, Lesley didn't think of herself as a little slip of anything. She couldn't help liking Pete despite his bear-hugging enthusiasm.

"Of course I care about her. I married her, didn't I?"

"You sure did, but then you said you was coming back with a wife if you had to marry yourself up with a polecat."

"Lesley's no polecat."

"I got eyes in my head," Pete said. "I can see that for myself."

"Good. Now, is the plane ready or not?" Chase asked, picking up two of their suitcases. He didn't look at Lesley and she sensed that Chase was annoyed by

Pete's remark about his determination to find a wife. She hadn't accepted his proposal under any misconception. If she'd turned him down, he would've found someone else. She'd known that from the first.

Pete grabbed the two additional pieces of luggage and winked at Lesley. "The plane's been ready since yesterday. I flew down a day early and raised some heck."

"Okay, okay," Chase muttered. He turned to Lesley. "Do you mind leaving right away?" he asked as they approached the four-passenger plane.

"No," she assured him with a smile. She was eager to reach her new home, and she knew Chase was just as eager to get back. It would've been nice to spend some time in Fairbanks, but they'd have plenty of opportunity for that later.

"So," Pete said to Chase after they'd boarded the plane, "are you going to tell me how you did it?" The two men occupied the front seats, with Chase as the pilot, while Lesley sat in the back.

"Did what?"

"Got someone as beautiful as Lesley to marry you."

Chase was preoccupied, flipping a series of switches. "I asked her."

Lesley was mildly insulted that he'd condensed the story of their courtship into a simple three-word sentence.

"That was all it took?" Pete seemed astounded. He twisted around and looked at Lesley. "You got any single friends?"

"Daisy," she answered automatically, already missing her neighbor.

"Daisy," Pete repeated as if the sound of her name

conjured up the image of a movie star. "I bet she's beautiful."

"She's divorced with two boys," Chase said, "and she recently started dating a guy she works with, so don't get your mind set on her."

Pete was quiet for a few minutes; silence was a rare commodity with this man, Lesley suspected. "I figured you'd get yourself a woman with a couple kids, liking the little rascals the way you do," he told Chase.

"Lesley suits me just fine." Chase reached for the small hand mike and spoke with the air traffic controller, awaiting his instructions. Within minutes they were in the air.

Chase hadn't told her he was a pilot; Lesley was impressed but not surprised. There was something so capable about him. So skilled and confident. She guessed that he was the kind of man who'd be equal to any challenge, who could solve any problem. Maybe that was typical of Alaskans.

"Won't it be dark by the time we arrive?" she asked.

Pete laughed as if she'd told a good joke.

"The sun's out until midnight this time of year," Chase explained. "Remember?"

Pete twisted around again. "Did Chase tell you much about Twin Creeks?"

"A little." Very little, she realized with a start. All she knew was that Twin Creeks was near the pipeline and that Chase was employed by one of the major oil companies. The town was small, but there weren't any exceptionally large cities in Alaska. The population of Fairbanks, according to some information she'd read on the plane, was less than forty thousand.

"You tell her about the mosquitoes?" Pete asked Chase, his voice low and conspiratorial.

"Mosquitoes?" Lesley repeated. She'd considered them more of a tropical pest. There were plenty in the Seattle area, but the air was moist and vegetation abundant. She'd never thought there'd be mosquitoes in the Arctic.

"Mosquitoes are the Alaska state bird," Pete teased, smiling broadly. "You ain't never seen 'em as big as we get 'em. But don't worry, they only stick around in June and July. Otherwise they leave us be."

"I have plenty of repellant at the cabin," Chase assured her, frowning.

"Twin Creeks is near the Gates of the Arctic wilderness park. Chase told you that, didn't he?"

Lesley couldn't remember if he had or not.

"We're at the base of the Brooks range, which is part of the Endicott mountains."

"How long does it take to drive to Fairbanks?" she asked.

"I don't know," Pete admitted, rubbing his beard as he considered her question. "I've always flown. We don't have a road that's open year-round, so not many folks drive that way. Mostly we fly. Folks in Twin Creeks mainly rely on planes for transportation. It's easier that way."

"I...see." Lesley was beginning to do just that. Twin Creeks wasn't a thriving community as she'd originally assumed. It was a station town with probably a handful of people. All right, she could live with that. She could adjust her thinking.

"Twin Creeks is on the edge of the Arctic wilderness," Chase said absently, responding to Pete's earlier remark about the town's location.

It was difficult to read his tone, but Lesley heard

something she hadn't before. A hesitation, a reluctance, as if he feared that once she learned the truth about living in Alaska, she'd regret having married him. But she didn't. It wasn't possible, not anymore. Their honeymoon had seen to that.

"What about the wildlife?" she asked, curious now.

"We got everything you can imagine," Pete answered enthusiastically. "There's caribou, Dall sheep, bears—"

"Bears?" She refused to listen beyond that.

"They're a nuisance if you ask me," Pete continued. "That's why most of us have caches so—"

"What's a cache?" Lesley interrupted.

"A cache," he repeated as if he was sure she must know.

"It's like a small log cabin built on stilts," Chase explained. "It's spelled *c-a-c-h-e,* but pronounced cash."

"Bears and the like can't climb ladders," Pete added. "But they do climb poles, so we wrap tin around the beams to keep 'em off."

"What do you store there that the bears find so attractive?"

"It's a primitive freezer for meat in the winter."

"I keep extra fuel and bedding in mine," Pete said. "And anything else I don't want the wildlife gettin'. You've got to be careful what you put outside your door, but Chase will tell you all about that, so don't worry. We haven't lost anyone to bears in two, three years now." He laughed, and Lesley didn't know if he was teasing or not.

She swallowed uncomfortably and pushed the thought out of her mind. "I think moose are interesting creatures," she said conversationally, remembering Lori's comment.

"We get 'em every now and then, but not often."
Once more it was Pete who answered.

By the time they landed, ninety minutes later, Lesley
was both exhausted and worried. After they'd parked
the plane in a hangar and unloaded their luggage, Pete
drove them to a cabin nestled in a valley of alder, wil-
low and birch trees. Lesley didn't see any other cabins
along the way, but then she wasn't expecting Chase to
live on a suburban street. Neighbors would have been
welcome, but he didn't seem to have any within walking distance.

"See you in the morning," Pete said, delivering two
of the suitcases to the porch. He left immediately, after
slapping Chase on the back and making a comment Lesley couldn't hear. She figured Pete was issuing some
unsolicited marital advice.

"You're meeting him in the morning?" Lesley asked.
Chase had told her he needed to be back at work. But
she'd assumed he wouldn't have to go in right away, that
he'd be able to recover from his travels first.

"He's picking me up," Chase said. "I have to check
in. I won't stay long, I promise." They were standing
on the porch and Lesley was eager to get a look at her
new home. The outside didn't really tell her much. She'd
seen vacation homes that were larger than this.

Chase unlocked the door and turned to her, sweeping
her off her feet as if she weighed no more than the suitcase. His actions took her by surprise and she gasped
with pleasure when she realized he was following tradition by carrying her over the threshold.

Lesley closed her eyes and reveled in the splendor
of being in his arms. They kissed briefly, then Chase

carried her into the bedroom and they sat on the edge of the bed together.

"This has been the longest day of my life," Lesley said with a yawn. "I could kill for a hot bath and room service, but I don't think I'd stay awake long enough for either."

"I've dreamed of having you in this bed with me," he said in a low voice.

Lesley cupped his face and tenderly kissed his lips. "Come on. I'll help you bring in the luggage."

"Nonsense," Chase countered. "It's no problem. I'll get it."

Lesley didn't object. While Chase dealt with their suitcases, she could explore their home. The bedroom was cozy and masculine-looking. The walls were made of a light wood—pine, she guessed—with a double closet that had two drawers below each door.

A picture was the only thing on the dresser and Lesley knew in an instant that the couple staring back at her from the brass frame were Chase's parents. The bed was large, too big for the room, but that didn't bother her. The floor was wood, too, with several thick, braided throw rugs.

There was a small guest room across the hall, simply furnished with an iron bedstead and a chest of drawers.

Moving into the living room, Lesley admired the huge rock fireplace. It took up nearly all of one wall. He had a television, DVD player and music system. She'd known there was electricity; she'd made a point of asking.

The furniture was homey and inviting. A recliner and an overstuffed sofa, plus a rocking chair. Chase loved books, if the overflowing bookcases were any indication. Between two of them stood a rough-hewn desk that held a laptop computer.

A microwave caught her eye from the kitchen counter, which was a faded red linoleum, and she moved in that direction. The huge refrigerator and freezer stood side by side and looked new, dominating one wall. Everything else, including the dishwasher and stove, were ancient-looking. She'd make the best of it, Lesley decided, but she was putting her word in early. The kitchen was often the heart of a home and she intended to make theirs as modern and comfortable as possible. From the looks of it, she had her work cut out for her.

"Well?" Chase asked from behind her. "What do you think?"

"I think," she said, turning and hugging him around the middle, "that I could get used to living here with you."

Chase sighed as if she'd just removed a giant weight from his shoulders. "Good. I realized as soon as I saw Pete that I hadn't really prepared you for Twin Creeks. It's not what you'd call a thriving metropolis."

"I've noticed. Are there neighbors?"

"Some," he answered cryptically. He held her close, and she couldn't read his expression.

"Nearby?"

"Not exactly. So, are you ready for bed?" he asked, changing the subject, but not smoothly enough for her not to notice.

"I've decided I'll have a bath, after all." She planned to soak out the stiffness of all those hours cooped up inside planes.

"There's one problem," he said, sounding chagrined. "I don't have a tub."

Lesley stared at him. "Pardon?"

"There's only a shower. It's all I've ever needed. At some point we can install a bathtub, if you want."

"Okay. I'll manage." A shower instead of a bath was a minor inconvenience. She'd adjust.

Chase needed to make a couple of calls and while he was busy, Lesley showered and readied for bed. Her husband of four days undressed, showered and climbed into bed with her.

The sheets were cold and instinctively Lesley nestled close to Chase. He brought her into the warm alcove of his arms, gently kissing her hair.

"Good night," Lesley whispered when he turned off the light.

"'Night." The light was off, but the room was still bright. She'd adjust to sunlight in the middle of the night, too, Lesley reasoned. But it now seemed that she was going to have to make more adjustments than she'd realized.

She rolled onto her side and positioned the pillow to cradle her head. She was too tired to care, too tired to do anything but sleep.

Chase, however, had other ideas…

Lesley smiled softly to herself as he whispered in her ear.

"You know what I want."

"Yes." She slipped onto her back and lifted her arms to him in welcome. She *did* know what he wanted. And tired or not, she wanted the same thing.

Chase was awakened by the alarm. His eyes burned and he felt as if he were fighting his way out of a fog before he realized what he needed to do to end the irritating noise.

Lesley didn't so much as stir. He was pleased that the buzzer hadn't woken her. He'd like nothing better than to stay in bed and wake his wife and linger there with her.

That wasn't possible, though. Not this morning. There'd be plenty of other mornings when they could. He looked forward to those times with pleasure.

Chase slipped out of bed and reached for his jeans and shirt. Wandering into the bathroom, he splashed cold water onto his face in a desperate effort to wake up. He'd report in to work, do what needed to be done and leave again. It shouldn't take more than thirty minutes, an hour at the most. There was a chance he'd be home before Lesley even woke up.

He smiled the whole time he made himself a cup of coffee. He sat in the recliner and laced his boots, put on a light jacket and let himself out the door.

Pete was just pulling into his yard when Chase walked down the two front steps. He sipped from his coffee in its travel mug and walked toward his friend.

"Trouble," Pete greeted him.

"What's going on?"

"Don't know."

"It isn't going to take long, is it?" Chase knew the answer to that already. Nothing was ever easy around the pump station.

"I gotta tell you," Pete said to him good-naturedly, "your arrival back couldn't have been more timely."

Chase released a four-letter word beneath his breath. He'd wait an hour or so, call Lesley and explain. This certainly wasn't the way he wanted their lives together to begin, but it couldn't be helped. Too bad she'd learn the truth so soon.

* * *

Lesley woke to blazing sunshine. That was how she'd gone to sleep, too. She turned her head toward Chase, surprised to find the other half of the bed empty. Swallowing her disappointment, she tossed aside the covers and sat on the edge of the mattress.

Chase had parked their suitcases by the bedroom door. Lesley decided to unpack first, and by the time she was through, she hoped Chase would be back.

She dressed, then looked in the cupboard for something to eat. As soon as Chase returned, they'd need to do some grocery shopping. Since he'd been gone for several weeks, they needed to restock the essentials.

The phone rang while she was munching on dry cereal.

"Hello," she answered enthusiastically, knowing it was likely to be Chase; she was right.

"Lesley, I've run into some problems here at the station."

"Will you be long?"

"I don't know. Do you think you can manage without me for a while?"

"Of course."

"I can send Pete if you'd rather not be alone."

"I'll be fine, and I certainly don't need a babysitter."

He hesitated. "Don't go wandering off by yourself, all right?"

"Don't worry. With bears and wolves roaming around, I won't be taking any strolls."

"I'm sorry about this," he said regretfully.

"I'll be fine."

"You're sure?"

"Chase, stop worrying, I'm a big girl."

"I've got to go."

"I know. Just answer one thing. We need groceries. Would you mind if I took your truck and drove into town and picked up a few items?" She eyed her bowl of cereal. "We need milk, eggs and so on."

She heard him curse under his breath. "Groceries. I didn't think of that. Hold off, would you, for a little while? I'll be back as soon as I can."

"I know." She was lonely for him already, but determined to be a helpmate and not a problem.

Another hour passed and she'd completely reorganized their bedroom. She consolidated the things in Chase's dresser to make room for hers and hung what she could in his cramped closet. When Chase had a few minutes to spare, she needed him to weed out anything he didn't need.

The sound of an approaching car was a welcome distraction. Hoping it was Chase, she hurried onto the front porch—to see Pete driving toward the house in his four-wheel-drive vehicle.

"Howdy," he called, waving as he climbed out of the truck. "Chase sent me to check up on you."

"I'm fine. Really."

"He had me pick up a few things on the way." He reached inside the cab and lifted out two bags of groceries and carried them into the house.

"I could've gone myself." She was disappointed that Chase didn't trust her enough to find her way around. Just how lost could she get?

"Chase wanted to introduce you around town himself," Pete explained. He seemed to have read her thoughts. He set the bags on the kitchen counter and

Lesley investigated their contents. For a bachelor, Pete had done a good job.

"What do I owe you?" she asked.

"Nothing," Chase's friend responded, helping himself to a cup of coffee. "Chase took care of it. He's got an account at the store and they bill him monthly."

"How...quaint."

Pete added two teaspoons of sugar, stirring vigorously. "Chase said you like to cook."

"I do," she responded. Since he didn't show any signs of leaving, she poured herself a cup of coffee and joined him at the kitchen table.

"There's plenty of deer meat in the freezer."

"Deer?"

"You never cooked deer before? What about caribou?"

"Neither one." Didn't anyone dine on good old-fashioned beef in Alaska?

"Don't worry. It cooks up like beef and doesn't taste all that different. You'll be fine."

Lesley appreciated his confidence even if she didn't share it.

"So," Pete said, relaxing in his chair, hands encircling the mug, "what do you think of the cabin?"

Lesley wasn't sure how to answer. It was certainly livable, but nothing like she'd expected. However, as she'd said to herself countless times, she'd adjust. "It's homey," she said, trying to be diplomatic about it.

"Chase bought it 'specially for you."

Lesley lowered her eyes. That couldn't possibly be true. He hadn't known her long enough to have chosen this cabin for her.

"He's only been living here a few months," Pete went

on. "He decided back in March that he wasn't going through another winter without a wife, so he started getting ready for one. The first thing he did was buy this place and move off the station."

"Do you live at the station?"

"Nope. I bought myself a cabin, too, year or so ago.

"Chase has lots of plans to remodel, but he wanted to wait until he found the right woman so they could plan the changes together."

Lesley looked around, the ideas already beginning to form. If they knocked out the wall between the living room and kitchen, they could get rid of the cramped feeling.

"Chase did all right for himself," Pete said, sounding proud of his friend. "I gotta tell you, I laughed when he told me he was going to Seattle and bringing himself back a wife."

"Why didn't he marry someone from around here?" Lesley asked. She already knew the answer but wanted to see what he'd say.

"First off, there aren't any available women in Twin Creeks. He might've met a woman in Fairbanks—used to go out with a couple different ones—but he figured his chances were better in Seattle. And he was right!"

"I'm glad he did go to Seattle."

"He seems pleased about it. This is the first time I've seen Chase smile in a year, ever since his father died. He took it hard, you know."

Lesley pretended she did. Although she'd told him about her own parents, Chase hadn't said much about his, just that they were both dead.

"So soon after his mother—that darn near killed him. He's all alone now, no brothers or sisters, and he needed someone to belong to the way we all do. I don't know that he's ever said that, but it's the reason he was so keen on marryin'."

"What about you?" Lesley asked. "Why haven't you married?"

"I did once, about ten years back, but it didn't work out." Pain flickered in his eyes. "Pamela didn't last the winter. I hope for Chase's sake you're different. He's already crazy about you, and if you left him, it'd probably break his heart."

"I'm not leaving." It would take a lot more than a harsh winter to change her mind about her commitment to Chase. She'd never taken duty lightly and she'd pledged before her friends and God to stand by Chase as his wife, his lover, his partner.

"Good." Pete's twinkling blue eyes were back.

"Chase sent you out to babysit me, didn't he?"

Pete laughed. "Not exactly. He was a little afraid you were gonna get curious and do some exploring."

"Not after the conversation we had about the bears." Lesley shuddered dramatically.

"They aren't gonna hurt you. You leave 'em alone and they'll leave you alone. You might want to ask Chase to take you to the dump and that way you'll get to see 'em firsthand."

"They hang around the dump?"

"Sure do, sorting through the garbage lookin' for goodies. We've tried plenty of ways to keep 'em away, but nothing seems to work and we finally gave up."

"I see." Lesley wasn't impressed. "Has anyone thought to bury the garbage?" The solution seemed simple to her.

"Obviously you've never tried to dig tundra. It's like cement an inch below the surface."

"What's wrong at the station?" Lesley asked, looking at her watch. It was well past noon.

"Can't rightly say, but whatever it is will have to be fixed before Chase can come home. Trust me, he isn't any happier about this than you. Chase isn't normally a swearing man, but he was cursin' a blue streak this morning. He'll give you a call the minute he can."

"I'd like to see the town," Lesley said. She was eager to meet the other women and become a part of the community. It was too late in the year to apply for a full-time teaching position, but she could make arrangements to get her certificate and sign up as a substitute.

"Chase will take you around himself," Pete said again. "It wouldn't be right for me to be introducin' you."

"I know." She sighed. "Tell me about Twin Creeks, would you?"

"Ah…there's not much to tell."

"What about stores?"

He shrugged. "We order most everything through the catalog and on the internet."

"There's a grocery store."

"Oh, sure, but it's small."

Well, she wasn't expecting one with a deli and valet parking.

"What's the population of Twin Creeks?"

Pete wasn't one who could easily disguise his feelings, and she could see from the way his eyes darted past hers that he'd prefer to avoid answering. "We've had, uh, something of a population boom since the last census."

"What's the official total?"

"You might want to talk to Chase about that."

"I'm asking *you*," she pressed, growing impatient. "A thousand?"

"Less 'n that," he said, drinking what remained of his coffee.

"How many less?"

"A, uh, few hundred less."

"All right, five hundred people, then?"

"No…"

Lesley pinched her lips together. "Just tell me. I hate guessing games."

"Forty," Pete mumbled into the empty mug.

"Adults?" Her heart felt as if it'd stopped.

"No, that's counting everyone, including Mrs. Davis's cat."

Eleven

"How many women live in Twin Creeks?" Lesley demanded.

"Including you?" Pete asked, looking decidedly uncomfortable by this time. He clutched his coffee mug with both hands and sat staring into it, as though he expected the answer to appear there.

"Of course I mean including me!"

"That makes a grand total of five then." He continued to hold on to his mug as if it were the Holy Grail.

"You mean to tell me there're only *five* women in the entire town?"

"Five women within five hundred miles, I suspect, when you get right down to it." If his face got much closer to the mug, his nose would disappear inside it.

"Tell me about the other women," Lesley insisted. She was pacing in her agitation. Chase had purposely withheld this information about Twin Creeks from her. Fool that she was, she hadn't even thought to ask, assuming that when he mentioned the town there actually *was* one!

"There's Thelma Davis," Pete said enthusiastically.

"She's married to Milton and they're both in their sixties. Thelma runs the grocery store and she loves to gossip. You'll get along with her just fine. Gladys Thornton might be kind of a problem, though. She's a little crabby and not the sociable sort, so most folks just leave her be."

"Is there anyone close to my age?"

"Heather's twelve," Pete replied, looking up for the first time. "She lives with Thelma Davis. I never did understand the connection. Heather isn't her granddaughter, but they're related in some way."

The woman closest to her in age was a twelve-year-old girl! Lesley's heart plummeted.

"You'll like Margaret, though. She's a real social butterfly. The minute she hears Chase brought himself back a wife, she'll be by to introduce herself."

"How old is Margaret?"

"Darned if I know. In her fifties, I guess. She doesn't like to discuss her age and tries to pretend she's younger."

"I...see."

"I'd best be heading back," Pete said, obviously eager to leave. "I know it's a lot to ask, but would you mind not tellin' Chase that I was the one who told you? We've been friends for a long time and I'd hate for him to take this personally. Me spillin' the beans to you, I mean."

"I'm not making any promises."

Pete left as if he couldn't get away fast enough.

An hour later, Lesley still hadn't decided what to do, if anything. Chase had misled her, true enough, but she wasn't convinced it mattered. She probably would've married him anyway.

No wonder he'd been so interested in Seattle's history

and the Mercer brides. Although more than a hundred years had passed since that time, she was doing basically the same thing as those women, moving to a frontier wilderness and marrying a man she barely knew.

Chase arrived shortly after one o'clock, looking discouraged. Lesley met him at the front door and waited, wondering what to say.

Without a word of greeting, Chase pulled her into his arms and his mouth came down on hers. The familiar taste of him offered comfort and reassurance.

"I missed you," he whispered into her hair, his arms wrapped around her waist.

"I missed you, too."

"Pete brought the groceries? Did he get enough of everything?"

Lesley nodded. "Plenty." She broke away from him. "I didn't know your parents died so recently," she said. She slipped her arm around him and led him into the kitchen. He had to be hungry so she opened a can of chili and began heating that for him. Keeping her hands occupied helped; she didn't want him to guess how much Pete's information had disturbed her.

Chase stood with his back against the counter. "My mom passed away less than two years ago. She died of a heart attack. It was sudden and so much of a shock that my father followed last year. They say people don't die of broken hearts, but I swear that isn't true. My dad was lost without Mom, and I believe he willed himself to die."

"I'm sorry, Chase, I didn't know."

"I meant to tell you."

"It was after their deaths that you decided to marry?"

"Yes," he admitted, watching her closely. "Does that upset you?"

"No." Her reasons for accepting his proposal hadn't been exactly flawless. She'd been escaping her love for Tony, running because she feared she was too weak to withstand her attraction to him. Recently those reasons had blurred in her mind, thanks to her doubts and the unexpected happiness she'd found with Chase. They'd bonded much sooner than she'd anticipated. They belonged together now and if it was Tony's craziness that had brought them to this point, that didn't matter. What did was her life with Chase.

"How's everything at the station?" she asked, placing the steaming bowl of chili on the table and taking out a box of soda crackers.

"Not good. We're going to need a part." He wiped his face with one hand, ignoring the lunch she'd prepared for him. "I hate doing this to you so soon, but it looks like I'll have to go after the motor myself."

"You're *leaving?*" She felt as though she'd been punched by the unexpectedness of it. "How long will you be gone?"

"I don't know yet. A day, possibly two."

It wasn't the end of the world, but she felt isolated and alone as it was. Without Chase she might as well be off floating on an iceberg.

"When do you have to go?" she asked.

"Soon. Listen, sweetheart, I don't want this any more than you do, but it can't be avoided."

Sweetheart. He'd never used affectionate terms with her before. He was genuinely worried, as well he should be. He was going to have to introduce her to the people of Twin Creeks sooner or later, and she knew he'd prefer to do that personally, rather than have her discover the truth on her own while he was away. Of course, he had no idea Pete had already "spilled the beans," as he'd put it.

"I'll pack an overnight bag for you," she offered, half waiting for him to stop her right then and explain.

"Lesley."

She smiled to herself, relieved at the hesitation she heard in his voice. He was going to tell her.

He moved behind her, wrapped his arms around her waist and slipped his hand inside her light sweater. "We won't be able to sleep together tonight."

"Yes, I know." Her voice sounded thick even to her own ears.

He caught her earlobe between his teeth. "One night can feel like a very long time," he said in a whisper.

"It won't be so bad."

"It could be, though."

"Oh." Brilliant conversation was beyond her when he touched her this way.

His lips nibbled at her ear and hot sensation spread though her. "I was thinking you might want to give me something to send me off."

"Like what?" Not that she didn't know *exactly* what he meant, but she was annoyed with him because he was so casual about letting her learn the truth.

"I was in a foul mood all morning," Chase continued, "hurrying because I wanted to get home." He laughed. "Wanting to rush home was a new experience."

"What was the big hurry?"

"Do you honestly need me to say?" He gave another throaty chuckle. "I can't get enough of you. We make love and instead of glorying in the satisfaction, I immediately start wondering when I can have you again. Have you put a spell on me?"

"No." If anything she was the one who'd been enchanted.

He groaned. "Pete will be here in five minutes."

She nodded, turning her head away.

"You're crying," he said with a frown. He held her face gently, brushing the hair from her brow, using his thumbs to wipe away the moisture on her cheeks.

She gazed up at him, blinking hard, hardly able to see him through her tears. Closing her eyes, she shook her head. "Go, or you'll be late."

"I'm not leaving until you tell me what's wrong."

"Pete's coming." She pushed him away.

"He'll wait. Lesley, tell me what's wrong." He reached for an overnight bag, stuffing it with the essentials he'd need as he waited for her response.

She didn't, couldn't, respond.

"You're upset because I have to leave you so soon," he said, "but, sweetheart, I told you. It can't be helped."

She was so furious by this time that she clenched her fists at her sides. "Pete told me his wife didn't last the winter. My sympathy was with Pete because of the weak woman he married. I was making all sorts of judgmental statements in my head, automatically blaming her. I blamed *her,* without the benefit of the doubt. I considered her weak and—"

"What does Pete's marriage have to do with us?" Chase took her by the arms, studying her intensely. A horn honked outside and he cast an irritated look over his shoulder.

"Go," she said again, freeing herself from his hold. "Just go."

"I can't, Lesley, not with you feeling like this."

She swiped impatiently at her tears. "It might've helped if you'd let me know Twin Creeks is nothing more than...than a hole in the road. There are only five women here. Three of them are years older than I am, the fourth is a twelve-year-old girl and the other one is...me."

The honking went on longer and more urgently this time.

"Go on," she said, squaring her shoulders. "Pete's waiting."

Chase wavered, took one step toward the door, but then returned to her. "Will you be here when I get back?"

She had to think about that for a moment, then nodded.

He briefly closed his eyes. "Thank you for that." He left without kissing her. Without touching her. And without saying goodbye.

Lesley ended up throwing out the chili she'd prepared for Chase. She'd never been fond of it herself, although Chase certainly seemed to be if his cupboard was any indication. There was an entire shelf filled with nothing but cans of chili.

She moved from one room to the next, feeling sorry for herself. She'd let the opportunity to really talk about their situation slip through her fingers.

Her cheeks burned at the memory. They'd kissed— and then fought. But their physical longing for each other hadn't diminished.

Their relationship hadn't started out that way. This

was a new development. One that had taken them both by storm.

Lesley delighted in how frequently Chase wanted her. Her joy was made complete by the ready response he evoked in her. But their mutual passion meant she not only needed him, she'd become dependent on him. This was the very thing she'd come to fear with Tony—this total giving of herself. Yet it was what she'd done with Chase. He ruled her head and her heart, as thoroughly as Tony once had. No, even more so.

Was this love? She didn't know. All she knew was that she couldn't be without her husband, but didn't want to lose herself in him.

Tucking her arms around her waist, she wondered how she'd ever manage to fill up the time without Chase.

Chase impatiently filled out the registration forms at the Fairbanks hotel. The sooner he finished, the sooner he could call Lesley.

He wanted to kick himself. He'd known from the moment he arrived home that something was bothering her. He'd seen it in her eyes and in the way she preoccupied herself with making him lunch. He should have settled things between them right then.

Once he had the key to his room, he glanced longingly at the coffee shop. He hadn't eaten since breakfast and that had been a quick cup of coffee and a blueberry muffin.

He'd eat later, he decided, after he'd spoken to Lesley, after he'd explained, if that was possible. He couldn't stand it if she left. She already meant too much to him.

He let himself into the stark hotel room and after dumping his overnight bag on the bed, sat on the edge of it and reached for the room phone. His hand was eager as he punched out the number.

She answered on the second ring.

"Lesley, hello." Now that he could talk to her, he didn't know what to say. The need to explain had burned in him the entire flight into Fairbanks, and now he was speechless.

"Chase?"

"I just got here."

"How are you? Did you have a good flight?"

"I suppose so. How are *you?*" He needed to know that before he proceeded.

"Fine."

The way she said it told him she wasn't. "I realize it's probably not a good idea to have this conversation over the phone."

"We'll talk later," she said, but Chase was afraid that might be too late.

"I didn't want this misunderstanding to ruin what we have."

"And what *do* we have, Chase?" she asked, her voice a mere whisper.

"A marriage," he returned without hesitation. "A fledgling marriage, which means we need to learn to communicate with each other. I'm going to need help."

"We'll learn," she said, and there was a new strength in the words that reassured him.

"I'm sorry I didn't tell you more about Twin Creeks. There always seemed to be other things to discuss and… it didn't seem all that important."

Lesley had no comment.

Chase pressed his hand to his forehead. "That isn't true," he said in a voice so low, he wondered if she could hear him. "I was afraid that if you did know you'd change your mind about marrying me." He was taking one of the biggest risks of his life admitting it, but that was what made honesty of such high value. It was often expensive. But Lesley deserved nothing less.

"There'll never be a teaching position for me here, will there?"

"No." Once more the truth stabbed at him.

"What did you expect me to do with my time?"

"Whatever you want. You can take correspondence courses, teach them if you'd like. Sometime you might want to start a business. The internet's created a lot of possibilities. Whatever you choose will have my full emotional and monetary support. More than anything else, I want you to be happy."

"That all sounds good in theory, but I don't know how it'll work in practice."

"Time will show us." He felt as though he was fighting for his marriage. Either he convinced her here and now that he was serious or he'd lose her. Maybe not now but later, sometime down the road.

He couldn't bear to think of his life without her. It seemed impossible that she could own his heart after so short a time. "Give us a chance—that's all I'm asking."

"All right," she agreed in a whisper.

Chase scowled at the phone. He didn't know if what he'd said had made a difference or not. All he could do was hope that it had.

Chase had told her there was beauty in every part of Alaska but that some of it wasn't immediately obvious. The beauty around Twin Creeks was dark—that was how she'd describe it. Lesley stood outside his four-wheel-drive vehicle. She couldn't shake the feeling that life was very fragile in this part of the world.

The colors she saw thrilled her. Wild splashes of vibrant orange, purple and red covered the grassy and lichened meadows. Pencil-thin waterfalls traced delicate vertical slopes, pooling into a clear lake. The valley wasn't like the rain forest of western Washington, but it was filled with life.

A moose grazed in the distance and she wondered if the great beast was plagued by mosquitoes the same way she'd been. Pete wasn't teasing when he'd warned her. These were the most irritating and persistent variety she'd ever encountered.

She'd found the keys to Chase's truck in a kitchen drawer. After less than twenty-four hours on her own, she was going stir-crazy. Chase had been adamant about not exploring on her own, but she didn't have much choice. If she had to stay inside the cabin one more minute, Lesley was convinced she'd go mad. Her books and other things hadn't arrived, and she didn't feel like emailing any of her friends. Not yet.

Anyway, it was time she introduced herself to the ladies of Twin Creeks, she'd decided, but she'd gotten sidetracked on her way into town.

The sight of the moose had captivated her and she'd parked on the side of the road to watch.

She'd soon become engrossed in the landscape. She lingered there, enjoying the beauty but aware of the dangers. After a while, she climbed back inside the truck and drove to town.

Twin Creeks itself didn't amount to much. She'd visited rest stops that were bigger than this town. She counted three buildings—a combination grocery store and gas station, a tavern and a tiny post office. There wasn't even a church.

The sidewalks, if she could call them that, were made of wooden boards that linked the three main structures. She saw a handful of houses in the distance.

Lesley parked and turned off the engine. A face peered out from behind the tattered curtains in the tavern. She pretended she hadn't noticed and got out of the truck, walking toward the grocery. If she remembered correctly, Thelma Davis ran the store.

"Hello," Lesley said to the middle-aged woman behind the counter, determined to be friendly. "I'm Lesley Goodman, Chase's wife."

"Thelma Davis."

Lesley glanced around. Thelma's business must be prospering. She not only carried food and cleaning supplies, but rented DVDs, sold yarn and other craft supplies, in addition to a smattering of just about everything else.

"Heard this morning that Chase got married," Thelma said, coming around the counter. "Welcome to Twin Creeks. Everyone around here is fond of Chase and we hope you'll be real happy."

"Thank you."

"Ever been to Alaska before? Don't answer that. I can see you haven't. You'll never be colder in your life, that much I can promise you. Some say this is really what hell will be like. Personally, I don't intend on finding out."

"How long have you lived here?" Lesley asked.

Thelma squinted. "We were one of the first ones to move up this way when word came that the pipeline was going through. I was just a young married. That's, oh, more than forty years now. We love it, but the winters take some getting used to."

That Lesley could believe.

"We'll want to have a party for you two. I hope you don't mind us throwing a get-together in your honor. There isn't a lot of entertainment here, but we do our best to have fun."

"I love parties."

Thelma's hands rested on her hips. "We'll have it at our house, since we've got the biggest living room in town. Are you and Chase thinking of starting a family soon? It's been years since we had a baby born in Twin Creeks."

"Ah..." Lesley wasn't sure how to answer that.

"Forgive me, Lesley, I shouldn't be pressuring you about babies. It's just that we're so happy to have another woman, especially a young one."

"I'm pleased to meet you, too."

"If you have a minute I'll call Margaret and get Heather and we'll have coffee and talk. Do you have time for that? Everyone's dying to meet you, even Gladys. We're eager to do whatever we can to make you feel welcome."

"I'd love to meet everyone." The sooner the better. If Chase was going to be away often, her link with the others would be vital to her sanity.

"I knew I was going to like you." Thelma grinned. "The minute Pete mentioned Chase had brought back a wife and described you, I knew we'd be good friends. I think Pete's half smitten with you himself, which to my way of thinking is good. It's about time the men in this community thought about getting married and starting families. That's what Twin Creeks really needs."

Lesley couldn't agree more.

She stayed to meet the other women and by the time she left they'd talked for two hours. Rarely had Lesley been more impressed with anyone. They were like frontier women—resourceful, independent, with a strong sense of community. After the first half hour with the others, Lesley felt as if she'd known them all her life. The genuine warmth of her welcome was exactly what she needed. When she returned to the house, she felt excited to be part of this small but thriving community.

Lesley wasn't home more than five minutes when the phone rang. She answered it eagerly, thinking it would be Chase. There was so much she wanted to tell him.

"Hello."

"Lesley, it's your mother." Their conversations invariably started with June Campbell-Sterne announcing her parental status as if Lesley had forgotten.

"Mom?" She couldn't have been more shocked if Daisy had arrived on her doorstep.

"It's true then, isn't it? You're married and living with some crazy man in Alaska."

"Mom, it isn't as bad as it sounds." She should've tried phoning them again, had planned to, but she'd been too involved in becoming familiar with her new environment.

"When Tony contacted us—"

"Tony?" Lesley said, fuming. Daisy had warned her that her former fiancé was up to no good, but she'd never dreamed he'd resort to contacting her family to make trouble.

"Tony was kind enough to call us and let us know you'd gotten married, which is more than I can say for you."

"Trust me, Mom, Tony did *not* have my best interests at heart."

"I don't believe that."

"He's being jealous and spiteful."

Her mother breathed in deeply as if she was trying to control her temper. "Is it true that you married a man who advertised for a wife on a Seattle billboard?"

"Mom…"

"It is true?"

"Yes, but I didn't answer his ad, if that's what you're thinking. I know you're hurt," she said, trying to diffuse her mother's disappointment and anger, "and I apologize for not letting you know, but Chase only had a few days left in Seattle and you and Ken were traveling and I tried to call your cell and—"

"As it happened, we returned early, but you didn't know that because you just assumed we were gone. You're my only child. Didn't you stop to think that I'd want to be at your wedding?"

"Mom, I'm sorry."

"Tony says you don't even know the man you married. That you weren't in your right mind. He sounded very worried about you."

"None of that's true. I'm very happy with Chase."

"I won't believe that until I see you for myself and meet this man you've married. Ken's already made the flight arrangements for me. I'll be leaving first thing tomorrow morning and landing in Fairbanks at some horrible hour. I have no idea how to reach Twin Creeks from there, but I'll manage if I have to go by dogsled."

"I'll fly down and meet you in Fairbanks," Lesley said, thinking quickly. "Then we'll fly back together." She wanted Chase to meet her mother, but she would rather have waited until they'd settled into their lives together.

"All right." Some of the defensiveness was gone from her mother's voice.

"If you'd like to talk to someone about me and Chase, I suggest you contact Daisy instead of Tony."

"It broke my heart when you ended your engagement to Tony," her mother said.

"Mother, *he* married someone else! I didn't end the engagement—he did. Despite the claims he's making now."

"Look what's happened to you. Just look."

"Mother! I'm married to a wonderful man."

"As I said, I'll judge that for myself. See you tomorrow." She gave her arrival time and Lesley wrote it down on a pad by the phone. Now all she needed to do was find a way of reaching Fairbanks and meeting her mother's plane.

Chase clutched his cell phone so hard, he was afraid he might break it. "What do you mean she isn't at the house?" he demanded, scowling at Pete's unsatisfactory response. He'd spent the most frustrating day of his life, first having to deal with the motor company and then attempting to contact Lesley. He'd tried repeatedly that afternoon with no answer.

There were any number of reasons she might not have answered the phone, but he'd started to worry. Two hours of no response, and he was beside himself. He'd called Pete and had his friend drive over and check out the cabin for himself.

"The door was locked," Pete explained, "so I couldn't get inside. What did she lock it for?"

"Lesley's from the city—they lock everything there," Chase said, trying to figure out where she could've gone.

"When she heard how small Twin Creeks was, she seemed upset," Pete said, sounding guilty.

"We already settled that," Chase said irritably. "Where could she be?" The dangers she could encounter raced through his mind. "Do you think she might have wandered away from the cabin?"

"No."

Chase stiffened. "What makes you so certain?"

"The truck's gone."

"The truck! Well, why didn't you say so earlier?"

He felt Pete's hesitation. "There's something you're not telling me."

"Chase, you're my best friend. I don't want to be the one to tell you your wife walked out on you."

"*What?* She left?" The constriction in his chest produced a sharp pain. "She drove?" His heart did a wild tumble as he calculated how long it would take him to rent a car and catch up with her.

"No," Pete said, "she went out to the field and parked the car there. She paid Jim Perkins to fly her into Fairbanks."

"Without a word to anyone, she just…up and left?"

"I'm sorry, Chase, I really am."

"What time will she be landing?"

"Not sure. All I know is what I heard from Johnny at the field. He only heard part of the conversation. What are you gonna do?"

"I don't know yet." Chase was in shock. His wife of less than a week had deserted him.

"You aren't gonna let her go, are you?"

"No." He'd find Lesley, somehow, someway, and convince her to give their marriage another chance.

Twelve

"Mom." Lesley ran forward and hugged her mother as June Campbell-Sterne entered the arrivals lounge. Unexpected tears sprang to Lesley's eyes and she blinked them back, surprised by the emotion.

The tears were most likely due to the restless night she'd spent in a hotel close to the airport. Apparently Chase hadn't returned to Twin Creeks the way he'd assumed, otherwise he would've seen her message or answered her calls. She'd tried the home phone *and* his cell, with no results. He must be someplace here in Fairbanks. Unfortunately Lesley hadn't asked him for the name of his hotel, since he'd originally planned to be in town only one night.

It seemed ridiculous to contact every hotel in town and ask for Chase. She'd probably be back in Twin Creeks before her husband.

"Let me get a good look at you," June insisted, taking a step back while holding Lesley's shoulders. Her mother had tears in her eyes, as well. "Oh, sweetie, how are you?"

"I feel wonderful. See! Married life agrees with me."

She slipped an arm around her mother's waist and together they strolled toward the luggage carousels.

"I'll admit to being curious about your husband. Honestly, Lesley, what kind of man advertises for a wife?"

Lesley laughed, remembering that her own response had been similar. "He's not crazy—just resourceful."

"I don't mind telling you, this whole thing has both Ken and me concerned. It just isn't like you to marry a virtual stranger and take off to the ends of the earth."

"It isn't as bad as it seems."

Her mother sighed expressively. She was exhausted, as Lesley could well understand. "When will I meet Chase?" was June's next question.

Lesley wasn't entirely sure. "Soon," she promised. "Listen, I got us a hotel room. You're going to need to catch your breath before we fly to Twin Creeks."

"I don't mind telling you, this felt like the longest flight of my life. I had to fly from Helena to Seattle, then wait for hours before I could get this flight." She shook her head. "I can't see you living in Alaska and liking it. You've lived in a big city all your life."

"You love Montana, don't you?"

"Yes, but that's different. Ken and I are retired."

"It isn't different at all. I've only been in Alaska for a short while and I love it already."

Her mother pinched her lips together as if to keep from saying something argumentative. "If it's all the same to you, Lesley, I'd prefer to push on. I'll rest once we reach your home and I meet this man you've married. Then and only then will I truly relax."

That posed a problem. "We can't, Mom."

"Can't do what? Meet Chase? I wondered why he

wasn't here to greet me. One would think he'd be eager to meet your family. I don't imagine you've met his, either, have you?"

"Mom," Lesley said impatiently. She was troubled by the way her mother was so willing to find fault with Chase and her marriage. No doubt that was Tony's doing. Even now, he was haunting her life. More and more she'd come to realize that Tony had never really loved her. Even more enlightening was the realization that she no longer loved him. She couldn't feel as strongly as she did for Chase if she loved Tony. She missed Chase terribly.

"What?" June snapped.

"Stop trying to make Chase into some fiend. He's not."

"You still haven't told me why he sent you to the airport by yourself," she said, in that superior way that had driven Lesley to the brink of hysteria as a teenager.

"Mother, Chase has a job. He was away on business when you called. And the reason we can't leave yet is that we can't get a flight until tomorrow."

"I will be meeting him later then?"

"Of *course*." Lesley just wasn't sure exactly when.

They stood at the luggage carousel for several minutes until June collected her one large suitcase and her cosmetic case. Lesley took the larger of the two bags and carried it outside to the taxi line.

Her mother was worn out, and by the time they arrived at the hotel room, Lesley was glad that Jim couldn't get them until the following morning. She was supposed to call this afternoon to confirm it.

"Would you like me to order you something to eat?" Lesley asked.

"No, thanks." June politely covered her mouth for a loud yawn. "If you don't mind, I'll lie back and just close my eyes."

"Of course I don't mind. Relax, Mom." Her mother curled up on the bed and was asleep seconds later. Lesley silently placed a sweater over June's shoulders and tiptoed to the other bed. Her intention was to read until her mother woke, but she must have fallen asleep, too, because the next thing she heard was the sound of running water.

Lesley stirred, opened her eyes and realized her mother was showering. With June occupied, Lesley reached for the phone and called Chase at both numbers. Again there was no answer at either. Discouraged, she replaced the receiver. Where could he possibly be?

"What exactly did she say?" Chase asked Jim Perkins. He found it frustrating to have this conversation by phone. Especially frustrating when he was sitting in a hotel room in Fairbanks. It would've been easier to read Jim in person. He spoke in a slow drawl and had never been one to reveal much, with either words or actions. If Chase could've talked to Jim in person, he might've been able to persuade him of the urgency of this situation.

Jim took his own sweet time answering. "She really didn't have a lot to say."

Jim was in his early forties and possessed a calm low-key attitude that had never bothered Chase before. But now he was desperate to learn everything he could about Lesley's departure from Twin Creeks.

"Surely you chatted during the flight."

"Yeah. She's the congenial sort. Personally I didn't

think much of this scheme of yours of advertising for a wife, but I was wrong. Half the men in town are talking about doing something like that themselves, seeing the kind of woman you brought back with you." He paused. "I don't suppose it would work with me, though."

"What did you and Lesley talk about?" Chase asked.

"Nothing much," Jim said. "Mostly she asked about you."

"What about me?"

He seemed to need time to consider this question. "Nothin' in particular. Just how long you've lived in Twin Creeks. Things like that."

"Did she mention she was staying in a hotel?"

"She might have." Another pause. "I don't recall her saying she was, now that I think about it."

Chase had difficulty not letting his distress show. It was bad enough that Lesley had left him so soon after her arrival in Twin Creeks. But he wasn't ready to announce to the entire community that his bride of one week had deserted him. If that was true, it would come out soon enough.

"I appreciate your help, Jim. Thanks."

"I don't think you need to worry about her," Jim added in that lethargic drawl of his. "Lesley's got a good head on her shoulders. She can take care of herself."

"Yes, I know." That, however, didn't ease his mind in the least.

No sooner had he finished with the call than the phone rang. Chase grabbed it so fast, he nearly jerked the telephone off the end table. "Yes?" he snapped.

"It's Pete."

"What'd you find out?"

"Lesley's staying at the Gold Creek Hotel by the airport," came Pete's reply. "Room 204."

"How'd you learn that?" Sometimes it was better not to know where Pete got his information, but Chase couldn't help being curious.

"I've got my sources. And listen, she may be having second thoughts because she hasn't bought an airline ticket to Seattle yet. Or anywhere else."

"You're sure about that?"

"Positive." There was doubt in his voice. "Did you get any sleep last night?"

Chase closed his burning eyes. "None."

"That's what I thought. You know, Chase, if she insists on leaving, you can't make her stay."

This had been the subject of an ongoing internal debate. He didn't want to lose Lesley, but he couldn't hold her prisoner, either. If she'd decided she wanted out of his life and out of their marriage, then he couldn't stop her. Even if it meant she'd decided to return to Seattle and Tony. But he was determined to have his say before he'd let her run out on him.

"What are you going to do?" Pete asked.

"I don't know yet. I'll probably go to the hotel and see if I can talk some sense into her."

"Sounds like a good idea to me. I suppose you want to do this on your own, but if you'd like, I'll come along for moral support and wait outside."

"No, thanks, but I appreciate the offer."

"No problem. That's what friends do." Pete hesitated as if there was something more he wanted to say.

"Anything else?"

"Yeah." Again Pete hesitated. "I don't make a practice of giving advice, especially when it comes to women.

My history with the opposite sex leaves a lot to be desired."

"Just say what's on your mind." Chase didn't generally seek other people's wisdom; he lived and learned by his own mistakes. This was different, though, and he was worried. He'd assumed everything was fine between them. That he could be so blind to her feelings was a shock.

"I wish now that I'd gone after Pamela," Pete said. It was the first time Chase had heard his friend say this. "I've wondered a thousand times over what would've happened if I'd taken the trouble to let her know how much I loved her, how much I needed her. If I had, she might've stayed and I wouldn't be regretting all the time that I didn't do everything I could to convince her. Don't make the same mistake."

"I don't plan on it."

"Good." Pete cleared his throat. "You love her, don't you?"

Chase wasn't sure how to answer. The physical desire they shared had overwhelmed them both. But their relationship had quickly become so much more.

When he'd first considered finding himself a wife, it had been to ease his loneliness. He was searching for a companion. A lover. A woman to keep him company during the long, dark winter months. He wanted a wife so he could bond closely with another human being. Since his parents' deaths, he'd felt detached and isolated from life.

Love had never entered into the equation. He'd never expected to fall in love this fast. Passion, yes, he'd expected that but not this kind of love.

This had been his error, Chase realized with a start.

Marriage to Lesley had altered everything. Because love had come to them—or at least to him—with everything she did, everything she said. Whenever he went to bed with her, he offered her a little more of his heart. A little more of his soul. Lovemaking had become more than a physical mating, it had a spiritual aspect. He didn't know how else to describe it.

He thought about Lesley lying in bed waiting for him. She was so incredibly lovely, with her hair spilling out over the pillow...

It felt like a knife in his belly to think that she'd walk out on him without so much as a word.

"I do," Chase said, answering Pete's question after a profound moment. "I do love her."

"Then do whatever you have to in order to keep her," Pete advised sagely. "Even if it means leaving Twin Creeks. You can always find another job, but you may never find another Lesley."

His friend was right and Chase knew it. Now all he had to do was come up with a way of convincing Lesley to give their lives together a fighting chance.

He showered and changed clothes, flipped through the Fairbanks phone directory for the address of the Gold Creek Hotel and ordered a cab.

It would've been better if he'd been able to work out what he wanted to say, but he dared not delay a confrontation for fear he'd miss her.

Chase was grateful to Pete. His friend had said he could find Lesley through his various connections faster than Chase would be able to do it. Chase hated sitting back and letting someone else do the footwork, but in the end it had proven beneficial. Pete had located her within twelve hours.

The taxi let him off in front of the hotel. His heart was beating so hard he could hardly hear his own thoughts. Even now he didn't know what he what he was going to say.

That, however, didn't stop him from pounding at the door of room 204. When she didn't immediately answer, he knocked again, louder this time, so loud that the lady across the hall stuck her head out to see who was causing such a commotion. She threw him an irritated look and went back inside.

The door opened and Lesley stood in front of him. Suitcases sat like accusations in the background, and suddenly he was angry. He'd considered Lesley decent and honorable, not the kind of woman who'd walk out on her husband without warning.

"What do you think you're doing?" he demanded, pushing his way into the room. Lesley was so startled that she stumbled two steps back before regaining her balance.

"Chase?" She closed the door and leaned against it, her eyes wide. The perfume she wore wafted toward him. He needed every ounce of willpower not to haul her into his arms and beg her to stay with him.

"I don't understand," she said, staring at him, her eyes so innocent that the struggle not to kiss her seemed to drain his strength.

"I may have made a few mistakes along the way, but I would've thought you'd have the decency to talk to me instead of running away."

"Running away? I just flew down to Fairbanks!"

"Without a word to me," he reminded her in clipped tones.

"I left you a note." Her voice was raised now, as well. She rested her hands on her hips and scowled at him.

"A note," he said as though he found that humorous. "What good is that when I'm here in Fairbanks?"

Lesley dropped her hands, clenching them tightly. "You didn't give me the name of the hotel where you were staying. And you didn't answer your cell. How was I *supposed* to contact you?"

Chase was embarrassed to admit that he'd left his cell phone charging and hadn't bothered to check for a message from her—because he hadn't expected one.

"So now it's my fault." Chase knew why he was arguing with her, because if he didn't, he was going to reach for her and hold her, kiss her.

"Yes, it's your fault," she cried.

"Lesley, who is this man?"

Chase whirled around to see an older woman in a bright red housecoat with matching red slippers. Her hair was wrapped in a towel.

"Mother..." Lesley sounded as though she was about to burst into tears. She gestured weakly toward him, before her hand fell lifelessly to her side. "This is Chase Goodman, my husband."

The woman glared at him as if he were living proof of every dreaded suspicion she'd harbored. "What's the matter with you, young man?"

"Mrs. Campbell-Sterne..."

"How dare you talk to Lesley like this! Have you no manners?"

Chase gave what he figured was an excellent imitation of a salmon, his mouth opening and closing soundlessly. He looked at Lesley, desperate for her to explain, but she'd turned her back to him.

"I'm sorry," he whispered.

"As well you should be. I can tell you I had my

concerns about the kind of man Lesley married. Now I can see that—"

"Would you mind if I spoke to my wife alone for a moment?" Chase interrupted. Lesley's arms were cradling her middle and she was staring out the window. She gave no indication that she'd heard him.

"I... I suppose not." Mrs. Campbell-Sterne flushed. "I'll go and dress."

"Thank you," Chase said. He waited until his mother-in-law had gone into the bathroom and closed the door before he approached Lesley.

He stepped behind her and went to rest his hands on her shoulders, stopping just short. He closed his eyes briefly, then dropped his hands to his sides. "I just made a world-class jerk of myself, didn't I?"

Lesley nodded, still refusing to face him.

"You left a note at the house?"

She answered him with another sharp nod. "And messages."

"What did they say?"

"That my mother had phoned and was worried about me and our sudden marriage. She was hurt that I'd gone through with the ceremony without trying harder to contact her. She decided to fly up immediately to meet you."

"Oh..." He didn't know what had possessed him to think she'd leave without some kind of explanation.

"Tony called Mom and Ken," Lesley went on. "He claimed I'd married on the rebound and that I'd made a terrible mistake. He was hoping to undermine our relationship." The way Lesley said it made Chase wonder if Tony had succeeded.

After the stunt he'd just pulled, he couldn't blame

Lesley for believing she *had* made a mistake. Apologies seemed grossly inadequate.

"You flew down to meet your mother." Once again he wanted to kick himself for being so stupid. No doubt her mother thought Lesley had married a madman and he'd quickly gone about proving her right.

"What's wrong with you, charging in here like a bull moose?" Lesley demanded, finally turning to face him.

His salmon imitation returned, and he couldn't manage a word, let alone a coherent sentence.

"I'm waiting for an answer," she reminded him.

"I… I thought you left me," he mumbled.

"You're not serious, are you?" Her eyes, which he'd always found so bright and beautiful, were filled with disdain.

It sounded so weak. "I couldn't let you leave."

"Why not?"

Now was the perfect opportunity to confess how much he loved her, how his heart wouldn't survive without her, but he couldn't make himself say it, not with her looking at him as if he should be arrested.

"What else was I supposed to think?" he flared. "You up and left."

"You left, too, and didn't return when you said you would, but I didn't immediately leap to some outrageous conclusion."

"That's different," Chase argued, although he knew that made no sense. He disliked the turn their conversation had taken. He didn't want to quarrel; what he yearned to do was pull her into his arms, bury his face in her neck and breathe in her scent.

"Can I come out now?" June asked from the bathroom doorway. She'd changed into blue-and-green-plaid slacks and a pale blue sweater. She was nearly as tall as Lesley, with the same clear, dark, intelligent eyes. And like Lesley, her thoughts were easy to read. Chase didn't have to guess what his mother-in-law was thinking. He hadn't impressed her, nor had he done anything to reassure her that Lesley had made a wise choice in marrying him.

The worst of it was that he couldn't blame her.

"It's all right, Mom. You can come out."

"You're sure?" She said it as though she was ready to contact the police and have Chase removed.

"I'm afraid I've made a mistake," Chase said, hoping he could explain what had happened and at the same time address her concerns about his and Lesley's relationship.

"You can say that again," June returned crisply.

"Perhaps we could discuss this over lunch." Feeding them both sounded like an excellent plan and once they were relaxed, he'd be able to smooth things over.

Lesley's mother didn't look too pleased about stepping outside the hotel room with him. She cast a guarded look in Lesley's direction. "What do you think, dear?"

"That'll be fine," Lesley said, reaching for a white sweater, neatly folded at the foot of the bed. Chase moved to help her put it on, then changed his mind. Now wasn't the time to be solicitous. Lesley wouldn't appreciate it.

Chase chose the hotel restaurant. Conversation over lunch was stilted at best. June asked him several questions, but his attention was focused on his wife. He answered June, but his gaze didn't waver from Lesley. He was hoping she'd say or do something, anything to ease his conscience.

He'd blown it. The door had been left wide open for him to explain why he'd reacted so badly. He'd been out of his mind, thinking he'd lost her.

Chase loved her. It didn't get any simpler than that. All he had to do was say it. How difficult could that be? Apparently more than he'd realized because he let the opportunity slip past.

"How long do you plan to visit?" Chase asked June, thinking ahead. He supposed he shouldn't have been so obvious, but he was already counting down the days, the hours and minutes, until he could be alone with Lesley.

"Five days," June returned stiffly. She glanced at Lesley as though to suggest that purchasing another plane ticket south would be highly advisable—for both of them.

"I was able to get the new motor this morning," Chase said to Lesley. "We can leave for Twin Creeks as soon as you're ready."

"Mother?"

"Anytime. I'm anxious to see your home, although heaven knows you haven't had much time to settle in, have you?"

"No." Lesley eyed Chase wearily.

"I'll leave you here and be back within the hour to get you," he said, reaching for the lunch tab. "Perhaps you'd care to come with me?" he asked Lesley. He tried to appear nonchalant about it, but his heart was in his throat.

"I don't think I should leave Mother," she said flatly.

Chase's shoulders fell. Her feelings couldn't have been more obvious.

Lesley couldn't remember being more furious with anyone in her life. Chase was a fool. She'd agreed to marry him, agreed to leave the life she'd made for herself, leave her friends, her career and most of her possessions, and he *still* didn't trust her. He assumed she'd walk out on him the minute his back was turned. That was what hurt so much. His lack of faith in her.

Lesley had spent the morning listing Chase's many fine qualities to her mother. By the time she'd finished, it sounded as if he were a candidate for sainthood.

Fat chance of that after the way he'd barged into their hotel room. He couldn't have shown himself in a worse light had he tried.

After Chase left, her mother was strangely silent. They sat on their beds, staring straight ahead. Every time Lesley thought of something to say, she changed her mind. Her mother would see through her efforts to make small talk in a second.

"He isn't always like this," she finally murmured.

"I certainly hope not."

"Chase is honest and hardworking."

"That remains to be seen, doesn't it?" her mother asked stiffly.

"You don't like him, do you?"

June paused. "I don't have much reason to, do I? I'm afraid you've been blinded, Lesley. How can you possibly love this man? You don't really know him… You couldn't. Tony said Chase disguised the truth."

"You can't trust Tony!"

"Why not? At least he called us when my own daughter hadn't bothered to let me know she was getting married. Now that I've met your husband, I can appreciate Tony's concern."

"Mother…"

"Hear me out, please. I've bitten my tongue for the

last hour, trying not to say what I should have earlier and didn't. You have nothing in common with Chase. You might have convinced yourself that you're happy now, and that you're going to make this ridiculous marriage work, but it isn't necessary."

"Mom, please, don't." It hurt that her mother thought her marriage ridiculous. Lesley was angry with Chase all over again for having put her in this impossible situation.

"I have to speak my piece or I'll regret it the rest of my life. I made the same mistake with your father." Her voice faltered slightly. "I knew the marriage wasn't going to work, almost from the first, but I was too stubborn to admit it. I convinced myself that I was deeply in love with him. I worked hard at making the best of the situation, giving more and more of myself until there wasn't anything left to give.

"After all that, after everything I did to hold that marriage together, he walked out. To see you repeat my mistakes would be the most tragic thing that could happen to me."

Lesley felt as if she was going to break into tears. "It isn't like that with Chase and me."

"I don't believe that, not after talking to Tony and meeting Chase for myself. He isn't right for you. Anyone with a brain can see that."

"Mom…"

"Are you pregnant?"

"No."

Her mother sighed as though relieved. "Come back to Montana with me," June pleaded. "If you want to start over, do it there. There's always a need for good teachers.

Don't make the mistakes I did, Lesley. Leave Chase now—before it's too late—and come back with me."

Lesley was so intent on listening to her mother that she didn't hear the door open. But she felt Chase's presence before she heard his words. He was studying her without emotion, without revealing a hint of his thoughts.

"Well?" he said. "Make up your mind, Lesley. What do you want to do?"

Thirteen

Lesley's mother was staring at her, too, pleading with her to cut her losses now.

"I... I thought we'd already decided to return to Twin Creeks," Lesley stammered.

June's shoulders sagged with dismay. Chase hurriedly reached for their suitcases, as though he expected Lesley to change her mind. That irritated her, too. Her mother was about to burst into tears and Chase was ignoring June completely.

The flight into Twin Creeks seemed to take twice as long as before. Chase flew the four-seater, concentrating as hard as if he were flying an F-14 under siege. Lesley made several attempts to carry the conversation, but it became painfully obvious that neither her mother nor Chase was interested in small talk.

When they landed at the tiny airfield, Pete and Jim were there to greet them. She knew Chase had let Jim know he'd be flying them home. But she didn't understand what was going on between Pete and her husband. The minute Pete saw her, he grinned broadly and gave

Chase a thumbs-up. Chase, however, didn't seem to share his friend's enthusiasm.

"This is where you live?" June asked, scowling, staring at the tundra that surrounded the town. "Why, it's... it's like stepping back a hundred years." The words were more accusation than comment. Lesley saw Chase's jaw tense, but he didn't say anything, which was just as well. Lesley doubted her mother would be receptive, anyway.

When they arrived at the cabin, Lesley waited curiously for her mother's reaction. June asked several questions, nodding now and then as Chase told her about his and Lesley's life in Twin Creeks. Lesley was pleased with his honest responses. She added what little information she could.

"The guest room is down the hall," Chase explained, leading them into the house. There seemed to be a détente between him and her mother, much to Lesley's relief.

June paused in the living room, staring curiously at the fireplace and the bookshelves and the desk in much the same way Lesley had earlier. Before leaving, Lesley had added several feminine touches to the house. A homemade quilt that had been her grandmother's was draped across the back of the rocking chair. A picture of her mother and Ken rested on the television and a small figurine of a harbor seal made of ash from the 1980 Mount Saint Helens eruption was propped against a Sue Grafton mystery in one of the built-in bookcases.

"This has a homey feel to it," June said grudgingly before following Chase down the narrow hallway.

Lesley bit her tongue and trailed after her mother. Already she could see that this was going to be the longest five days of her life.

* * *

Chase was forced to wait until after dinner before he had a chance to speak to his mother-in-law privately. While Lesley was busy with the dinner dishes, Chase casually suggested a drive into town.

June hesitated, but it appeared she had things she wanted to say to him, too, and she agreed with a nod of her head.

Chase walked into the kitchen. Under normal circumstances, he would've slipped his arms around Lesley's waist. But these weren't normal conditions. He was afraid of touching her for fear of being charged with not behaving in a circumspect fashion. He swore his mother-in-law had the eyes of an eagle and the temperament of a polar bear.

"Your mother and I are going for a drive," he said as casually as he could, hoping Lesley would leave it at that. He should've known better.

She hurriedly finished rinsing the pan she'd used to bake biscuits and reached for a hand towel. "I'll come with you."

"Don't be offended, but we'd both rather you didn't."

Lesley blinked and leaned against the sink. "I don't know if talking to my mother when she's in this frame of mind is a good idea."

"We either clear the air here and now, or all three of us are going to spend a miserable five days."

"But, Chase…"

"Honey, listen." He paused and glanced over his shoulder. June had gone for a sweater, but would return at any moment. "You and I need to talk, too. I'm sorry about starting off on the wrong foot with your mother. I promise I'll do my best to make things right. I owe you that much—and a whole lot more."

Lesley lowered her gaze.

"I realize June's not the only one I offended," he said gruffly, walking toward her. If he didn't kiss her soon, he was going to go stark raving mad. Lesley must have felt the same way because she moved toward him, her steps as eager as his own. His heart reacted immediately, gladdened that she wanted to end this terrible tension between them.

He clasped his hands about her waist and caught her, drawing her into the shelter of his arms.

The sound of June clearing her throat behind him was like a bucket of cold water tossed over his head. He released Lesley and stepped away from her.

"We won't be long," he said, as evenly as he could.

June was fussing with her sweater when he turned around, smoothing out the sleeves. Her back was straight with unspoken disapproval. She looked prim and proper and determined to save her daughter from his nasty clutches. Chase sighed inwardly and prayed for patience.

Lesley followed them out to the front porch and watched as Chase opened the passenger door and held out his hand to help June inside. His mother-in-law ignored him and hoisted herself into the front seat.

So that was how it was going to be.

Knowing what to expect, Chase threw a look over his shoulder at Lesley and shrugged. He'd do his best, but he wasn't a miracle worker. He couldn't *force* Lesley's mother to accept him as her son-in-law, nor could he demand she give her approval to their marriage.

He climbed into the seat beside her, and started the

engine. "I don't know if Lesley had a chance to tell you, but Twin Creeks is a small town," he said, as he pulled onto the dirt and gravel road. "The population is around forty."

"Forty," June repeated, sounding shocked. "Did Lesley tell you she was born and raised in Seattle?"

"Yes."

"There were almost that many students in her kindergarten class. What makes you think a woman who's lived in a large populated area all her life will adjust to a place like this?"

Chase was ready for this one. "Lesley knew Twin Creeks was small when she agreed to marry me." True, she hadn't known *how* small, but she'd had the general idea.

"You haven't answered my question," June said primly, her hands tightly clasped.

"I'm hoping love will do that," he said simply.

"Aren't you asking a good deal of a woman you've only known a few weeks?"

"Yes, but—"

"It seems to me," Lesley's mother interrupted, "that neither of you has given the matter much thought. Lesley won't last a month in this primitive lifestyle."

Chase was fast losing his patience. "It seems to *me* that you don't know your daughter as well as you think you do."

"I beg your pardon," she snapped. "Do you suppose I don't realize what you did? You seduced my daughter, convinced her to marry you and then practically kidnapped her to get her to move north with you."

Chase pulled over to the side of the road. He couldn't concentrate on driving and hold on to his temper at the same time.

"Lesley mentioned that you'd spoken to Tony. I gather you're repeating what he said. Unfortunately you and I don't know each other well enough to be good judges of the other's character. You see me as some psychopath who's tricked your daughter into marriage."

"You can't blame me for that, after you charged into our hotel room, acting like a lunatic."

Chase closed his eyes with mounting frustration. When he collected himself, he continued in a calm, clear voice. "Arguing isn't going to settle anything. You believe what you must and I'll do my best to stay out of your way." He started the engine, intent on turning the vehicle around and heading back to the house. He'd tried, but hadn't lasted five minutes with June hurling accusations at him.

"Listen here, young man—"

"The last person who called me 'young man' was my junior high teacher," Chase retorted. "I'm a long way from junior high, so I suggest you either call me by name or keep quiet."

She gasped indignantly, and Chase wondered how it was possible to love Lesley so much, yet feel so negative toward her mother.

"What you fail to understand," he said, after a lengthy pause, "is that we have something in common."

"I sincerely doubt that."

"We both love Lesley."

"Yes, but—"

"There aren't any qualifiers as far as I can see," he interrupted. "She's your daughter, the woman you've raised and nurtured and loved all these years. I don't have the same history with Lesley, but I love her. Right now those may be only words to you, but I'd rather die than hurt her. If your main concern is that she won't adjust to life here in Alaska, then let me assure you, we'll move."

"This all sounds very convenient. You're telling me what I want to hear."

"I'm telling you the truth." His anger flared briefly, then died down just as quickly. "We were wrong not to make more of an effort to contact you about the wedding. If you want to blame someone for that, then I'll accept the guilt. I was in a hurry—"

"You rushed her into making a decision."

Chase had another argument poised and ready, but he'd recognized early on that there was nothing he could say that would alter June's opinion of him.

"I don't think we're going to be able to talk this out," he said, not bothering to disguise his disappointment. "I'd never keep Lesley here against her will, that much I promise you. You've raised a wonderful woman and I love her more than my own life. I can't offer you any greater reassurance than that."

His words were greeted with silence.

"You and your husband will always be welcome here, especially after we start our family."

She turned and glared at him as if he'd said something offensive, but Chase was tired of trying to decipher this woman's thoughts.

"If Lesley wants to visit you and your husband in Montana, she can go with my blessing," he added. It went without saying that *he* wouldn't be welcome. "I apologize for making an idiot of myself earlier. I don't blame you for thinking ill of me, but I'd hoped we'd be able to put that behind us and start again. Perhaps before you leave, we'll be able to do that." He switched gears, turned the vehicle around and drove back to the house.

Lesley was knitting in the rocking chair when he walked inside. She glanced up anxiously, but must have read the defeat in his eyes, and the disdain in her mother's, because she sagged against the back of the chair.

"What are you knitting?" June asked, revealing some enthusiasm for the first time in hours.

"A sweater for Chase. One of the ladies in town sells yarn, so while I was there I picked up a pattern and everything else I was going to need."

"You met Thelma?" Chase asked, claiming the recliner next to his wife.

"I had tea with all the ladies," Lesley informed him. She was trying not to smile. Her mouth quivered and the need to kiss her felt nearly overwhelming.

So she'd gone into town on her own. Chase should've realized she was too anxious to meet the others to wait for him to introduce her.

"It's stuffy in here," June announced.

"There's a chair on the porch," Chase suggested. If his curmudgeon of a mother-in-law wasn't standing guard over them, he might be able to steal a few minutes alone with his wife.

"I think I'll sit out there for a while."

"Good idea," Chase said with just a smidgen of glee. To his credit, he didn't lock the door behind her.

"What happened?" Lesley asked in a breathy whisper the instant her mother was out the door.

"She thinks I seduced you into moving up here with me."

Lesley batted her long lashes at him. "You did, didn't you?"

"I'd certainly like the opportunity to do so again," he said, waggling his brows suggestively. "I'm not going to last another five days without making love to you. Maybe not even another five minutes—"

"Chase!" Lesley whispered, as he moved toward her. "My mother's right outside."

"She already thinks I'm a sex fiend as it is."

"You are!"

Chase chuckled, but his humor was cut short by a piercing scream from the front porch. Never in his life had Chase moved faster. Lesley reacted just as quickly. Her knitting needles and yarn flew toward the ceiling as they both raced out the front door.

June was backed against the front of the house, her hands flattened over her heart. Even from several feet away, Chase could see she was trembling.

"What happened?" he demanded.

June closed her eyes and shook her head. Luckily Lesley was there to comfort her. She wrapped her arms around her mother and gently guided her toward the door.

"Something must have frightened her," Chase said. He debated going for his hunting rifle, then decided against it. Whatever the danger had been, it'd passed.

"It was…huge." The words were strangled-sounding.

"A bear, Mom. Did you see a bear?" Lesley's eyes widened with fear, but her mother shook her head.

"It must've been a moose," Chase speculated. He recalled the first time he'd come nose to nose with one. It was an experience he'd rather not repeat.

"No." June shook her head again.

"A wolf?" Lesley pressed.

"No," his mother-in-law moaned. Lesley led her into

the house and urged her down in the rocker while Chase went for a glass of water.

"It was a...a *spider*," June said, gripping the glass with both hands. "A black one with long legs. I... I've never liked spiders."

Judging by June's reaction, that was an understatement.

"A spider?" Chase whispered. The woman had sounded as though she'd barely escaped with her life.

His wife shrugged and rolled her eyes.

"Suggest she go to bed and rest," he said in hushed tones.

Lesley's lips quivered with the effort it took to suppress a smile.

"Maybe you'd better lie down," Lesley said in a soothing voice.

"You're right," June murmured, clearly shaken by the encounter. "I don't usually overreact like this. It's just that this spider was so *big*. I didn't expect there to be spiders here in Alaska, of all places."

"We all have a tendency to overreact under certain circumstances," Chase said, using the opportunity to defend his own behavior earlier in the day. "Later we realize how foolish we must have looked to everyone else. People generally understand and forgive that sort of thing." As far as sermons went, he felt he'd done well. He was no TV evangelist, but he figured he'd got his point across. He only hoped June had picked up on his message.

"I do feel like I should rest."

"I'll check out the room first," Chase offered, "and make sure there's nothing there." All he needed was for June to interrupt him and Lesley. He didn't know how well his heart would stand up to another blood-curdling scream.

"Thank you," June whispered as he hurried out.

When he came back to signal that all was clear, Lesley accompanied her mother to the bedroom. After five minutes Chase was glancing at his watch, wondering how long this was going to take.

Another ten minutes passed before Lesley returned to the living room. "Mom's resting comfortably. I gave her a couple of aspirin to settle her nerves."

"I need something to settle my nerves, too," Chase said, reaching for her and pulling her onto his lap.

"Chase." She put up a token struggle.

"Kiss me."

"I… I don't think that's a good idea."

"Considering what I *really* want, a kiss seems darn little. Don't be stingy, Lesley, I need you." If they'd been alone, he'd have had her in bed fifteen seconds after they got home. As it was, he'd been forced to sit through an uncomfortable dinner and then deal with her dragon of a mother before and after the spider attack. A kiss was small compensation.

He nibbled at her ear. He'd settle for kissing her. It was all he wanted right now, just enough to satisfy him until he could tell her all that was in his heart.

He could feel her resistance, the little there was, melt away.

She turned her head until their lips met. The kiss was slow and deep. It demanded every shred of stamina he had to drag his mouth away from hers. By then, Lesley's arms had circled his neck and she was sighing softly. She laid her head on his shoulder and worked her fingers into his hair.

Now was the time to tell her. He forced his mind from the warmth of her body pressing against his, her moist breath fanning his neck.

"When I spoke to your mother..." The words wouldn't come. Maybe this would be easier after they'd made love.

"Yes?" Lesley lifted her head, curiosity brightening her eyes.

"I told her something I've never told you." Their eyes met and her mouth widened with an enticing smile.

"I love you, Lesley." There it was, out in the open for her to accept or reject. His heart was there, too, along with his dreams for their future.

Lesley tensed, her hands on his shoulders. "What did you just say?" Her voice was barely audible.

"I love you." It sounded so naked, saying it like that. "I realize blurting it out might make you uncomfortable, but I didn't think it was fair if I told your mother how I felt and said nothing to you."

She was off his lap in a flash. Tears glazed her eyes as she backed away from him.

"I was sure of it when I thought you'd left me," he explained. "I'd tried to reach you by phone and when I couldn't, I had Pete go to the cabin. He told me the truck was gone and that Jim had flown you into Fairbanks. I didn't know what to think. Now it seems ludicrous to leap to the conclusions I did, but at the time it made perfect sense."

"I see." One tear escaped the corner of her eye and rolled down the side of her face.

"Say something," he pleaded. His heart was precariously perched at the end of his sleeve. The least she could do was let him know if she was about to pluck it off and crush it beneath her feet.

"I knew when we got married that you didn't love me," she said, without looking at him. "When we were in Victoria—I knew you didn't love me then, either."

"Don't be so sure," he returned, frowning. He understood the problem, had always understood it. Tony. She was in love with her former fiancé and that wasn't likely to change for a long time.

Her head snapped up. "You were in love with me on our honeymoon?"

He shrugged, unwilling to reveal everything quite so soon. He wished she'd express her feelings for him.

"Were you?" she asked again.

Chase stood and rubbed his hand along the back of his neck, walking away from her. "Does it matter?"

"Yes."

"All right," he muttered. "As near as I can figure, I loved you when we got married. It just took me a while to…put everything together." He shoved his hands inside his pockets. This wasn't going as well as he'd hoped.

"I tried to reassure your mother, but that didn't work," he continued. "Tony's got her convinced you married me on the rebound and that it was a mistake."

"I didn't."

Now it was Chase's turn to go still. He was afraid to believe what he thought she was saying.

"You *aren't* in love with Tony?" he asked breathlessly.

"That would be impossible when I'm crazy in love with you." She smiled then, the soft womanly smile that never failed to stir him. Her love shone like a beacon.

Chase closed his eyes to savor her words, to wrap them around his heart and hold on to the feeling. It happened then, a physical need, a craving for her that was so powerful it nearly doubled him over.

They moved toward each other, their kisses fuel to the flames of their desire.

"Chase," Lesley groaned between kisses, unbuttoning his shirt as she spoke. "We can't... Mother's room is directly down the hall from us. She'll hear."

Chase kissed her while trying to decide what to do.

"The cache," he said, grateful for the inspiration. It wasn't the ideal solution, but it would serve their purpose.

Lesley's legs seemed to have given out on her and he lifted her into his arms, pausing only long enough to grab the quilt from the rocking chair.

He gathered her in his arms, holding her close with a fierce possessiveness.

"I love you." Each time he said it, the words came more easily.

"I know." She spread a slow series of kisses along his jaw.

"Your mother..."

"Don't worry about Mom. She'll come around, especially when she's got grandchildren to spoil."

"Children," Chase said softly.

"Is this a new concept to you?"

"Not entirely." He grinned and she smiled back.

"Good." Her teeth caught his lower lip. "Soon I hope," she said a moment later.

"How soon?"

Lesley raised her head and her beautiful dark eyes gazed down at him. "No time like the present, is there?"

Chase sucked in his breath. He'd thought they'd wait a year, possibly longer, to start their family, but he couldn't refuse Lesley anything.

"Will I ever grow tired of you?" he wondered aloud.

"Never," she promised.

Chase instinctively knew it was true.

Epilogue

"Grandma, Grandma." Three-year-old Justin Goodman tore out of Lesley's grasp as they stepped into the small airport and he ran into the waiting arms of June Campbell-Sterne.

June hugged her grandson and lifted him from the ground. "Oh, my, you've gotten so big."

Justin's chubby arms circled his grandmother's neck and he squeezed tightly.

"Justin's not the only one who's grown," Chase said, slipping his arm around Lesley's thickened waist.

"You would have, too, if you were about to have a baby," Lesley reminded her husband.

Chase chuckled and shook hands with Ken Sterne.

"Good to see you again," Ken said. "June's been cooking for three days. You'd think an army was about to descend on us."

"Hush now," June chastised her husband. "How are you feeling?"

Lesley sighed. How did any woman feel two months before her delivery date? Anxious. Nervous. Eager. "I'm okay."

June put down her grandson and kissed Chase on the cheek.

His eyes met Lesley's and he gave her a know-it-all look. It had taken time, but Lesley had been right about the effect grandchildren would have on the relationship between her mother and her husband. When they'd first met, four years earlier, her mother had been convinced Chase was some kind of demon. These days he was much closer to sainthood.

"How's Twin Creeks?" Ken asked, steering the small party toward the baggage area.

"The population has doubled," Lesley informed him proudly. It had started soon after her arrival. Pete had gotten married the following spring and he and his wife already had two children and another on the way. Even Jim had married, which surprised them all. A widow with four children had found a place in all their hearts.

It seemed there was a baby being born every few months. The community was thriving. Lesley believed Chase was the one who'd put everything in motion; his venture into Seattle to find himself a wife was what had started the process. Soon the other men working at the pump station were willing to open their lives.

Chase, however, was convinced that once the other men saw what a wonderful woman *he'd* found, they'd decided to take their chances, as well.

Whatever the reason, there were fifteen more women residing in Twin Creeks. Ten of them had apparently made it a personal goal to populate Alaska.

She placed one arm around her husband and smiled softly to herself. How different her life would have been without him. Each and every day she thanked God for that crazy billboard she'd seen on her way to the store.

BRIDE WANTED.

Their marriage was meant to be—because he'd chosen her although she hadn't answered his ad. And he'd let her know in a million ways since that *she* was the bride he wanted.

* * * * *

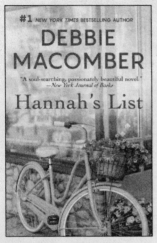

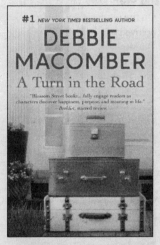

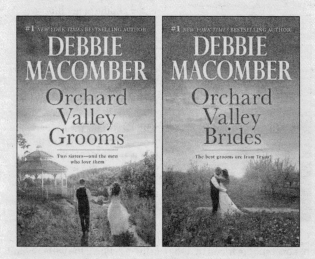

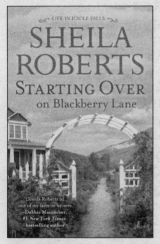

Turn your love of reading into rewards you'll love with

Harlequin My Rewards

**Join for FREE today at
www.HarlequinMyRewards.com**

Earn **FREE BOOKS** of your choice.

Experience **EXCLUSIVE OFFERS** and contests.

Enjoy **BOOK RECOMMENDATIONS**
selected just for you.

PLUS! Sign up now
and get **500** points
right away!

Earn
FREE
REWARDS
Join
Today!
HarlequinMyRewards.com

MYR16R

DEBBIE MACOMBER

33019	ALASKA HOME	___	$7.99 U.S.	___	$9.99 CAN.
32918	AN ENGAGEMENT IN SEATTLE	___	$7.99 U.S.	___	$9.99 CAN.
32798	ORCHARD VALLEY GROOMS	___	$7.99 U.S.	___	$9.99 CAN.
31894	ALWAYS DAKOTA	___	$7.99 U.S.	___	$9.99 CAN.
31888	DAKOTA HOME	___	$7.99 U.S.	___	$9.99 CAN.
31883	DAKOTA BORN	___	$7.99 U.S.	___	$9.99 CAN.
31868	COUNTRY BRIDE	___	$7.99 U.S.	___	$9.99 CAN.
31864	THE MANNING GROOMS	___	$7.99 U.S.	___	$9.99 CAN.
31860	THE MANNING BRIDES	___	$7.99 U.S.	___	$9.99 CAN.
31829	TRADING CHRISTMAS	___	$7.99 U.S.	___	$9.99 CAN.
31580	MARRIAGE BETWEEN FRIENDS	___	$7.99 U.S.	___	$8.99 CAN.
31551	A REAL PRINCE	___	$7.99 U.S.	___	$8.99 CAN.
31441	HEART OF TEXAS VOLUME 2	___	$7.99 U.S.	___	$8.99 CAN.
31413	LOVE IN PLAIN SIGHT	___	$7.99 U.S.	___	$9.99 CAN.
31341	THE UNEXPECTED HUSBAND	___	$7.99 U.S.	___	$9.99 CAN.
31325	A TURN IN THE ROAD	___	$7.99 U.S.	___	$9.99 CAN.
31917	BECAUSE IT'S CHRISTMAS	___	$7.99 U.S.	___	$9.99 CAN.
31535	PROMISE TEXAS	___	$7.99 U.S.	___	$8.99 CAN.
33018	ALASKA NIGHTS	___	$7.99 U.S.	___	$9.99 CAN.
31624	ON A CLEAR DAY	___	$7.99 U.S.	___	$8.99 CAN.
31903	WEDDING DREAMS	___	$7.99 U.S.	___	$9.99 CAN.
31907	THE KNITTING DIARIES	___	$7.99 U.S.	___	$9.99 CAN.
31926	THE SOONER THE BETTER	___	$7.99 U.S.	___	$9.99 CAN

(limited quantities available)

TOTAL AMOUNT	$ _____
POSTAGE & HANDLING	$ _____
($1.00 for 1 book, 50¢ for each additional)	
APPLICABLE TAXES*	$ _____
TOTAL PAYABLE	$ _____

(check or money order—please do not send cash)

To order, complete this form and send it, along with a check or money order for the total above, payable to MIRA Books, to: **In the U.S.:** 3010 Walden Avenue, P.O. Box 9077, Buffalo, NY 14269-9077; **In Canada:** P.O. Box 636, Fort Erie, Ontario, L2A 5X3.

Name: _____

Address: _____ City: _____

State/Prov.: _____ Zip/Postal Code: _____

Account Number (if applicable): _____

075 CSAS

Harlequin.com

MDM1217BL

*New York residents remit applicable sales taxes.
*Canadian residents remit applicable GST and provincial taxes.